For you

No v Michelle

MW01252031

CHA-CHA-CHA

A Novel of Politics

MELCHIZEDEK MAQUISO

ISBN: 1-4140-4330-9 (e-book)
ISBN: 1-4140-4328-7 (Paperback)

This book is printed on acid free paper.

Printed in the United States of America
1st Books
1663 Liberty Drive, Suite 200
Bloomington, IN
First Printing -------------2004
Website http://www.1stbooks.com

1stBooks - rev. 02/21/04

To:

Jesus Melchizedek,
Nikolai Raymond,
Uyok Benfelino
and their
generation

CAST OF PRINCIPAL CHARACTERS

ADMINISTRATION PARTY

Sergio Imperial Rosales	President of the Republic and Party Chairman
Meandro Destino	Presidential Adviser
Robustiano Toledo	Executive Secretary
Serafin Andolana Davide	Secretary General and Presidential Aspirant
Jack Tibogol	Chief of Staff
Gil Ceasar Malasuerte	Campaign Manager
Timostocles Sipula	Coordinator, Support Group
Leopoldo Mondejar	Bagman

OPPOSITION PARTY

Juancho Mahalina	Presidential Aspirant
Ruperto "Fatso" Santos	Campaign Task Force Chairman
Patricia Gan-Alfonso	Campaign Coordinator
Randolf Patis Cruz	Media Bureau Chief
Raul Pangilinan	Academician

OTHER PRESIDENTIAL ASPIRANTS

Marshall Alonzo Dimalasa	Secretary of National Defense
Arturo Tan-Kong	Former Police Officer
Juan Carlos Enriquez	Former Governor
Naomi Ganzon Santolan	Senator
Vicente delos Ajos	Perennial Presidential Candidate

BUSINESS MOGULS

Ferdinand Tancho	President of the Other Central Bank of the Republic
Don Felipe Aboitez	Industrialist
Ruperto del Pardo	Chairman, Metropolitan Business Club
Winthrop Lopez	Mindanao Business Tycoon

MILITARY GENERALS

Gen. (Ret.) Delfin Quintos	Strategist, Oplan Twilight Zone
Gen. Alexander Pecson	Chief, Presidential Security Battalion
Gen. Napoleon Cornelio	Commander, Southern Command

REBEL COMMANDERS

Ahmad Jamil	Field Marshall Fox, Moro Liberation Front
Ali Tausug	Chief of Staff, MLF
Ka Rollie	Commander, People's Watch and Revolutionary Army (PWRA)
Ka Alex	Task Force Commander, People's Watch Brigade, PWRA
Ka Lulu	Task Force Commander, Bomb and Explosives Division, PWRA
Ka Piccio	The Assassin

NATIVE WARRIORS

Datu Joshephus Sibugong	Supreme Datu, House of Agyu
Tomasing Labaongon	Heir to the Throne

RELIGIOUS LUMINARIES

His Eminence Pedro Alingasa	Cardinal
Father Rudy Nicolas	Priest
His Eminence Luigi Toscanini	Cardinal of Bologna, Italy
Rickie Balete	Most Exalted Brother, Brotherhood Of Faith in Jesus Movement
Father Morales, S.J.	Mob Psychologist

MEDIA STARS

Katrina Avila	Journalist
Feliz Salamanca	Columnist
Richard Martin	Foreign Correspondent
Tina Gomez Latorta	Talk Show Hostess
Vito Sta. Dolores	Talk Show Host
Fred Palanca	TV Anchorman
Gina delos Reyes	TV Anchorlady

OTHER PROMINENT CHARACTERS

Marissa Gantuico	Social Worker
Humphrey Bogart Putto	Senator
Rustico Kapunan	Secretary of Interior and Local Government
Racleto Albanos	Majority Floor Leader, House of

	Representatives
Ephraim Bejarde	Speech Instructor
Pablo Tabile	Barangay Captain, Barrio Kadugay
Simeon Sempron	Barangay Councilman
Cardo Roque	Barangay Councilman
Rushmore Stockman	Resident Ambassador, American Embassy
Marvin Reed	Consul
Claudia Palomos Davide	Wife of Serafin Davide
Priscilla Batungbakal	Urban Poor Activist
Charlene Divinagracia	Singer
Jason Angelo	Son of Mahalina
Jessica	Daughter of Mahalina
Filipinas Cruz	Letter Writer

PARANORMALS

Madame Carla Madonna Omen	Crystal Ball Gazer
Professor Hagibis del Yuta	Earth Shaker
Sonny Boy Profeta	Barometer

TV COMMERCIAL MODELS

Kidd Batuta	Sandwich Eater
Luningning Morena	Lingerie Model
Steve Karate	Rum Drinker

1
TO BE OR NOT TO BE

The convention hall of the International Plaza Hotel suddenly fell silent. Up on center stage behind the presidential table, Sergio Imperial Rosales, president of the republic and chairman of the administration party, stood and walked in measured steps toward the rostrum. After scanning his notes in front of him, he took a deep breath and then, in his famous flat monotone, addressed the delegates of the administration party.

"Esteemed delegates, my friends," President Rosales began, his blood-shot eyes darting back to his notes after a quick survey of the crowd. "It now falls on my shoulders to decide who among the five aspirants will become the presidential standard bearer of our party in the coming national elections. In this regard, I have created a 31-member Selection Committee to set the criteria on which I will make the final decision. The creation of the committee has the imprimatur of the National Directorate."

The president paused, slowly scanning the rows of party officials and delegates directly below him. At the front row to his left sat Marshall Alonzo Dimalasa, secretary of National Defense. When their eyes met, Dimalasa raised his right arm and simulated a fast surreptitious military salute. As he did that, he manufactured a grin as his pale face flushed.

To the president's right sat Serafin Andolana Davide, secretary general of the party. When their eyes met, Davide gave his signature double thumbs-up from the top of his knees. As he did that, his doe-like eyes shone; his grin widened; and his oversized ears flapped like sails in the winds of glee.

Looking back at his notes, the president continued.

"Please understand that what we had to undergo in the last three days was a most taxing one, to the point that we threatened ourselves with walkouts, resignations and all sorts of emotional outbursts. But I believe all this is an integral part of the democratic process and indicates clearly that our party is indeed a dynamic party."

The president paused again.

"All of us in the party have only one common aim and this is to win the elections in May. But we have different ideas how to achieve this common aim. This is where the Committee of 31 will help me unite all the different ideas to achieve our common aim."

The president once more paused, feeling the uneasy silence. Then his voice rose with the sharp crack of authority: "I have given the committee two weeks from now to submit its recommendations. One week after that, I will call a press conference and announce the official decision."

President Rosales slowly folded the notes in front of him, feeling the uneasy silence grow heavier.

"I thank you and may God bless us all," he finally said. His jaws firm and his head up, he walked back toward his seat at the center, behind the presidential table.

The reactions of the 1553 delegates throughout the convention hall were spontaneous and varied. "Then why were we called to this convention?" a mayor from one of the remotest towns in Southern Mindanao fumed, hastily pulling out a handkerchief from his back pocket and sneezing into it. Obviously, the air-conditioned hall had a negative effect on his sinuses. There was not one air-conditioned office in his municipality.

"Sonnamagun!" a governor from the Bicol Region cursed. "This is what you call the chaotic process of democracy, democrazy, democrazzzy." He accompanied his repetitions with twirling fingers, moving in opposite directions around his balding head.

"Yeah, that's the government of the people, because you buy the people, to make poor the people," a delegate garbed in native costume said, chewing a betel nut in his mouth. A matron beside him raised an eyebrow, wondering what the man from one of the mountain tribes, was talking about.

"What a waste of money!" a delegate from the women's sector exclaimed, her mouth spewing some trickles of saliva. Fumbling for a tissue in her purse, she found nothing. "The same story—we're being used again."

"The President is really a genius," a congressman from the Visayas offered. "He knows when to get in and when to get out and when to get in again!" the congressman ended his declaration by repeatedly nodding his head, a clear suggestion he knew something that the others didn't.

"What do you mean by that?" his seatmate, another congressman, asked.

"Just watch, my friend. The best is yet to come."

"Or is it the worst is yet to come?" the seatmate said, as both delegates regarded each other in the eye.

"I'm lost. I'm simply lost!" cried another female delegate. Large and heavy by any standard, she was trying to wriggle out of the thick crowd that now scampered for the exit doors.

"How can you be lost when you don't know where you're going?" a voice said on the side.

The November national convention of the administration party ended up in chaos as President Rosales had observed.

The chaos was brought about by the intense rivalry between the supporters of Serafin Andolana Davide, secretary general of the party and Marshall Alonzo Dimalasa, secretary of the Department of National Defense in the Rosales Cabinet. Each desperately wanted to be the standard bearer of the party. However, the national directorate knew that if a choice were to be made in this convention which meant forcing a showdown, the loser, whether Davide or Dimalasa, would still run for president of the country in the coming May polls. That would split the administration party and spell disaster for everyone. Only President Rosales could prevent that from happening.

The chaos began when the supporters of Dimalasa started spreading the rumor that he, Dimalasa was the personal choice of the president. The supporters of

Davide countered by saying the allegation of the Dimalasa camp was simply outrageous—it had to be Davide, they said, for Davide fought with Rosales when the latter was still an unknown presidential candidate. It was Davide, they added, who stuck with Rosales through that tortuous and uncertain presidential campaign. At that time, Dimalasa who was still in military uniform was stuck in his own field command and was not known to have any political ambition.

From there, the political weapons of mass distraction started firing their poisoned bullets of mudslinging and character assassination.

Dimalasa's supporters accused Davide as "the classic example of a tradpol or traditional politician, a corrupt businessman and one who makes promises in billions every time he opens his mouth."

The supporters of Davide hit back by accusing Dimalasa of "being an opportunist." Dimalasa's presidential ambition, they said, was "just too high and mighty compared to his proven mediocrity," sounding like their intelligence was greatly insulted. Dimalasa, they prattled on, was "a stooge of big business in Makati whose record as a military general was full of hesitation and indecision exemplified by his speech stutters."

"Davide has been buying the votes of the delegates," Dimalasa's supporters babbled back, claiming that Davide's brokers not only gave cash but also entertained the delegates nightly with wine, GROs (Guest Relations Officers) and exotic dancers.

"Dimalasa has been spreading lies and promising positions left and right," Davide's supporters cried, claiming that Dimalasa himself personally promised Cabinet positions and government contracts to whomever was within whispering distance. "How presumptuous of him!"

"What a SAD story," Dimalasa's supporters sighed, their eyes rolling, referring to the initials of Serafin Andolana Davide.

"You're all MAD!" Davide's supporters countered, referring to the initials of Marshall Alonzo Dimalasa.

In the first hour of the second day, after Davide and Dimalasa were nominated on the floor, another delegate moved to close the nominations, which prompted another delegate to shout his objection. When the latter was recognized, he ran toward the standing microphone in the middle aisle of the convention hall and at the top of his voice, shouted: "You are all sons and daughters of a whore!" That sent the rambunctious convention hall in the quiet of a funeral parlor. That also prompted the president of the party, the presiding officer, to declare a recess, angrily banging his gavel, after uttering an inaudible profanity. The wooden symbol of administrative authority broke in two.

The topic of conversation that night was the delegate who shouted his profanities and aborted the election of the presidential standard bearer of the party. It was later established that the spoiler was Robinson Lastik, president of the National Federation of Jeepney Drivers and Operators.

There were two versions why Lastik did what he did. One said Lastik was a staunch supporter of another presidential candidate, thus he went wild when another delegate moved to close the nominations. The second version claimed that Lastik, a fanatic of President Rosales, wanted to nominate the president on the floor, but he wasn't sure if Rosales himself would like the idea. Like most delegates, Lastik knew the president was barred by the constitution of the land from running for a second term. "Perhaps, in his confusion, he got wild," one delegate ventured to say. Neither version could be confirmed since Lastik could not be found that night or, for that matter, until the convention of the political party in power adjourned.

"What a shame!" "What a tragedy!" "This spells the end of our party." The lamentations were endless.

But there were delegates in the convention hall and they were not a few, who believed that united or not, the party was not the problem. Davide or Dimalasa had no chance whatsoever against the opposition candidate, the overwhelmingly popular Juancho Mahalina. This tragic truth, they claimed, was as undeniable as the sun rises in the east and sets in the west. Like hardened political animals, they never believed in alliances with losers. Against Mahalina, all were losers. This was their pure and simple prognosis.

To some who did not fully comprehend the political undercurrents behind the intense rivalry between Davide and Dimalasa and the role of President Rosales in that rivalry, the whole exercise was simply a combination of a circus, political image positioning and democracy at work.

Some 40 minutes after the convention chairman banged his new gavel to end the three-day event, three stalwarts of the Rosales Cabinet met for coffee at a small café in the heart of Makati. Rustico Kapunan III, secretary of the Department of Interior and Local Government, Marshall Alonzo Dimalasa, secretary of National Defense and Robustiano Toledo, executive secretary, were huddled in a corner table.

"It was a good thing the old man accepted the idea of a selection committee," Kapunan said, clicking his fingers in the air with obvious delight. "With Ruby and me in the committee, it's smooth sailing from hereon," Kapunan declared, lifting his cup and savoring the brew. Sitting down, Kapunan still towered over his companions. At 37, he was the youngest in the Rosales Cabinet and the most handsome, according to his female fans who did not fail to admire his mestizo features.

"Rusty, are you sure that ah, ah the closing statement of the President will now end all speculations that he has no more, ah interest?" Dimalasa asked, gazing from Kapunan to Toledo and back. To Dimalasa, nothing was over until it was over. At 63, Dimalasa was slow with words and some say low in intelligence, but he was ambitious in a grand scale. He had that lean and hungry look and projected the image that he was a man of destiny.

"Well, let's stop trying to read the old man's mind," Kapunan pointed out, drumming his fingers on the table. "That's counterproductive. All we need to do now is watch our back and proceed from there."

"That's correct," Ruby Toledo agreed, signaling a waiter for a refill. At 49, the "Little President" was the shortest of the three. He dressed like a peasant as no suit ever seemed to fit him. Probably it was the shape of his shoulders or the structure of his torso or simply his primitive bearing that did not, to his detractors, give justice to his exalted position in the Rosales cabinet. If Kapunan lectured with words flying and Dimalasa stuttered, Toledo garbled his words like he had a toothache.

"And do you think you will be able to ah, sway the whole committee, in our ah, favor?" Dimalasa asked, again gazing at his companions from one to the other. The Committee of 31, Dimalasa correctly observed, was composed mostly of tradpols, with the exception of Toledo and Kapunan.

"I don't think that's difficult." Toledo asserted, sipping his refill. "What's difficult is if the old man will use the committee for his personal agenda. You know, he is never wanting of options."

Dimalasa shrugged, looking intently at Toledo.

"That is why we are in the committee," Kapunan said, his voice rising. "That gives us all the opportunity to keep a close tab on everything." Kapunan smiled, the quick indulgent smile of a man infatuated with his own intellect, imagined or not.

"You really think the President will ah, ah go for me?" Dimalasa asked, his apprehensions rising. "I, ah, ah…"

"C'mon, Mars." Kapunan interrupted, waving a deprecating hand. "How many times do you have to ask that same stupid question? You know its not good for our health. What would people think?" As he spoke, Kapunan's face reddened. Why was he supporting this political neophyte who was famous for his indecisiveness and hesitations, Kapunan asked himself, peering mockingly in the face of Dimalasa. Why? Kapunan could not sense the real essence of the man except that he knew Dimalasa was moral to the tip of his hair, in contrast to Davide who was a tradpol to the core of his bones.

"I'm sorry," Dimalasa said, dabbing his forehead, wiping off perspiration beads that started to trickle down his neck. "It's just that I can't ah, sleep what with Pin Davide working his ah, ah evil charms on the President."

"Well, can we stop him from spewing his evil charms on the President?" Rusty Kapunan snapped. "Look Mars, you seem to be unsure about a lot of things." Kapunan paused, breathing harder. "Are you with us on this or not? Are you going to be with us on this?"

Dimalasa didn't appear to have any answer. He stared at his shoes. He took off his glasses. He rubbed his chin. He scratched his ears.

"I will ah, try…" the words finally came out.

"No, you will not try. You will do it," Kapunan hissed like a schoolmaster demanding homework from an underachieving pupil.

"What's really bothering you, Mars?" Toledo asked, offering a gentle smile and a patronizing gaze.

"Ah, ah its just that I feel the President owes Pin Davide a lot. Except for my loyalty to the President, I really have nothing else ah, ah to offer."

That prompted a spell of silence as Kapunan and Toledo ordered more refills. While sipping their refills, both agreed in their own thought that Dimalasa was honest, at least. That was rare among men with great ambitions.

"Any new development from somewhere?" Toledo asked, breaking the mood.

"Damn!" Dimalasa said, slapping his hand against his temple. "Don Ipe is, ah with us now. We had ah, ah long huddle last night. In fact, he said he'd ah, call the President and tell him he could not, ah stand tradpols, that's why ah, he is for me."

Dimalasa could not contain his excitement. Don Ipe was Don Felipe Aboitez, the builder of the financial capital of the country and the biggest real estate developer in the entire region. It was universally recognized that whomever ran for the presidency with the financial backing of Don Ipe, the throne in Malacanang Palace was his for the taking.

"That's the best news I've heard in a long time," Toledo declared as he stood. "Let's move!"

"Right on," Kapunan stood as Dimalasa also stood.

They exchanged high fives. Anxiety was shaken off and adrenalin flooded into their bloodstreams.

About an hour after the three stalwarts of the Rosales Cabinet left the café in Makati, Presidential Adviser Meandro Destino entered his apartment along chaotic San Marcelino Street in Ermita. Haggard, hungry and thirsty from driving through heavy traffic, Destino felt relaxed after two shots of Chivas, his mind back to what happened at the convention and the closing statement of the president.

As presidential adviser, Destino's primordial concern was the legacy of President Rosales—to secure his rightful place in the history of the nation. Everything, yes, everything emanated from there.

Destino was no great fan of President Rosales. As an academician throughout his professional life until he became presidential adviser in the palace, Destino had learned to look at both sides of every coin. He judged people and events after examining their good and bad sides, their pros and cons, their strengths and weaknesses. In the almost six years he served the president, Destino had come to the conclusion that indeed every national leader had something odd and distasteful about him. "Great men have great aberrations," he remembered that. But there was no doubt about it—President Sergio Imperial Rosales, P-SIR, had in his short term in office cast a long shadow in the behavior of men and institutions in the country. This was P-SIR's legacy.

At 53, with a receding hairline and a slight bulge in his midsection, Destino was a man who enjoyed his solitude. Destino, despite his prominent position in the president's orbit, disliked the glitter and glamour of palace parties. He thought they were a waste of time in which flattery was exchanged in prodigious quantity. And he hated manicured nails and salon facials, the latter a recent preoccupation among men in high places. Perhaps, it was his upbringing. He grew up in a farm. He went through school as a working student and he had no love for material things.

Most of the time, he took only three cups of coffee for breakfast. For lunch, he usually ate at a ramshackle restaurant opposite his apartment with fried goat meat spiced with lots of garlic as their specialty. For dinner, he cooked assorted vegetables from the vendors that lined the sidewalk towards his apartment. Each dinner was always preceded by two to three shots of whiskey, most of the time, local and on rare occasions, stateside. Destino never liked wine. He went for the much stronger stuff. And he smoked, as his friends would say, like a chimney. He was never afraid of cancer. If his life span were reduced by five years because of smoking, it was a tradeoff worth taking. To him, cigarette smoking was another companion in his solitude.

After his biological clock woke him at three o'clock the following morning, Destino took a quick hot shower, prepared his coffee, opened his laptop and began tapping the keyboard. The president should get this memo by fax in time for the breakfast meeting of his inner circle at six. This was a Tuesday, another Tuesday in the life of the president and the president's men.

After the second ring, Destino picked up his landline. "Yes, Tim... go ahead. Yes, hmmm... how many? Okay... Got it. Yes, my fax is on auto. Okay, you better do it fast. See you. Good work. Till then."

Destino lighted another cigarette after checking his watch. He still had two-and-a-half hours before he'd get the data from Tim. He checked the fax machine when his cell phone trilled. "Hello... 'Gaya... right. That's correct. So it's for Saturday... first flight in the morning... that's okay. Just make sure those papers are out of the office by Friday. Clear the desk; clear the desk every weekend, okay? Good girl... Bonus? You must be kidding... Christmas is still light years away! Ha! Ha! Okay... keep in touch."

Destino's fingers swiftly ran through the keyboard.

CONFIDENTIAL

Memo to	:	P-SIR
From	:	Meyan D.
Subject	:	Assessment of Delegates' Reactions (Party Convention, November l0) and Recommendations
Date	:	November 11

A quick survey conducted last night by our coordinators showed approval rating of your decision at 53%, disapproval at 37% and non-committal at 10%. (Please see details in Table l, page 2 of this memo.)

Outside of survey, reliable info indicates Davide camp distributed loaded envelopes, believing an election of the standard bearer by the general assembly would push through. Dimalasa camp did not distribute any but spread the rumor that the decision was not to be arrived at via the ballots of the delegates but by the president's sole decision, adding that the President, meaning you, Sir, is for Dimalasa.

Over and above those who have expressed their support for either Dimalasa or Davide, the great majority of the delegates are still hoping the President remains in office beyond his current term, by whatever means.

A check earlier with leaders in business, civil society and the military showed the great majority is in sync with the common sentiments of the delegates and vice-versa. (Please see Table 2, page 3 of this memo for details.)

Recommendations:

Destino paused, staring at the screen. He clicked file, save, start, shut down, then OK. Lighting another cigarette, he stretched on the long couch with his hands clasped behind his head and stared at the ceiling, trying to phrase his recommendations. From the corner of his eye, he saw the writings on the screen: 'It is now safe to turn off...' He closed his eyes. Sleep came in brief naps, interrupted by long periods of staring at the ceiling.

S erafin Andolana Davide knew President Rosales was indebted to him. That fact, the party also knew and acknowledged. But he also knew the president had the statistics to show his chances of winning were as dim as formally marrying his common-law wife Claudia. He had, by mutual consent, separated from his first wife but the law of the land and the canons of the Church told him a formal union with Claudia was an impossible dream.

Davide at 63, short in height with a puffy round face and a pair of doe-like eyes that made him look harmless, buttoned his shirt as he slowly closed the door behind him. Claudia was still asleep, tired and yet so lovely in her flawless skin. As in many late nights, he had tried time and again to make it with her but his boundless energy, exhibited in public, exhausted him in private.

As he entered the reception hall cum dining area of his mansion, the guests filling the hall from table to table suddenly stood from their seats. They'd been eating with much relish and appreciated their breakfast at his home, served by hired caterers and uniformed waiters. Davide of course knew they did not just come for the sumptuous menu ordered from the most famous restaurant in Makati. He knew that more than their appetite for good food, they came for the shopping bags he was notorious for dispensing during election campaigns. During Christmas, similar shopping bags contained ham, century eggs, a bottle of imported wine, chocolate candies and a pocket-size calendar made of glossy plastic with the colored picture of him and Claudia seated in front and his two sons standing at the back. This time, election campaign time, similar shopping bags did not contain the usual Christmas goodies. They contained cold, hard cash.

"Good morning, Mr. President," chorused his guests, heartily clapping their hands in greeting. It was the kind of greeting that reenergized Davide. Pumping hands with everybody, whispering a word here and there or horselaughing along the way, Davide made everybody feel he missed them like they were his high school classmates of bygone days.

As if on cue, 15 of his guests followed him to the conference room at the west-end of the reception hall. In this conference room, confidential party caucuses were held, issues debated, political careers decided and favors given in cash.

Davide scanned the faces around the oval conference table where his guests were now seated, sipping his first cup of brewed coffee for the day. Of the 15, he could only count on seven; the rest were known in the trade as certifiable political beasts.

"Well, gentlemen, the fate of the nation is once again on the shoulders of President Rosales," Davide orated, manufacturing a politician's smile, opening the informal caucus. Davide was shorter than most of those who sat around him. But his voice was booming and radiated a sense of authority and power. "If my calculations are correct, President Rosales will make the announcement within two weeks but not beyond three weeks. Meanwhile, I'm interested to know at this time—first, your reading of the President's latest pronouncements and second, the public pulse out there in your respective regions."

"It's really hard to say," Racleto Albanos, the majority floor leader of the House of Representatives, representing Region IV in the party, pointed out. "It's really hard to say what the President is thinking. He's still a sphinx to me. But I can tell you this… you are guaranteed 51 percent of the votes from my region."

Albanos was much taller than Davide. And older too, at 69. He wore a wispy mustache on a face that was flat as his hair was flat, combed neatly down from his forehead to the nape of his neck.

"Why 51?" Davide's doe-like eyes alighted on Albanos. "Why not 60 or 70 or 90 percent?"

"Well, let's be realistic," Albanos said, sounding sincere and overly concerned. "The upscale depends on how much we deliver. As of today, everything is volatile above the 51 percent."

Davide pretended to give full attention but his mind was somewhere else. This guy was really a full-blooded political animal. The lower he started with his figures, the more shopping bags he expected to harvest.

"All right," Davide said, sounding totally convinced. "It's a deal. The delivery system follows immediately after the official announcement by the President that Serafin Andolana Davide is the official standard bearer of the party."

"But we have to have running ammo!" His guests said it almost at the same time. They were clever enough to sense a smokescreen.

Davide anticipated that. In such moments, Davide was always ahead of the pack. From nowhere, Claudia entered the room as a whiff of her perfume filled the air. Everybody stood to greet her. Claudia responded with her signature smile as she glided toward her husband who buzzed her and then whispered something to her. Claudia at 43, was two inches taller than Davide, her hair dyed extra gold and special blonde ash flowing down smoothly, her eyes a little bit sunken but glistening below her thick natural lashes.

It took her only a few minutes to reenter the room, an aide following with five full shopping bags. The room suddenly went hush. Without any preamble Claudia with her long nimble fingers, scooped three bundles from the first bag. Each bundle was wrapped neatly in coupon bond and held together by masking tape from end to end. Claudia then carefully placed them in front of the majority floor leader of the House who was seated right next to her husband. As she moved from one guest to another doing the same thing, no one dared open or touch the bundles in front. It was obvious each one was mentally noting no one got two or four but specifically three—each with the same size and thickness. Everyone was sure about that.

"Well," Davide finally broke the silence, his doe-like eyes twinkling in total amusement. "You just got your running ammo. Until then, my friends, when the President makes the official announcement. See you around, gentlemen."

The loud hallelujahs that followed echoed in the room.

As Claudia left him to conduct their guests out of the conference room through the reception hall and into the garden, Davide pushed a button of the hidden elevator that took him to the third floor, got out and walked towards the balcony overlooking the garden. The guests appeared to be admiring the roses and orchids as Claudia pointed to this or that variety, proudly showing them her latest collection. As soon as they noticed him up the balcony, Davide waved his arms, ending with his signature double thumbs-up.

Four million five hundred thousand pesos. That meant P300 thousand each. Chicken feed, Davide chuckled to himself in time to see two of his security guards close the massive gate below.

To Davide, money was not a problem. His first venture in the Middle East built this mansion, one of the most expensive edifices in Forbes Park, the enclave of the rich and the famous. Not only that. The killing he made out of his venture also provided the vast capital that established his businesses here and in three countries in Southeast Asia. Those did not include the substantial stocks he held in many national and international corporations. Yes, Claudia was loaded, too. Her family controlled the movie and entertainment industry in the country. But he had, time and again, told his father-in-law he would have none of Claudia's money for political purposes.

Aside from prestige, power and influence, politics was really good, lucrative business. You earned much more than you spent with no sweat. Yes, a lot of saliva but no sweat. The P4.5M he just dispensed with some 15 minutes ago was yes, a minute grain in a barrel full of tiny sand that was delivered to him in seven sacks the other night, after only one phone call. Seven sacks that looked like garbage collection sacks but contained cold, hard cash.

Politics was really good big business, Davide repeated to himself. When he ran for the first time 22 years ago as congressman of the first district of his province, he only spent one half of the total contributions he obtained from friends and his party. The rest he invested to start a small transport business. He did not only win, he also profited. When he ran for reelection, he spent only one-fourth of the total contributions from friends and his party. The rest he spent to start a business venture in Taiwan with local Chinese businessmen in partnership with their friends in that country. He did not only win overwhelmingly and pulverized his opponents. He also gained large profit margins and the respect of the international business community for his shrewdness.

Now as he pondered further on the possibilities, Davide concluded he could easily gain P2.5 B, win or lose. Win? No, that was no longer possible. All he needed was the president's endorsement. It was more than a trade-off. It was absolute guarantee.

Overwhelmed by the impeccable logic of his inner thought, Davide did not notice Claudia who had been observing him from the low sofa by the corner of the balcony. Sensing what she was thinking, he sat beside her as he gently squeezed that tender flesh below her right armpit, that portion he knew was her primary erotic zone. Definitely, he told himself, it was not the money he just distributed to his

10

political allies. Claudia was used to that. Definitely, it was not also his failed attempts to make it with her last night. Claudia was used to that, too, for she immediately followed each failed attempt with a soft kiss on his forehead and a smile of understanding. That she also did last night.

To Claudia the ascent to the presidency was the best she could possibly expect of her man. There would be no turning back. And win or lose, it had to be fought with dignity. She had been theorizing about this since both of them agreed there was no other way for him to go but up.

What would her friends say to her? What would happen to her social and civic projects? What would happen to their marriage that until now could not even be formally solemnized?

Claudia with her innate beauty and natural charm could have easily been a movie star, what with the money and influence of her father. Instead, she remained unassuming and sincere. That was what totally endeared her to him.

But Davide had to think of the future, the future of his two sons, now of college age. Many had referred to each of them as Serafin Andolana Davide, Jr. because both looked like him, spoke like him and moved like him though they were not twins and were two years apart in age. Davide concluded since he had no chance whatsoever to become president, the billions he would amass could easily be multiplied in the years to come, in time for either of his two sons to get to that position.

But he dared not tell this rambling in his inner thoughts to Claudia. His sons were not her sons.

So… that's it!" the professor concluded, switching off the microphone as he stepped down from the lectern, then settled on the chair behind the small table at the middle of the stage of the amphitheater.

"Any questions?" he then asked.

Some 15 arms went up in the air. The professor pointed to a female student at the third row from the back.

"Sir, your stress on competence is rather obvious. But my question is, what kind of competence is needed to judiciously govern? How can that competence be 'imaged' or given a face so it can be grasped by the masses as clear as popularity? What is its form or structure, if any? Is my question clear, Sir?"

"Clear as day. Miss…?"

"Chonana Villa, Sir."

"Yes, clear as day, Miss Villa. But you said a mouthful there, young lady. If you were present during my third lecture in this series, I stressed that competence could only be acquired by going through the rigors of how to become a philosopher-king, before anyone should even dare to run for public office. The form or structure for competency was clearly outlined by Plato in his *Ideal Republic*. That structure if I may recall, Miss Villa, started with <u>G</u> and ended with another <u>G</u>; that is, from Grammar to Governance. In short, the education for competence for one who aspires to be philosopher-king starts from the time the baby is ready to talk, to the time the grown man is ready to govern."

"But Sir, we don't have that kind of academy in this country?"

"That is why to paraphrase John Osborne, the world is mad because we have ambitious people who aspire for public office but who are not trained for it."

"Sir," a bespectacled male student stood from the front as soon as he was recognized. "What I have discovered, Sir, is your stress on the training of leaders while you completely ignored the education of the masses or the great majority of the electorate. If this is so and correct me if I am wrong, could you blame the masses for electing officials for their popularity rather than for their competence?" His classmates rolled their eyes.

"Well taken, Mr.?"

"Dennis Latigo, Sir."

"Well taken, Mr. Latigo. But that is really beyond the scope of my lecture series. Moreover, I must qualify that the issue here is not popularity versus competence. This is not an either-or proposition. In this context, popularity means universal acceptability and competence means qualifications for the job. Do you get the point?"

"I'm sorry, Sir, if I muddled the issue. But I think it is only fair that you share your thoughts on the masses, on the basis of their competence to vote for the right leader, for the right job. It takes two to tango, you know. For where would the leader be without the people and where would the people be without the leader?" Latigo thought he had forcefully made his point. His classmates seconded with their "Ohhmmm."

"You're right. It takes two to tango," the professor assured Latigo. "Since there are no academies to train would-be philosopher-kings after Plato, so are there no schools for the masses to judiciously elect their leaders. Indirectly, however, our schools and educational institutions have been teaching us that to arrive at a decision, we have to consider the pros and cons of any situation or problem. This is readily demonstrated in the question—True or False? Right or Wrong? Unfortunately, this rationality is never totally independent. It is in fact, often overshadowed by stronger influential factors that predominate in our society and culture such as family ties, indebtedness and the like. So that in the end, when we exercise our right of suffrage, we decide what is false is true and what is wrong is right." Some of the students nodded their heads.

"Are you saying the masses are incompetent to elect their leader?" a voice from the back, almost a shrill, rang in the hall.

"The question should have been—are the masses generally incompetent to judiciously elect the right leader?" the professor dabbed his forehead. "No, I didn't say that... though I might have insinuated that, remembering the divine rights of kings as the precursor of the idea. At the time, strong leaders felt it was their right to govern because the masses were ignorant and incompetent."

"But that was still in the Middle Ages!"

"You are Mister..."

"Miss, err Mr. Juanita, eh, Juanito Matis, Sir," the lanky student with long hair in a ponytail demurred, fondling the earring on his left ear. His classmates snickered.

"Right you are there, Miss, eh, Mr. Juanita, eh, Mr. Juanito Matis," the professor smiled as laughter roared throughout. "True, that was still in the Middle Ages but the ambitions of men and their insatiable quest to follow their stars have not died since then," the professor paused. "Our very own dictator-president some years ago is a classic example. He had to declare martial rule to stay in power, believing he and he alone, could make this country great again. But as he ruled in absolute terms, he became a megalomaniac, so with his wife, so with his cronies."

"Professor! Professor!" almost half of the class raised their arms, their eager voices competing for attention. The professor recognized one from the front who immediately glided to the middle aisle where the standing microphone was located.

"Thank You, Sir. I am Arlene Rebongue. I am glad you mentioned the megalomaniac dictator-president, for he always reminds me of a great writer who once said 'power corrupts and absolute power corrupts absolutely'. Moreover, I'd like to point out there is a consequence, something like poetic justice, to absolute power and this, I believe, is absolute downfall. This was demonstrated clearly in our own people-power revolution some years back. What is your comment on that, Sir?"

For the first time, the professor fidgeted in his chair. The very topic he wanted to avoid rather than engage in finally came out.

"A most intriguing observation, Miss Rebongue," he finally blurted out.

The professor then stood, detaching the small microphone from its stand on the table. In measured tone, he continued. "Your observation, Miss Rebongue, of absolute power and its consequence, absolute downfall, almost like 'poetic justice', did you say, brought about by the so-called 'people-power revolution' however needs qualification. Truth to tell, the so-called people-power revolution, was not really 'people-power' in the truest sense of the term. In fact and in deed, that so called people-power was actually the accidental coalition of, by and for certain vested interest groups that did not benefit during the dictatorship or were victims of that dictatorship.

"In fact, the sudden rise of the first woman president of this country was a deliberate cabal whose motive was revenge for the murder of her husband, a rising political icon at the time. All in all, that motive of revenge gained the support of a moribund religious institution that wanted to reassert itself and the military establishment that wanted reforms, as well as the opportunists from the business community who wanted to recover their losses. Altogether, this unlikely coalition of forces, yes, finally did the dictatorship in.

"TV footages of ordinary folks storming Malacanang were not actually there on ideological grounds. Most of them were actually plain and simple looters, who were made to believe through radio broadcasts earlier, that millions of cash, trunks of jewelry and crates of gold bars were left in some rooms and in the basement of the palace. That was of course after the dictator and his family suddenly abandoned fame and glory to save their own thick hide."

"Sir," Miss Rebongue was on the verge of tears. Finally, she managed to say "Sir, I think you have become irreverent. I think you are trying to rewrite history in your own terms. Isn't that what you are doing, Sir?"

Reactions were varied and some hoots were heard.

"In fairness to Miss Rebongue," the professor said as the noise subsided. "The word 'irreverent' is rather alien to me, the word being commonly used by blasphemers of religious dogma. And Arlene, with due apologies, I am not a historian, so how can I possibly write, much more rewrite history?"

Some in the audience chuckled. Arlene's face flushed.

"And seriously speaking now, when Miss Rebongue earlier equated absolute downfall with poetic justice, I was enthralled. Poetic justice as taught in your Literature classes is a literary explanation of a phenomenon as in the Greek tragedies. In modern times, we often allude to that as self-destruction. But note, the dictator-president did not pluck his own eyes out of their sockets, as King Oedipus did, after becoming aware of his fatal human flaw. On the contrary, the dictator-president made no single act of self-retribution. Instead, he stuck to his alibi to the end, that he was stealthily flown to Hawaii instead of to Paoay, his hometown in the north, so that he could get away from the noise that some people were making at EDSA. Do you see the point, Miss Rebongue?"

"Sir! Sir! Sir!" More arms were raised as Miss Rebongue, her head bowed, her stride measured, went back to her seat.

"Okay, I will entertain one more question. Yes, the gentleman in faded crimson, please."

"I am Luis Valdevil. Sir, did you imply that the world famous people-power revolution was a pseudo-revolution, a sham? That it was not actually a revolution of the masses against the dictatorship?" Valdevil turned to his classmates. He thought he had made a brilliant statement.

"As you stated earlier, Mr. Valdevil, people in the streets, the common people themselves, already realized long ago that the so-called people-power revolution was not their revolution. In fact at present, the major players themselves who are still alive and kicking, are taking a nonchalant attitude every February 25, the day designated to commemorate the event. Let me see... I've got here in my notes one editorial from a national daily and I quote: '...the sense of EDSA's historicity had wilted under the sweltering heat, its spirit obscured by the antics of clowns.' And may I continue—'Year after year, the celebration has dwindled into a crowd of *uziseros* (or curiosity seekers) and aspiring VIPs and a prancing mob of unknowns trying to upstage each other before the TV cameras and what have you.' There you have it."

"So where does all this lead us, Sir?" Valdevil asked. His voice said he was lost.

"To nowhere," the professor answered, "unless and until our people are truly empowered. That means the masses are empowered socially, economically and politically. When that will happen requires a wilderness of question marks. People empowerment in the context of a democratic state is a tall order that necessitates sustained development, a point I stressed in my second lecture. You just can't change priorities from one leader to another, otherwise the tendency is to remain static or you take more backward steps than forward."

The professor paused, gathering his notes on the table.

"Our lecture today stressed on governance although we took a lot of detours due to your spirited reactions in the discussions that followed. Let me now make some conclusions at this point in our lecture series. First, successful governance requires competence. I think that is obvious. Second, competence and popularity are the ideal twins to guarantee good governance since with competence judicious decisions are expected to emanate and popularity ensures support from the people, the governed. And third, the leader must have a strong sense of history. A person who seeks public office, most especially the highest position of the land, the presidency that is and gets it, must always be conscious of the fact that whether he likes it or not, he will, after his term, be leaving a legacy."

"Sir! Sir! Sir!" Most were now standing, raising their hands for recognition.

"May I remind you of your assigned essay on the aspects of politics in your own hometowns. See you on the 27th, same time, same room for the next lecture. Thank You."

In spite of the rumor that grew louder from day to day, there was subdued silence in the military establishment. The rumor even got louder when six retired military generals occupying top positions in government corporations were seen having breakfast together in a corner table at a bayside restaurant fronting Manila Bay, the morning after President Rosales delivered his closing statements at his party's convention in the International Plaza Hotel.

"The air is getting dense," Gen. (Ret.) Delfin Quintos, president of the National Power Company observed, sipping his third cup of coffee. "I strongly feel Oplan T-Z be activated now." Popularly known as GDQ, the tall and lean retired general spoke, impatiently drumming his fingers on the table. GDQ was known to be very close to President Rosales. In fact, he was once the president's official military adviser.

"I fully agree, Mistah," the second man left of GDQ pointed out. He was the chairman of the board and CEO of the National Mining and Exploration Corporation. "Oplan Twilight Zone is the answer to all these leaks, rumors and gossips." The man repeatedly nodded his balding head. He wore a thick mustache that partly covered a scar on his upper lip.

"Are we absolutely certain the Oplan cannot be traced to Group G-3?" The third man farther left asked, referring to the nation's military academy class that did not participate in recent coups. The man was now the president of the National Airport Authority. He was squat, had a bulging belly and sported a long hair.

"That is what the Oplan is all about," GDQ reminded his former classmates at the academy. "While foot soldiers are involved, they are not really involved!"

Everyone laughed.

"What's bothering me is the President. Are you sure he got the blueprint?" the fourth man right of GDQ mumbled, wiping his mouth with a table napkin. The dark glasses he wore covered his eyes. He was known to be merciless, taking with him no prisoners when he was commanding officer of the southern command in Mindanao. He was now president of the National Maritime Company.

The silence that followed was now and then interrupted by the occasional sounds of clinking teaspoons and coffee cups, knives and forks slicing over pancakes and clicks of lighters to burn more cigarettes.

"Well, I'm sure the President already got the blueprint," GDQ confidently said, cracking the interregnum. "Meyan Destino assured me."

"But did the President approve it?" the others asked, one after the other.

"I have no means of knowing. But Meyan Destino assured me he'd relay the message as soon as he gets the signal."

The retired generals spent the next 45 minutes reviewing the critical operational steps of Oplan T-Z. Nodding at each other to indicate they were now in full agreement of the details, GDQ punched buttons in his cell phone and waited as he threw a conspiratorial wink at his colleagues. Leaning on his chair, he placed the cell phone closer to his right ear.

"It's ringing," he winked again. "Hi, there Meyan... yeah, its GDQ. How are things going? Yeah... I understand. Are you free anytime within the week? Okay for Thursday, did you say? Yes, today is Tuesday, old boy... you must really be very busy... that's what you get for being a think tank. Need another massage? The place is yours, old boy... No? Some other time, eh. Okay, Thursday then, yes at seven at the usual place. Of course, I'll come alone, one on one. Right, till then... thank you, Meyan. I owe you one, bye."

"So there you are," GDQ heaved a deep sigh of relief, picking his almost empty pack of cigarettes from the table. "Let's have another breakfast meeting, Friday. Till then."

The air was getting more dense as the tension grew.

"Don't Tinker With Constitution!"
"Six Years—Enough is Enough!"
"No to Martial Law!"
"No to Coup D'etat"
"No to Cha-Cha"
"Never Again!"
"Extension? No! No! No!"

Banners. Streamers. Placards. All in red... thousands of them. From end to end along Ayala Avenue and across Paseo de Roxas in the financial capital of the country, the demonstrators shouted and chanted their indignation; some say anxiety, against the possible extension of the term of President Rosales, whether through cha-cha or charter change, martial law or coup d'etat.

"The Cardinal is on the way! The Cardinal is on the way!" boomed the loudspeakers. Hurrahs and applause rang throughout as showers of confetti flew from the windows of tall buildings. Nuns representing various religious orders mixed with the crowd, uttering words of encouragement. Fair skinned men and women, some in business suits, moved from one group of demonstrators to another, distributing snacks.

"Brothers and sisters in Christ..." the voice of the Church, the self-anointed arbiter of right and wrong in the politics of the republic, began. "Today, we are again faced with the foul hand of evil, the evil of some men, who because of their greed like to perpetuate themselves in power. As dutiful Christians, we shall resist this threat to peace and stability. Let us all go and tell our brothers and sisters who are not with us today, to join us, in this time and day of infamy. Let us tell them, we resist and God will be with us."

The crowd roared as more confetti flew from the windows. Banners, streamers and placards shook and fluttered above the heads of thousands.

E lsewhere, the stench of garbage and the cries of another horde of demonstrators swelled in the air as rains fell at high noon. Soon thereafter, the hot sun burst, scorching the concrete pavement and mud puddles along Congressional Road in Quezon City.

"Amend Constitution Now!"
"Now or Bust!"
"We Want President Rosales!"
"Let's Move Forward, Not Backward!"
"Church Interference—A Cardinal Sin"

Banners. Placards. Streamers. All in blue. Thousands of them shouting, calling for cha-cha, to allow President Rosales to run again. Their battle cry: six years was too short for a good president but too long for a bad one.

"Amend the Constitution Now! Amend the Constitution Now!" the demonstrators shouted and chanted.

"We are here to maintain peace and order," the loudspeakers on top of the main gate of the House of Representatives boomed. "You are clogging traffic and you have no permit. Please let our lawmakers pass through and let them do their job. We are therefore asking you now to disperse peacefully."

"Amend the Constitution Now! Amend the Constitution Now!" the demonstrators boomed back in defiance.

I n private homes, coffee shops, billiard halls, restaurants, bus terminals, hotel lobbies and public places where people converge or lounge after a hard day's work, television sets were tuned in to "Truth or Tale", the most talked about TV talk show in town. Aired from seven to eight o'clock in the evening every Wednesday of the week, the talk show was regarded as the redeeming factor to the inane and sappy television programs that pervaded the airwaves.

To the A-B-C crowd, "Truth or Tale" was the most educational and entertaining, current national issues being its main menu. Its male host, Vito Sta. Dolores projected the image of an owl, knowledgeable and articulate on any issue of national importance. His lady co-host, Tina Gomez Latorta projected the face of the curious innocent, her eyes rolling into some kind of an inverted arc every time she pouted her lips to ponder at a question or to wonder at a statement. In time, the D and E crowd became fans of "Truth or Tale" as national issues became simplified either by the carefully selected guests or the prodding of Vito and Tina who always managed to translate complicated issues into common language for all types of audiences to appreciate.

The guests had already expressed their expert opinions on the hottest issue of the day and Vito, now zeroed in on his summary.

VITO   So there you are folks. We have a constitution that prohibits the incumbent president to run again because he is restricted to only one term but the same constitution also allows amendments, one of which may allow him to run again. I think that is clear enough for our viewers to understand. Tina?

TINA   Clear as day, Vito. To our viewers, our telephone numbers are now in your split screens. Vito, are we ready for the first caller?

VITO   Yes, we are.

VOICE I am Amelita Lucas, housewife, from Cubao. I just want to know why some people are forcing the issue on constitutional prohibitions, when the same prohibitions were of their own design. And now, they are the leaders of some of these demonstrations. Like it or not, these demonstrations are simply counterproductive.

VITO   Mrs. Lucas, to whom are you addressing your question?

LUCAS Probably, to the congressman in your panel.

VITO   Congressman Dimaano?

DIMAANO As Chair of the House Committee on Constitutional Amendments, all I can say is if the people want to amend the constitution, then so be it. However, we do not have enough time necessary for such an exercise nor the huge amount of money required for it. You know, this is an election year. As a matter of fact, the COMELEC is already complaining that not enough money has been released yet for the printing of ballots, etc. Now, if we conduct the plebiscite to amend the constitution within this year then that means tons of money because all the voters will be involved.

VITO   Mrs. Lucas observed that demonstrations are counterproductive. Any comments? Why don't we ask Professor Tirso Iglupas of the National State University?

IGLUPAS Demonstrations are part of the democratic right of the people to air their grievances. Demonstrations only become counterproductive if they end in violence. Nevertheless, even in that context, the right of the people to express their opinions through demonstrations still needs to be respected. If they allow themselves to be used by some vested interests, then they only have themselves to blame.

LUCAS I really don't know what you are talking about, Sir. But most of those who join demonstrations are not there in pursuit of legitimate issues but for the fund of it.

IGLUPAS Excuse me?

LUCAS I said for the f-u-n-d of it, not for the fun of it. You see what I mean?

IGLUPAS Fund of it… Oh, I see!

VITO   You sure about that, Mrs. Lucas?

18

LUCAS Well, can't you see? Demonstrations are growing by the thousands every day because many people make demonstrations their livelihood. They don't only get allowances but they also get free meals, free rides and pocket money.

VITO Well...

TINA Well, well... we have another caller from Cagayan De Oro in Mindanao.

VOICE I'm Antonio Almira. As I was about to say, I am simply bothered by the silence of President Rosales. It is becoming clear that his silence is fueling all these demonstrations. Some people are demonstrating because they want him to be President for life while others are also demonstrating because they don't want him to serve beyond what is legally allowed by the constitution. So both sides are right—wrong? Or is it, both sides are wrong—right? This is where I agree with Mrs. Lucas that all these demonstrations are counterproductive.

VITO Yes, why do you suppose the President is keeping mum, I mean, why is he silent in all this? Oh yes, Prof. Restituto of the National Forecast Service Institute, please.

RESTITUTO I remember that several years ago, a similar question was asked by the Center for Strategic Studies based in the Netherlands. About 63 percent responded that in crisis situations, most great decisions are made by a single person and those decisions are almost always made at the peak of the crisis.

TINA Now, that sounds very interesting. Do you imply that the silence of the president could mean he is waiting for the right time?

VITO Meaning, he would allow all these demonstrations to go on until some form of crisis emerges, so by that time, he will have a clear idea whether to act or not to act? Like Hamlet asking the eternal question—to be or not to be?

RESTITUTO Maybe. You know, Hamlet was also a king as portrayed by Shakespeare, perhaps the equivalent of our president today. But in fairness to President Rosales, our situation is not yet in crisis. The demonstrations against charter change are actually apprehensions of what I call the dictatorship syndrome—that people suspect President Rosales would like to perpetuate himself in power just like our former dictator-president. The demonstrators for cha-cha, I think, believe that since President Rosales has performed well, then let's change the charter and allow him to run again.

TINA What if those against and those for cha-cha clash and there is violence?

RESTITUTO Then that is what we call a crisis situation.

VITO We have another caller, Tina. Go ahead please...

VOICE General Quintos mentioned earlier in his opening statement that the possibility of a coup d'etat is very remote if not impossible at this time. Will he please elaborate on the matter?

QUINTOS As I said earlier, I am already retired and may not be as updated as those in the field. I was then in the active service when the series of coup d'etats was then staged against the regime of former President Caridad Anilao

Castro. The reason for that was the general discontent of the men in uniform. But today, during this regime, there is no discontent. On top of that, the military is busy with the war in Mindanao, not to mention the recent sparks of hostilities in some parts of Luzon and the Visayas being instigated by the once moribund New People's Watch and Revolutionary Army. That is why, I said, a coup d'etat at this time is not only very remote but also almost impossible.

TINA   State your name and address please, Sir...

VOICE I am Silvestre Autanan. I'm calling from Iloilo City.

My follow up question is, does it take the whole military force to launch a successful coup d'etat?

QUINTOS I would not dare comment on that except that a successful coup should have the support of the troops in the field, otherwise there will be a lot of bloodshed.

AUTANAN How about martial law? You also mentioned that earlier but did not elaborate on it.

QUINTOS Well, again, the present circumstances would not allow the declaration of martial law. Remember, martial law is only declared when the state is endangered.

AUTANAN Why, isn't the war in Mindanao endangering the security of the state?

QUINTOS The war in Mindanao could lead to the declaration of martial law but actually that war is isolated and has so far not even threatened the security of the central government. In addition, it may be noted the demonstrations referred to earlier are being led by known civic and religious leaders.

VITO   Excuse me, Father Ben Morales... Did you want to say something?

MORALES If Mr. Autanan would allow me...

AUTANAN Yes, Father.

MORALES I like to believe I was invited as one of the guests here, because of my book on the psychology of demonstrations. The issue raised by Mr. Autanan is a valid one. Demonstrations that start as peaceful ones usually end in violence because of what we call mob psychology. While I recognize the observation of General Quintos that the leaders of both demonstrations are known civic and religious leaders, implying they are rational men and women, there is actually no guarantee that the current peaceful demonstrations will not end in violence. A small stone thrown to the other side could lead to some retaliatory moves and before you know it, violence erupts. In some cases, violence started with just a simple joke. But, of course, many of us know most demonstrations that erupted in violence were infiltrated by provocateurs, planted there deliberately by some evil forces or would you say, vested interests to create chaos.

TINA   Are you saying Father Morales if chaos occurs, that could justify the declaration of martial law?

MORALES Maybe, Tina, maybe.

VITO   Let's have a word or two from our sponsors.

TINA   Please don't go away, we'll be back.

As the studio scene fades out, the prince of local movies and darling of TV commercials, Kidd Batuta looms on screen, taking a big round bite of his favorite jumbo sandwich, his dimples flashing. Then, Luningning Morena, Miss Universe 1st runner-up and local supermodel glides on the fashion ramp, her eyes glistening their cutie, little stars as her oh-so-slim body displays the latest lingerie for all women of all ages, above and below her open midriff. Then, Steve Karate, the bone-cracking martial arts villain-hero and international movie star, his grin so macho cool, withdraws the glass of sparkling liquid gold rum from his lips and sighing with satisfaction, says: "Only in the Philippines..."

TINA   Welcome back to "Truth or Tale", the most talked about talk show in town. Vito?

VITO   Thanks, Tina. This time, we'll entertain questions from our audience in the studio. There you are... the young lady in white shirt, yes, she with the long curly hair.

YOUNG LADY I'm Roxanne Federico, a student from Marikina. I'd just like you to know we students are getting tired of leaders who keep on saying their policy is transparency. But when it comes to issues related to their personal position, they all keep us in the dark, so we have no choice but to speculate, speculate and speculate. Now, that is really counterproductive. We students find this whole thing absolutely unfair to us who voted these people to office. So I propose that once and for all, if your term of office is six years then you should only serve six years, period, period and period. Once is enough, enough, enough and enough!

VITO   Ha! Ha! I see the president of the National State University student council did not react to what Miss Federico just said. Mr. Gascon, would you like to comment?

GASCON I really cannot understand why Roxanne's comments drew laughs and chuckles. Roxanne was not only stating a personal conviction but also the conviction of many students. What she actually pointed out is the façade of duplicity many of our leaders display. It might be good politics to them but bad role-modeling for us.

TINA   Vito, there's another lady from the audience...

VITO   Please, Ma'am. Yes, the lady with the scarf...

LADY WITH SCARF I am Mrs. Rosalinda Jamores, elementary school teacher. I'd like to take a contrary view to what Miss Federico stated a while ago. My position is this: if a leader has demonstrated for six years that he or she can deliver, then for God's sake, let him or her become the president for life. I repeat, this is my position whether the constitution says so or not, whether the cardinal says so or not, whether the poor or the rich say so or not, whether the students say so or not. Let us not allow our emotions to override our rationality. It is absolutely insane to change a leader who has already proven his or her mettle, so to speak. What if the new elected leader performs like a monkey or a clown? So in this case, one good leader is enough. One election is enough. Once is enough!

The guests once again erupted in laughter.

TINA   Ha! Ha! Ha! Oh, my God. Ha! Ha! Ha! Just a minute. Vito, we have a VIP on the line. She's been insisting ...

VITO   Who?

TINA   It's Senator Santolan.

VITO   Magnify the audio. Magnify the audio!

VOICE This is Senator Naomi Ganzon Santolan. Let me tell you immediately that what you are showing in public is a toxic insult to the sanctity of the constitution of this land. Your hyena-inspired laughter and hen-like cackles further deepen the injury. For your information, the constitution is explicit and you cannot just change that through magic and manipulation. Let no man, whether he is president or not, put his own personal rapacity over the rule of law. Because if he is allowed to do that and no one cares, then I will personally see to it that he and his hallucinations will end in the dungeons of shame and ignominy. Thank You.

VITO   Let's have a station break.

TINA   Don't go away—it's never enough to say, we'll be back.

Off camera range, the honorable guests look at each other, this time without a hint of laughter or a sign of a cackle.

"I believe we've covered everything there is to cover," Fatso said, lowering his reading glasses at the tip of his nose. "Now, to the last topic of the day. Any bright ideas?"

The speaker was the chairman of the task force to Elect Mahalina for President or EMPRES. Fatso or Ruperto "Fatso" Santos was known as a brilliant lawyer who earned his moniker not because he was obese, although lately he was a little bit like that. Well, he was known as "Fatso" because of the fat fees he charged his clients, mostly political fat cats and business hotshots who were known tax evaders. A two-term congressman representing the lone district of the home city of Mahalina, the two became close friends over the years. To his credit, Fatso was one of the few who finally persuaded Mahalina to run for president. That was nine years ago. He was also one of the few who kept calling Mahalina, "Mahal" which meant "Love" until that moniker stuck for him, the most popular candidate for president representing the opposition and the most feared by the administration party.

"Okay, so far we have ascertained three options for President Rosales to hold on to power beyond his term. One, through a constitutional amendment; two, through a coup d'etat; and three, through the declaration of martial law. From the discussions that followed, it appears the cons are overwhelmingly stronger than the pros. But just in case Rosales pushes hard to effect any one of these options, we have the strategy, the means and the wherewithal to counteract and frustrate him."

Randolf Patis Cruz who just did the running summary was the media bureau chief of EMPRES. Randy, as he was called, was a newspaper columnist whose attacks on corrupt government officials were considered classic in the trade, well-researched exposes written in sarcasm and bile. He also did not spare his colleagues who were suspected of being ACDCs—the Attack-Collect, Defend-Collect operators whose "envelopmental journalism" as he called it, enabled them to live a comfortable life. His attacks on his wayward colleagues did not endear him to them but they had no choice. Randy had become powerful in his own turf, had strong political connections and they knew it.

"Are there other options?" Fatso asked.

"I don't think this is an option but I think it is a possibility. What if the president suddenly dies or is assassinated? Bitten by a cobra? Or, by an act of God, is hit by lightning?"

"Jesus, Raul! What are you saying?" Patricia Gan-Alfonso snapped. If there was anybody in the task force of Mahalina that had real battle experience in the so-called "war zone" that was Malacanang, Gan-Alfonso was it. A frail-looking woman of 41 who looked five years younger than her age, Gan-Alfonso never retaliated openly when attacked but used the backdoor direct to the office of past presidents, two of whom she had served. Gan-Alfonso exuded a personality that drew attention and a voice that moved in slow accented cadences, assets that threw off skeptics in arguments and impelled others not similarly engaged, to look and listen. She served as coordinator of the task force.

"Raul" was Raulito Pangilinan, the academician of the group. Except for his thick sideburns and the slightly protruding dentures that now and then would jump out of his gums every time he got excited, certainly not his fault but that of his dentist, Pangilinan looked the typical university professor. Thin and lean, he walked with a stoop but when he looked up, his face stayed there as if the answers to all the questions dangled from the roof of the sky.

"You must be kidding!?" Cruz echoed Gan-Alfonso's sneer.

"No, no, I'm serious," Pangilinan answered. "It happened to many heads of state before. Who would have ever thought Lyndon Johnson would become president of the U.S. until John Kennedy got hit in the head? I don't need to review here the history of assassinations to prove my point!"

"Okay, okay," Fatso said. "Since this is a very serious matter, why don't we request Raul here to write a treatise about it and send it directly to Mahal—For His Eyes Only. We don't need to review that here. As I said it is very serious and very sensitive. Leaks could jeopardize our position and of course, Mahal's position. Will you take that, Raul?"

"Absolutely, yes, I will do just that," Pangilinan nodded, pleased.

"Now back on track. As agreed earlier, our legislative agenda include but are not limited to the following major concerns: gambling and other forms of amusement as revenue-generating projects, creation of a department of housing and urban development and amendment of the law on poverty alleviation. The latter, I find too bureaucratic in its organizational set-up to effect efficient and coordinated delivery of services."

"Are we really serious on gambling…?" Gan-Alfonso interjected.

23

Fatso Santos did not reply. Dr. Randy flipped through the pages of the legislative agenda. Pangilinan surveyed the ceiling.

"Are we really serious on gambling?" Gan-Alfonso repeated, clearly sounding irritated.

"I think we are sailing into stormy waters," Pangilinan recited. "But we need not sink if we can steer the ship to safety." He then stood and paced the floor.

"C'mon, Professor," Gan-Alfonso cut in. "Why don't you stop talking in metaphors and instead tell us what you want to say in plain language? The masses will not understand you that way."

"The masses is not the right term, Pat, if I may say," Pangilinan replied, laying his predicate. "I am sure that you allude to the masses in this country who live below the poverty line, whose votes would give Mahal total victory. These are not the masses, Pat. These are the Great Unwashed who exhaust 95 percent of their time scrounging for food to survive. And what is left, that is five percent, is spent to seek entertainment. In short, a little time for happiness is what they need. Don't you think Pat, that they deserve a little time for happiness? Even God rested on the seventh day."

Pangilinan paused, pushing his tongue against his gums. "So, with that little time, the Great Unwashed seek entertainment instead of taking a bath. And what is that entertainment? It is gambling, Pat. Gambling! Why? Because it's the cheapest kind of entertainment they can afford while imagining, dreaming that by chance, they might win some substantial amounts of money and live a happy life thereafter, beyond mere survival. This quest for entertainment in gambling is part of the culture of poverty. So no matter what you do to suppress it, gambling will stay. Therefore, the best way is to legalize it to make everybody happy; the small-time gamblers constituting the Great Unwashed in this country and the government for the additional taxes it will earn!"

Gan-Alfonso did not say anything.

"No wonder, Mahal is partial to gambling," Cruz connected. He did not say that Mahalina was a compulsive gambler.

"I think Raul's arguments are convincing enough," Fatso concluded. "Okay, Dr. Randy, do the spin on it but don't use the term the Great Unwashed."

"No problem," Cruz said, nodding his head while looking at Gan-Alfonso. Pangilinan flashed a smile, his dentures sinking back in place.

"Are we sure, all of these are the priorities of Mahal?" Pat Gan-Alfonso asked, deliberately making a detour as she leafed through the pages in front of her.

"These are all in your copies, pages 9-14. It doesn't matter," Fatso said, pushing back his glasses in place. "Mahal has to have a comprehensive program of governance. And I suggest, very strongly, all these be incorporated in his campaign speeches. Now, you are to work very closely with the subtask forces under your charge. They have already been created and are ready to go as soon as you give the green light. The checklist of the subtask forces, their respective members and their functions, see pages 17-26. Also, note the deadline of each and the work schedule of all concerned for our review."

"Are we sure Mahalina would like all these included in his speeches?" Cruz asked.

"It doesn't really matter," Fatso pointed out. "What is important is we have papers to present to media so the public may know of the programs of Mahal."

Meandro Destino stared at his laptop but all he could see on its screen was not the last paragraph of his memo to the president, but the face of Marissa Gantuico on the carpet floor. Would she or would she not? Admitting to himself he was out of focus at the moment, he switched off his laptop and decided to sleep. He would finish the memo early in the morning.

In bed, he could not sleep. The face of Marissa Gantuico stuck with him in the dark. Would she or wouldn't she tell on him?

Nineteen days ago, Meandro Destino delivered the speech of the president in an international symposium. In the open forum that followed, Marissa Gantuico, in a dark blue business suit, her long ebony hair cascading around her neck and ending just at the top of her heaving breasts, made a statement. Three things he could not forget that busy afternoon—the unique personality that glowed in the woman, the brilliance of her statement and the certain way she regarded him. On this third, she gave him the impression he was nothing to her but another tape recorder of the president.

Within 48 hours after, Meandro Destino thought he had a complete profile of the woman. She was one of two daughters of a former senator. She had married a foreigner while studying abroad but divorced him after she finished her master's degree in third world sociology. They had no children. After that marriage, Marissa Gantuico was known to shun men. She lived alone and had no social life. She had a burning interest—devoted herself to social work specializing on malnourished children. She was also a successful businesswoman who traveled extensively abroad. Not a few men, married or unmarried were in hot pursuit to win her but she denied all of them the privilege.

Seventy-two hours after he first met her, Destino made his move. He called her office and told her over the phone the president was so impressed by her reaction, that he, the president would like to meet her and discuss with her the merits of her statement. The result could lead to a presidential policy pronouncement on the issue.

To his surprise, Marissa Gantuico was cold and aloof. While she was flattered by the president's invitation, she said, her statement during that symposium wasn't really worth it. She was not a politician, she added. And besides, she would be out of the country in the next two weeks. Destino asked where she would be in the next two weeks, sounding as if she was just presenting an alibi. Again, to his surprise, Marissa Gantuico told him she was flying to Frankfurt and then to The Hague, then London and finally to Hong Kong on the way home, mentioning the hotels she was booked to stay along the way. Destino felt that her matter-of-fact enumerations were clothed in veiled sarcasm but he took that as a sign of a professional who knew her place in the sun. At that time, Destino knew he had to make his final move.

The early flight to Hong Kong somehow made him groggy. Lack of sleep and the two memos he wrote to the president deprived him of sleep, plus the third one he underlined *personal*, explaining he had to be in Hong Kong in the next two days for a personal reason. It was easy to get a flight reservation but it took a lot of haggling before he finally got his room on the same floor of the Four Seasons Hotel where Marissa Gantuico said she was staying.

For the first time in his 53 years, Meandro Destino felt like the tight little veins in his loins would burst. By just thinking of Marissa Gantuico, rehearing her voice, imagining her in his mind—all that excited him to the bone. His separation from his wife of 15 years had somehow turned him into a freak. True, he had made several attempts on young and attractive call girls in the last five years or so but the moment he thought he would explode, his manhood suddenly went limp, his embarrassment turning into soaring anger. Hell hath no fury like a man unable to perform even if the mocking laughter that followed came from a virgin-whore.

In room 727, Meandro Destino had stayed stuck on the sofa, mumbling to himself whether to proceed or not to Room 725 where the reception desk clerk said Miss Gantuico had checked in seven hours earlier. What if this move failed? What price would he pay for the daring, for the scandal to himself and to the office of the president?

Destino splashed his third untouched shot of Chivas on the sink and before he knew it, found himself in front of Room 725. On his second knock, he heard the latch slide as the door opened.

"Dr. Destino!" Marissa Gantuico gasped in surprise, backing hastily away from the open door.

"May I come in?" Destino asked uneasily, noting that she was not wearing her glasses; that she was in a dark blue silk robe that punctuated the pinkish white glow of her skin; that her breasts were heaving mightily as she moved hastily away from him, slumping on her seat behind the desk. On top of the desk were several sharpened Mongol pencils that were strewn here and there, over a yellow pad paper. Apparently, she had been writing before his intrusion.

Her dark brown eyes were all over him, as he closed the door behind and found himself seated at the single chair fronting the desk.

"Well, what can I do for you, Dr. Destino? This is rather an unusual surprise for me!" her tone of voice did not hide its venom.

"Marissa, I mean, Miss Gantuico. I had to fly here to see you. I had to see you because I lied to you... about the President." He swallowed hard, trying to control his discomfort.

"So you came to tell me, an ordinary citizen that... apparently using government time and money that you lied! What crap are you peddling, Mr. Presidential Adviser?" She was fuming. She was in rage.

"Miss Gantuico, no, Marissa, that's what I'm going to call you from hereon, whether you like it or not. No, no, I used my own time and money to fly over and see you. And you are not an ordinary citizen to me and 'crap' is not in my vocabulary. I repeat—I lied to you about the President. I used his name for the simple excuse to see you again. I wanted to see you again because I have never felt like this before, in my whole damn lonely life."

As he said that, the veins in his loins burned and the ache made him pause. He had said what he wanted to say in the last 16 days and 15 nights. Now, he was ready for the consequences.

All of a sudden, Marissa picked one pencil as she stood and hissed, trying hard to control her rage. "Dr. Destino, you will have to leave right now and please close the door behind you."

"Marissa," Meyan Destino pleaded as he stood, slowly circling the desk and placing his arms around her shoulders. "Marissa, I need you. Please hear me. I know that in time, you will also need me."

Marissa stiffened as he tightened his arms around her. Her anger had engulfed her. But she would not shout neither would she stab him with the sharpened pencil in her right fist which she now clinched even tighter. His voice, the way he looked at her and the way he held her could only mean this man did not come to be humiliated. He had come to do what he wanted to do. A wound or two would not stop him. And she could not stand the sight or smell of blood. And violence.

"Marissa, please..." the heat of his mouth on her nape startled Marissa; she unknowingly dropped the pencil from her clasp. "Marissa, please..." the heat of his body against her back startled her even more, as the days and nights of living alone flashed through her... as he slid his arms into her robe and turned her firmly but gently toward him.

"No, no, no!" Marissa tried to scream but only hisses came out of her throat. His whispers, his pleadings and his grip dominated her. "Marissa, I want you now... I want you forever."

Marissa stayed composed even in her nakedness as he gently but firmly laid her down on the carpet floor. With eyes shut, she folded her arms around her breasts and tightened her right thigh over her left.

The first thrust and flow splashed over her upper right thigh. The second thrust and flow watered the upper flesh of her navel. The third thrust and flow sought her as he plunged deeper and deeper into her being.

Except for the loud breathing, there was total stillness in what seemed to be an eternity.

"You're an animal! You're a rapist of an animal!" Marissa moaned, whimpering, her arms and thighs limping languidly on the carpet floor.

After some seconds of unexplained relief, Destino slowly rose, took his handkerchief from his pants on the floor and went to the sink where he rinsed it in hot and cold water. Marissa was still on the floor, in fetal position as he gently rubbed the misplaced remains of his rage and desire off her flesh.

"Marissa," Meandro Destino said as he kissed her on the forehead. "I'll pay for this. I'll pay in whatever way you want me to pay. All I ask is to spare the President from any embarrassment. Just remember one thing. I did what I had to do because I need you and I want you to also need me."

Destino bent and fell on his knees. It took him a long time to extract something from his wallet.

"Here's my card. At the back you'll see my confidential phone number and the address of my apartment where I stay alone. I'll see you in Manila."

Destino woke up at exactly one-thirty in the morning. At 53, his biological clock was accurate. All he did was set up his interior clock in his mind anytime he wanted to wake up in the morning and voila, it kept ringing on the hour. And here he was, sitting upright on his bed, his bare feet planted on the linoleum floor, fully awake and totally conscious but not quite sure of himself.

Where was he last night? Yes, he was into the last paragraph of his memo but Marissa was on the screen. Today was the fourth day after Hong Kong. Would she or wouldn't she tell on him?

A cold shower and five cigarettes later, the screen on his laptop told him the memo he had written was formidable. Whether the president would buy it or not was not his problem. His main job, he reminded himself many times, was to think of at least three options to any issue or problem from which the president might make his choice. Glad to know, he told himself, in almost six years he served as adviser, the president's choice always came from within those options or a combination thereof.

Where would Marissa be right now? Would she or wouldn't she tell on him? Destino kept asking himself as he faxed his memo at three in the morning. At three-fifteen, his cell phone trilled. A presidential aide was calling to remind him of his one-on-one with the president at five o'clock, the breakfast meeting with his inner circle at six, the meeting of the cabinet clusters at one, the cabinet meeting at three and then the press con at five.

At three-twenty five, his doorbell rang. As he opened the door, Marissa Gantuico, still smelling of bath soap, her hair still wet but neatly combed down to her heaving breasts, plunged into him, grabbed the front of his boxer shorts as she kicked the door behind her. The violence with which she attacked him and the equally violent way he responded threw all forms of inhibitions there were between them. There were no terms of endearment, no nicknames, no family names, no recall of position papers in a symposium and no words. Except that it was everything else as she tore into his flesh and as he tore into her flesh with increasing intensity—from the floor to the sofa, from the sofa to the kitchen and from the kitchen to the bedroom. He pushed and he pulled and she clung and she clung, her mouth in his, his mouth in hers. Her legs were locked around his waist, his hands were clamped against her rear, as they struggled from bed to carpet, from carpet to bed until their mutual cries of desire and ecstasy exploded in climax then receded—then gradually returned to the normal beat of the heart.

As he stood smoking a cigarette, Meyan Destino gazed at Marissa lying in fetal position at the edge of his bed, her eyes closed, her face askance in a certain smile, her heaving breasts partly pressed against the pillow. "Those are the breasts that could topple empires," Destino whistled softly, remembering Richard Burton's description of Elizabeth Taylor's great bumpers. It was absolutely strange— Destino muttered to himself as he headed for the bathroom that Marissa who would not even smile to a greeting acted like a tigress in heat in the arena of mating. And it was doubly strange that he, a freak in the last many years also raged like her except that he was the hungry tiger. At 53, with the work he was engaged in and his discouraging experiences with women, Destino had about forgotten his manly needs until Marissa came into his life. Now, he trembled at the power of his loins.

When he returned from the bathroom, Marissa was gone. There was no note, no hint, nothing. Destino hurriedly dressed for his appointed hour with the president.

"Good morning, Mr. President," Destino spoke his greeting as he tiptoed toward the chair in front of the president's desk. It was exactly four minutes past five o' clock in the morning, Tuesday.

When the president did not answer but simply gestured to the chair in front of his desk, Destino immediately felt something different was in the air this morning.

As soon as he was seated, the president put the pen back on its cap, removed his glasses and wiped his eyes with a handkerchief. "You look thoroughly reinvigorated this morning, Meyan," the president suddenly said, beaming at him over his glasses. "Did you sleep well last night?"

How did he know? Destino asked himself, slowly nodding his head, his mind's eye on the heaving breasts that could topple empires.

"Meyan," the president's voice suddenly sounded official. "Are you a part of Oplan Twilight Zone?"

"No, Mr. President," Destino swallowed as he answered. "Upon the request of GDQ, I agreed to personally hand carry the blueprint to you, Sir."

After some silence, the president asked, "What do you think of the Oplan?"

Is the President considering it? "I believe it will work, Mr. President. My research work on nonviolent coups that succeeded tells me the Oplan as blueprinted will work." Destino found the opportunity and shifted in his chair.

"Granting that Oplan T-Z is executed and consummated," the president said, obviously still in his own thoughts, "how do you equate its success to the legacy of this presidency that your latest memo stressed, should be 'safeguarded and freed from all suspicions of guile, greed and guilt? That is, if the legacy of performance and commitment to the people of the Rosales Presidency is to be assured its rightful niche in the future history of the nation.' Did I quote you right?"

Destino gasped. *Where is he leading me?*

"Mr. President, you asked me what I thought of Oplan T-Z. My answer, I believe, mirrors a logical conclusion and, therefore may be considered objective. My memo to you that stressed on securing your legacy is a personal opinion, hence may be considered subjective, though I derived that same opinion from the history of guile, greed and guilt that documents the rise and fall of world leaders from fame to shame."

The president slowly swayed his swivel chair backward, pulling out from his right front trouser pocket a piece of coupon bond paper folded lengthwise that he now set before him on the desk. Uncapping the red pentel pen, the president began to write on top of some old notes that were earlier written there before Destino got into the study.

Destino did not want to assume that what the president just wrote had something to do with what he just said. For again in the last five and a half years, he had observed that the man was capable of pursuing multilateral thoughts in space, time and motion. While listening to reports in closed door meetings, or to speeches in big auditoriums or during briefings above the clouds in the presidential plane—he was also at the same time whispering instructions to an aide while writing some notes on that piece of paper in red over black. Surely, the president had the uncanny ability to tune in to several conversations at once.

"Now, Meyan, which of our party's presidentiables, do you think, is winnable?"

Destino was startled at the sudden shift. The president seldom did that without any signal.

"Against Mahalina?" this time, Destino was startled at himself. He seldom reacted like that, asking another question over the president's own.

"All surveys, Mr. President, show no one has any iota of a chance against Mahalina. That includes our own unpolluted surveys. That being the case, I feel you shouldn't be bothered about it. On the contrary, my advice is we invoke the democratic process as part of this whole exercise—win or lose."

"Which means?" the president cut in, leaning forward.

"Which means, Mr. President, the contest must go on as called for by the constitution, unless, of course, there are other situations that would justify a different course of action. Either way, what is paramount is the legacy of your presidency."

"In operational terms, Mr. President," Destino found himself connecting after the president stayed silent, "if you take the first option which presupposes you have no choice but to name your successor, you have to use all the powers of your office and the resources of your party to really campaign hard for him on the ground."

The president took a sip from the glass of water beside him.

"Actually, many of us are bothered, Mr. President," Destino took advantage of the lull. "Pin Davide may end up at the tail end of the contest. That would not be a good reflection of your leadership, Sir." Destino suddenly felt a lump in his throat.

Like many others, Destino knew that Davide's chance of winning was like squeezing juice from a dry leaf. The man was simply not marketable to the electorate. Destino felt that the president was partial to Davide but would the president endorse him, knowing that Davide had no chance whatsoever against Mahalina? Dimalasa was worse. Yes, he was known as a moral man but he was weak. If a choice had to be made, where would this lead to? Would the choice be between putting up a façade of respectability on one hand and suffering total humiliation, on the other?

After some silence, the president stood and paced the floor.

"Meanwhile, let's confine ourselves to the four hot issues this afternoon. I'll see you at breakfast."

As soon as Destino stood to leave, the president went back to his desk and said after him. "Kindly tell GDQ to hang on. I will call him when the proper time comes."

"Yes, Mr. President," Destino answered, tiptoeing out of the presidential study. Out in the yard, it took him a few minutes to wonder at the fallen leaves on the ground before he lighted a cigarette.

From the palace gates, journalists of all persuasions, both from the local and foreign media rushed to their designated seats at the Heroes Hall, ground floor of the palace.

"Ladies and gentlemen, the President of the Republic His Excellency President Sergio Imperial Rosales." the press secretary announced, just in case there was a visitor from Mars. "Mr. President, the members of the Press."

"Thank you, Mr. Secretary," the president acknowledged, looking at his notes. "Ladies and gentlemen of the press, good afternoon to all of you."

"Good afternoon, Mr. President," chorused his audience. Some said it loud enough, the others simply muttered.

"After a careful review of certain standards, I have decided, in concurrence with my party stalwarts in the Committee of 31, to adopt three criteria which I think are most relevant to our situation. I hope that after revealing all three, all speculations should stop. I'm not saying that some of you in media are also fond of making speculations."

Some laughter could be heard in the hall.

He is really becoming sarcastic! Katrina Avila muttered to herself, scribbling some notes on her notebook.

"Number one," the president looked at his notes again. "Loyalty to the party must be incontestable and consistent over the years."

The hint was almost conclusive, most of those present thought. Serafin Andolana Davide was it. He was one of the founding fathers of the party in power, along with the president. He was also its incumbent secretary general.

"Number two," the president went on. "The candidate must pledge to continue the programs and projects this administration already started. This commitment to continuity must be adhered to, at all costs, by the candidate to ensure the country's continuous development as planned by this administration."

There were whispers. There was a general agreement all the aspirants would easily qualify here. "The third and final criterion," the president said, raising his head up, "is that the candidate who will be my successor... "the president paused again, "has a clean and spotless public record."

The rumble of hisses and whispers suddenly filled Heroes Hall. Those who thought Davide was it, now thought Dimalasa was it.

"Mr. President!" voices competed with each other, arms shooting up in the air and bodies standing up to gain recognition.

"Honorable ladies and gentlemen of the press," the press secretary's voice rose above the din. "May I remind you that the President has yet to make his concluding statement."

That sent all the bodies back to their seats as silence followed. That also sent the president grinning, pleased at the vigilance of his press secretary.

"Ladies and gentlemen of the press, the three criteria I mentioned, I will apply in making my final choice for the official presidential candidate of the party. In three weeks, I will make the final announcement. That is all, Mr. Secretary. Thank you."

After she was recognized, Katrina Avila of TV channel 6 asked as she stood. "Mr. President, the three criteria you mentioned, do they have equal weights or different weights?" Katrina Avila was known as the sweetheart of the press. At 33 and almost five-five, she was more than a pretty face. She was in fact a well-known TV personality and a popular ramp model. Her gray-brown eyes were the envy of many, not to mention her pulsating personality and quick wit.

"I have not mentioned weights, young lady. What I mentioned are the three general criteria which I will, as I said, use to assess the qualifications of our aspirants." Like most men of knowledge, the president believed in telling media the truth but not the whole truth or everything about it.

"Which implies, Mr. President, despite the three general criteria you mentioned, the final decision would still be highly arbitrary," Katrina Avila quickly observed as hisses and whispers filled the hall again.

"I'd rather not respond to your highly speculative conjecture," the president forced a smile, winking on the side.

Some laughter, this time a little subdued, could be heard again as Katrina Avila went back to her seat, shaking her head in disgust.

"From the Orient Business Daily," the press secretary recognized another.

"Thank you. Mr. Secretary," the reporter raised his voice over the standing microphone in the middle aisle. "Mr. President, it appears all the aspirants in your party will easily qualify using the second criterion, that is the criterion of commitment to continuity from what your administration started. However, it appears again, that among all the aspirants nobody will ultimately qualify using the other two criteria. What do you say to this, Mr. President?"

Everybody wanted to ask that same question in one form or another. "Silence, please," the press secretary raised his voice, motioning to those who were already standing to go back to their seats.

"Your reaction simply tells us all how difficult it is to make decisions from up here," the president forced a grin, trying to contain his irritation. "Your consolation is that it is not your difficulty. That is mine and mine alone to make. I appeal to you, therefore, to report or editorialize this whole burden with compassion and understanding. In this way, our people will be fully informed of such burden and, therefore can make their final decision who to vote for in the coming presidential elections."

From the corner of the hall, Richard Martin, foreign correspondent of the Asian Times Journal, rushed out of the gate, hailed a taxi and consulted his notes. He had to seek out his old sources and cover more ground. He wondered if he had the time.

Commander Ahmad Jamil pressed the red button on the remote as the TV screen went blur, then blank. Had the president finally decided to give up? Or was that press conference another ploy to cover his tracks? So what? It was the same rigmarole. Criteria or no criteria, whoever became president of the republic ended up power-hungry, selfish and helpless.

Jamil puffed on his cigarette. It was more than two decades ago. He was a fresh high school graduate from a Christian missionary school, when he was whisked to an island farther south to be trained as a *mujahedeen* or holy warrior. Jamil topped what was known then as the Class of 36. Smoking with his eyes closed, Jamil remembered clearly what happened on graduation day. It was exactly ten in the morning. There was no wind and the bright sun warmed the bodies of his class who stood at attention on the parade ground of the camp in their full battle gear. The ceremony was about to start when two government F81 fighter planes suddenly thundered from above as their missiles whammed all over the place. Anti-aircraft mortars and grenade launchers from the ground responded, but it was too late. Exactly 24 from Class 36 were ripped apart by the missiles, including five of their instructors from the Middle East, two of whom were from Libya. Jamil and his eleven classmates survived, their uniforms bloodied and their faces splashed with the scattered flesh and guts of their dead comrades. From the Class of 36, the survivors became known as the Dirty Dozen.

After barely four months of extensive operations, the Dirty Dozen and their heavily armed men, wrecked havoc in the countryside that killed many government troops and burned many villages. It did not take long for Commander Jamil to become known as Field Marshall Fox. There were many occasions when government military forces thought they had cornered him, but the fox always eluded them. Until one day when Jamil was caught. Totally elated, the dictator-president wanted the world to see the captured fox who was heavily guarded in the confines of Camp Wala-Wala, the headquarters of the Southern Command. But between the skies of Manila and Mindanao and to the consternation of the local and international media that he had invited to fly with him in the presidential plane, the dictator-president received word by radio the fox had escaped again, this time burning the whole camp behind him, including the camp commander and exactly 42 of his men. The rest were hog-tied and dumped one kilometer from the razed camp, stripped of their uniform, their weapons and their pride.

To the surprise of many, retaliatory government military operations against the rebels did not follow. There was silence too from the dirty dozen and their men. Then exactly two weeks after the Camp Wala-Wala carnage, the dictator-president announced the government's offer of total amnesty to Commander Jamil and his men, in exchange for their surrender. For every firearm turned over to the government, depending on kind and make, a commensurate loan package was to be made available to develop the land grants that went with the package. Above all, the dictator-president boldly announced, half of the reward money allotted for the capture of the twelve commanders would be given to them in cash, the other half to be invested as start-up capital in any small business venture that they might want to put up with government assistance

Five weeks after the historic announcement, the rebels surrendered, the 11 commanders one after another, laid down their arms and received their cash in different points in Mindanao. Commander Jamil and his immediate command were flown to Malacanang as flashbulbs popped and TV cameras converged around the dictator-president and Jamil who shook hands and hugged each other like they were long lost brothers suddenly reunited.

In addition to the amnesty award of P400,000 originally intended for his capture, an old duffel bag containing P5M in cash was delivered to his hotel room that night by some of the dictator-president's special security detail. Commander Jamil remembered the last parting words of the dictator-president— "I have something personal to give you later. Shalom!"

That magnanimous gesture of the dictator-president gave Jamil an idea, an idea that entirely changed the character of the relationship between the government and the rebel forces.

A year and four months later, the fox and the 11 other commanders went back to the hills. Commander Jamil announced he had no choice. The land grants could not be made productive because the loan packages promised were not released. Much paper work was required and too many government agencies involved. In many cases when some loan packages were actually released, the amount was no longer enough to start a venture, since much had to be deducted to pay private loan sharks for the follow-ups.

"My men are starving because of government's broken promises," Jamil told media that now hounded him like a superstar.

The impact of Jamil's return to the hills was far more devastating to the dictator-president. Jamil did not only make a fool out of him; he had also exposed the inefficiency of his government.

The dictator-president was known as the most brilliant head of state ever in the history of the republic. But because of his superego, he failed to recognize that Commander Ahmad Jamil had institutionalized the game of blackmail upon him and his government. Throughout their relationship and until the dictator-president's exile and eventual death, Commander Jamil had surrendered three times—in the process, taking with him millions of cash. All this, plus additional tons of promises from the government of land grants, business ventures and more concessions that until the present were still being claimed by the rebels.

Jamil stuck another cigarette to his gold plated holder and lit it with the table lighter. Puffing the stateside nicotine, he felt young again; exhilarated and totally amused he had outsmarted the most brilliant president ever in the history of the republic.

Scratching the itch in his butt, a habit acquired through the years in the hills which he believed was originally caused by leeches, it occurred to him now that the itch could have been actually caused by the complaining soul of the dead dictator-president, to remind him of the millions he had taken away from him. "I only took a fraction of the billions you embezzled from your own people, Mr. Dictator-President," Jamil hissed at no one in particular, scratching the itch in his butt with more enthusiasm. "Anyway, you are an infidel and you deserve nothing but to rot in hell." Commander Jamil spat again, hitting the center of the waste can.

Just then, an aide entered and saluted. "Field Marshall Fox, Task Force Commander Tausug and his men already left for the mission you ordered."

"Excellent," the Fox exclaimed. "Allah Achbar!"
"God is Great!"

At Home
Apartment No. 201-A
243 New York St., Quezon City

Dear Angela,

Greetings from your home country! How are you my childhood friend and first cousin? This is my fourth letter and I still have to hear from you! Except for the postcard you sent from that zoo you last visited, there is not a word from you that would lift my spirits over here. Tell me, what have you been doing lately?

Anyway, keep on earning dollars and save a lot when you finally come for your vacation. But when is that? This is now the third year of your adventures abroad and you are still there and never here. Wow, you must really be enjoying yourself.

I failed to visit your kids as I promised in my last letter. Bicol is now 23 hours by bus from here. Well, as you know it used to be 14-18 hours but they've lengthened traveling time by those road repairs that suddenly come about every election year. Politics, politics, politics. Gosh!

Times are really getting harder here. I just got back shopping from the corner grocery store. You know what? I really got depressed—my weekly supply of grocery items which used to be only P500 now cost me P900! Now, this is really outrageous—that wasn't so two months ago!

The political situation over here looks pitiful. I mean you have a very good performing president, yet he cannot continue serving this country because of a constitutional provision that limits his term to only six years. Of course, there are many who are also interested in that position. But you know what? Many are saying the further our country has moved from its colonial to its independent status, the smaller our leaders have become in stature. Well...

You remember when I was president of our college student council, do you? Didn't our college president change the rules (of course with the support of the studentry) so that I could continue since I was that good, right? You won't forget that Angela, since you were my secretary in the council. Those were the days.

Remember the guy I was writing you about? Well, I had to finally ditch him. I have to admit he is tall, dark and ah, ah not too handsome (Ha! Ha!) but he seems to have no future as an insurance agent. While he kept on ensuring me that with his love we could have a bright future, I could not really see anything beyond my nose that his sweet promises would become a reality. I found out too, he was supporting two younger brothers to school!

35

While this is a very noble aim on his part, what does it do for me and Tony Boy?

I think you're right Angela. Forget about love. All I have to do is to have a fling now and then. Watch me.

Tony Boy is all right. You'll be surprised that at seven he could already spell a lot of words and add numbers with the speed of light.

I really miss our hometown, our relatives, especially Papa and Mama who had already gone ahead of us, our friends, Lolo Didong and Lola Besing, much as I miss you. Sometimes, I think I have no future here because my roots are not here. Most of the time when I wake up in the morning I just feel like going home to our hometown. It's strange but I do feel strongly that some force is beckoning me to get back home and start a new life from there. Should I or shouldn't I? What do you think?

Angela, please say you haven't forgotten me. Please write then, ok? By the way, I have not yet received that perfume you promised to send. Joke only.

I have to rush. Work is still three hours away through heavy traffic.

Your cousin and best friend,
Fili

2
IS THAT THE QUESTION

"May I join you?" Richard Martin gestured toward the vacant seat, bending his head while peering at the two ladies seated around the table in the Malacanang Canteen overlooking the Pasig River.

"All the time, sure," Feliz Salamanca said. "Dick, this is Katrina Avila of TV Channel 6. Katty, Dick Martin of the Asian Times Journal. You two haven't met before, have you?"

"No, we haven't," Martin said, extending his hand and shaking Katrina's. "But I think I know her pretty well. Who wouldn't? Two-time investigative journalism awardee and ramp model, very pretty on magazine covers and I would say right now, much, much delectably prettier in person." Dick Martin was tall, very tall in an appealing way. His beard was thick, very thick that somehow compensated for his receding hairline. His eyes were Caucasian blue and when he shook the hand of Katrina, his smile exploded disarmingly as he looked at her. Obviously, Salamanca surmised, the American was totally mesmerized by the smell or was it the sense of Katrina's femininity.

"Now there, Dickey. Be careful... Katrina is already engaged," Salamanca said, theatrically crushing her cigarette butt on the ashtray. Katrina Avila blushed. "And besides," Salamanca said, winking at Martin, "I don't think Katrina here would fall for a depraved man like you, Dickey. Twice divorced, who drinks bourbon like water and who, in the guise of journalism is actually a CIA spy!" Salamanca was known as the most abrasive woman columnist in the country. Her sharp nose, penetrating brown eyes, the extra-large earrings that dangled from her earlobes and the ubiquitous cigarette in her mouth always attracted attention. But Salamanca was much more than her accessories. She charmed men with the lethal combination of huge breasts and excessive modesty. When she opened her generous mouth, her fierce brown eyes would seem to squint with intense, intelligent combativeness. "Hmmm, hmmm. Delectably prettier! Hmmm, hmmm." Salamanca hummed, lighting another cigarette.

Martin's smile dimmed several watts lower. "Now, Feliz. I don't exactly rue the day I met you but please, don't blow my cover in public. It's difficult nowadays to get fired and hunt for another job," Martin sighed, looking at his empty cup.

While excusing himself to get a refill at the counter, Katrina asked Feliz if Martin was really CIA. Her friend explained she was not sure but they'd been in that kind of banter before and Dick Martin did not seem to mind her open suspicions. Anyway, Feliz added, they'd known each other for a long time, met in Vietnam, Cambodia, Indonesia and in some other foreign assignments and consulted with each other as friends in the profession.

"What do you think of the President's press con?" Katrina asked as Dick Martin rejoined them.

"You're asking me!" Dick Martin exclaimed. "Why don't you ask Feliz? Her column this morning says, those criteria were as murky as the Pasig River down there." The blue eyes surveyed the black river, turned to Salamanca and went back on target. "Why, you were the first to ask the President, weren't you?"

"Well, I'm interested in your opinion, especially now that I know you are with the Agency," Katrina Avila said, winking at Salamanca.

"Now, now, now," Martin shrugged, sipping his coffee. "You know, Feliz, that's what I really like about you. You don't only influence people with your column, you also influence them quite quickly with your conspiratorial whispers." Salamanca shrieked, totally tickled.

"Okay, as a journalist, not as CIA," Dick Martin chuckled again. "Seriously, I think the President had to make that announcement of the criteria in direct response to public suspicions that he was not scheming to perpetuate himself in power. I think the old man had really no choice but to come out of the cold."

"So you think the President is that serious?" Feliz interjected, inhaling more nicotine.

"No doubt about it, that's my personal opinion," Martin averred. "What happens after that, assuming something goes wrong, would no longer be directly attributed to him."

"What do you mean by that?" Katrina cut in, her gray-brown eyes alert, darting from Salamanca to Martin.

"To me, the criteria are of no moment. It is the announcement that is the substance. By publicly announcing he has these criteria, he had indirectly admitted he has neither scheme nor dream to perpetuate himself in power. That he is now ready to give way to his successor."

"What if nobody will qualify?" Katrina probed some more.

"That's what I wanted to point out," Martin said, lighting a cigarette. "Assuming nobody qualifies, the next steps, I am sure, will be taken by others. If that happens, I'm doubly sure, the President will act as a statesman—and not just a politician who wants to extend his term beyond what is legally allowed."

"Now, Dickey," Salamanca said, crushing her cigarette butt in the ash tray. "I think you're making things murkier. Why don't you cut that shit and just come out with something convincing. I suspect you're part of a conspiracy!"

"Well, Katrina here asked me for a personal opinion so I'm giving it to her for free!"

"Well, what Dick Martin is really saying," Salamanca said, lighting another cigarette, "is this. If nobody will qualify, there will be chaos but the President has nothing to do with it. The possibility of a coup d'etat or martial law is still there and so if that suddenly takes place, the President still stays on top as a statesman and everything is under control. Right, Dickey?"

"Assuming that indeed happens, what would be the stand of the CIA, the U.S. government?" Katrina interjected.

"Now, now, now. Is that the question?" Martin blew smoke toward the ceiling. After looking at his empty cup of coffee, he then peered into the face of Katrina. Her eyebrows were small works of art, he now discovered, plucked and shaped into elegant, thin curves. They might have been painted by one of the old masters, so little did they resemble ordinary human eyebrows. She raised one gracefully.

"You are absolutely beautiful, aren't you?" Dick Martin blurted out, sighing deeply.

"You are absolutely a blue-bloodied Caucasian flirt, aren't you, Richard Martin?" Salamanca exclaimed, cackling loudly like a hen that had just laid an egg.

"Well, isn't she?" Dick Martin rolled his eyes toward the ceiling. "She's not only absolutely beautiful in the face but also in the mind. Imagine, asking me about the CIA and the U.S. government! Well, why don't you come to dinner with me, Katrine and I'll give the dope to your difficult but intriguing question."

"Hmmm," Feliz Salamanca hummed. "Kat-rinnne, eh?"

"Why not?" Katrina said, rolling her gray-brown eyes. "But only with Feliz!"

"Holy mackerel!" Martin blurted out, pretending to groan. They all cackled hilariously as the floating debris of water lilies and all types of unmentionables swayed and danced on the surface of the murky Pasig River below.

"It is now exactly thirty-one minutes to seven," Rusty Kapunan announced over the microphone, pointing to his watch. "The call of destiny, my friends, is at hand!"

The crowd of about 250 guests cheered. As everyone knew, President Rosales would appear on national television at newscast time to announce the administration party's official presidential candidate. Those who felt their political and related fortunes depended on that decision, waited with bated breath on the wide manicured lawn of industrialist Don Felipe Aboitez.

From somewhere, four men in overalls carried a huge television set while a fifth was dragging the extension cord, careful not to unplug the connection along the way. The huge TV set was then mounted on its improvised platform behind the middle of the long banquet table. The whole lawn was groaning with food. At the far end just before the gigantic swimming pool, a roasted calf was dripping with sauce and fat over red-hot charcoal. The aroma of a thousand and one gastronomic concoctions filled the air. Mouths began to water.

Hanging from the gigantic balcony that jutted out of the white marble mansion was the gargantuan streamer, screaming "Congratulations! Marshall Dimalasa for President!"

"Meanwhile, ladies and gentlemen, let us all drink, be merry and be sober, aha, for tomorrow is the dawn of a new day!" Everybody cheered.

Rusty Kapunan, in red shirt, khaki pants and dark brown loafers then strode toward the round table immediately fronting the banquet table to join the group that was toasting each other, laughing and evidently enjoying each other's company.

To his left in blue shirt was Robustiano "Ruby" Toledo who recently resigned as executive secretary to run for senator. Next to him in light blue silk shirt, with sleeves folded up to his elbows, sat Teodoro "Tex" Cortez, incumbent secretary of trade and industry. Next, was Efrain Co, print and media mogul who was exchanging banter with a justice of the Supreme Court. Next, in red short-sleeve shirt sat Marshall "Mars" Dimalasa, the man of the hour, the very reason for this fiesta. By his side, in black shirt was "Don Ipe" Aboitez, the biggest land developer not only in the country but also of the entire region. In his mouth dangled a large cigar, its thick gray smoke belching in the open air. He was the sponsor and host of this fiesta and it was on his lawn that his guests were now cavorting and enjoying themselves.

As Rusty Kapunan scanned the guests immediately around him and beyond the round table, he glowed inside and felt thoroughly elated. No one and no one in this crowd had ever been openly accused of graft and corruption, no scandal, no dark past brought out in the open. No tax evaders here. These men here, he insisted to himself were leaders in their own right and might. The battle cry of this campaign was "The Moral Crusade for the Presidency." Even Father Rudy liked the battle cry very much. "It is time for the moral man to be president of this country," Father Rudy had told him many times.

"This is getting exciting," Efrain Co said, sipping his Johnny Walker. "Why don't we switch that thing on and listen to those political analysts?"

"Policy, policy, Ef, my friend," Rusty Kapunan crooned. "We agreed not to switch it on until the final hour, right? I got the remote here, see? Just cool it, my friend. It's nice to be in the dark once in a while."

Everybody laughed at that except Ruby Toledo. Although nobody seemed to notice his present discomfort, Toledo was paranoid. He had argued four days ago when Kapunan hatched the idea of holding this fiesta that the president did not categorically say he was for Dimalasa. Kapunan and Cortez, however, insisted the president did say so. That made him wonder because he was seated immediately to the president's right while Kapunan and Cortez were three seats away from the president's left during the Committee of 31's final caucus.

Ruby Toledo's recollections were suddenly interrupted by Kapunan's excited voice over the microphone.

"And now, my friends, the great moment has come! [All the rest now stood] 10, 9, 8 [All were now counting in unison as Kapunan raised his left hand up and down, up and down as an orchestra conductor would] 7, 6 [Kapunan extended his right arm that held the remote toward the TV] 5, 4, 3, 2, 1!" Kapunan pressed power, then the channel button as the wide screen lighted up.

Silence.

"That's it, ladies and gentlemen," the TV anchorman said, his voice jolting with excitement. "President Rosales is now in front of the rostrum, behind him the top guns of his administration. This is it!"

The president's full image zoomed in as the anchorman's faded out.

"My countrymen," President Rosales began, looking straight at the camera. A slight drizzle began to fall. Kapunan's right arm with the remote was firmly extended toward the TV. He felt the drizzle and he thought God's blessing was at hand.

"The Committee of 31 of the party has bottomed down its recommendations to two candidates out of the original five, the other three having withdrawn at the last moment to give way to Serafin Andolana Davide and Marshall Alonzo Dimalasa. It is the consensus of the Party that either one will assure our victory in the coming polls."

The drizzle continued to fall. Somebody hollered for a tent or umbrella to shed the TV but Kapunan motioned everybody to freeze, pressing a button on the remote to increase the volume.

"So the fate of the party and that of the nation is now in my hands," the president said, eyeballing the camera while flipping a page in front of him. "Marshall Dimalasa is my personal choice [Kapunan thought it was thunder as the tidal wave of applause and cheers swept all over the lawn] but based on an extensive secret survey I conducted [Kapunan's voice again boomed for silence] the great, great majority of the party favors Davide. It is, therefore on the basis of this reality that I must abide.

"Based on the powers vested in me, I now declare and officially announce that Serafin Andolana Davide is the official presidential candidate of the party. I urge…"

The drizzle somehow ceased as the last sentence of the president cut across the funereal silence that now reigned in the lawn. Everybody was stunned to even utter a cry or a curse, but only for a millisecond.

With all the force he could muster, Kapunan slammed the remote against the TV screen shouting, "Liar!"

The TV screen popped as electronic sparks flew. It then went blur, then blank.

"Shit. We were deceived!" Cortez cursed.

"Goddamned, lying old bastard!" Kapunan hissed, throwing his fists on the air.

Dimalasa, the man of the hour and the very reason for the fiesta, lowered his head until his chin was an inch off his chest. Then like he was hit by a powerful kick from behind, he groaned like a wounded elephant. "How could, ah, ah he do this to me?" As his whole body shook in disbelief, some lump of creamy liquid flowed freely from the inside caverns of his nostrils down to his upper lip and farther down to his mouth and chin. "How could he do this ah, ah to me? How could he ah, ah, ah do this to me!" Dimalasa croaked, unashamedly wept and then vomited.

As the shock and rage showed from one face to another, the press people, photographers and cameramen converged quickly around Dimalasa.

"Mr. Secretary," one asked. "What did President Rosales exactly tell you when you asked for his endorsement, if you don't mind, Sir?"

Dimalasa could not reply immediately. He was stunned. "He told me ah, to go ahead, that it was now, ah my time." He managed to finally say, sniffing for more air to fill his beleaguered lungs as he swiped off the sticky liquid from his mouth and chin with the back of his hand. Kapunan by his side, watched in horror.

"And whereto from here, Secretary Dimalasa?"

"The battle lines, ah have been drawn," Dimalasa moaned, wiping his whole face with his handkerchief that was now completely wet and sticky. "From here on ah, ah, ah it's war!" Saying that, he clinched the handkerchief into a ball inside his fist and squeezed it repeatedly, now and then slamming his fist against his breast.

Father Rudy Nicolas who had been fidgeting on the side, wedged himself into the middle as he said, his voice pleading, "Please, let us form a circle and hold each other's hands." As the circle was formed, Kapunan the last to oblige, the press people scampered out to send their dispatches to their editors.

"Let us pray," Father Rudy intoned, making the sign of the cross. "Almighty God, forgive us for we have sinned. For as you have repeatedly reminded us, you are a generous Father and you will always forgive us." The good priest had to pause. Dimalasa was now whining. "We have sinned because our hearts are in turmoil. This occasion, O Lord, is held to celebrate a moral crusade, to be led by dedicated men and women who are praying with me now to seek your guidance. Tonight is the beginning of this moral crusade. Please give us the light to move toward a new horizon of hope that with your guidance, we shall pursue to the end."

The good priest had to pause again, this time much longer. Dimalasa was not only openly crying now. He was also shaking, like he had lost control of his body parts. The whole scene was becoming bizarre: the good priest invoking the Almighty for mercy in the tone of a supplicant, Dimalasa providing the background sonata of hysterical despair. "Finally, Almighty God, please grant us peace in place of turmoil, courage instead of outrage and wisdom instead of obsession. In the name of the Father, the Son and the Holy Spirit, Amen."

"Amen."

Dimalasa's amen thundered above the rest. It was an amen of defiance, of anger and complete abandon. Kapunan who earlier was full of rage was now full of regret. To Kapunan, a hysterical woman was bad enough but a hysterical man of Dimalasa's stature was simply insufferable.

Richard Martin, correspondent of the Asian Times Journal sat quietly under the solitary tall tree beside the gigantic swimming pool. It was his fourth doubles of bourbon. The roasted calf some two meters to his left smelled good but he wasn't sure if he would have the opportunity to dig his teeth into some of that delectable meat. For one, there was no more sauce and fat dripping from it. The once red-hot charcoal below it was now in dying embers. "Coffee, please, black," he signaled the lady in apron and white cap nearest him.

He continued writing in his notebook: "Earlier, supporters of Dimalasa claimed that President Rosales himself was for Dimalasa, thus the fiesta as an advance celebration of his victory. It turned out the fiesta was not only a premature toast—it was a fiesta that bombed."

Martin folded his notebook and inserted it in his inside coat pocket. The rain began to pour like cats and dogs as he hit the side-road out of the massive gate and hailed a taxi.

The full statement of President Rosales and what immediately followed after that on live TV went through unimpeded in the safe house of Task Force EMPRES.

"That's it! That's it!" Fatso Santos cheered, punching the red button on his remote and slumping back on his chair.

"That's how the cookie crumbles," Randolf Patis Cruz sang, heartily grinning at everyone.

"Okay, let's get down to business," Fatso Santos declared, flipping through his notes. "The latest survey confirms what I had been saying all along that for Mahal, it's an optimistic high of 55 percent and a pessimistic low of 40 percent of the total votes, that is against the five other presidential candidates. Davide, Rosales' stooge, will only get at most 15 percent, the rest to be split among the four. In real terms, this means a lead of at least eight million votes over Davide. Question—do we still need to campaign?"

Except for Gan-Alfonso, the rest guffawed at Fatso's witticism.

"Of course, we should," declared Gan-Alfonso. "I think you all have a copy of my proposal on that. If I may summarize…"

"I think there is no need for a summary," Pangilinan interrupted, grinning from ear to ear, hoping to win Pat over to his side. "Pat's idea is clear. There has to be a semblance of seriousness here. Mahal's campaign sorties should be so scheduled so the rest of our national candidates will have more or less the same exposure, in tandem with Mahal's, without of course overshadowing Mahal and his megastars and superstars."

"Don't put something in my mouth that I didn't say!" Gan-Alfonso snapped. "I never mentioned megastars and superstars." Pangilinan's jaw dropped, his dentures almost jumping out.

"I agree in principle," Cruz said, "except that for me the paramount concern is for Mahal to win and to win with the greatest margin. The rest is secondary."

"Now, just a minute there," Gan-Alfonso cut in, raising her voice. "I think I made it clear in my paper that equal time is equal time. We also need our vice-president, our senatorial candidates elected. They should, otherwise, that would weaken our strong hold in the middle level power substructures. I fully agree, that like it or not, Mahal will be elected. So the best strategy is to take advantage of Mahal's bandwagon and carry everybody to a convincing victory."

There was a moment of silence.

"Okay, but we have to be realistic in operational terms," Cruz interposed. "You know Mahal. For one thing, he does not feel comfortable sitting on the same stage with those highly educated senatoriables, with those lawyers and Wharton-educated businessmen. Mahal will be in his elements if he's with the movie stars. Do you get my point? And besides, Mahal has to cover a lot of ground to get that 55 percent that Fatso mentioned. Put Mahal on the same stage with those senatoriables and I bet you, he'd feel ensconced, caged and gagged."

The spin-doctor had spoken.

"And Mahal will be bored to death listening to all those senatoriables deliver their speeches. Remember, as presidential candidate, he is the last to speak because after him there will be no crowd. He is the main attraction, the main event!" Fatso connected.

"That's it," chimed in Cruz. Mahal's style is to walk the ground, press the flesh, put his arms around the shoulders of whomever, kiss babies and embrace the ladies. Oh, how they would love that, hug the mothers, or if they are old enough, kiss their hands. That's how Mahal would get the shrieks, the euphoria, those precious votes. That's his charisma!"

43

"But..." Gan-Alfonso was now exasperated.

"Okay, okay," Fatso Santos interrupted, noting the flushed face of the lady. "How do we reconcile all of these? Both sides have their valid points."

"Why don't we just fly him over in time for the last speaker to wind up his speech? When Mahal goes up the stage, he raises all their arms as a symbol of his endorsement and that's it!" Cruz pointed out.

"But is that possible in the provinces?" Gan-Alfonso asked, incredulously. "I mean who will constitute the audience of our national candidates without Mahal on stage?"

"I have a sure fire solution," Pangilinan said, pushing his tongue harder against his gums. Everybody looked at him.

"Really," Pat Gan-Alfonso said, removing her glasses and raising an eyebrow.

Pangilinan saw it but he was undaunted. "Bring in the clowns and the starlets with lots of boobs and butts," Pangilinan said, winking suggestively. "In this way, we're guaranteed we've got an audience. And when Mahal arrives, he'll love it, too!" In his excitement, Pangilinan's dentures jumped outward but his practiced tongue was faster, pushing everything back in place and just in time.

"Yeah, why not?" Fatso Santos joined in, chuckling.

"That's right," Cruz agreed. "That'll make it a lot easier for our local candidates to bring in the crowd. No sweat!"

Pat Gan-Alfonso was now fully exasperated, her pale face reddening. Her intellect had been ravished. But she did not say another word. There was another time for that.

"Your Eminence, it is my sincere feeling that the purpose for which we have come to your domain is laudable and is acceptable to you. The Moral Crusade will surely be a great success with your blessing." Father Rudy Nicolas placed his right palm over the other, stretched his back discreetly and waited.

His Eminence Cardinal Pedro Alingasa gently stroked his chin as the golden ring around his index finger glistened.

"Thank you, Father Rudy for your concern," His Eminence said as his forefinger left his chin and started to press that portion of the flesh fronting his right ear just below his velvet cap. "I also believe it is time to launch a moral crusade of the kind you have elaborated on. But let me ask my guests if indeed this moral crusade is credible since it is supposed to be launched during this presidential campaign and those leading it are political aspirants." The sagging eyelids of His Eminence flickered as his small round eyes opened and rested on Marshall Dimalasa.

Dimalasa wanted to respond but Rusty Kapunan beside him began: "Your Eminence, the moral crusade is credible because the country needs it. The country needs it, in the sense that unless the aspiring politicians who stand on high moral ground, the people and the Church unite together to denounce immorality, then the presidential aspirant who practices and in fact flaunts immorality, will inevitably become the president of this country. God forbid!"

"And may I ask my other guest what he thinks about all this?" His Eminence inhaled deeply as he spoke.

Dimalasa watched the gaze of His Eminence and he trembled inside. He felt that the prelate who would control his immediate destiny was contemplating him with evident distaste, if not outright indifference. All the words that he so carefully prepared and rehearsed now remained frozen in his larynx. But he was a general, he reminded himself and the Cardinal was just a priest. Was he not the noted military general in the battlefield of Wala-Wala who sent the enemy scampering out, with their tail between their legs?

After he discreetly swallowed a droplet of saliva to clear his throat, Marshall Dimalasa began. "Your Eminence, the tragedy of the world, as one great philosopher said, is when in times of great challenge, men of, ah good will, ah, ah choose to do nothing. I believe, Your Eminence, that I, an aspiring politician as Your Eminence has, ah referred to me earlier, am the person who will lead this moral crusade. My training, my, ah discipline and my abiding faith in the Almighty, I believe prepare me for this, ah ah, great challenge, with your blessing, Your Eminence."

Dimalasa finally delivered his prepared speech and felt relieved.

Kapunan, who was, as always, watching his ward, felt the crying and hysterical insufferable had somehow recovered from his trauma, except for his despicable stutter.

With his great bulk, His Eminence slowly stood, smoothened his priestly vestment with the gentle touch of his palms and paced the floor, clasping his hands behind his back. By the window overlooking the palace grounds, the prelate pondered on the pronouncements of his guests.

"Pray tell me," His Eminence asked without looking at his guests, "who among the politicians, the people, the church should be united to lead this noble crusade to fruition, aside from your good selves?"

"Besides us, we have the commitment and support of over a thousand national NGO's with international linkages," Kapunan elaborated. "But more than all this, what is desperately needed, Your Eminence, is to make a smashing statement in the streets that our demands for moral governance can no longer be deferred." Kapunan felt he had exceeded his limits but in the same vein, he believed, he had burrowed in convincingly.

"We are also, ah hoping, Your Eminence," Dimalasa chimed in, "that Arturo Punzalan Tan-Kong will, ah join us with the support of former President Caridad Castro. With your blessing, Your Eminence representing the Church, the moral crusade is assured of success and the future of our children will be, ah bright, Your Eminence."

Kapunan now felt Dimalasa had fully recovered. Dimalasa was not only a moral man; he was also a noble man, Kapunan concluded.

His Eminence twitted the fleshy lobe of his right ear with the tips of his thumb and index finger while scanning the manicured lawn below. Something was missing somewhere. Something was missing at the end of the path that led to the small chapel.

45

"What makes you think Tan-Kong will support this undertaking? My understanding is, the good man will pursue his candidacy on his own terms—or am I in the throes of speculation?" His Eminence was still looking out of the window, his back to his guests.

Kapunan and Dimalasa exchanged furtive glances as Father Rudy felt his palms tighten.

"Your Eminence," Kapunan suddenly said, "Father Rudy here, went to see Arturo Tan-Kong about the crusade…" he failed to finish his speech.

"And so the good Father has also been busy lately!" the Cardinal said, his back to his guests, his head still facing the garden below, looking for something that was missing there. "Am I correct, Father Rudy?"

"Yes, Your Eminence," the good priest's eyes darted from Kapunan to the back of His Eminence. "Arturo Tan-Kong told me that yes, he would join the crusade but only with your blessing, Your Eminence."

"Aha, there you are!" His Eminence gleefully muttered, seeing the gardener push the wheelbarrow with two pots of full bloom white chrysanthemums. He had instructed the gardener during his regular early morning rounds that the two pots of roses had to be changed since they looked wilted and needed some refurbishment.

Kapunan, Dimalasa and Father Rudy watched His Eminence pace the floor again, until he returned to his chair in front of them. As His Eminence picked up his glass and sipped his orange juice, the three also did the same.

"Pray tell me," His Eminence said, returning his empty glass down on the low table. "Which one of you is willing to sacrifice, in the name of the moral crusade, his aspiration for the presidency and run instead as vice-president of the other?"

The impact of the words of His Eminence hit the three like Moses before the burning bush. Marshall Dimalasa's glass froze just before his mouth, Kapunan's dangled midway his mouth and the surface of the low table and Father Rudy's shook on top of his open palm.

The anteroom was barely enough to accommodate a medium-sized table with six chairs around it and served as the conference room of Gil Ceasar Malasuerte, the campaign manager (CM) of Elect Davide for President (ED4PRES). That the space was small and limited was understandable enough. This was in the east wing of the Manila Hotel and the rent was exorbitant. But to the low-income folks who were involved in the campaign, the choice of the location was plainly outrageous, inaccessible and anti-poor.

The group of Timostocles Sipula, national coordinator of the support group arm of the Davide campaign was made to wait for almost three hours at the lobby of the hotel, along with two other groups and some five individuals. All of them had appointments with the CM.

"Why don't we all split? The campaign manager is treating us like shit," one of the companions of Sipula said, daring everybody within hearing distance.

"No, we don't. We won't. We can't." Sipula declared, lifting the folder he carried in his right arm. "Otherwise, the future of this country which is in this folder will all be in deep shit."

At 34, Sipula looked like he just graduated from college. Boyish looking, his thick black hair was always impeccably combed. His close associates regarded him as smart-ass, though nobody could question his organizational skills. An ex-seminarian, he was the president of a nationwide coalition of inter-fraternity alumni associations known as the Alliance of People's Organizations or APO. APO was recognized by those in the know of its strength on the ground and its network of volunteer campaigners in all provinces of the republic.

"The boss can't be bothered right now since he's on the phone with Sec-Gen Davide," the office secretary announced, closing the door to the inner room behind her. "The boss says you may start the briefing soon as the Chief of Staff (COS) comes in. The COS is on the way. He's just probably delayed by traffic. You know how it is. The boss will join you later." With that, she went back inside, closing the door behind her, bloody red fingernails ablaze.

The briefing was actually the presentation of the support group arm's proposed budget. This was the fourth and hopefully, the final presentation and Sipula and his team were prepared for it.

Sipula checked his watch. He was now 22 minutes into his presentation but the CM was still not around.

"Next frame, please."

Frame 12 appeared on the screen.

STRATEGY	F/12
(How to get the votes: precincts are the key)	
Volunteer Coordinator per precinct	3
Target Votes per Coordinator	24
Target Votes per Precinct	72
Total Number of Precincts	145,000
Total Votes Targeted	10,440,000

"As you can see on screen," Sipula continued, "the key to these operations is the precinct where the voters are. The 10.4 million targeted votes look big, but will turn out to be very small, if we take stock of the fact that we need only 72 votes for every precinct in the country! I repeat, we need only 72 votes for every precinct in the country to clinch victory for Sec. Gen. Davide!

"To achieve that we only need three coordinators per precinct, each to target only 24 votes. Now tell me—is that difficult to get? Our preliminary headcount shows we have many precincts where only one, repeat, only one coordinator can easily get 72 votes! Family ties, neighbors and friends—that's why. And that is the unwritten strategy here—get those relatives and neighbors for Davide. Our assessment is: this is the only way to counter those blind votes that go to entertainer-candidates, the blind votes caused by euphoria and fanatical idolatry for movie stars and their kind."

"Excuse me, Tim," COS Jack Tibogol interrupted. "Could you please go back two frames earlier?" Tibogol asked. Unlike the top guns in the Davide campaign,

Tibogol was an anachronism: he had a pockmarked face, his speech was full of profanities and his manner was pedestrian, not to mention the ubiquitous cellular phones and pager that dangled from his belt.

"Manila, Manila, Manila, oo, Manila..." Tibogol's right cell phone blared the opening bars of the popular hit song.

Ala Fernando Poe, Jr., the fastest gun alive in local movies, Tibogol suddenly stood, pivoted, then wriggling his fingers, swiftly drew the cell phone from his right. "Hello! Jack Tibs here, chief of staff of incoming President Davide of the Repub..."

"Bayang Magiliw, Perlas ng Silang..." Tibogol's left cell trumpeted the opening bars of the national anthem of the republic.

With the phones on both ears, his mouth was now servicing one and the other and back. Suddenly aware that eyes were stabbing him from all directions, the chief of staff of Davide darted out of the room, yelling instructions or excuses, accompanied by profanities to whomever was at the other end of the line.

Frame 10 was projected back on screen.

FOOT SOLDIERS ON THE GROUND   F/10

To organize, recruit, swear in and mobilize 435,000 (3 coordinators x 24/precinct x 145,000 precincts nationwide) Foot Soldiers on the Ground to win over 10,440,000 target voters on election day.

"Where will you get these coordinators, these foot soldiers as you call them?" one of Tibogol's aides asked, a follow through of Tibogol's early query.

"Actually, half of that number are already on the ground since the Rosales campaign. All we need to do is reactivate them and help recruit the rest for Davide. As of today, the RSACs (Regional Affairs Committee Coordinators), the PSACs (Provincial Sectoral Affairs Committee Coordinators) and the DSACs (District Sectoral Affairs Committee Coordinators) are already in place—the same set-up during the Rosales campaign."

The CM finally came in, Sipula nodding his head to acknowledge his presence. "Please continue," the CM said as he settled on the chair reserved for him. Scanning the faces around him, he seemed to see nothing, but his body language told everybody the entire campaign rested solely on his shoulders.

"How do you square this set-up with the Party List?" Tibogol asked, coming back in as he slid back on his seat, his eyes on Malasuerte.

"As we know the party list is a new thing," Sipula observed. "We are still in the process of establishing a convergence with those who are running under the Party List. Let me show you the next frame."

Scenario: Party List Projections	F/13
*Projected votes for the party list	10,440,000
*Minimum no. of votes to get 1 seat (2%)	200,000
*Total seats targeted	52
*Total votes needed to win 52 seats	10,400,000
*total registered voters	35,000,000
*% of total voters needed to win 52 Party list seats	30%

"As you will note," Sipula continued, "the total votes targeted here jibe with the total votes targeted for coordinators in Frame 12, that is 10.44 million votes. We are simply saying that if there is a convergence, if the old set-up, RSACs and down the line and the new Party List work together, then the greater possibility of attaining the overall target of 10.4 million votes. Presently, the COMELEC is still in the process of accrediting Party List applicants. Once the accredited listings are finalized, we shall be able to pinpoint where this convergence will occur in specific places and in specific terms. If we run short of the 52 party list seats in the House as projected, then the old set-up will simply take care of the gaps in order to meet our target votes, which constitutes 30% of the registered voters nationwide," Sipula thought he made his point.

"Just how reliable are your coordinators?" one of Tibogol's aides again asked, his face frowning.

"The question is not actually new," Sipula said, his confidence rising. "The same question was repeatedly asked by the politicians themselves during the initial stages of the Rosales campaign. It was their position then that the volunteer army of coordinators would only complicate the political set-up that is already on the ground, on the local level, particularly."

"Yes, I also heard about the tensions that followed," the CM observed, leaning forward, his eyes on Tibogol.

"Correct," Sipula agreed. "Most of the local politicians did not at first appreciate the concept. When the campaign went full blast, there were many complaints that this volunteer army was intruding into the affairs of the local political candidates. Then candidate Rosales was undaunted and insisted that the campaign should be run like a 'two-rail transit system" of a campaign machinery: One rail to represent the political arm, the other the support group arm—both heading toward the same direction. On his instructions, Dr. Meandro Destino pushed the support group arm hardest on the ground." Sipula paused, loosening his tie. "President Rosales won because as he strove hard to get more politicians to help him, he also relentlessly built a strong army of volunteers who toiled tirelessly, though silently, on the ground. It was this two-way transit system that spelled the difference. Political giants even from the opposition, among others, publicly acknowledged that it was indeed this machinery that spelled the difference.

Rosales, himself, declared many times that this army of volunteers catapulted him to the presidency."

After some silence, CM Malasuerte again asked. "You said earlier that this army of volunteer coordinators can't be bought. Are you sure about this?"

"You mean to tell us Tim that these volunteers do not require any cost at all?"

"I am not saying that. Even as volunteers, they also have to eat. They also need some allowances."

"And how much will that entail?"

"On pages 17 and 18 you will see the projected cost." Sipula said after flipping some pages. "As you can see, said amount is not even a drop in the bucket of some P6 billion to run a presidential campaign."

The CM and his aides flipped to the mentioned pages. Immediately, some went through the figures with their calculators.

"The amount asked for would constitute and, therefore, could slice off some 17 percent of the budget allocated for the local candidates. What would they say?" one of the aides addressed the CM.

"That's small," Sipula jumped in before the CM could react. "That's really nothing considering what our volunteer coordinators can deliver."

"That's what you say," the CM retorted. "The local candidates will certainly squawk. Once that happens, there will be lots of chaos on the ground."

The room subsided into silence.

"Has Meyan Destino discussed this budget with either Pin Davide or President Rosales?" the CM asked, after the lull, knitting his forehead and adjusting his tie.

"I believe he did," Sipula said. "To my knowledge, President Rosales already instructed Sec. Gen. Davide to release the amount."

"That's surprising," the CM said. "Pin Davide has not said a single word about this. I was with him at lunchtime. And the focus of our talk was the budget."

Sipula was stunned. He was about to say something when Tibogol's cell phones trilled and blared.

"You're a jackass, don't you know that?" Sipula hissed at Tibogol.

"Hello! Hello! Hello!" Tibogol bellowed over the phones.

"Goddamit!" CM Malasuerte shouted, slamming a fist on the table.

In his penthouse on the 31st floor of an old, unpretentious building in the heart of Binondo known as Chinatown—the Chinoy (Chinese-Filipino) stronghold in the republic, sat Ferdinand "Ferdie" Tancho, sipping his afternoon tea with his two guests. Tancho's building was known as the other central bank of the country; the official central bank being the financial institution of the republic. When the two central banks clashed, the government's bank ended up defending its policy position before media while Tancho's bank got the cash and the dividends. Among power-wielders, Tancho carried the title of "Kingmaker" in the world of political patronage and corporate dominance.

Robustiano Toledo sipped his tea. He was waiting for an opening, the reason he and his friend Efrain Co came to visit the king. Co was a close friend of Tancho, their friendship going way back immediately after World War II when they were pushing carts, selling discarded bottles and old newspapers in the potholes of Binondo and nearby markets. Those were the days of sweat and sacrifice, of eating nothing but noodles for breakfast, lunch and supper, to save on every centavo that built the legends of the Chinoy taipans in the country. It was Co who suggested they meet with Tancho to resolve Toledo's predicament.

"As a lawyer and former executive secretary of President Rosales," Tancho asked, "what do you suppose the old man is hatching right now?"

"President Rosales is always hatching something," Toledo declared. "What that is all about, I really do not know. He is still a sphinx to me. That's why I had to resign. You know the rest of the story."

After they'd taken their snacks of hot *pan de sal* and Spanish sardines, Tancho's favorite, Co stood and excused himself. "I've got to make two phone calls," he said, walking toward the door.

"It's the pink one for outside calls, right side of the anteroom," Tancho hollered after him.

"It's okay, I've got my cell with me," Co said, turning his back and patting his inside left breast pocket. Then winking at Toledo, Co joked, "Besides, how do I know if this place is bugged?"

That sent the three of them chuckling as Co closed the door behind him.

"So what is your decision?" Tancho suddenly asked, lowering his voice, the pair of slit black eyes digging at Toledo's.

Toledo got his opening and he dug in. "I cannot run anymore under the team of Dimalasa," Toledo said, also lowering his voice, "after what happened."

"So?" Tancho asked again, his somber eyes did not even flicker.

"I was entertaining the idea of running under Mahalina's team but I was informed his senatorial slate is already complete," Toledo said, his voice slightly quivering. Tancho thought Toledo garbled his words and surmised his visitor had a toothache.

"I can arrange things… if you want." Tancho connected, his eyes boring in on Toledo's. "So?"

Having dug in, Toledo now fortified his gain. "Oh yes," Toledo said, staring back at Tancho's face. "I already talked to Undersecretary Fajardo. He was my recommendee for that position. He's in charge of the tax evasion cases against you." The words flowed smoothly.

"So?"

"If he gets the position of Justice Secretary when Mahalina assumes office, I'm sure he would be of great help to you."

Tancho slowly shifted in his seat, his eyes still on focus. Slowly leaning forward, his face very close to Toledo, he slowly whispered: "Do we have a deal?"

"Done," Toledo said. This time he did not blink. "My pleasure, Mr. Tancho. My pleasure, Sir," Toledo added, trying to control the convulsion inside him.

Jack Tibogol, chief of staff of Davide, presided over the final meeting of the seventeen committees tasked to organize and ensure the success of the grand proclamation rally for ED4PRES. To his right was Gen. (Ret.) Ramil Placer, former chief of staff of the Rosales campaign years ago. Placer was pinch-hitting for Gil Malasuerte, the campaign manager, who was, according to Placer, with Davide in an emergency party caucus. To his left, slouched on his chair was Justine Pulido, media bureau chief.

Many had wondered how Placer could play second fiddle to Tibogol who undoubtedly was operating separately from Malasuerte, the campaign manager.

"Three-hundred seventy-five buses from 19 points all over Metro Manila with 70 warm bodies per bus," the chair of the transportation committee intoned.

"Check!" Echoed the one in charge of the monitoring committee from the right corner of the war room.

"26, 250 packed meals including soft drinks for all those warm bodies of the 375 buses, at 70 each." The chairman of the food and refreshment committee said. "Check?"

"Check," echoed monitoring.

"Courtesy of caterers from the Chinoy connection, check?"

"Check."

"Plus 250,000 with packed meals, including soft drinks to those who will converge on their own designated zones on target hour. Check?"

"Check."

"The main crowd of 500,000 will arrive in their own buses and their packed meals taken care of by the BFJM. Check?"

"Check."

Additional reports came in as monitoring checks followed.

Placer finally stood and positioned his laptop. At six-foot one, Placer was a giant of a man. After several clicks on the keyboard, the facsimile of the makeshift stage for the rally and the backdrop flashed on the front wall of the war room. The seats on stage were numbered.

"Here, Number 1 in the center, the President will sit," Placer began with his laser pointer emitting red dots on the wall as he went along. "Numbers 2 and 3 will be occupied by our presidential and vice-presidential candidates, respectively. While sitting or giving their speech, their image will be magnified in the giant backdrop screen up there, so even the farthest spectator from all sides out front can see. The rest of the seats in Rows 1, 2 and 3 will be occupied by the senatoriables. The seats on the sides will be occupied by other party VIPs."

"How about Rickie Balete? I don't see any seat assigned to him?" the media bureau chief asked.

"You're right," Placer said. "The Most Exalted Brother (MEB) of the Movement has refused to sit on stage. The script here says that after the emcee announces his name, the spotlight will seek him out in Zone B and the spotlight will be on him all throughout until he reaches this spot here on stage where Davide will meet him. They hug. Then they approach President Rosales. Then the President and the MEB raise the arms of Davide as the three of them move toward the center of the stage, here..."

"Manila, Manila, Manila, oo..."

Tibogol drew from his right. "Hello, hello!"

"Beep... Beeeepppp..."

Tibogol now had one cell on his ear and the pager before his eyes as he darted, flying out of the room.

"Then the crowd roar and roar, to be led by our barkers on stage and below with their powerful megaphones.

"After his endorsement speech, where would the MEB go?"

"No, no, no. The MEB will not deliver any speech or something like that," Placer said, after checking his script. "What he will do is offer a prayer, seeking the Almighty to give the victory to our candidates..."

The exchange went back and forth. Nothing was left to chance.

As more reports were presented and details discussed in the war room of the ED4PRES, another meeting was being held at a penthouse of the Brotherhood of Faith in Jesus Movement (BFJM).

"I notice Brother Attorney, that you have not even taken a sip of your coffee," Brother Isaac Gopez, third in rank in the BFJM observed. "That brew is the favorite of the Most Exalted Brother." Brother Gopez was a small man and the huge tie hanging from his neck made him look even smaller. But he was not a small man in the BFJM. He was its financial wizard.

Atty. Leopoldo Mondejar fidgeted in his chair, eyeing the cup of coffee in front of him. Why was this guy addressing him "Brother?" As a lawyer and banker, Mondejar didn't like it. But he seemed to have no choice.

"It is all right, Brother Isaac. Thank you. I prefer to take my coffee cold." He had addressed Gopez "Brother." Well, he really had no choice—that was one of his instructions. He was feeling his cup with his fingertips and was glad it was still warm. "As I said earlier, Brother Isaac, the campaign chest right now can only afford P150 million for this rally. We've exhausted all avenues to raise the original amount agreed upon, but to our great frustration and embarrassment could not."

As he uttered those words, Mondejar, the bagman of Davide felt lost. Two hours ago, he recalled, he refused to come to this meeting. "I am sure, Brother Attorney, the Most Exalted Brother will be most surprised indeed at this turn of events," Gopez said in a very low, conspiratorial voice. "You know and Brother Serafin Davide knows, the Most Exalted Brother is a very sensitive man. He never backs away from any agreement."

Mondejar took a sip of the coffee, thinking hard what to say next. Would he assume the rest of the amount? But he knew there was enough, more than enough to meet the original agreement. What had caught him rather by complete surprise was the eleventh hour instruction of Davide to bargain for half. Asked why, Davide simply told him he needed more contingency funds to shell out to his leaders. "They are now growing by the hundreds of thousands, that's why." Those were Davide's last words.

The grand proclamation rally was only 37 hours away. Mondejar reminded himself. If the Most Exalted Brother and his throng of half a million followers would not attend, then that would surely sabotage the whole event.

53

"Brother Isaac, the P150 million I mentioned earlier, is all we could raise at this very hour," Mondejar found himself repeating as he put down his cup of cold coffee. "They're right here in my brief case, in manager's checks. If the Most Exalted Brother will consider, the other half of the total amount originally agreed upon will be delivered to you within 72 hours after the rally."

He finally said it.

"Well, Brother Attorney," Gopez said as he stood with Mondejar. "As I mentioned earlier, the Most Exalted Brother is a sensitive and honorable man and he would never back away from an agreement. Please tell Brother Serafin Davide to call the Most Exalted Brother right away, after say, two hours from now. The Most Exalted Brother cannot be bothered in the next two hours—religious duties, you know. Praise the Lord!" With that, the two shook hands, Gopez ushering Mondejar out of the door.

Taking the elevator from the penthouse to the ground floor, Mondejar felt like vomiting.

The grand proclamation rally to Elect Davide for President started as scheduled. The buses arrived and disgorged their passengers in their designated zones on the largest expanse of the reclaimed area fronting Manila Bay. The entertainers had sung and danced for one and a half hours as additional buses and their cargo of loyalists also arrived, courtesy of the local government executives of the administration party from Metro Manila and adjoining provinces. Banners, placards and streamers of all sizes and make waved and fluttered over the heads of thousands of sweating and screaming humanity. The opening salvo of the administration party campaign was now taking off.

At exactly seven in the evening, the emcee, backed by the barkers, boomed the arrival of the president as the presidential chopper appeared from above the Folk Arts Palace, hovered over the roaring crowd, pivoted gracefully, finally landing on the far side of the huge parking lot. Unbeknownst to the crowd, Serafin Davide, the presidential candidate, was whisked from his limo to the back of the stage, where at the agreed signal, he and the president met at the east wing of the stage, mounted it together, as the emcee, seconded by the barkers, announced the president and his successor were now mounting the stage. As both started pumping hands with the senatoriables, the party dignitaries and all that mattered on stage, the giant backdrop erupted in lights, the magnified images of the president and Davide looming magnificently on the gigantic screen. The emcee and the barkers led the tumultuous shouts of praises and welcome as the crowd burst into a deafening roar.

The roaring subsided as the president mounted the rostrum. This was a political campaign so he was careful to begin his speech by mentioning everyone that mattered on stage. Facing the crowd, the president began: "Esteemed citizens, the fate of this nation lies not in the brilliance of a few men and women but by the commitment of the great majority of our people in the growth and progress of their children and their communities…"

As the president waded through in his famous monotone, packed meals began to be distributed at the outer zones. It was past eight o'clock in the evening and the crowd were feeling hungry, thirsty and uneasy. From backstage, CM Gil Ceasar Malasuerte ordered the distribution of packed meals and cold drinks after the insistent calls of his assistants through their handheld radio who were posted in the different zones. Sensing that food was being distributed, those in the middle zones started to get unruly.

"I, therefore, urge the great majority of our people to pursue that commitment. The programs necessary to jumpstart that commitment are already in place. The program on..." The president continued, starting to enumerate the priority programs he had pursued during his incumbency.

"Foxtrot, Foxtrot, this is Eagle," Malasuerte barked into his handheld radio. "Do you copy?"

"Copy, copy. This is Foxtrot. Go ahead, Eagle."

"Foxtrot, you tell the emcee to go back to Plan C. Repeat, back to Plan C, immediately after the Horseman's speech. Do you copy?"

"Done."

From his perch on top of the hidden platform above the giant backdrop of the stage, CM Malasuerte could see people from the outer zones begin to disperse. "Damn," he cursed. "After eating, they're leaving. What kind of people are these?"

"Continuity of the programs my administration has started is therefore, a must, to ensure development. We cannot afford to move backward. We can only afford to move forward..." the president's voice rose. His antennae were quite advanced in picking up the warning signals. He could see people in the outer zones dispersing.

"Thank you, Mr. President, thank you, Sir for that very challenging speech!" the emcee boomed, soon as the president dismounted the rostrum. "Ladies and gentlemen, there is a slight change in the program. Instead of calling our beloved presidential candidate Serafin Andolana Davide to deliver his acceptance speech and to disclose his platform of government as soon as he assumes office by June 30 this year, may I call right now the young and lovely upcoming superstar of them all, to entertain us with her latest hit. Ladies and gentlemen, Charlene Divinagraaacia and the CyberRocketssss!"

The bright lights on stage gradually dimmed as the powerful spotlight zoomed to the left and the right. From the sides, the CyberRockets swiftly took their choreographed positions, swinging and pointing their arms toward the center. From the middle of nowhere, Charlene Divinagracia, in her strapless black gown glided toward center stage, a cordless microphone in hand, her long legs swinging in and out of their thigh-high slits, the background music blaring into the hundred and one giant baffles mounted all over the length and breadth of the campaign grounds. As the background music soared in intensity, Charlene's shoulders shook, her hips swaying, her long legs swinging much faster now, in and out of the thigh-high slits. The Cyber Rockets flew on air, landing on the floor on split legs, their open palms toward Charlene, as the upcoming superstar opened her sultry opening lines of her hit: "Luv me or luv me not... lime, lime, limme... luv you or limme... limme ..."

From his perch, CM Malasuerte saw the crowd rushing back, multitudes now pushing and stampeding toward the stage, shouting for more of "Limme, limme, limme…" Through the chaos, the Emcee barked and begged louder for order.

When Serafin Andolana Davide finally mounted the rostrum and with his stentorian oratory started to enumerate his development programs and the billions he would sink into them—the crowd at the outer zones completely disappeared. Four minutes into his speech, the crowd in the middle zones started thinning out.

From his seat on the press section, Richard Martin maneuvered himself through the packed platform until he got to Meyan Destino who was smoking a cigarette at the far right side of the stage.

"Hi, there Meyan," Dick Martin whispered in greeting as he lit his own stick. "I notice the President was not so fired up tonight. He looks spent. What's going on?"

"The Boss just got back from his 14th regional cabinet meeting, Dick."

"Really? You know I also noticed the President mentioned Davide only once, and that was during the salutation. Was that deliberate?"

"Now Dick, don't be naughty. The President knows what he's up to."

"Up to? And how come the messiah, the Most Exalted Brother and his multitude of faithful followers have not arrived?"

"Who told you the messiah was coming?"

"C'mon, Dr. Destino, stop pulling my leg, okay? I also have my impeccable sources, you know."

At about three o'clock in the afternoon a few days later, in the same expanse where the administrations party's grand proclamation rally was held, a gigantic white cross was erected at the back of the gargantuan stage. The stage was occupied by members of BFJM's One Thousand Voices choir. True to their calling, the members of the choir were all in immaculate white gowns, their heads bowed, their hands clasped together, their eyes closed in prayer. Behind them loomed the gigantic white cross that seemed to reach up into the blue skies yonder.

Out front, on center stage, stood the charismatic Rickie Balete, the Most Exalted Brother, in his signature ministerial garb: tight fitting silky white jeans, silver sports jacket that wrapped his small frame, polka dotted bow tie and three inch white boots. Before Balete a man was kneeling; his head bowed, his eyes closed, his palms clasped together in prayer, his elbows resting slightly over his large jutting belly. He was a big man with broad shoulders, a thick forest of black hair and well-trimmed mustache. He was garbed in *jusi* Barong Tagalog, black pants and black shoes. His whole posture was that of a penitent.

Balete raised his sights up to the skies and once more, intoned.

"Bless this man, oh Lord-Jesus, for without your blessing, there is no future for the poor in spirit, the downtrodden, the jobless, the children in the streets, the laborers, the farmers, the fishermen and the urban squatters. In short, oh Lord-Jesus, the great, great majority of our people who have been marginalized and ignored in this country for a long, long time."

"Amen."

"Bless this man, oh Lord-Jesus for without your blessing, there is no future in this country because all the signs that you have given us so far, tell us this man is the leader of all leaders who will lead this country to greatness in accordance with your will."

"Amen. Amen."

"For as the Almighty Father said in the good Book of Isaiah Chapter 25, Verse 4, 'when the children of God have forgotten their creator, there is trouble in the nation'."

"Amen. Amen. Amen."

"For indeed, Lord-Jesus our former leaders have forgotten your children and thus we seek your blessings for this man who will follow the law of the Lord-Jesus."

"Amen."

"Thus, Lord-Jesus, in accordance with your will, I now place my right hand on top of the head of this man, as a sign that your blessing is now upon him and we rejoice because of your blessing, oh Lord-Jesus."

"Amen, Amen, Amen."

"Almighty Father, as in the good book of Genesis, creator of heaven and earth, the seas, the stars and all those who walk upon the earth, your apostles, your followers, Lord-Jesus, now bear witness to this blessing. May I hear from the East Zone?"

"Hallelujah!"

"May I hear from the West Zone?"

"Hallelujah!"

"The South Zone?"

"Hallelujah!"

"May I hear from the West, the East, the North and the South Zones?"

"Hallelujah!"

"There, Father in Heaven, you have heard the loud, yes loud voices of your people. They are one in praying to thank you through your son, the Lord-Jesus for the blessing of this man."

"Amen."

"For what did the Prophet Isaiah profess when the Almighty Father asked 'Whom shall I send?' The Prophet Isaiah immediately replied, 'Here I am Lord, send me.' The good Book of Isaiah Chapter 6, Verse 8."

"Amen."

"Do you see this humble man, kneeling before the Lord-Jesus, with my right hand over his bowed head, as a symbol of the blessing he has just received from the Lord-Jesus? As with the Prophet Isaiah, this man is now also praying, 'Here I am Lord, send me.'"

"Amen."

"For as in the good Book of Psalms Chapter 113, Verse 1, 'Oh, let us now give thanks unto the Lord because His mercy endures forever.'"

"Amen. Amen. Amen."

"Let us pray. Almighty Father in Heaven through your only Son, the Lord-Jesus, we present this your servant, Juancho "Mahal" Mahalina who has, like the Prophet Isaiah, prayed to you 'I am here, oh Lord, send me.' We beseech thee, Almighty Father through your only Son, the Lord-Jesus to send him now, to send him to the highest position in this land to save our people from the clutches of deprivation and poverty and to make this land your land of milk and honey."

"Amen."

"Almighty Father, what did Solomon ask of you before you made him King? He only asked for 'an understanding heart' so he could discern good from bad. And you were most pleased, Almighty Father, because Solomon did not ask for riches, for glory, for honor, for long life. And because you were most pleased, Almighty Father because Solomon only asked for an understanding heart, you gave him more than that, you gave him riches, the kingship of Israelis so that as you said, 'there shall not be any among the kings like him, unto thee all the days.' You gave him wisdom, you gave him wives and concubines, you gave him sons upon sons and daughters upon daughters and you gave him the blessing' so that 'the throne of David shall be established before the Lord forever.' From the good Book of Kings, Chapter 2, Verse 45 and Chapter 3, Verses 1-14."

"Amen. Amen. Amen."

"And now your humble servant, Juancho "Mahal" Mahalina is asking you love so he could feel forever the heartbeat of our people. Bless him Almighty Father through your only son, the Lord-Jesus."

"Amen. Amen. Amen."

"Now, may I request this humble man to please rise and now wave his arms to acknowledge our brothers and sisters who are his witnesses of the blessing upon him by the Almighty Father?"

As the presidential candidate rose and waved his arms, the throng of over a million faithful followers of the Brotherhood of Faith in Jesus Movement rose in one thunderous roar, "praise the Lord!"

And before the next round of exaltation came out of their throats, Balete, now sweating profusely from his three-inch high boots, darted to the left of the stage and raising his head up to the heavens, likewise raised his right fist that clutched a hand microphone, faced the crowd in that direction, then at the top of his voice bellowed "brothers and sisters in the Lord-Jesus, do you bear witness to the man now waving his arms in acknowledgment of your prayers and your support?"

"Amen!"

And before the next round of exaltations came out of their throats, Balete darted to the right side of the stage, repeating the same gestures and the same question. Before they could respond to another "Praise the Lord," Balete darted toward the stage apron out front, the candidate in tow, as he, Balete raised the right arm of Mahalina toward the sky, shouting "Praise the Lord!"

"Praise the Lord! Praise the Lord! Praise the Lord!"

Then in a voice that completely contrasted from his previous exaltations, Balete suddenly mumbled into the microphone: "Brothers and Sisters in the Lord-Jesus, the time is now, the time to spread your white handkerchiefs to receive the blessings of the Lord-Jesus. Now, upon your open palms, raise your handkerchiefs, your vessels of faith up, up, slowly now up, up, up toward the heavens because the blessings of the Lord Jesus will soon fall forth upon your white handkerchiefs, your vessels of faith. Are you ready?"

"Amen."

"Are you ready to receive the blessings of the Lord-Jesus?"

"Amen! Amen! Amen!"

"Father in Heaven, creator of heaven and earth, we now beseech thee to bestow your blessings upon your children who with their vessels of faith are now raised up, waiting for your benevolence and your love. For as you keep on reminding us in the good Book of John, Chapter 3, Verse 16, 'For God so loved the world that he gave his only begotten son for whosoever believeth in Him shall not perish but have everlasting life.'"

"Amen."

Silence followed. Then as a soft breeze from the still waters of Manila Bay began to whisper in the afternoon calm, Balete suddenly leaped upwards. Landing back on the floor, he shouted, "Can you now feel the holy breathing of the Lord-Jesus, upon your vessels?"

"Praise the Lord-Jesus!"

"Praise the Lord-Jesus!" Balete was now beating to the chant.

"Now, Brothers and sisters in the Lord-Jesus, slowly lower your vessels, together now, in the direction of the man before us, his head bowed, his hands in prayer. Now there, are you ready?"

"Amen!"

"Now tilt your vessels of faith, slowly toward the incoming president of this country... there, now, pour, pour, pour the holy breathing of the Lord-Jesus in your vessels. Pour, pour, pour upon Mahal—Hallelujah!'

"Hallelujah! Hallelujah! Hallelujah!"

"Praise the Lord-Jesus for Mahal!"

"Mahal! Mahal! Mahal!"

"Amen."

In his suite at the Holiday Inn overlooking the prayer rally at the distance, before the panoramic Manila Bay that was now bathed in harbor lights, Richard Martin switched off his remote as the TV in front of him went blur, then blank. "That's it!" he muttered to himself and began running the keyboard on his laptop.

The lecture hall was only good for 175 seats but those inside could double that number. Thirty minutes before the time, the aisles on the extreme sides were already occupied by sit-ins, most of them squatting on the floor.

"I am totally impressed," the professor began, "by the inputs you submitted in answer to the question—'What aspect of politics is dominantly practiced in my hometown?' assigned to you at the beginning of this lecture series. "Moreover, as I am totally impressed, so am I terribly dehydrated, emptied, exhausted. You know why? It's because I spent so much energy trying to put some sense, some order in your varied inputs in the last four days." When the professor paused, giggles and laughter from the students in "Contemporary Politics and Politicians" filled the large lecture hall. "Now, give me a few minutes to write down on the board a summary of these inputs in tabular form."

ASPECTS OF POLITICS

Grp.	Terms Used in Essays	Aspects of Politics	Freq.	%
1	Rule, Regime, etc.	Governance	60	39
2	Company, Corporation, etc.	Business	56	36
3	Amusement, Comedy, etc.	Entertainment	18	11
4	Cardinalism, Priesthood, etc.	Religion	14	9
5	War, battle, etc.	Armed Force	8	5
Total			156	100

"There you are," the professor faced his students. He continued. "Let me tell you that I am completely amazed at this discovery. For one thing, all the textbooks and all the references I used in this lecture series give prominence to Governance as an aspect of politics, but wittingly or unwittingly fail to highlight the four other aspects. Or, probably are simply silent or unaware of their existence in practice.

"The inputs, therefore, that emerged from the simple question 'what aspect of politics is dominantly practiced in your hometown' are very revealing. As I said in the beginning, "aspect of politics" was never defined nor did our lecture series so far touch on anything that resembled aspects or faces of politics. We did touch on politics as science and art and how it is practiced but that was all there was to it. All right, any questions so far?"

Throngs of arms shot up in the air.

"I am Carmena Pacasum, Sir," the student spoke in front of the standing microphone in the middle aisle as soon as she was recognized.

"Sir, it appears that the aspect of politics as practiced in my home town is 'Armed Force', that is Group 5 as indicated in the board. But the term I used in my essay is "war" because that is really what is happening in my hometown, not because of local politics but because of a national policy that resulted in war in my hometown. What do you say, Sir?"

"Thank you, Miss Pacasum for your observation. I do think you are right in using the term "War" because as you said, that is the reality in your hometown. Moreover, please note that other terms were also used by your group which include Battle, Bloodbath, Conflict and the like. I believe "Armed Force" will not only appear distinct in comparison with the other aspects, but approximates the contexts and nuances of the other terms."

"Sir," another student stood as soon as he was recognized.

"Sir, it means now…"

"Excuse me, please state your name first, that's our policy here, right?"

"I'm sorry. I'm Tommy Villaflor. As I was about to say... I belong to Group 2. To be honest, I really think, Sir that 'Business' as an aspect of politics is inadequate to pinpoint with some accuracy what is being practiced. I suggest this be changed to 'Monkey-Business' because that is what it is! 'Business' is too mild a term to represent an industry famous for crooks, crocodiles and ah, ah monkeys."

That sent everyone giggling and laughing.

"Okay, Miss Martino, what were you saying?" the professor pointed to a student at the far end of the front row who was mumbling loudly and calling for attention.

"Sir, the figures on the board clearly show the closeness of Groups 1 and 2 on one end and those in Groups 3, 4 and 5 on the other. Do such closeness imply something, Sir?"

"Okay, they do imply two things. One, that there is some kind of a race, yes, a competition. You may recall that in my earlier lectures, I pointed out that religion used to be at the top of organized groups or communities. Starting with paganism, the priest or priestess was the ruler who set the rules. When government took its present form, religion was somehow cast aside, but not without a whimper. That brought about the conflict between church and state. And two, the closeness you observed could mean a conspiracy. Governance and business for instance, conspiring together to hold on to power, to share the wealth that goes with it. Now, this conspiracy, for absence of a better word, could be either beneficial or harmful to the people. Beneficial, if the wealth is shared with the citizens or harmful, if the wealth is only shared exclusively between the two conspirators." The professor paused, looking at his student. "Miss Martino, are we talking on the same wavelength now?"

"I think so, Sir. It's getting clearer. What about the relative closeness of Entertainment and Religion? I note that there is a difference of only two percentage points between them, as against three percentage points between Governance and Business."

"Now, class, did you notice that? Miss Martino should have helped me in statistics!"

The lecture hall became alive again.

"Levity aside, I think that does not apply here. Remember, our point of departure or springboard of analysis is politics. Therefore, all other aspects should be seen in the context of politics. That'll keep us on track."

"Sir! Sir! Sir!"

"Sir," the student in red shirt practically ran to the microphone at the center aisle as soon as he was recognized. "Sir, I am Benjamin Casilang. I am intrigued by your conspiracy theory. I remember reading somewhere the so-called 'military-industrial complex' in the U.S.; that the military and business or industry are always in conspiracy to create war in order to make money. Do those entries on the board somehow tell us something about that, in one way or another?"

"Now, this is really getting to be intriguing," the professor chuckled, turning his back toward the board. "Hmmm, let me see... No, the answer to your question is

MELCHIZEDEK MAQUISO

not on the board. But you raised a valid point and I have to respond. The conspiracy of the military-industrial complex is real, not only in the U.S. but also in other highly industrialized countries where to make money, they have to make war. Note that business or industry manufactures weapons but they cannot make money out of these weapons if the military cannot use them. And if the military cannot use them, the generals and the soldiers become useless in the scheme of things. So, since both are affected, they have to conspire to build an armed force that leads to war. Note further, that when conflicts arise, the military emerges from its catatonic state of un-use and assumes its role as aggressor, with business pushing for intensified conflict to make more money. From that point on, the conspiracy of two becomes a conspiracy of three, Governance becoming the junior partner. But, and this is a big but, if Governance is saddled with unemployment problems and the economy is down, it can make a deal with business to employ the unemployed, get them to work and help boost the economy. Once an agreement is made, Governance becomes a senior partner in the conspiracy of three."

"Sir! Sir! Sir!"

"Okay, we have time for one more question," the professor said, after looking at his watch. "The young lady with spectacles, please."

"Sir, I am Titania Villamor. Looking at the board, I am really amazed why Entertainment has become an aspect of politics and to think that it got 11 percent, even higher than Religion or Armed Force. How do you explain this phenomenon?"

"Now, this is really getting to be more intriguing," the professor chuckled. Villamor's classmates nodded their heads.

"Well, let me tell you, Miss Villamor that when I went through the essays related to Entertainment as an aspect of politics, I almost died laughing. The early history of politics and politicians tells us that Entertainment has never been there except perhaps for the clowns and court jesters, they were called then, who were hired by the king to make him laugh if he was confronted with problems. Now, if the clown or court jester succeeded in his job, he was then awarded acres of land or a knighthood in some cases. But if the clown failed to do his job, he was immediately beheaded."

"Gosh, how could they do that? It's cruel!" a fat lady sporting an Afro hairdo, obviously a sit-in at the back, cried.

"So, it is easy for you to see that that kind of medieval entertainment could never be classified as an aspect of politics. On the other hand, the kind of entertainment as manifested in your essays is a different one, a recent phenomenon. I say, recent because never have we witnessed the emergence of entertainers and celebrities in the field of politics. As one columnist wrote, 'politics and showbiz are now nakedly intertwined in the country.' If you will recall, I mentioned in my earlier lecture the criterion of popularity that one must have to get elected.

"The popularity of entertainers among the masses could be the key to explain the phenomenon. But let us qualify immediately that this is a different kind of popularity. It is not associated with greatness of stature, wisdom or genius. The popularity of entertainers that get them elected in office, on the other hand, is closely associated with passion, mania for hero-worship or obsession with the world of make-believe. All these are caused by the constant exposure on TV, in movies and in radio that no mayor, priest or pastor, corporate CEO, or military general can ever hope to equal. This kind of exposure inevitably begets popularity and lo and behold, when election time comes, the 'factor of recall' comes to the fore and the entertainer-candidate gets most of the votes. In a poetic way of saying, entertainment has narrowed the field of battle because it doesn't have to conquer the brain, only the heart."

The professor paused.

"The infatuation of politics by showbiz types has practically rattled the country's establishment. As one columnist writes, 'Movie stars are a clear and present danger to national security. They can all run in the next elections and then we have a senate filled with movie stars.'

"Anyway, a vice-mayoralty candidate, a famous actor and game show host, apparently appalled by the clear and present danger, once said, that people have become wary of the so-called intelligent and educated politicians who had done nothing for them, so they tell themselves, why not a *bobo* (stupid) for president so long as his heart is for the masses?

"Actually, there are entertainers who accept their limitations in spite of their proven popularity. If America has a Bob Hope, we have a Dolphy here, right? Well, it was bruited about that Dolphy was asked not once but many times: Why are you not running for any public office when you know that you will surely win? You know what Dolphy said in reply? 'That's scary,' he simply said."

"I never thought Dolphy has a social conscience!" muttered a young lady at the front row.

"Sir!" a bespectacled young man came forward as soon as he was recognized. "Sir, I am Giovani Sinco. Sir, the five aspects of politics that have been discussed here, I find to be most interesting. But I think they are inadequate to reflect accurately the political landscape in this country. The addition of another aspect will complete that picture."

"And what is this other aspect?"

"Media, Sir. Media, the fourth estate," Sinco said. "I believe that nobody can deny the force of media in the politics of this country. To ignore media as an aspect of politics is simply unreal!"

"Now class," the professor scanned around for some reactions. "Has anyone mentioned media as an aspect of politics in any of your essays?" There was no reaction. "Do you think media can be considered as an aspect of politics, in the light of the five that have been revealed to us so far?"

"I think, Sir, that media is distinct from the other five," Giovani Sinco said. "It is a force by and of itself."

"Any reaction?" the professor asked again.

"I think media is a sub-aspect of the five major ones, rather than an aspect of and by itself," Miss Villamor said, joining the exchange.

"Please explain," the professor prodded Villamor.

"Well, I said sub-aspect, "Villamor said, "because media is a tool rather than an entity or an institution for that matter, of and by itself. Governance uses media as propaganda, business uses media to sell its products, religion uses media to propagate the faith, armed force uses media to tell the world it is winning the war even if that is not correct and entertainment uses media to, to eh, win elections!"

Her classmates roared.

"You certainly have a poor regard for media," Sinco said to no one in particular.

"Well," the professor interjected. "I think, eh, Mr. Giovani Sinco brought up a very interesting topic here while Miss Villamor has taken a strong argument to buttress his position. Considering the time constraints, I think, it is best to confine ourselves to the five aspects of politics, as you yourselves have identified as practiced in your hometowns. Moreover, let me say immediately that I am not completely dismissing the point raised by Giovani here.

"Sir! Sir! Sir!"

"I'm sorry class but we have already exceeded our time. 'Til next lecture, class. Bye for now."

As the professor walked down from the lecture hall to the parking lot, an eager voice hollered from behind. "Dr. Destino! Dr. Destino! Can I have a minute with you, Sir?"

"Yes?"

"Dr. Destino, I am Ephraim Bejardo, Sir. I teach fundamentals of speech in the College of Arts and Sciences."

"What can I do for you, Ef?"

"Sir, I am one of those sitting in, in your lectures. You're great, Sir, simply great!"

"Thank you. What can I do for you?"

"You know, sir, right after your first lecture, I got this idea of assigning my students to deliver their speeches as if they were the presidential candidates, approximating the candidates' style of delivery and the content of their proposed platform of government, once elected. What do you think?"

"How long will each speech go?"

"Five minutes. Could be shorter but not beyond."

"Would that not require a lot of research work?"

"To the extent, yes."

"Must be a lot of fun!"

"That's the rub. After every speech, there is critiquing so it would be a lot of fun. In that way too, we go through another actual learning because the class can correct mispronunciations, gestures and even content."

"Looks okay to me. How many students do you have?"

"Well, for this particular class, I have only 18, so three for each presidential candidate, since there are six of them, right?"

"Right. So actually it's not just fundamentals of speech but some kind of political awareness of the candidates via content?"

"Absolutely, yes. And of course, plus their manner of speaking, gestures, body language, etcetera."

"I bet that would be most interesting. Now, what can I do for you?"

"Sir, if it is all right with you and if you have the time and I know you are very busy, could you act as senior critic, with particular focus on content?"

"When will it be?"

"It's three weeks from today. Actually there will be two sessions. Just pick one and we'll be most appreciative."

"Now, I cannot guarantee you but remind me in my next lecture. I understand you will be there?"

"Of course!"

"You know the schedule?"

"Definitely. I already checked with the department."

"Fine. And good luck to your young presidentiables. See you."

"Thank you very much, Dr. Destino."

As the famous Manila Bay sunset sank in the horizon and dusk loomed over the Luneta and the whole stretch of Roxas Boulevard, a couple alighted from a taxi, held hands and walked leisurely on the pavement toward Rizal Park. Both wore black leather shoes with soundless rubber soles.

Just like hundreds of couples at this late time of day, Rizal Park was the place to stroll and relax. Touches and whispers of intimacy were part of the scene. As the couple finally settled on a vacant park bench just below a lamp post, a cigarette vendor approached but was shoved away. The cigarette vendor uttered a low curse, scratched his head as if to say one more rejection and he would head for home. Then he sat by the armrest of another vacant park bench some five meters away from the couple. A few seconds later, another vendor, this time carrying a Styrofoam box with "Ice Cold Pineapple Juice" printed out front, approached the couple who nodded as a sign that they were interested.

As the vendor opened his box, his knees on the pavement, he began to speak in a casual, low voice.

"Long time no see, Ka Alex, Ka Lulu." "Ka" was short for "Comrade." "I see you are both in good shape," the vendor picked two packets of juice with accompanying straws and extended them to his customers. His hands free, he felt for the .45 Colt automatic that was taped at the bottom of his box. The vendor was Ka Rollie, a.k.a Commander Cobra, the top gun of the People's Watch and Revolutionary Army (PWRA). In appearance, Cobra didn't look like the man that he was. He was squat and tubercular except for his eyes that stared long and hard like that of a coiled viper before the strike.

"Thank you, Ka Rollie," Ka Alex acknowledged the compliment, receiving his packet of juice and inserting the straw in it. "You look in good shape, too." He started to sip his drink. Ka Alex, a.k.a. Task Force Commander Sawa was the chief of the People's Watch Brigade, the dreaded assassination group of the PWRA that specialized in eliminating corrupt government officials and big businessmen who failed to pay their monthly revolutionary tax. Sawa was taller than Cobra and a lot huskier. No one could miss the massive hands that he now and then formed into balls of steel. Sawa was known to have no need for guns. He eliminated all his victims with his powerful hands.

"I agree," Ka Lulu nodded, also sipping her drink. "Actually, I didn't recognize you immediately, Ka Rollie. Your mustache really looks real and your wig, too!" Ka Lulu further said, emitting a peculiar laugh. Ka Lulu, a.k.a. Commander Lourdes Dalisay, was the explosive division chief of the PWRA. She majored in chemistry at the National State University, joined the PWRA and trained abroad to further hone her skills. Ka Lulu could easily mix in a crowd. She had a common face and a common countenance. It was when she laughed that she became totally unique.

"Well?" Ka Alex asked as he continued sipping his drink.

"The cargo is on its way," Ka Rollie said, taking one packet for himself. "It is ready for pick-up at ten tomorrow night, at the usual rendezvous."

The cigarette vendor who was sitting on the armrest of another park bench, shifted his gaze toward the Rizal Monument as he felt for the .45 Colt automatic under the false bottom of his cigarette vendor's box. He was Ka Piccio, a.k.a. the Assassin. With that gun, he could shoot and hit anything that moved 30 yards away.

Ka Piccio was Ka Rollie's point man. He had cased the joint earlier and his trained eye told him his three comrades were safe for the moment. His left eye was no longer functioning. It was pierced with a rusty jute sack needle by his military interrogators years ago, the first and only time he was caught and incarcerated. He lighted his first cigarette for the evening.

"Anything else?" Ka Alex asked again, signaling the cigarette vendor for a stick. Ka Piccio obliged, taking one stick from his box and extending it to Ka Alex, then lighting it with his lighter as soon as Ka Alex had it between his lips. The assassin returned to his post without any sign that he knew the three and neither did the latter.

"The Chairman was specific. He said that once the cargo is delivered to its final destination, the fewer collateral damage of innocent people, the better. The cargo is meant only as a second and last warning."

"Did the Chairman say anything about my last message?" Ka Alex asked again, inhaling his cigarette.

"Yes, he did but as second priority, immediately after this cargo."

"Who is going to deliver the cargo to its final destination?" Ka Lulu asked, pointing to the box for another packet of juice.

"It is you, Ka Lulu," Ka Rollie said, extending her another packet. "I am sorry, I was about to say that earlier. The Chairman was specific. It is you and your commandos."

Ka Lulu shifted in her seat. "Did the Chairman say the fewer collateral damage, the better? I cannot guarantee that, Ka Rollie. I have no control over the flow of traffic and the cargo is very heavy."

"That is your problem, Ka Lulu. But I will guarantee you full backup. You will have three escorts immediately in front and two immediately behind."

"How about the exit, immediately after the final delivery?" Ka Lulu asked again.

"My men and I will provide the first zone of defense. Ka Alex and his men will provide the second. The Chairman will meet us 11 days after this mission. Ka Piccio over there, will contact you about the exact time and place of that meeting."

As Ka Rollie stood and collected the empty packets and the used straws, he drew two bundles wrapped in plastic bags from inside his box, gave one to Ka Alex, the other one to Ka Lulu. From a distance, each bundle looked like it contained some five packets of juice piled on top of one another inside each bag. "Cash from the Chairman. That's more than enough to carry out the mission from start to finish and the daily needs of our comrades directly under your command."

Ka Lulu opened her bag, got a P20 note and handed it to Ka Rollie, the pineapple juice vendor. Her gesture and the innocent-sounding laugh that followed caught the attention of an elderly couple passing by. The couple stopped to pause, then went on their way giggling, no doubt tickled by the innocent-sounding laughter of Ka Lulu.

Ka Rollie, a.k.a. Commander Cobra, the top gun of the PWRA, nodded his head several times in gratitude, for effect. He then walked away in the dark.

At Home
Apartment No. 201-A
243 New York St.
Cubao, Quezon City

Dear Angela,

Two months and still no letter from my best friend and first cousin (if you still remember). Wow!

Sorry, I failed again to visit your kids and your mother. But I was able to talk to her on the phone. Well, among others, she told me Reynante had written her to say that there was no need for him to send his regular monthly obligation for the children. His reason—your mother finds this sad—his business has gone kaput Also, he said, according to your mother again, your trial separation of three years had since lapsed. Not to mention your having failed to even write. Well, it's your personal life. If it was a mistake marrying the guy as you said it was, then so be it. A mistake is a mistake, right? No wonder, we are the best of friends. Ha! Ha!

Remember the guy I told you about, the one I just ditched? Well, I really think I made the right decision. I also found out, he's actually married! Gad, who says trust is always a virtue?

Know what? I saw Julia Roberts again, in Erin Brokovich. She's really good, isn't she? Except that she seemed thinner with her cheekbones becoming more prominent. But wow, look at those *boobs! (Not far from mine, eh! Ha! Ha!) I've read somewhere she's already paid more than $20 M per picture. Gad, can you imagine how much that money would mean to us here? Simply unbelievable!*

The presidential campaign here is getting hotter everyday. What does the Filipino-American community there think about our presidential candidates? Would you know their preferences by now? How about yours?

I promise, again, to visit your kids this weekend. Also, I promise to keep on calling you Angela instead of Angeling until you finally answer my letters. I'll be taking ballroom dancing lessons next week—will also tell you all about it.

Bye and always the best for you.
Fili

3
WHO AM I

In his English 101-B class (Fundamentals of Speech), Instructor Ephraim Bejarde wrote the following, in big block letters at the center of the board—'WHO AM I?'

As soon as he finished, he faced his freshman class.

"The semester is about to end and we have come to a point where each of you will deliver a speech posing as a candidate for president of this country."

A ripple of excitement filled the air as those scheduled to deliver their speeches concentrated on their memory work. This was the hour they were waiting for. "It's now or never," mumbled one, closing his eyes as if in prayer.

"As announced earlier, you will be graded according to content, style of delivery, *pronun-cia-tion* and your ability at repartee. Now, to further refresh your memory, you have five minutes to tell your audience not only who he is or who she is, the candidate's personal *cir-cumstances* but also what the candidate intends to do once elected."

Bejarde paused, adjusting the solid red tie hanging from his bull of a neck. His collar was so tight it pinched the skin on his neck in excruciating-looking little creases. He was a big man, had a round puffy face made more pronounced by his crew cut. "Every statement in your speech substance-wise, should be backed by references, recorded speeches, TV interviews, newspaper quotes, autobiography, biography, if any. Remember, your ability at repartee during the critiquing will also be graded. This will show speech patterns that were not practiced earlier. Do you know what I mean?" Bejarde paused again, scratching a portion of his posteriors.

"Finally, there are six official candidates for the presidency. Each one of you has been given the freedom to choose which candidate you prefer to portray, your instructor being a true believer of democracy."

Bejarde went back to his seat, scanning his notes and his attendance record.

"Okay, let's start with Tomas Villafranca as candidate Dimalasa. Let's give him a big round of applause even if we haven't heard him yet!" The applause followed.

"This is it!" Villafranca mumbled to himself, striding toward the front, waving both his arms, then executing a stiff military salute, ala Dimalasa, the ex-general, now presidential candidate. Setting aside the lectern to indicate he had memorized his magnum opus, he demurely smiled at his instructor, inhaling deeply as he had learned from this class then began.

"My fellow countrymen, ladies and gentlemen," Villafranca's voice shook a little. "I am Marshall Alonzo Dimalasa, former secretary of national defense, 66 years old and married to the former, ah Evangeline Osario, daughter of one of the ah, outstanding senators that this, ah country ever had. We have ah, two sons and two daughters, all ah, ah professionals now, except ah, the youngest who is in ah, third year college. From a lowly soldier who fought in ah Korea, I earned my ah, ah three stars, retired and served ah, in the cabinets of two ah, administrations from which I ah, earned the highest ah, ah commendations for ah, distinguished service."

Villafranca paused, shifting the fulcrum on his left leg. Never hesitate to move your body every time you felt like it, he had learned in this class. He just did that rather smoothly, didn't he?

"I have been attacked by my rivals as a crybaby. They based ah, their accusations after they ah, saw me crying on TV, crying after ah, President Rosales announced I was not his choice. Let me tell you—the man you saw crying on TV was the ah, man who finally became ah, ah liberated from false promises, so he could follow his own ah, path towards his own destiny. What is pushing me ah right now are the people, the people of this ah, country, who want me ah, to be their President.

"I am running for President on the basis of morality and my vehicle is ah, the moral crusade." Villafranca's voice quivered. He was now on the verge of tears. "It is ah, time this country elects ah, a leader who is ah, ah moral. It is the time that ah, we denounce immorality, leaders who have mistresses ah, illegitimate sons and daughters, nay, even one ah illegitimate son or daughter. Immorality starting ah, in sex indiscretions gives birth not only to ah, illegitimate offspring but also to ah, illegitimacy in public service, graft and corruption and all the sins and ills familiar ah, ah, ah in government.

"Once elected president with the help of the Almighty," Villafranca paused, pushing both his arms upward as if bearing the cross of martyrdom and slowly closing his eyes as if in prayer: "I, your ah humble servant, pledge ah, to denounce all immoral persons and all ah, their immoral acts. So help me God. Ah, I thank you."

His speech ended, Villafranca opened his eyes again, bowed his head once, then twice, then thrice until he heard the complimentary applause from his skeptical classmates.

"Hmmm," Speech Instructor Bejarde nodded his head in slow motion. "Critique, anyone?" Obviously, he was not pleased with the performance of Villafranca.

"Sir," a student from the second row raised her hand. "Is it really true Dimalasa cried when President Rosales dumped him for Davide? I cannot imagine…"

"If I may answer your question, madam voter," Villafranca volunteered with confidence. "I cried upon ah, realizing I was ah used; hence, that feeling of ah, ah liberation dawned upon me. During ah, my entire military career, it was not ah, rare to see soldiers cry ah, in the field of battle. Soldiers crying in war is not ah, sign of weakness but ah, ah a sign of anger, rage that adds ah, ah, ah more adrenalin, that vital force that ah drives one to seek the enemy and sends him scampering away with his ah, ah, ah tail between his legs."

"Candidate Dimalasa, Mr. Dima…" simultaneous voices rose as laughter and applause went full riot in the room.

"Mr. Dimalasa," one voice finally came out in the ruckus. "Mr. Dima… what's wrong with your speech? Why do you always say ah, ah, ah, ah, ah?"

70

"Order, order!" Instructor Bejarde cried. As the room came back to some kind of normalcy, Villafranca stood there in front, unaffected by it all. He was now the real Dimalasa: a soldier and a gentleman, candidate for president of his beloved country, launching the moral crusade. "My countrymen, the ah, stutter that goes with my ah, speech," he orated, "is not a defect out of ah, childhood, but a scar of battle that ah, ah I got when I, together with four others left in our ah, company after an ambush that sent most of our companions to kingdom come, ah, ah defended the hills of Wala-Wala against the ah, superior force of the ah-nemy."

The laughter and applause grew louder and louder.

"Mr. Dimalasa! Mr. Dimalas…!" a student shouted above the din. "Some say it is the height of madness that you are running for president without any political experience, that you are actually MAD for doing so. What can you say to that?"

"If you are referring to my initials, then you are the one that's ah, ah, ah mad yourself!" Villafranca cried.

"You will notice, class, that Mr. Villafranca has done his research on his subject," Bejarde interrupted. "Let's give him a real big round of applause." Villafranca as candidate Dimalasa executed a military salute as his classmates clapped and cheered.

"Thank you. We shall now hear from Mr. Artemio Pikotan as candidate Tan-Kong. Let's give him a big hand."

Pikotan strode forward, his shoulders ramrod straight. Facing his classmates, he raised his neck and pressed his index fingers to his temples, drawing them back as his eyelids began to close. He wanted to project the slit eyes of candidate Tan-Kong and he thought he had partly succeeded since his classmates began to snicker.

"My fel-low coun-try-men, I am, Arturo Tan-Kong, 71 years old, a wi-dow-er and re-cent-ly married to this no-ble quest for the pre-si-den-cy." Pikotan began, raising his neck again and half-closing his eyes. "I have no mis-tress-es, children or re-la-tives who bo-ther me, nor cro-nies to pres-sure me be-cause e-ven if I have them, I will not al-low them. I s-star-ted my go-vern-ment ca-reer as a police-man, then be-came chief of police, then be-came the head of the natio-nal inves-ti-ga-tion agen-cy of this coun-try. In all the thir-ty years I spent on the force, I have no re-cord of she-na-nig-gan, mal-fea-sance or de-re-lic-tion of du-ty ex-cept as my ac-cu-sers say, I am a vio-la-tor of hu-man rights. Well, I tell you this, when a cri-mi-nal is ar-res-ted, put to jail, e-ven if there is no war-rant, have I, the ar-res-ting of-fi-cer, vio-la-ted the cri-mi-nal's hu-man rights? Does a cri-mi-nal, a vio-la-tor of h-man rights, have any hu-man rights? See? The pro-blem with my ac-cu-sers is that they are making an is-sue of a non-is-sue that is ty-pical of born lo-sers. See?"

Pikotan paused. His throat was getting dry. He had exhausted his reserves of saliva by pronouncing almost every word in monosyllables. And he was beginning to have a stiff neck. "I am run-ning for pre-sid-dent to once and for all, bring about peace and or-der in this vio-lent and wild-wild west coun-try of ours. We have so ma-ny re-ci-di-vist fe-lons roam-ing a-round who ought to be in jail: ra-pists, mur-de-rers, thieves, crooks, smug-glers, ad-dicts, drug-gists… name it, we have it. Just s-can our dai-ly news-pa-pers, lis-ten to the ra-dio, watch TV… what do you see? Cri-mi-nals here, cri-mi-nals there, cri-mi-nals everywhere, a fo-reign-er can ea-si-

71

ly say we are a big jail-house of a coun-try, with-out cells and iron bars! To the cri-min-nals, who have vio-la-ted the hu-man rights of the law-abi-ding ci-tizens of this coun-try, your days are num-bered! Once elec-ted and sworn to of-ffice, Arturo Tan-Kong will end your days of a-buse and bu-ry your no-to-rie-ty into ob-li-vion. So help me God. I thank you." Pikotan barely made it. His throat was now completely parched. He was beginning to have a headache.

"All right," Instructor Bejarde said. "Applause for candidate Tan-Kong." Pikotan's classmates clapped their hands. "Thank you. Critique?"

"Mr. Pikotan, ah, Mr. Kang-Kong, eh Tan-Kong," a student from the back eagerly stood. "I notice you zeroed in on the issue of human rights when the real issue against you is, that you are allegedly not a natural born citizen which if proven true, will automatically disqualify you as a presidential candidate!"

"I thought about that when I was wri-ting my speech," Pikotan paused, scratching his throat. "Then I con-clu-ded that iss-ue is not as mag-ne-tic as the issue of hu-man rights, which is the cur-rent rage a-mong ma-ny peo-ple. See?"

"But what could be more magnetic than a constitutional violation? Everything starts from there, see?"

"With due res-pect, I am a na-tu-ral born ci-ti-zen of this coun-try. My an-ces-tors are from Shang-hai, see? Ma-ny in this room are also from China. Just look at their eyes, see?"

Some of his classmates chuckled. Some peered sideways to examine the eyes of their classmates.

"Sir," one student observed. "I think Mr. Pikotan has his facts confused. Tan-Kong claimed his ancestors come from Taipei. I heard him say that on TV!"

"Oh yes," Pikotan countered. "His p-arents—yes, but his an-ces-tors—meaning those ahead of his parents came from Shang-hai. See?" Pikotan pressed his temples. The headache was becoming unbearable.

"You are both right," Instructor Bejarde interrupted. "Any more critique?"

"Mr. Kong," another student asked. "I've noticed that your delivery is very slow, with many pauses in between and is rather dull. Is that really the style of candidate Tan?"

The room burst in confusion. Some shouted, "Kang-Kong," some "Kong-Tang," some "Pak-Kong."

"To be frank with you my friend, I, Arturo Tan-Kong, can-di-date for Pre-si-dent has real dif-fi-culty in s-peaking Eng-lish." Pikotan scratched his throat again. "I have to go slow—to be a-ble to say what I mean and mean what I say. See? The re-sult of this is a bles-sing, for I am clear and speak to the point, un-like o-thers who s-peak fast without tan-kong, eh thin-king. At least I don't ah, ah, ah. See?" He pressed his temples again.

That sent the whole class hooting.

"All right, all right, that is enough, children!" Instructor Bejarde had to wipe his eyes from shedding more tears of laughter. "Let's give a round of applause to Mr. Pikotan for doing a great job." A burst of applause followed as Pikotan hurriedly went back to his seat, one hand scratching his throat, the other pressing his temple.

72

"Thank you," Instructor Bejarde said, loosening his tie. "Now to the next speaker, may I call on Rustico Advincula as candidate Enriquez."

"Ladies and gentlemen, I am Juan Carlos Enriquez, popularly known among friends as JCE, 65 years old, married with seven children and 28 grandchildren. Of all those aspiring for the presidency of this country, I am the only one who really knows what politics is all about, politics being in the Enriquez blood for generations now. As all of our people know, my grandpa was once the president of this country. My father was a senator for three terms. My brother is an incumbent senator. My wife has been a congresswoman whose district one of our sons now occupies. This is now my third term as governor until I have to vacate the post to run for the highest post in the land.

"Of all the candidates now seeking the position of president nobody has been a governor. In the United States of America, most of its presidents started as governors. Why is that? The answer is simple—it is the governor that runs the affairs of the state, the state being almost autonomous. The governor is the politician who is most familiar with governance; not the congressman, not the senator, not the military general, not the policeman.

"The name Enriquez is a household word. Besides Rizal and Quezon, most towns and cities in this country bear the Enriquez Street, in honor of my uncle's good performance in office, the kind of honor that all of us, the living members of the clan, dignify.

"Politics has become a bad word in this country because those running the government do not understand what politics is all about. Thus, I am running for President to give back dignity to politics, which in its most basic sense means the art and science of governance.

"My detractors allege I have made myself richer by cornering every government contract I could lay my hands on. That I am rich, I will not deny but that I have been cornering every government contract, I will deny most vehemently. The truth of the matter is—my family owns vast tracts of lands some of which we had to sell so government can build airports, national highways, ports, housing projects and other needed infrastructures. And what are the results? High employment rate, high per capita income, efficient transport system and efficient facilities for trade and commerce.

"Once elected president, I will transform each of the other 75 provinces of this country into a boom town, just like my province. That simply means I will cut the umbilical cord that presently ties the provinces to the dictates of imperial Manila. As former governor of the most progressive province in the country, I have confidence that with your support, my vision for the entire country will see fruition in the next few years. I thank you very, very much. *Muchas gracias!*"

Advincula stopped. He had done it, fast and easy. The applause that followed confirmed his remarkable performance. And surely, he would vote for Enriquez in the coming elections. No doubt about that.

"Thank you," Bejarde clapped as the students followed.

"Critique, anyone?"

"Mr. Enriquez," a student in the front row stood even before he was acknowledged. "I am most impressed by your speech and delivery. However, I would like to ask you a question which I think is in the minds of most voters. The question is—How come you still aspire for president when you and your family have already everything in the world?"

Advincula was familiar with Enriquez' vintage answer to that question. "You know my friend, that is one advantage of being rich. Once he becomes President, he won't steal anymore. Unlike the others who have to recoup whatever they spent in the campaign."

"Is that right?" another student said, as he rose from his seat. "So, it is not the money but the perpetuation of your political dynasty!"

"Political dynasty? I've never mentioned that in my speech!"

"Oh yes, you don't need money but you have to secure your family and perpetuate your family dynasty to protect your money. You and your Castilian greed!"

"Sir! Sir!" Advincula cried. "The inquisitor is getting out of bounds!"

"Both of you are out of bounds," Bejarde grinned. "Although both of you are doing all right. Any other critique?" Bejarde slowly scanned the faces of his students while scratching a portion of his posteriors, this time as surreptitiously as he could.

"Sir," a female student rose from the third row. "I mean, Mr. Enriquez. It just occurred to me that as far as I can recall, this will be the first presidential elections wherein we have ah, ah, pseudo-multiracial fight. We have a Spaniard, a Chinese and some native-looking candidates. How come we don't have a Muslim and a Lumad?"

Advincula had not anticipated that. And what had that issue got to do with his speech?

"Okay," Advincula said. "I think the Muslims and the Lumads—I think, this is not their time yet. In the near future, perhaps."

"Which is really next to impossible," the previous inquisitor jumped in. "Unless people like you with your Castilian greed stop acting like Pacman, the Muslims, the Lumads and all those marginalized will never have a chance in the near future and until eternity!"

"But..."

"Thank you," the speech instructor cut in.

Advincula slowly went back to his seat. He knew his delivery was perfect, almost perfect but most of his answers to the queries were corny. Why? Advincula asked himself. Because the queries themselves, Advincula concluded, were corny.

Speech instructor Bejarde continued: "I am confident that those of you who are on deck, will have enough time during the weekend to improve your speeches in the light of what we've witnessed today. But before I'll let you go, we still have a few minutes left, let me look at my notes. Ah, here are my comments, mostly on your *pronun-cia-tions*. On Candidate Dimalasa..."

Filipinas Cruz just made it on time, that was, for the second part of the one-hour session. Damn that traffic, she muttered to herself, hurriedly slipping the cream colored jeans out of her long, shapely legs. After depositing her jeans in the locker, she adjusted her leotards. Examining herself before the inside wall mirror, a salacious smile of satisfaction washed over her face: "You still got them, Babe. You still got them!" She then blew a kiss at the stunning figure in front of her.

Filipinas or Fili to her friends was about 33, five feet two in height, with long black tresses now dyed brown and gold. She had a face that always caught a second look, a pair of come-on chinita eyes and a countenance that prompted men to whistle to themselves over her high spirits and sexual exuberance. Slamming the locker door behind her, she sneaked from the back to the third row in the dancing hall and took her place. The music was in full blast.

"All right, all righttt! Dahlings, let's do it all over again, okay? You in the third row from the back, form a straight line, pleassse! Now, follow me. Number 1, left step forward and back, gyrate; Number 2, right foot backward and back, gyrate. Number 1, repeat, left step forward and back, gyrate. Repeat Number 2, right step backward, then back, gyrate. Stop... stop! Stop music, too, pleasssee!"

The Dance Instructor (DI) paused, sweating profusely while fanning himself. He was in a loose white cotton shirt and red silk hot pants that clung to his buttocks. He stood on black high heels, their pointed toes in pink. A silk bandanna was wrapped around his head, red as the paint on his lips. He moved and swayed like a ballerina.

"Okay, dahlings, okay, let's take a breather. Now, as I said many times, ladies and girls, the cha-cha-cha is a dance, a dance, a dance! Most of you do the fundamentals like you were in a military parade. I told you, you have to have grace, not the grace of a female water buffalo. Ouch! Joke only, dahlings. Okay? Now to be sexy, you do it this way. You sway your body this way, with a subtle angling of your hips, this way, then glide forward with your first step and your arms and your fingers this way, like you were saying, come on baby, come on, with your beautiful face looking this way as your left eye twinkles that way. Got it, dahlings? Okay, music, pleassee!"

The ladies took their positions in their respective rows. The DI then swiftly turned his back to his students, facing the vast wall-to-wall mirror that reflected all of them in the wide dancing hall.

"Now, ready—there it is!" the DI hollered, hips swaying, legs gyrating as the music began. "Number 1, left step forward then back, gyrate. Number 2, right step backward then back, gyrate. Okay, you at the third row, more of the hips! All together now, let's go with the beat, dah, dah, dah, cha-cha-cha, yes, cha-cha-cha, yes, gyrate. That's it, yes, cha-cha-cha, there, hips, face, look, cha-cha-cha, fingers this way, hips, hips, first row, hips, you third row, angle, angle, cha-cha-cha, headwork, hips, gyrate, there, very good! Now go, go, go, go, cha-cha-cha, hips, hips, dah, dah, dah, la, la, la, hips, two steps backward, then back, cha-cha-cha, hips, eyes, look, headwork, you're doing great! C'mon girls, c'mon ladies, cha-cha-cha, hips, hips, look, arms, arms, cha-cha-cha, dah, dah, dah, gyrate, forward... Wow! Wow! Let's clap our hands together. Stop... stop! Music, stop!"

More than half of the dancers collapsed on the floor. The rest heaved and heaved, especially the near-obese and the super-thin. In situations like this, the ubiquitous face towel was the most helpful. "Damn, I forgot my towel in my hurry!" Fili complained to the matron squatting on the floor by her right.

"That's okay, sweetheart. With that body of yours, you don't really need a towel. You don't even need those leotards!" the voice was hoarse and the eyes were glassy. Filipinas Cruz stared at the matron.

"Okay, girls, okay ladies. We still have about 19 minutes," the DI announced, profusely fanning his front and back. "Now listen to this while you rest. The cha-cha-cha is a dance, a dance, a dance like the tango. But, but, but unlike the tango where you completely lose your identity, the cha-cha-cha projects your personality in the way you move on your own and in relation to your partner. Unlike the tango where the female is the conquered and the male is the conqueror! Remember dahlings, in the famous tango dip, it is always the man on top, never the woman. Is that true in real life? Of course not! But shhh, don't tell him huh? Ha! Ha! In the cha-cha-cha, you and the man are equal! After the fundamental steps, one forward, then back, then gyrate, then backward and back, then gyrate, the next moves will now depend on you, whether you want to be the conqueror or the conquered, because taking the next forward steps, or the next backward steps, if you don't know it yet, is part of the game of seduction. Did you get that, dahlings? Therefore, when you are able to do that, you take gradual control of the pace and from there, hmmm, depending on the grace of your body and the sunshine of your personality, the man, your partner is now ready for your conquest. Grrrr... kill him! Ha! Ha! Wow! For it takes two to cha-cha-cha, right dahlings? But you don't want to do that unless you want to project yourself as an exhibitionist. Ouch! Joke only."

The DI paused; profusely fanning himself again as some strands of hair fell from his wig. Raising his jaws, he flipped a strand of stray hair aside as his eyes rolled and his penciled eyebrows arched. The gesture was unmistakably feminine though the voice, husky and throaty remained. "So, the cha-cha-cha is the most challenging dance for the female beauty!" The DI continued, his hands on his hips. "Never mind me because I prefer to be in the middle, between you and your man. Wow! How sexy! One last reminder, reminder, huh? The few backward steps of seduction should not be overdone otherwise you'll fail to gain enough space to move forward for the kill, because if you keep on moving just one step forward and two steps backward, you'll end up like an idiot, like a drunken idiot! Got it, dahlings?

"All rightttt! Back to your rows! Take your position now for the fundamentals and be ready to take the right steps towards conquest. Grrrr. Music! We sing our version of the cha-cha-cha and dance to the beat of Querico Bacelon. Now, dahlings, here goes... louder that music pleassseeee.

Cha-cha-cha, I've got you by the hands,
Cha-cha-cha, I've got you by the waist—
Cha-cha-cha, My hips are brushing yours,

Cha-cha-cha, We're dancing now in heat!
Ta-la-la, Ta-la-la, Ta-la-la, la
Ta-la-la, Ta-la-la, Ta-la-la!

"C'mon dahlings... Go, go, go cha-cha-cha! First step forward, back, gyrate, two steps backward, back gyrate, now, forward, now forward! Now more... Grrrrr, kill him! Now there, hands, hips, eye, headwork, more hips, cha-cha-cha hips, go! Angle, angle, hips, hips, cha-cha-cha, go, cha-cha-cha..."

Cha-cha-cha, Querico Bacelon
Cha-cha-cha I've got you by the waist—
Cha-cha-cha, My hips are brushing yours,
Cha-cha-cha, We're dancing now in heat!

"Good afternoon, class."
"Good afternoon, Sir," chorused the college freshmen in English 101-B.

"All right. We have four candidates today, in the order of Davide, Santolan, Mahalina and delos Ajos. May I remind... "Instructor Bejarde said, looking at his notes.

"But Sir, delos Ajos has just been disqualified by the COMELEC!" a student from the second row pointed out.

"Never mind," Bejarde declared. "I also know that. Anyway, I have a big surprise for all of you. When I heard of the disqualification of delos Ajos, I got this idea—why not invite him to this class and deliver his speech here? So I exerted all efforts to contact him only to find out he is my neighbor!" his eyes danced in orbit. "To my surprise, he readily agreed, saying he would be most happy to deliver his speech in this class. He said he would be here promptly at one-thirty this afternoon."

Wows could be heard throughout.

"All right," Bejarde's voice boomed, obviously pleased with the reaction of the class. "May I now call on Pablo Lampaso as presidential candidate Davide? Let's give the candidate a big hand."

Almost everybody snickered as Lampaso walked up front. The way he moved restlessly, the way he twitted his ears and the way he waved his right arm by way of greeting, reminded everyone this was indeed the real McCoy.

"My countrymen," Lampaso began, bowing and extending his arms, palms up. "I am your humble servant Serafin Andolana Davide, 63 years old and married to the most attractive and understanding woman, the one and only Claudia Palomos. I have two sons. I am proud of my sterling record in Congress, having been the principal author of 122 bills and co-author of 327 others. Thus, I was always voted one of the Ten Outstanding Congressmen every year throughout my career in the august halls of Congress.

"I am proud to be chosen by His Excellency, President Sergio Imperial Rosales to be his successor. This only means our president, recognized all over the world as having caused the miraculous turnaround of our economy in his less than six years in office, has total confidence in my ability to succeed him and continue his excellent record as president of the republic."

Lampaso arched his body backward, pushed his right arm forward and raising his voice, bawled: "I've been attacked by my rivals as a tradpol, which I accept but not in the negative sense my rivals are in fact, guilty of. I am a tradpol in the sense that I dispense favors to my constituents, in the same manner that worthy politicians all over the world dispense favors to their constituents, a practice that morally binds the elected and the electorate. For I say, if you don't dispense favors and sustain them, who will vote for you?"

Lampaso paused, taking two steps forward, raising his voice still higher. "If elected, I promise to continue the programs of President Rosales."

Lampaso took another step forward, raised his voice much higher, his arms now swinging alternately, his eyes bulging in their sockets.

"I also commit myself to transform within the next six years our country from its present reputation as the sick man of Asia to one of the most successful tiger economies in the world! My friends, gone are the days when our foreign friends would look down on us—for there, there in the horizon shines a new dawn, a new hope, a new Shangrila! There, there we shall show the world this country is peopled with great men and women, comparable to any proud race in the whole world where each family should at least earn, at the end of my term, the meager, I say meager sum of only $4,000 a month, which, with the current foreign exchange rate would mean P200,000 a month or P2.4 million a year for every family, with at least six children! All this would guarantee not only a sumptuous meal for everyone in the family, education for the children, kitchen appliances for mama, a Mercedes Benz for papa but also a lovely palatial home that is more than enough to accommodate relatives, guests and close friends from the provinces during fiestas."

Lampaso stepped backward, inhaling air, then lowered his voice as if to whisper a secret: "And how do we achieve all these?" He paused again, pacing the floor, twisting his body to the left. Then raising his voice to the max, he answered his own question: "By exporting I.T. or Information Technology! At present levels, the world needs $135 B worth of IT software and hardware. Within my term, if elected, we will supply one fourth of that demand. Can we do that? Yes, because we have thousands of bright young men and women in this country who are practically untapped! Elect me and I will tap them! Elect me and I will send all of you to the United States of America! My countrymen, Ladies and gentlemen, vote Davide for Davide is the best! Praise the Lord!"

English Class 101-B would never be the same again. At one o'clock noon when everybody was supposed to sleep, the classmates of Lampaso exploded in standing ovation. Lampaso himself, already through with his speech, was still stabbing the air with his fists, his eyes swelling out of their sockets, his whole body shaking ala Hitler, Charlie Chaplin and Jackie Chan. "My goodness!" Instructor Bejarde stood, massaging his chest with his right arm. "My goodness, Lampaso, you almost killed me with your antics!"

"Your humble servant, Sir, is not Lampaso but Serafin Andolana Davide or SAD, candidate for president. SAD because everyone of my rivals will be crying when I win and they will all be pulverized into smithereens."

"All right, all right!" Instructor Bejarde shrugged his shoulders in surrender, nodding, sitting back on his chair. "Any critique?"

"Vote Davide for president!"

"Down with Davide and his billions!"

"What a SAD story!"

Lampaso bowed three times, raised his arms, gave the double thumbs-up and darted back to his seat, gasping for breath.

"Okay, that's enough," Instructor Bejarde cried, scanning his notes. The riot had subsided. "Okay, at this time, let us call on Arlene Ramirez as Senator Naomi Ganzon Santolan, the only woman candidate for president. Let's give her a big hand." The clapping followed.

Ramirez glided toward the front in her mini-skirt, subdued whistles following in the heels of her stride. When she turned around to face her classmates, silence ensued. The guys in the front row watched in admiration. The guys at the back rows strained for a peek.

"Ladies and gentlemen, I am Senator Naomi Ganzon Santolan, the only woman candidate for president among men of questionable characters," she began, cracking the quiet. "Don't ask me about my age, but all the men, including all the pretenders in this campaign generously ogle at my legs and that's only one of my assets. I graduated magna cum laude from the National State University, took graduate courses in constitutional law at Harvard, was a former regional trial court judge who sent felons rich or poor to jail and served as senator for three uninterrupted terms. I got elected president of the republic but failed to serve only because I was cheated in the counting."

Ramirez went through her opening lines ala Santolan, the vowels she rolled in her tongue like round marbles, her delivery fast but controlled as mouths went agape.

"Ladies and gentlemen, people who could only be associated with my rivals have thrown everything from their toilet bowls at me, to prevent me from the fulfillment of my destiny. One of these is the stink that I am supposed to be suffering from brain damage. Well, let me tell them it's their buffoonish brains and pitiful IQ's that's causing them to panic. It is their inability to grasp complicated issues and solomonic problems that can only explain the slings and arrows of outrageous lies they are hurling against Senator Santolan."

Ramirez paused, raising her right index finger, her eyes unblinking. "Once elected with the votes counted correctly in my favor this time, I will send all the political buffoons in jail and the idiotic candidates running for public office back to elementary school! Believe me, immediately after I am sworn into office on June 30, all these pretenders will make your day and mine a memorable feast." She paused and inhaled, her eyes staring in space.

"Let me end by remembering and paraphrasing Shakespeare when he said, 'My friend, your tomorrow is in your stars.' That is the misfortune of all the others who innocently seek the highest position of this land, without knowing their tomorrow is the end of their superegos and mega-ambitions! As for me, I need not state the obvious. I thank you in advance for your votes and see you at the inaugural, with a special request for the ladies to wear their miniskirts. I thank you and kisses to all of you."

When Arlene Ramirez ended her speech by blowing kisses, the boys in the class also blew their kisses toward her, whistling and hooting in obvious delight.

"All right, you've heard Candidate Santolan... any critique?"

"Sir! Sir!" Ramirez suddenly thumped her feet on the floor. "They're ogling at my legs!"

"Now, boys you behave!" Instructor Bejarde hollered, winking at the boys. Looking at her, he then asked, "Who are you, actually?"

"Who am I?" startled, Ramirez asked, blurting out, "Of course, I'm Arlene, Arlene Ramirez!"

"Oh no, you're not," the instructor said, making a face, his large eyeballs swerving out of their orbit, his right arm vigorously scratching his behind. "You are candidate Naomi Ganzon Santolan with the beautiful legs, right boys? It just happens you also have them, Miss Ramirez! Hmmm."

Ramirez darted back to her seat, practically all red in the face. Bejarde lectured: "Now, that is a lesson all of you should never forget. When in actual situations, you are on stage delivering your speech, always maintain your composure even in the midst of distractions. Now, let me ask you—what would the real Naomi Ganzon Santolan have done under the circumstances? *Cir-cumstances*, with accent in the first syllable, don't forget. Well, I assure you that at the first sign of ogling, she would pause and then bend to look down for something that is not there, exposing her knees in the process. When the whistles come, she would then move forward a little bit, adjust the belt around her waist and raise the hem of her skirt a little bit more. That would send the crowd into a riot. Well, let me tell you, there's nothing vulgar about that. Santolan is just taking advantage of the situation, just like all other effective speakers who want to get the full attention of their audience."

Bejarde adjusted his solid red tie. Some flesh in his flabby neck protruded out of his collar. Obviously, he had more neck than he needed.

"Now, in fairness to Arlene whose legs are actually more attractive than those of Candidate Santolan, ehem, her delivery was almost perfect Santolan style: the clipped accent, the voice of venom when attacking her rivals and even the eyebrows that curled when talking of her vision and destiny. Let's give Arlene Ramirez a big round of applause."

The whistles simmered down. Bejarde remained standing. "Okay, we're down to the last two candidates. May I now call Roman Tomador as Candidate Mahalina?"

Tomador lumbered toward the front, sporting a fake mustache. Bejarde saw it while noting the jutting belly of the young man. *This guy must be a real fan of Mahalina... belongs to a fraternity of beer drinkers, too.* Bejarde mused.

"Sir," Tomador asked, "may I use the lectern? I'm going to read my speech, just to make sure." He scratched the mustache. *Must be itchy...* Bejarde thought, correctly. "Go ahead."

"My friends, my classmates, the beautiful ladies before me, the poor but good people of this country, good afternoon. I am Juancho "Mahal" Mahalina. I am 63 years old but look at me, the ladies will tell you I still look like sweet sixteen. I do not pretend to be a virgin, for I have loved many. I do not deny, I have sons and daughters outside my marriage. But I have amply provided for all of them because my love for all of them is the same: true and sincere.

"Leaders of the Church are accusing me of being immoral—that I am a sinner. Now, let me ask you—who among us mortals are not sinners? Who among the leaders of the church are not sinners? Who among the candidates for the presidency are not sinners? If any one of them will deny he is not a sinner, then he is a hypocrite—including the priest. Your father confessor, too, the one who keeps on saying he is no longer a sinner after he has confessed his sins every Sunday.

"I think it is time we forget this issue of immorality—this hypocrisy. It is in fact time to have a serious look on who among the candidates, once elected, will lovingly care for the poor, the downtrodden, the oppressed, the ignored, the street children, the squatters, the dislocated, the prostitutes, the pimps, the small time gamblers, cock fighters and the many families in our country who cannot have three square meals a day.

"I am not fondly called Mahal for nothing. My buddies, casual friends and classmates, even enemies call me Mahal because they recognize my love for all of them. I am, therefore, running for president to devote my love for everyone and for this country that I want to serve in love, for love and with love.

"It is love that this country needs. Once elected, I will show everybody that the most effective program of government can only be based on love. That's for you and for all of us. From Mahal, with love, I thank you from the bottom of my loving heart. Tsup, tsup, tsup."

The speech did not impress his classmates. Only a few clapped.

"Critique, any one?"

"Mr. Mahalina," a bespectacled female student finally asked, after some silence. "Your program of love is very nebulous to me. You said Mahal is love. Mahal loves the masses and the masses love Mahal and all that. Isn't that rather corny?

"Corny? Sonnamagun! You can have your corned beef. The masses love rice." Tomador replied, snickering at his own repartee.

"May I continue?" the female student asked, indifferent to the repartee. Tomador nodded.

"Thank you. It is public knowledge and you have admitted in your speech, that you have loved many—that you have a mistress here and a mistress there. Isn't that anomalous? Your statements are an insult to the women of this country. What can you say to that?"

"May-nay? I don't love a May-nay. Miss Tress? I don't have a Miss Tress here or a Miss Tress there. What I have are my Mrs. here and my Mrs. there." The class snickered.

"Yes, the student from the back," Bejarde acknowledged the raised hand.

"Mr. Mahalina, what is your plan for the economy? The country is still in turmoil economically unlike Singapore, Taiwan, South Korea and others that are positively recovering from the present economic onslaught. Do you think there is a chance for us becoming a tiger economy?"

"Are you ending?" Tomador asked, seemingly startled.

"What ending?"

"Your long question?"

"Yes, will you please answer my question?"

"What question?"

"My question of us possibly becoming a tiger economy."

"Tiger?" He scratched his mustache. "Sonnamagun! We don't have tiger here. We have horse, carabao, but no tiger."

The snickers turned to laughter.

"Mahalina," another student from the back came forward as soon as he was recognized. "I really don't care about the content of your speech because that would be improved over time, what with so many speechwriters and advisers when you become president. To be honest, I was a little impressed with the way you delivered your lines, as you read through your speech. But I am just curious—how come you are very economical with words; that is, if you are not reading your speech?"

"Less talk, less mistake. No talk, no mistake."

The laughter became a riot of hoots and cries.

"Mr. Mahalina, eh, Mahal, may I call you Mahal?" another student from the front row stood as he asked.

"Yes. Mahal means love and love is a many splendored thing."

The hoots and cries became thunder.

"Thank you. What can you say about your opponents in the fight for the presidency? Are they also sinners as you said all mortals are, including yourself? If so, why can't they also reveal some of their indiscretions, their hidden skeletons in the closet?"

"Are you ending?" Tomador asked again, seemingly puzzled.

"Yes. That's the end!"

"What is your question?"

"Why can't your opponents also reveal their hidden skeletons in the closet? That would make them human, too, wouldn't it?"

"Closet?"

"Yes."

"Sonnamagun! No, not closet. Confessional, yes. In the confessional, it's a sin to tell a lie."

The thunder became an explosion.

"I think it is obvious from your tumultuous reactions," Bejarde observed, wiping his eyes from tears of so much laughter, "that Tomador did a very good job, not necessarily in delivering his speech, but with his one-liners which Candidate Mahalina is famous for. If for anything else, that simply implies the considerable research work Tomador did on his subject."

"Sir," Arlene Ramirez raised her hand then withdrew it but Bejarde saw it. "Yes, Miss Ramirez."

"In real life," Ramirez said, "do you really think the masses will vote for Mahalina, simply on the basis of those one liners, on the basis of his anomalous relations, on the basis of…"

"Let me cut you off right there, Miss Ramirez," Bejarde interposed, vigorously scratching a portion of his posteriors. "I will not really comment on that, except to say that academic theories are often incompatible with the realities of politics." Having said that, Bejarde shrugged his shoulders and stared at the ceiling.

There was an interregnum of silence.

"Good afternoon! I'm here! Presidential Candidate Vicente delos Ajos!" Bejarde almost fell from his chair when the voice boomed from the open side door parallel to the platform where he momentarily sat in reverie. The source of the thunder was a small creature of a man, the students in English l0l-B found it difficult to accept the thunder could erupt from the bowels of his lungs. On top of his head was a panama hat made of recycled plastics from the garbage dumps of Payatas. When he took off his hat and his shades to introduce himself, the room seemed to suddenly brighten up. His bald, oval pate radiated its own solar system. On one of his abnormally large ears—the flagship of longevity, was pinned a tiny precious stone that sparkled every time his head or his shoulders moved.

"Class," Bejarde said, recovering from his shock. "It is my honor to introduce…"

"Cut the formalities, Professor," delos Ajos snapped, cocking his head toward Bejarde, the precious stone sparkling. "I already introduced myself." Inserting his dark glasses in his breast pocket, he peered at his watch. "Just in time. May I now begin?"

Before Bejarde could answer, delos Ajos was facing his audience and ready to go. Holding his hat with both his hands in front of him, the self-proclaimed presidential candidate began.

"My children, whom Rizal had consigned as the hope of the fatherland, I am your Lolo Inting. A very pleasant good afternoon to all. I am 84 years old and married recently to a 23 year-old bride who can attest to my strength in both flesh and spirit. All in all, I have 39 grandchildren, offsprings of my four previous wives, now all in the bosom of Abraham. Bless their souls."

His audience could not believe what they were hearing. Lolo Inting was definitely a geriatric, yes, but his voice flowed effortlessly and was full of conviction. And he stood erect and proud like the Rock of Corregidor.

"The COMELEC disqualified me from running as an official candidate for the presidency, saying that I am a nuisance. Who are they to say I am a nuisance candidate? Is it because I don't have a party?

"I am running for president of this republic to bring back family values that had been erased by the likes of the real nuisance candidates, the political crocodiles and all those who think they are Solomon to solve the problems of this country. I have proven myself to be a strong family man. If you have any doubt, count my legitimate children and grandchildren and you can count on me with or without the COMELEC."

Wows and whistles could be heard.

"My platform of government, therefore, is to put the family together again, let it blossom and multiply, as the God of Abraham in the Old Testament instructed us to do. Once that is done, with or without the COMELEC, the real father of the nation will emerge. Need I say more to convince you—that the family is the beginning of everything, that the right family values are the springboard of all development to bring forth a productive and caring government? Trust your Lolo Inting. I thank you."

English class 101-B was surprised at the sudden finish. It was obvious that its eager ears wanted more.

"Thank you, Mr. delos Ajos, Sir," Bejarde said, clapping his hands. "Would you like to answer some questions from your ah, grandchildren?"

"That's what I'm here for. That's why I had to shorten my speech," Lolo Inting snapped. His audience clapped their hands heartily.

"With due apologies," a pretty coed from the second row asked as soon as she was recognized. "I am completely amazed that a man of your age would still insist in running for president, not to mention that you had just been disqualified. Would you please tell us your reason or reasons for this tenacious burst of enthusiasm on your part, Mr. delos Ajos?"

Snickers could be heard. Lolo Inting scanned the faces of his young audience, his gaze finally settling on the pretty co-ed who asked the question, whose face now flushed, obviously feeling remorse. Had she insulted grandfather? She thought, wrongly.

"I thank you. I do feel tenacious just by looking at you," Lolo Inting said, unleashing a killer smile that would have been fatal during his salad years. "For you remind me of my current wife, Estrellita, my fifth, who is always young and whose eyes, similar to yours, are like stars in the night." Lolo Inting paused, his eyes twinkling, the boys whistling, the co-ed's flushed face melting into a cute winning smile, the rest of the girls giggling. "Well, the reason for all this tenacity is the family, which is the focus of my present campaign, to develop the right values for the family. And to tell you honestly, in the words of Ambassador Carlos P. Romulo, age doesn't really matter for as long as the matter doesn't age."

Snickers were much louder now.

"I hear your snickers there boys, but Ambassador Romulo could have meant 'matter' as the brain which is the fountain of wisdom, not the kind of matter that you are thinking about, although I say that the matter you are thinking about also matters here… with due apologies to the sweet young lady that started all this."

The young lady rushed out and kissed the bald cranium. The room burst into applause.

"Thank you," the eyes twinkled. The head swayed, the tiny precious stone sparkled. "Anyway, where was I? If you recall, Adam, the first man God created lived to be 930 years and his great, great grandson, Methuselah lived to be 969 years. Why is that? The reason is they had to live that long to procreate and populate the first nation on earth. Mao Zedong, the father of more than a billion people lived to be over 90 and Deng Xiao Peng, the father of modern China also lived to be over 90. Look around you when you go back to the provinces. You see big trees there—the older those trees, the bigger they become and the bigger they become the more oxygen they exude, because they are the lungs of the earth. Without them, we will all die. But it does not end there. Once cut into lumber, they become beautiful material for furniture, wall paneling and many other useful things because they are seasoned; their grooves distinct and shiny, their surface once polished, becomes smooth and slick. It's like wine. The more it's aged, the more it ignites the fire that goes down your throat to your intestines like ambrosia, the drink of the gods, suave, ingratiating and smooth as silk."

Mouths went wide open.

"Now, where was I? Oh yes, why am I running when I am disqualified? Actually, this is not the first time I am running for president of this beloved country of ours. This is actually my third time. The first was a mistake because at the time my platform of government was to lick graft and corruption. Well, that was a mistake because you can never lick graft and corruption in this country. Like AIDS, this sickness is already endemic in our society, perpetuated by politicians. The second was also a mistake because at the time, my platform of government was to annex our country, to be one of the states of the United States of America. Nobody really knew my secret agenda at the time. All they knew was, I was for progress, development and all that which could have been a reality now, if you look at Hawaii and Alaska. But my secret agenda at the time, which I will reveal to you now and for the first time was that once annexed, I would, as president of this country automatically be appointed as governor of the United States. After that, I would qualify to run for President of the United States!"

Almost all jaws dropped.

"Where was I? Okay, now I remember. But as you know, we are a people of different breeds. We do not only have short noses, except the Castilian candidate around, you know who, but we love independence so much, we drove the Spaniards, the Americans, the Japanese out of our shores—although up to this time we are still begging them to give us aid."

Some were clapping their hands. Some swore.

"Where was I? Oh, I'm running for the third time even if I got disqualified because I know I am fighting for the right family values... the kind that will..."

"Sir, Sir! Time is past four minutes!" shouted somebody from the back. "We still have to go to our next class!"

"My goodness!" Instructor Bejarde exclaimed, his large eyeballs rolling, a hand vigorously scratching his behind. "I've been totally mesmerized by the musings of aged wisdom. Thank you, Lolo Inting. Until next time, class... dismissed!"

Most people in the republic turned on their TV sets to watch "Presidential Debate—Live", the much publicized and the most awaited spectacle on Channel 4. In living color, the presidential candidates were in their Sunday's best, their faces aglow, no doubt made up by the best facial salons in town, their eyes on their notes. This was their first public encounter, their first blood and each wanted to make a lasting impression.

Fred Palanca was the anchorman and Gina delos Reyes, the anchorwoman. Fred and Gina were two of the most popular TV personalities and enjoyed celebrity status. Fred was now at the end of his summary on the rules of the debate.

FRED And so, ladies and gentlemen, let me sum up the rules of this debate. One, each candidate will only be allowed at most two minutes to every question asked. Two, the sound of the buzzer will tell the candidate his time is up, sounding off the candidate next to his left, that it is his time to answer the question asked. Third, the candidates will not be seated alphabetically but by the order of their pre-drawn numbers. Professors Bobby Quebral and Webster Salas of the National State University will be our moderators.

GINA This is really getting to be exciting, Fred.

FRED That's right, Gina. We'd like to inform our viewers that due to unavoidable circumstances, candidate Mahalina could not be with us today in this debate. Mahalina's spokesman just phoned in that he could not make it due to a very personal reason.

GINA Wow. Isn't that very disappointing? His many fans will surely miss him. Fred, do we know the personal reason?

FRED Now, now Gina, I can see the naughty twinkle in your eyes! Our reporter on the spot confirmed a while ago that Mahalina, together with his top aides, is in his mother's eh, ancestral home. Our reporter suspects that Mahal's mother who is already 94 may not be feeling well.

GINA Could that be the real reason? Now Fred, what was I about to say? Oh, yes we have a total of five candidates in this debate, excluding Vicente delos Ajos or Lolo Inting to his fans. The COMELEC just disqualified him for being a nuisance candidate.

FRED Right. Before we turn you over to our moderators, let's have some words from our sponsors.

GINA Don't go away. We'll be back. This is TV Channel 4.

Unbeknownst to anchorpersons Fred and Gina, Mahalina was comfortably sitting and watching TV Channel 4 in his boxer shorts, his favorite drink by his side which he sipped now and then, oblivious to the young lady who was pedicuring his toenails. It was the 11th hour counsel of Fatso Santos that Mahal dodge the debate. In Fatso's words, actually capitalizing on one of Mahalina's one liners, "On TV, less talk, less mistake. No talk, no mistake."

Fatso sat next to Mahal with his notebook ready before him. Around them in the wide sala sat Mahal's other advisers, along with his buddies and classmates from way back in high school days.

Also unbeknownst to anchorpersons Fred and Gina, Vicente delos Ajos was also watching Channel 4, sitting on his rocking chair in his pajamas. When the anchorman mentioned his name and his disqualification, Lolo Inting suddenly stood and cursed as the child on his lap fell and hit the floor. This caused all the other children to shriek and panic as Lolo Inting yelled for Estrellita, his young wife to take care of the child in distress.

On TV Channel 4, cameras zoom in on the presidential candidates who are now seated in their best pose and posture behind the long table.

QUEBRAL Ladies and gentlemen, welcome to "Presidential Debate—Live!" on Channel 4. Before you, are our five presidential candidates who have come to honor us with their presence, in spite of their busy campaign schedule. My co-moderator, Webster Salas will now present the first issue.

SALAS The problem in Mindanao is getting to be very serious and is attracting more international headlines than the present national elections campaign. What is your position on the matter?

DAVIDE   Thank you, Professor Salas. Our viewers probably don't know Webster is a province-mate of mine. Webs, you still remember our swim in the Agno River when we were still kids? Without anything except our birthday suits? Ha! Ha! Anyway, the problem in Mindanao is not only getting to be serious. It has already reached its catastrophic level of damage to the economy. (His voice rises, his right hand shoots up) The reason is total neglect of the welfare of our brothers and sisters in Mindanao (the left arm points south), which the present administration had started to address with full force (the right arm forms a fist) but because of time constraints, could not yet be fully accomplished. That is why I am running for president (the right palm taps the heart) to continue what the Rosales administration started.

Once elected (the voice rises), I will build two more international airports: one to link Mindanao (the left arm points south then waves all over that direction) to Sabah, Malaysia; and another for international flights via Cebu, Cagayan de Oro and Manila. This will only cost an initial outlay of P120 billion. (the voice booms, both arms flying and shaking) Along with that, I will build the first circumferential railroad in Mindanao (the voice booms some more, both arms flying and shaking) that will have waiting stations in every town and city in that island. (the torso turns halfway facing south, the arms moving in circles) My Japanese contacts, not to mention my European friends, have indicated interest to build that railroad through the Build-Operate-Transfer scheme at an initial cost of only P215 billion.

QUEBRAL (After pressing the buzzer) Sorry, Sir.

(Dimalasa eyes the moderator to confirm if he is next. Getting Quebral's nod, Dimalasa fingers his buttoned collar, checks his watch, then starts to say his piece.)

DIMALASA The serious problem in Mindanao is ah terrorism. It's as simple as that. That is why it is getting ah more headlines in the international press, terrorism being the ah, ah main threat to world peace. This is now the major ah, concern of the United States and the rest of the world. (He unbuttons his collar) The recent kidnapping of foreign tourists in Malaysia is ah, actually the work of Muslim rebels in Mindanao. The bombings ah, kidnappings, killings, rape of women, ah, all these are the handiwork of those terrorists in Mindanao. It is really, ah, ah as simple as that.

(After watching Quebral about to press the buzzer, Santolan stretches herself, cuffs a stray hair above her brow, clicks her fingers to check if the table microphone in front of her is working, then raises her senatorial jaws upward. After inhaling air to fill her lungs, she opens fire with her automatic missiles of words in her peculiar, riveting accent.)

SANTOLAN While I consider the so-called problem in Mindanao serious, it is only a diatomic pest compared to the more serious mad cow disease which if uncontrolled would escape from its biological confines and lead to loco dementia. I am, of course, referring to some people whose perceptions of the problem in Mindanao are either skewed to the right or the left but never focused at the center. You see (her extended eyebrows arch as her eyes roll), the local and international press as well as my competitors here, regard Mindanao as if it is a small place occupied by some rebels. But for their information, Mindanao is such a vast, rich land composed of 14 provinces and nine cities and thousands of municipalities.

(Mouths are agape as ears are extended. Santolan has fired her initial salvo with stinging missiles, a whole, rolling, unfamiliar register of sounds that is instantly identifiable as sophisticated to the learned or simply "stateside" to the semi-literate.)

The problem you are referring to is only happening in exactly three towns in just two specific provinces! What does this mean? If you allude to the whole of Mindanao as the problem, you also bloat your figures into billions and exhaust the limited budget of the Department of National Defense to fight terrorism, all because of skewed perceptions. What a waste (the head swings like a pendulum), waste of money and saliva and…

QUEBRAL (He presses the buzzer.) Sorry Ma'am…

SANTOLAN Just a minute, just a minute, I thought this was a debate! (The tongue kicks "debate" into two distinct syllables.)

QUEBRAL Sorry, Ma'am. Next please…

(Tan-Kong slowly tilts his head backward, his slit eyes peering at Santolan to his right. Then Tan-Kong faces the camera.)

TAN-KONG What is hap-pe-ning in Min-da-nao… ex-cuse me, in those three towns in Min-da-nao, I tend to agree with Se-na-tor San-to-lan here—is a les-son that I can-not e-ver for-get when I was in the po-lice force. (The slit eyes widen in recall) When you deal with kid-nap-pers, bank rob-bers, har-dened cri-mi-nals and the like, you have no choice but to deal with them in the way they deal with their vic-tims. (The right fist tightens) It's the Bib-li-cal dic-tum of an eye for an eye and a tooth for a tooth. All the more be-cause the prob-lem in those three towns, is not just a-bout ter-ro-rists but ter-ro-rists whose a-genda is to dis-mem-ber this re-pub-lic. So, it is not just ter-ro-rists who kid-nap their vic-tims for ran-som, be-head their vic-tims if there is no ran-som, kill our mi-li-ta-ry men and wo-men at will but ter-ro-rists who want a por-tion of this re-pub-lic their own. See? (The slit eyes are now shut) This is not only a vio-la-tion of our na-tio-nal pa-tri-mony but they are also doing vio-lence—to our Cons-ti-tu-tional in-te-grity. See? (The eyelids withdraw as the slit eyes resurface)

SALAS Candidate Enriquez, please.

ENRIQUEZ I think we have to look at the problem in a very sober way if we intend to solve that problem. Emotionalism also breeds violence, if I may say. I believe among the candidates here, I am in the best position to say something rational because I have many friends and associates in Mindanao, everyone in my family speaks the common language of Mindanao, unlike my friends here who are unfamiliar with the nuances of that language, with the exception perhaps of Senator Santolan who may understand it but couldn't speak it anymore... since she had been schooled in a foreign tongue as her accent can attest. (Enriquez pauses, looking at Santolan whose nostrils suddenly flare, her eyes eyeballing Enriquez.) I agree with most of the noble intentions of my fellow candidates here, but noble intentions are never enough. What is needed is a specific, doable solution. My position has always been to give the problem to the local government to solve. The problem in Mindanao has become serious because imperial Manila is always overacting, not to mention its colossal ignorance in dealing with the situation in Mindanao. That's how we get adverse reports from the international media.

QUEBRAL Thank you, Madame senator and gentlemen. That ends the first round of "Presidential Debate—Live!" on TV Channel 4.

FRED Let's have a word or two from our sponsors.

GINA Don't go away—We'll be back.

As soon as they are out of camera range, Candidate Santolan immediately stands from her seat, threatening to leave. "I don't like this," she says. "You've cut me off before my time!" The moderators explain their stopwatch is functioning well. "I don't care! You've got to let me finish first before you press that buzzer. You're being discourteous not only to a senator of the republic but also to the only lady in this forum!" Candidate Dimalasa pleads. "Ah, ah Naomi, please, ah, ah, I think they will consider your ah, ah, request ah..." To which Santolan immediately cuts him off. "Now, Marshall, if you cannot speak straight to me, then you better salivate that stutter. It's jarring to my ears!" The other candidates snicker; Dimalasa's face flushes.

GINA We're back to "Presidential Debate—Live!".

FRED Ladies and gentlemen, the honorable presidential candidates are back on their seats after a breather backstage, after the grueling first round. I shall now turn you over to our moderators—Professors Bobby Quebral and Webster Salas.

SALAS Now, to the second hot issue in this debate. There is a noticeable standstill in the economic front in the country. Investors are pulling off their punches. They are saying the political front is not stable, therefore they do not want to take high risks. What is your position?

DAVIDE   As a businessman and a politician, I fully understand the apprehensions of our investor-friends. Humbly speaking (the right palm taps the heart), I can fully comprehend what is going on because I am the only (the voice hits the ceiling) candidate who is an economist. 'It's the economy, stupid!' was the battle cry of Bill Clinton, who by the way was initially ignored since he was from that very small state known as Arkansas—many Americans couldn't even spell that since its pronunciation is Ar-kan-saw. Ha! Ha! (A quick shrug of the shoulders is accompanied by a pout of the lips) Let me repeat (the head moves forward as the hands are stretched, palms up), no one but Davide (the right arm withdraws and taps the heart) is an economist among the presidential candidates here. And that is the reason why investors are apprehensive if I lose. Candidate Enriquez is not an economist, he inherited...

QUEBRAL (Presses buzzer) I'm sorry. Candidate Dimalasa, please...

ENRIQUEZ I think, you should ask me, instead, Prof. Quebral. Candidate Davide specifically mentioned my name—I have to respond.

QUEBRAL I'm sorry, Sir. We have to stick to the rules.

DIMALASA Ah, ah I am sorry but I cannot ah, agree with Candidate Davide. President Rosales who ah, pushed Davide to be the ah, official candidate of the party in power, is not an ah, economist but Rosales was able to turn around the poor state of the ah the economy during his time, to be ah, fair with him even if he wasn't ah, fair with me. My own reading of investors ah pulling off their ah punches right now is not really ah, for economic reasons. Their apprehensions are caused by the ah phobia that a tradpol (Davide's ears flap sidewise), an alien (Tan-Kong's eyes widen), or one with some ah mental defect might ah be elected president. (Santolan's extended eyebrows arch skyward, her jaws jutting forward and backward)

SANTOLAN Tradpol? Alien? One with mental defect! (The piercing eyes roll in their orbit) Economist! The problem with us is, we tend to be subjective, hence the dominance of impertinence and irrelevance when we tackle issues. The issue propounded here, if I may review it for the deaf is— what is causing the economic standstill? According to investors, it is because the political front is unstable. And what is the political front—the crying face of a candidate? the hooked nose of a candidate? the mouth of a candidate that spews billions of promises? the slit eyes of a candidate? the mustache of a candidate? Or, the stunning legs of a candidate? (She smiles to herself) No, no, no! (The head swings like a pendulum) By political front is meant the collective political situation, not the personal...

QUEBRAL (Presses the buzzer) Am sorry, Ma'am...

SANTOLAN Let me just finish... (Both arms spread-eagle as she stands, the face up in heaven)

QUEBRAL But Ma'am, the rules…

SANTOLAN Just one sentence—it's the collective political situation, stupid, that calls for policy imperatives and not personal impressions of subjective egos! Thank you. (The piercing eyes never leave the camera as she sits triumphantly back on her chair)

SALAS Candidate Tan-Kong, please.

TAN-KONG Thank you. E-ven if Se-na-tor San-to-lan allu-ded to me as the can-di-date with slit eyes, I bear no ill will against her. Be-cause ac-tual-ly to be ho-nest, I am one of her fans, not only be-cause of her stun-ning legs… (Leans backward, looking down at his right)…but also be-cause of her bril-liant mind. See? (Looks at the face that is staring at him, its nostrils vibrating.) I ful-ly a-gree with the lady senator. The po-li-ti-cal front re-fers to the col-lec-tive po-li-ti-cal sit-ua-tion and that calls for po-li-cy im-pe-ra-tives which with her le-gis-la-tive pro-wess could be trans-la-ted into laws, to en-sure the eco-no-my moves for-ward and not back-ward, or for that mat-ter stand still. When I become Pre-si-dent, I will im-ple-ment with full force all the laws that Nao-mi San-to-lan will le-gislate in the Se-nate. See? A-ny-way, I am ve-ry hap-py she men-tioned my slit eyes be-cause they mean more votes, since there are many Chinoys all over the country, see?

SALAS Candidate Enriquez?

ENRIQUEZ Many Chinoy voters and lots of Chinoy money! Right, Art? Ha! Ha! Ha!

TAN-KONG Right… may-be.

ENRIQUEZ I think we've got to straighten some things in here. First, I vehemently object to Pin Davide's insinuation that if my name is associated with wealth—it is not because I am an economist but because I only inherited such wealth. Now, I like to inform everyone that I studied economics abroad but in the third year, I dropped out. Why? Because I found half of what they were teaching me in college were the same things my father taught me when I was still in high school—the other half were all macroeconomics food-for-thought, not food for the pocket. Second, I won't deny I inherited a lot of wealth from my parents but I used that as my capital to create more wealth with blood, sweat and tears. The issue here is not the investors—it is the government's failure to formulate the right policy so investors will not hold their punches. That's my…

QUEBRAL (Presses the buzzer.) Sorry, Sir. Your time is up.

FRED That ends the second round. Gina?

GINA Wow! This is really an education for all of us. Let's have a station break. We'll be back.

(As soon as they are off camera range, Davide stands immediately, vigorously pumping the hand of Enriquez. "You 're still the smartest practitioner of economics, aren't you, Juan Carlos, old boy! How's Renee, my comadre?" Davide then slings his left arm over the shoulder of his taller friend, guffawing as he did. "Smartest, my ass!" Enriquez guffaws back. "Now, don't ever twit me with your smart-ass insinuations, Pin. You can never get away with it, from me, you know." Both laugh like horses. "Renee is okay, campaigning as usual for her good husband. Just like your Claudia, my comadre." Enriquez guffaws again.

At the other end of the table, Arturo Tan-Kong and Naomi Santolan are similarly engaged. "I didn't know you had a wry sense of humor, Art?" Santolan quips, pretending to admire the slit eyes. "I meant what I said, you know, my be-ing one of your fans," Tan-Kong explains. "You mean because of my stunning legs and brilliant mind?" Santolan says, her extended eyebrows arching. "Of course, of course!" Tan-Kong agrees, vigorously nodding his head several times. "But more than that, be-cause of your le-gis-la-tive pro-wess, I was think-ing, why don't you shift o-ver and ins-tead run as my vice-pre-si-dent?" "How dare you!" Santolan shoots back, her nostrils vibrating as she returns to her seat. To her right, Marshall Dimalasa sits alone, impervious to everything, Santolan thinks. She is wrong. "If you weren't a woman, I'd ah … Dimalasa mutters to himself without looking at her… "ah, ah kick those legs of yours till you'd cry ah, ah ah."

While "Presidential Debate—Live!" gets hotter on TV, another debate is going on in the sala of the ancestral home of Mahalina. Fatso Santos has argued against the other advisers' insistence that Mahal should make a call to TV Channel 4 and say something, if only to maintain presence and visibility, even if it is only his voice.

FATSO That is Mahal's decision. But I am still taking the position that less talk, less mistake. No talk, no mistake.

1st ADVISER But he would be reading from this prepared script!

FATSO Well, as I said. it's Mahal's decision. But as you can see, he is already dozing off in dreamland. You want to wake him up and get his goat?

It was mid-April, the height of summer and the peak of the national campaign season. From its opening salvo in Metro Manila, the political campaign blazed its trails in the provinces and the countrysides. Like flies after the smell of fish, media went after the presidential candidates at every twist and turn.

Sorsogon, Sorsogon. After barnstorming 54 isolated towns and cities in the region, presidential candidate Marshall Dimalasa finally reached this capital town of the province definitely haggard and exhausted but full of high hopes. In his speech last night before some 7,000 loyal province mates, Dimalasa promised to pursue his moral crusade with unstoppable vigor and military zeal, promising the good life and uplifting poverty in the province and the region. Asked of his chances of winning, Dimalasa confidently said that there was no question about it. He cited figures that his region was the third vote-rich in the country, which meant 15 percent of the total votes. With the votes of the military forces and their families behind him, the followers of former fellow cabinet secretaries also behind him, constituting another 10 percent, that would mean 25 percent and with the other four candidates who would split the rest of the votes, Dimalasa averred, victory was his for the taking. Dimalasa was former secretary of national defense in the Rosales Cabinet.

Dimalasa was accompanied by six of his senatorial candidates, Father Rudy Nicolas, his spiritual adviser and four former cabinet secretaries led by Rusty Kapunan who also acted as his campaign manager. *(News dispatch from Alran Pendon and Luz Montojo.)*

University Town, Catbalogan, Samar. Dressed in flaming orange blazer over black shirt and black miniskirt showing her stunning legs, the fiery and sharp-tongued presidential candidate, Naomi Ganzon Santolan lashed at her rivals for their "idiotic dreams" and "grave-worm promises" to lift the country from its present "state of stench" and "cemetery-like dormancy." Santolan who practically promenaded around the stage while displaying her legs to advantage before she spoke to the four thousand students under the blazing summer heat, promised "intellectual relief" to the dismal state of education in the country. Asked about her chances of winning, the senator simply blurted out her often repeated claim that if not for the cheating in the counting of votes in the last presidential elections, she would have already been president.

"But this time," Santolan orated, "the people will instigate a revolution if you deprive Santolan of her God-given right. And let me warn them further that this woman, the only lady among pretenders of questionable characters who are running for the most exalted position of this land is never afraid. For the information of everybody, threats are never new to me. I smell them everyday as I breathe fresh air and explore new ideas every day."

Candidate Santolan was, as always accompanied by her doting husband. Both did a boogie-woogie on stage that sent students into wild cheering after her much applauded speech. Five of her senatorial candidates were also with her. *(Andres Caritas. PDS. Visayas News Bureau.)*

Baguio City. "How can I possibly lose when I am the administration party candidate?" this was the assertion of presidential candidate Serafin Davide after his meeting with the Rotary Clubs of this city. According to Davide, his party had to forego the scheduled *miting de avance* today in this city due to the full support of all congressmen and local government executives in the entire region as expressed in their resolution. Instead, Davide said, he would fly later today to Cagayan de Oro in Mindanao to meet all the congressmen and local government executives there, who he claimed, also passed a similar resolution of full support for his candidacy and the entire slate of his party.

Many are wondering however why President Rosales has not been seen lately with Davide in the latter's public appearances. Also, many are asking why crowd are dwindling during Davide's provincial sorties. (*Reports by Norberto Sales and Maricelia Unabia, Northern News Bureau.*)

Davao City. Accompanied by the former lady president of the republic, ex-president Caridad Anilao Castro and two senatorial candidates of his party, presidential candidate Arturo Tan-Kong emerged from the San Miguel Cathedral, this city, confident that he would win the presidency, although he admitted—by a small margin. The mass presided over by Archbishop Conrado Castaneda and attended by the rich and prominent personalities as well as the poor folks of this city, was held in honor of the former lady president and presidential candidate Tan-Kong. The former lady president had not made any public statement, not yet anyway, but it was quite obvious that she was endorsing Tan-Kong. In his homily, the Archbishop praised the virtues of the former lady president while exhorting the faithful to always remember the sincerity and good public record of candidate Tan-Kong. Both had the blessings of the Divine Providence, the Archbishop claimed.

After mass, Tan-Kong went straight to the Bankerohan Mall and Shopping Arcade in this city as guest speaker of its eleventh anniversary celebration. "With your support," Tan-Kong said, "and God's blessings there will be no impediment to my quest for the presidency." He then went on to expound on his program of government, anchored on peace and order.

At 71, Tan-Kong appeared in excellent health and at the height of his elements. A widower, he is rumored to marry a high-profile widow in both the business and political world, one week before election day. "This would radically change the entire ballgame of this campaign because the marriage will be the wedding of the century. It will become a fairy tale. People especially the masses will simply be awed and bewildered. And before anyone realizes what's going on, loyalties will shift and voters will flock to Tan-Kong," a close aide of the candidate confided on condition of anonymity. (*Reports from Dante Sinco, Rac Collado and Larry Deveza.*)

ZAMBOANGA City. "Never before in the history of this city has a phenomenon of the kind been witnessed!" boomed the voice of the local radio announcer. He was referring to the thousands of people who practically went into a rampage to get near the Mahalina chopper as it landed in the middle of this city's sports complex. When Juancho "Mahal" Mahalina alighted from the chopper, the horde of his fans rushed forward shouting "Mahal! Mahal! Mahal!" as bodies got trampled upon and children pushed out of the way. As he was whisked on top of the stage, borne on the shoulders of people he even didn't know to the frustration of his bodyguards, Mahal's dark glasses flew out of his face and his flaming red blazer torn out of his bulky frame. Young ladies and mothers alike planted lipsticks on his face and those who could not reach his face, on his shoulders and even on his jeans.

When order was restored after Mahalina finally managed to stand erect on stage, his arms still stuck to some ladies' waist or neck, the mothers and young ladies on stage and those who failed to mount the stage shed tears of uncontrollable joy. They've seen and touched Mahalina. Mahal has become Mahatma Gandhi, the Pope and John Travolta in one.

As in his other sorties, Mahal did not give any speeches. It was not necessary. The people have spoken. They shouted, cheered, cried and rushed to meet and be near their idol Mahal. The election in this city is finished before it started.

Meanwhile, in the city's famous Insular Hotel where presidential candidate Juan Carlos Enriquez was scheduled to speak before a gathering of his supporters, the *merienda grande* reserved earlier for 300 supporters was practically untouched by the 50 guests who arrived, mostly belonging to the rich Castilian clans and business moguls of this city. "We made the horrible mistake of scheduling this event with the coming of Mahalina," said one of the organizers on condition of anonymity. (*Reports by Romulo Nieto, Solidad Bohin and Dona San Juan, The Sunshine Daily.*)

The wall clock in the presidential study said it was five forty-five in the morning. The hot issues marked for the cabinet had been identified and classified. Time to go, PA Meandro Destino told himself, arranging his notes and stuffing them in his briefcase.

"Not yet," President Rosales said. "We still have some other issues to discuss." Destino straightened himself on the chair and waited.

"I am concerned about the cabinet," the president continued. "Looks like we are left with nothing but technicians."

"I've been pondering on that, too, Mr. President," Destino averred. "But I always end up accepting the awful truth that, most cabinet members have inevitably come to believe they deserve no better than to become a senator, a vice-president or president, for that matter. Lofty ideas for the country are the main menu in the cabinet and that must have given them some inspiration."

"That's interesting," the president joined Destino in his musing. "Former corporate managers, academicians, technocrats, retired military generals and what have you, end up wanting to be politicians. And to think almost everyone at the beginning expressed some kind of loathing against politics and politicians."

"Perhaps, you've directly or indirectly encouraged them, Sir," Destino paused, smiling uneasily. "Perhaps, after their exposure to public life, they thought they could also institute needed reforms as you did in such a short time and leave their own legacy of achievements, imagined or not, to the next generations."

"Really?" the president was obviously amused, chuckling on the side as he removed his glasses.

"That's the upside, Mr. President," Destino connected. "The upside, the noble side."

"And the downside?" the president said, chuckling louder.

95

"The downside is the ignoble side, Mr. President. That's when men in the corridors of power begin to develop voracious appetites for food, flash and fantasy."

"Hmmm… did I hear that somewhere?" the president said, returning his glasses at the tip of his nose as he leaned forward. "I mean the three F's."

It was in such moments when Destino suddenly felt comfortable and relaxed. He sensed the president was now in the mood for banter.

"It's kind of difficult to explain, Sir why most if not all around your orbit prefer food in five star hotels, what with their grease and all. Why take coffee in the lobby of five star hotels when you can take it in the comfort of your office, at lesser cost and lesser trouble?"

"And the second F?" the president accompanied that with a cackle.

"That's the flash in the dash… "Destino said, examining his fingernails. "Or is it the dash in the flash. It's our preoccupation with sartorial elegance, the flash of the palace ID, the flash of the rotating orange light on the roof of the car and many other flashes."

"And the third F?" this was followed by a presidential wink.

"You might have noticed, Sir, most of us are enjoying the fantasy that sometime, someday, we might be like you. From up here, it is not at all difficult to engage in fantasy. The impossible dream seems not too far away from up here."

There was an interval of silence.

"Something wrong with all that?" the president asked, wiping the lenses of his glasses and blowing tiny spurts of air on them.

"Nothing really, Mr. President, except those preoccupied with food, flash and fantasy end up very busy doing nothing."

A smirk slid over the president's face.

Destino was sure the president knew them all, he knew what his men had done and worse, he knew what they had never done. It was bruited about and this was not a joking matter, that the president had a huge blackboard in a corner of his brain that was chalked with all necessary information, including the totals of all the sins and virtues of all those closest to him.

"So… you are saying," the president broke the silence, "having been exposed to the workings of government at the top, most have developed ambitions far beyond their capacity to attain?"

"It appears, Mr. President." Destino quickly answered, believing it was the right thing to say.

"Does that include you, Meyan?"

"Oh, no, Mr. President," Destino suddenly said, obviously taken aback. He was about to add he'd rather drink of the bowl of poverty and suffer graciously. But he didn't want to sound like a martyr.

"Why not?"

Destino remembered that many wanted him to run and be included in the senatorial slate of the party. Davide himself had offered him a slot. "Just say it Meyan and it's yours for the taking." But Destino did not want to be beholden. Besides, he needed millions to contribute to the party and he didn't have any.

"I like politics very much, Mr. President. But I don't like to be a politician," Destino finally blurted out. That sent the president chuckling until he coughed.

"What do you think of the chances of Ruby Toledo?" the president asked after taking a sip of water from a glass on his desk.

"Very dim. But I don't think that is his problem right now. In the opposition camp, some of them suspect him as your spy. I think his conscience is bothering him. He realizes this late the opposition is using him more than he thought he could use its popularity for his own purposes. My feedback is all is not well with him, even with former close colleagues, Mars Dimalasa and Rusty Kapunan. Ruby is left alone in the cold now—without real friends."

"Why do you think he did what he did?" The president asked, his voice almost bitter. He was shaking his head.

Destino remembered that the president blew his top when he came to know that Ruby Toledo made a deal with the business tycoon Ferdinand Tancho, for Toledo to be included in the senatorial slate of Mahalina. Destino did not know exactly the specifics of that deal, but he knew from an impeccable source that it was in exchange for Toledo to work on the tax evasion cases against Tancho. Destino recalled that during the Rosales campaign, Tancho had on many occasions tried to wrangle an appointment with then candidate Rosales, apparently to offer his contribution to the campaign fund. In fact, two of Tancho's lieutenants had approached Destino not once but several times. The amount promised for the campaign and for his own pocket was so big, Destino almost chocked in disbelief and anxiety. When Destino monitored the offer, Rosales did not say anything. Destino did not know what happened after that. After he won, President Rosales ordered the Department of Justice to pursue the tax evasion cases against Tancho.

"Well, as you had observed, Mr. President, Ruby Toledo developed ambitions both noble and practical. Perhaps, he thought that as your executive secretary, he had nowhere to go but up. He forgot gravity. That was his undoing."

"Some say he was misled?"

"Maybe, but I find it difficult to believe that, Sir. I still hold on to the general impression that Ruby was one of the cleverest men in your cabinet except that at the height of a major political impasse when a presidential decision had yet to be made, he missed to read the president's mind, your mind Sir, probably blinded by his overwhelming ambition and that did him in. From there, instead of up, he had nowhere to go but down."

Destino did not blink as the president stared at him. He knew the president was pained by Ruby Toledo's defection to the opposition, by Rusty Kapunan's personal attacks against him and by Mars Dimalasa's public pronouncements that he was the personal choice of the president, unduly preempting the decision of the president at that time.

"As they say, in politics..." Destino hesitated but he had to say it anyway, "there are no permanent friends, only permanent interests ..." the president joining him in an early morning duet whose lyrics they knew by heart even without the background music.

"What is irritating," the president went on, "is that important bills I certified as urgent long ago are frozen because most congressmen are running for reelection and are in their respective districts campaigning. The senators are vacationing elsewhere or very busy doing nothing as you said, except the reelectionists who are also campaigning. Don't you think, Meyan it is easy to live out the presidency in the last few months practically not leading, not governing but simply politicking, at the same time thinking what chapters in the presidency need to be included or excluded in his memoirs?"

Destino did not exactly know what to say except to shrug his shoulders.

"What do you think should be done, Meyan?"

"Mr. President," Destino found his opening. "Why don't you start revisiting the major projects you started in selected cities and provinces, the projects that are closely identified with your administration's thrusts? Take along the First Lady. The locals would be ecstatic. It would be a happy reunion with your people on the ground, Sir."

The president's eyes suddenly glinted. "That's not a bad idea, Meyan. Okay, plan out the itinerary. Let's start it a week from now."

The conference hall of the Southern Paradise Apartelle was packed with ED4PRES volunteer coordinators from all over Mindanao. They were engaged in process evaluation and updating campaign strategies. All enthusiasm however suddenly fizzled out when Timostocles Sipula, national coordinator of the support group arm of the ED4PRES returned to reveal that the mobilization funds approved in the budget were no longer forthcoming.

The workshop groups were then convened into a plenary session. After a heated debate, some speakers mincing no words to express their frustrations, the assembly passed a resolution tendering their resignation en masse and expressing disgust over the party's unfulfilled commitments. The writing of the final resolution took half a day. The following morning, Gil Ceasar Malasuerte, the campaign manager of the Davide campaign suddenly arrived, with his entourage of six young men and two ladies, all in bright blazers of violet and yellow colors, heralding at the front and back, "Davide for President."

Malasuerte immediately mounted the platform of the conference hall. He looked kind of strange in his dark sports jacket over yellow shirt. A red baseball cap that seemed too large rested on his small head.

"Good evening my friends," Malasuerte began, after he was introduced by Sipula as the "savior of our present woes" and "one if not the most trusted confidant of presidential candidate Davide." Probably because he did not get a hearty applause, Malasuerte ignored Sipula's introduction.

"It was a good thing Pin Davide allowed me to fly over here to attend to your 11th hour call. I need not tell you the campaign in the south is doing very well. True, we don't have millions of hysterical voters cheering our candidate but we have the local government executives backing us all the way. And that, in the final analysis, is what counts, let me tell you."

Malasuerte paused, his staff nodding their heads in agreement.

"Let me also tell you that the non-appearance of the Most Exalted Brother in the grand proclamation rally does not make any difference in our total equation. As a matter of fact, that was not factored in. With or without him, it does not matter. We are on top of the situation and will remain so until Davide takes his oath of office on June 30 as the next president of this country."

His staff clapped their hands.

"Why do I keep saying that? Why does the Party keep on saying that? Why do most of us in this campaign keep on saying that? I'll be brief."

The CM's "brief" lasted almost two hours, extolling the virtues of Davide, attacking the other candidates as a bunch of nincompoops and the inevitability of victory for the party. He ended his brief by pledging full funding support for the volunteers.

The silence that followed the exit of Malasuerte and his staff ended the session.

He picked up the red phone on the fourth ring. Totally exhausted from too much hustling on the campaign trail and with no sleep, Gil Ceasar Malasuerte wanted very much to be left alone. But this was the phone with the unlisted number. Only four people knew this number. So this call must be important.

"Hello," Malasuerte said as casually as possible.

"Hello there, Gil. Sorry to call you at this ungodly hour," the voice was self-assured that Malasuerte almost hated it. But this was Presidential Adviser Meandro Destino and it could only mean he had a message from the president.

"No problem, Meyan," Malasuerte found himself saying. "In this job, there is no rest. You know how it is." *To hell, what is it this time?* Malasuerte cursed. "What can I do for you?"

"The President instructed me to check this report about the growing unrest among our support group. Can you feed me on that?"

"Err, yes Meyan. Can you hold on a minute? I'll get my glasses—just a minute." Actually, he already had his glasses on. *Damn, where are those cigarettes?* Having found them at last, he hastily lighted a stick and got back on the phone.

"Yes, Meyan okay," he pretended to flip the pages of his notebook and made sure the sound would get to the other end. "...Two weeks ago these guys were demanding the third tranch of their approved budget be released immediately. To my knowledge, to this very hour, the rest had not yet been released. I consulted Pin Davide about it. What he told me, I followed."

"Now, Gil. Don't you think you should release what you promised these guys? I know these guys. I know them way back when the president was still a candidate. These are the guys that deliver."

"But Pin Davide told me top priority should be the congressmen and mayors! They're our powerbase on the ground."

"Now, now Gil. Who said they aren't? What I am saying is at this time, meaning five weeks before E-Day, it is still too early to coddle the local executives. You might just be wasting your funds. The support group is the most reliable."

"Excuse me, Meyan, but are you saying the congressmen and mayors in our party are not reliable?" Malasuerte tried to temper his voice but it was already out. He dragged deeper into his cigarette.

"No, I didn't say that, but I might have insinuated that. It's the reality of the political ballgame, Gil. Local politicians shift loyalties depending on the perceived success of any candidate at the last two minutes of the campaign. That happened many times before."

"Is that also the position of the President?"

"Absolutely. As I said, I had to call you upon the president's instructions."

"But the president did not say the local executives should be given second priority, did he?"

"He did not. But the message is clear, both should be given equal treatment."

Okay, Meyan. I think I got you. But let me say this and please don't quote me. Funds are not coming in as expected."

"Are you pulling my leg? C'mon Gil, you must be kidding!"

"No, I'm not. What the heck. You may tell the President I said that."

"Okay, I believe you. What do you think is causing that?"

"Honestly, I could not pinpoint other possible causes at this time," Malasuerte said, dragging more nicotine. *Damn this nicotine—it's hurting my throat!*

"Now Gil, you may or may not confirm this but some well placed people are saying campaign funds are being kept in some vaults…"

"Who said that?" Malasuerte suddenly blurted out. But he could not continue. A large lump seemed to clog his throat.

"How about Pin Davide?" Destino broke the long silence. "The president has joked one time it could be his penchant for making mountains of promises that is turning voters off. Don't you think that's the major cause or just one of the causes?" "So what do I tell the president?" Destino pursued.

Are you threatening me? You're not only a pest. You're an asshole, too! In his anger, Malasuerte suddenly stood, in the process lifting the phone handset off its cradle as its stretched cord sideswiped the ashtray off the desk and unto the floor.

"Please tell him what we promised the support group—they'll get it today, right after I take my shower." Malasuerte said, crawling on the floor to gather the cigarette butts that were scattered all over.

"Now, you're talking Gil. That' s the real campaign manager talking. Happy campaigning! See you soon."

Once again, the visitor stared at the old man. It was now four o'clock in the afternoon. In a few minutes, he expected the old man to wake up. Soon it would be another night, the second night.

"Don't you worry, Sir," the nephew told the visitor. "The Supreme Datu will be awake soon."

The old man better be, the visitor told himself. He had to have some definite answers and he had to catch the morning flight if he expected to be back in Manila the next day, in time for the press conference that had already been set for the purpose. He was told and he was convinced this "secret" mission if accomplished would be a major coup for Davide in his quest for the presidency.

The old man groaned and muttered. The nephew bent over. Everyone present leaned over to catch his words but they were too garbled. Every now and then, the nephew nodded, the old man muttering on and on.

"The Supreme Datu asked if you had rested well last night," the nephew addressed the visitor. "He also told me to thank you for the food and drinks you brought us."

The visitor nodded, pleased.

"Please tell the Supreme Datu, yes, I did and yes, there is no problem with the food and drinks. Those are really nothing." For the food and drinks, yes, those were really nothing, he told himself. But for the rest, damn. How could he sleep last night with all the crickets and those strange voices in the night? Owls? Birds? Animals? But this was not really the reason for his unease. Nothing was clear yet, as far as this mission was concerned. The visitor knew not one word of the mountain tongue.

The visitor nodded casually, accepting the bottle of gin from the man to his left. Another drinking ritual began. He should have brought only a few cases of the gin. But he was advised earlier to bring as many—for to them, these natives, meetings or negotiations always began and ended with alcohol. And that meant he had to drink, too and stay sober to accomplish his mission. He took a gulp of the gin and passed it on to the man on his right, another tribal chief who grimaced back at him, like a thirsty boar before a watering hole.

"The Supreme Datu says he's tired," the nephew simply said. The old man's head nodded, then wobbled and rested on his shoulders.

The visitor fidgeted in his buttocks. Was this a signal that the old man would go to sleep again?

"The Supreme Datu says he's tired of all the promises. He also instructed me to tell you he is too tired to make the trip to Manila."

Atty. Leopoldo Mondejar, the visitor, could not believe what he just heard. He gulped his second round as he passed on the bottle to the man on his right. "Please tell the Supreme Datu I fully understand his sentiments. But please also tell him that every thing has already been set. The presidential proclamation for the release of your ancestral domain claims is ready for signing, but the Supreme Datu has to be physically present at the Palace. I have a true copy of the presidential proclamation." With that, he unzipped the small black bag beside him, took a folder and handed it over to the nephew. He then drank the mineral water in front of him to soothe his burning throat.

"The Supreme Datu tells me to request you to please take a walk outside as the tribal chiefs of the descendants of the House of Agyu examine your document. If you please…"

Mondejar quickly stood and walked out of the hall, nodding to everyone to express his appreciation. The sunset outside was a golden ball, the mountain breeze a biting cold. His buttocks ached from squatting on the hard floor for hours and his stomach was empty. Unzipping his black bag, he took out two packed ham sandwiches. He had to fill his stomach not only because he was hungry. He had to sustain it for more rounds of the cheap, despicable gin. Mondejar, the banker, was used to imported brandy in a champagne glass. But he had to drink with these natives and straight from the bottle, if he intended to accomplish his mission.

From where he sat, now smoking his fifth stick of Marlboros, Mondejar could hear the arguments. Most voices were loud and angry. Only the sober voice of the nephew gave Mondejar some confidence. The nephew, the direct heir, was the only educated person in the entire tribe. A third year law student, Mondejar was told, the nephew had to stop schooling to tend to the wishes of the old man. The nephew was clearly trusted by the Supreme Datu.

Almost two hours passed. After two ham sandwiches, two bottles of mineral water and six cigarettes, the nephew appeared on the hall and signaled Mondejar to return inside.

Before he could squat back on the floor, a half filled bottle of gin was passed on to him from the left and he gulped his turn. The gin felt good and he was ready.

"The Supreme Datu, concurred in by the descendants of the Twelve Tribes of the House of Agyu, objects to two major provisions in this proclamation," the nephew declared.

Mondejar stared straight at the old man, pretending not to be jolted. He now began to realize how stupid this mission was. And the more he looked at the old man, the more uncomfortable he became. Naked from the waist up, he was shrunken, shriveled, his ribs standing out against his flesh. His buttocks and flanks were loose and flabby, no doubt brought about with the failures of time. His cranium was wrinkled, his eyes were distant and stringed beads of multicolored forest seeds from ankle to knee wrapped his tiny, bony legs.

The nephew continued: "The first is the provision that relates to the ancestral domains as a property of the government to be leased to the House of Agyu through the Supreme Datu for a period of 25 years, renewable only after half of them are fully developed. The objection is on the lease provision. The Supreme Datu makes it clear, with the concurrence of the descendants of the Twelve Tribes that the property in question has always been our ancestral domain. Thus, the term lease is a misnomer and is in fact an insult to our legitimacy and dignity as a people. Instead of lease, the term should be 'return'; that is, the lands in question should, by force of tradition and cultural heritage, be returned by the government to the original owner, the House of Agyu without conditions. I repeat, without conditions. The Supreme Datu would like to remind the government the House of Agyu has been here centuries ago—long, long before your government even took its present form." Mondejar was shocked but did not blink. He felt an ant or was it a spider crawl on his right leg under his pants, but he did not move.

"The second objection pertains to the signing of a peace pact among the so-called contending forces in Mindanao, the negotiations of which should start immediately after the signing. The Supreme Datu with the concurrence of the descendants of the Twelve Tribes of the House of Agyu, stresses that we have never been in conflict or at war with any group or force. We are a people of peace and to refer to us as one of the 'contending forces,' a euphemism for warring groups in

Mindanao is again another insult to our legitimacy and dignity as a people. To also refer to us as Lumads, parallel to the Moros of the forces of Ahmad Jamil, parallel to the private armies of the Christian land grabbers in Mindanao is more than we can take."

Mondejar tried to focus. The cheap gin was taking its toll. His eyelids were about to drop and his eardrums were almost failing him. The ant or was it a spider under his pants didn't seem to crawl anymore. But he was sure it was still there.

"Those are the two objectionable provisions the Supreme Datu wants entirely deleted from the proclamation."

This won't work, Mondejar now told himself.

"But there is a third point," the nephew took a deep breath, dropping an arm that held the document. "which is not in this document. The Supreme Datu observes there is no provision for the granting of schools to our children and grandchildren. Your government has granted Madrasah schools to the Moros of Ahmad Jamil, Christian schools to the land grabbers, even Chinese schools to the Chinese but no schools for our people. The House of Agyu concludes this omission is a deliberate attempt to keep our future generation ignorant. This omission, is indeed and in fact, worse than the treatment the American Indians got from their European colonizers who grabbed their lands, raped their women, kept them drunk, confined them in reservations and shot their buffaloes and their horses in wild abandon."

Mondejar tried harder to focus. The old man was now nodding to himself, his eyes on the floor, as if he understood what his nephew was saying in English, his wrinkled cranium going up and down like an old lizard signaling assent.

Mondejar turned his attention around and saw nothing but empty bottles of gin held high by all those around, their tongues out, a sign they were still thirsty. Or were they taunting him? Some were shaking empty bottles over their mouth, a sign the bottles were dry and wanted more gin. Mondejar noted the Supreme Datu was now fast asleep and snoring heavily, his empty bottle clasped between his hands as the nephew continued his enumeration.

This is how we lose an election, Mondejar cursed silently, motioning his driver-bodyguard who stood by the hallway to get more cases of gin. Feeling lost, Mondejar decided to really get drunk and the easiest way to achieve that was to drink more of the cheap, despicable gin.

Mr. Winthrop Lopez adjusted his safety belt. Out front, the stewardess was announcing the take-off at exactly eight fifteen in the morning. Seated beside him by the window was Atty. Leopoldo Mondejar who didn't seem to care what was going on and appeared preoccupied doodling on a legal pad. Obviously, he had nothing to write about, except perhaps the terrible hangover in his head.

The jet was shaking a little, Lopez observed, but that stopped when the clouds parted from his view and the streaks of sunburst took over the sky. "We are now at 35,000 feet... You may unbuckle your safety belts and relax. Coffee and sandwiches will be served in a few minutes."

Lopez had the urge to smoke. But the "No Smoking" sign stared at him from the roof, so instead he reached for the lower pocket of his sports jacket and chewed one of the peppermints in his mouth. "So how was it?" Lopez asked.

"Bad news," Mondejar said.

"So I heard," Lopez observed, shifting his right leg over the other.

"Pin Davide will certainly be very disgusted in all this. And the president, am sure as hell will be embarrassed."

"Don't sound desperate, my friend," Lopez said. "I just talked to Pin Davide over the phone before I hit the airport. He said we should not worry about it. We still have all the time in our hands, he said, given the options available to us. He also said, he'd take care of the President."

"And I thought I was given the full authority to handle this," Mondejar said incredulously, staring at his seatmate. This was going out of control, he cursed silently, regretting why he had accepted this mission. Claudia, his niece, had begged him to undertake this mission, reminding him that he was the proponent of this presidential proclamation, long before President Rosales announced Davide as the official candidate of the party. Unbeknownst to most people, his personal interest was the thousands of hectares of unclaimed lands for gold exploration, adjacent to the ancestral domain claims of the natives. "Please, uncle." Those were the last words of Claudia, his favorite niece.

Lopez took another peppermint in his mouth "That is correct, but I had to tell Pin before he hears your bad news from some polluted sources. This is different, my friend," Lopez said, pulling out a magazine from the seat pocket in front of him as he pretended to read.

Mondejar did not connect. He knew when to open or shut his mouth. This guy beside him was not only a close friend of Davide and the president. He was also a very powerful man. "How about the press con?" Mondejar asked.

"I also had that cancelled. Pin already knows about it."

"Coffee or juice, Sirs?"

"Yes, please, coffee for me. No sandwich. How about you?" Lopez said, nodding at the stewardess and then looking at Mondejar.

"Just coffee. Thank you."

The one thing good about hot steaming coffee was that it went deep into your stomach and reactivated your frayed nerves, Mondejar consoled himself.

"Do you think the supreme datu's sudden turnaround will affect Pin's campaign?" Lopez asked, sipping the brew and flipping through the magazine. "Greatly, I think," Mondejar said. "The publicity will undoubtedly cause a big boost to what otherwise is a losing proposition."

"Are you saying if Pin Davide does not get the endorsement, he is sure to lose?" Lopez sounded like he was making a statement, not asking a question.

"I think it is already a given."

"Then why is he still running?"

"I think…" Mondejar paused but what the hell, "I think you know the answer to that question more than I do."

104

Lopez smiled, signaling the stewardess for a refill. "Anyway, what could be the reason behind the sudden turnaround? You were the visitor. You must have your own impressions."

Mondejar could not react immediately. Were there some undercurrents to the statement? Was there sabotage somewhere? Was the Supreme Datu enticed earlier with an offer much greater and could not refuse? What was at stake, really? Who were responsible?

Arriving at his suite at the Manila Hotel, Lopez stripped, took a quick cold shower, donned his robe and dialed a number.

"Ferdie, how is it with you, my good friend? Yes, I just got in. So, how is it with Mahal?"

"Positive. Mahal likes the whole idea."

"Oh yeah?"

"Well, Mahal says you can have your choice of any of two positions in the Cabinet."

"Sounds great, huh? Ferdie, I owe you one."

"That's nothing, my friend. So how was your trip?"

"Great, great! You can have them any time after the inaugural."

"You mean all the adjacent areas out there for gold exploration?"

"Definitely. Who can refuse the offer of Ferdie Tancho, the King?"

The two big tycoons roared from both ends of the line.

Commander Ahmad Jamil stuck another fresh cigarette into his gold-plated cigarette holder. The report about the rejection of another peace pact was not new to him. In fact, he was glad it was now in the open. That wily old Manobo knew his place and what would happen next. Another peace pact would lead to another conflict and another conflict would lead to another peace pact. There was no end to this rigmarole.

And besides, how could the supreme datu reject his initiative? He, Ahmad Jamil came from the blood of Princess Urduja, the Manobo princess who became the most favored wife of Sultan Sarip Kabungsuwan, the first Muslim leader who came to these mountains centuries ago. Many people did not know this and Ahmad Jamil preferred to keep it a secret. Among the Christians, only Winthrop Lopez knew this secret. And the scoundrel and infidel who smelled of roasted pig proved to be good at his word, so far. Lopez was Jamil's conduit for buying guns from the corrupt military generals.

He had great respect for the supreme datu, Jamil admitted to himself. His men were loyal to him. His word was law, the only law. While they worshipped their gods in those trees and on those rivers, the act of war or the call for peace, only came from their supreme datu. Jamil also recognized the power of the supreme datu to wield together in one solid command, all the chiefs of the twelve tribes of the House of Agyu. Only that, Jamil again chuckled to himself, they had no guns, real modern weapons to sow terror if they wanted to.

And they were almost totally ignorant. Most of them did not know how to read or write. They lived like birds in the trees and wild pigs on the ground. They survived mostly on root crops. And yes, they had no love for guns. Yes, bows and arrows maybe, even air guns but not real guns, Jamil almost laughed to himself. The supreme datu's recent defiance would take many generations to have its impact on his people. And with no guns, everything would be a wild voice in the wilderness.

If only he could unite his own people into one big, solid force, Jamil sighed, recognizing the supreme irony. With one united front and the force of modern weapons, his dream for Mindanao would become a foregone reality. The Maranaos or the people of the lake up north, the Maguindanaos or the people of the mountains in the midlands and the Tausugs or the people of the sea down south, all of them, his brothers—if only they would unite into one solid force.

There was no difference. These so-called Christians were as greedy as the mayors, congressmen and military generals. Actually, he told himself, the more dangerous and ravenous among them were the land grabbers, the likes of Winthrop Lopez, whose private army had no accountability to the government. But there was no problem there. This private army could easily be contained and he, Jamil had no accountability either on that score. Jamil cursed, picked the garbage pail from the side of his feet and spat into it.

Jamil once more scanned the map in front of him. He had earlier marked seven red spots on that map. Three of them would get simultaneous raids one week hence and the last four would get the biggest explosions ever as scheduled 'til election day. That would surely put the government and its military forces in a very embarrassing position and cause a lot of votes against the administration party. Jamil chuckled, squeezing the cigarette butt in the ashtray.

Carefully pinning the map on the wallboard beside his desk, Jamil sat back and stared at the red spots and counted the hours when the strikes would begin. He then slowly swung his swivel chair backward, removed his shoes and put on his imam's cap. It was time for prayer as he faced Mecca in the east and sank his knees on the wooden floor. He thanked the Almighty Allah for the dedication of his comrades-in-arm, their courage as warriors who never truly surrendered, who fought fiercely and proudly to die in the name of the Almighty Allah. This was their greatest advantage because their legendary ferocity and sacrifice had carved a permanent wound in the heart of the enemy. "Allah be praised!"

Meandro Destino woke up and checked his watch. Gad, it said six-thirty in the morning! Jumping out of bed, he went straight to the window, parted the drapes, the bright glare of sunlight hurting his eyes. Shading them with his palm, he looked down from his seventh floor apartment. The parking lot was almost empty. Gad! What happened last night? Destino asked himself. Nothing, he told himself as he walked slowly toward the coffeemaker, switched it on, lighted a cigarette and then again looked over the window.

He had his second cup of coffee when he realized for a week now, his biological clock had somehow malfunctioned. About this time, he could hear the rattling of a key, then that door would swing inside. Marissa would suddenly come in, kick that door shut with her heel and attack him. Unless it was a burglar, that door would not open now, not tomorrow, not ever.

He had sought her in the last so many days but Marissa just disappeared. Marissa was indeed a strange person. And now she was nowhere to be found.

His daily early morning remembrance of Marissa made him wonder if this was indeed a part of his subconscious resistance against male menopause. Was there such a thing? Or was it andropause? But he was sure of one thing—Marissa's instinctive ingenuity and passionate intensity as a lover had taken him to regions he had not known before. And every time he got there and peaked, he experienced the explosion, the full, unimpeded explosion of the flesh.

After taking a long cold shower and relieving himself of the memory, Meandro Destino went to his desk and started going over his diary. When did all this begin? Slowly, a part of his past slid into the present.

"Tomorrow at 0700 hours," the Chief Protocol Officer (CPO) continues his briefing, *"the presidential party will take off from the back of the Premier Guest House for the Smokey Mountain. Remember, this is the first public appearance of the president,"* the CPO reminds his hearers, *"after he took his oath as President of the Republic a week ago. As your advanced briefing papers say, Smokey Mountain is referred to by the international press as an 'anomaly...an inhumane habitat only a government without any regard or any compassion for its citizens can tolerate.' It is important, therefore, that you show nothing but concern and compassion for the 15,400 families holed up in that mountain of garbage brought daily by no less than 2000 dump trucks from the bowels of the five cities and 17 municipalities of Metro Manila.*

"You are reminded not to use any handkerchief to cover your nose when that starts dripping because of the stench; not to rub your eyes when they start itching because of the fumes emitted by decaying garbage; and not to massage your chest so as not to vomit because of the human excrement, dead rats and cats that you will surely encounter as you move from one step to the next. The President himself will have nothing on him but an unlighted cigar in his mouth. That, I think, is his advantage. (giggles and laughter) And so, with the first lady who will carry neither fan nor umbrella. (Wows follow.)

"Remember, the garbage in that mountain is the livelihood of those families. That is all for now. Any questions?"

Dr. Meandro Destino, newly appointed presidential adviser, raises his hand and asks. "Can we smoke over there?"

"You may," the CPO answers, *"but do not add another cigarette butt to the garbage."* That sends the ladies giggling and the men chuckling.

The breakfast at the Premier Guest House is served at exactly 0600 hours. But for two or three, the rest of the presidential party only takes coffee, some smoking cigarettes. At quarter to 0700 hours everyone is in his or her designated seat as the President and the First Lady take theirs in the lead bus. As soon as he has the cigar in his mouth, the head of the Presidential Management Staff hands over a folder to the President. It is his briefing papers for the day.

As the president and the first lady alight from their bus, the throngs of people from all sides of the garbage mountain wave their arms and shout their welcome. Placards and streamers made of discarded jute sacks and cardboards are raised everywhere, with signs welcoming the president and his party. The sight is grotesque: thousands of men, women and children in tattered clothes, on top of thousand tons of garbage some two kilometers wide from east to west and some 700 meters high from sea level up to the sky.

The executive secretary starts scratching his throat. The secretary of the Department of Natural Resources and Environment starts rubbing his eyes. The secretary of the Department of Social Welfare and Development starts twitting her nose. But one furtive side-glance from the president sends their perspiring necks up and their manufactured smiles out, in greeting the crowd that is now swarming closer to the president and his party.

The first stop is at the shack of Barangay Captain Alfredo Cura, a makeshift structure of plastic and cardboard on top of an abandoned skeleton of what was once a World War II U.S. army jeep.

"Welcome to our home, Mr. President, Madame First Lady," Capitan Cura hisses, two front teeth missing as he introduces his wife beside him. He is about 48 with hair heavily coated with gel. His wife is about half his age, thin as an ice drop stick and pale as a plastic sheet. "This is Sonia, my wife, with our latest," Cura grins with pride, as Sonia sways the baby back and forth in her arms to stop it from shrieking. "The baby is only seven weeks old. The five boys and one girl in front— yeah, they are still eating their breakfast, are also our children. The eldest is my junior—he's nine years old, Mr. President, Madame First Lady." The five young boys wear no pants. Their young sister is naked above her soiled panties.

Cura points at Junior who just scooped a large amount of rice from a cracked basin where the other toddlers pick their own food. Destino observes the first lady's eyes moisten. The president starts to chew his cigar in a way that gives Destino the cue to break the sudden uneasy quiet.

"Capitan," Destino asks, "how do you find life here?" Though he sounds as casual as he could, Destino wonders if that is the right question to ask at the moment.

"Unbelievable, Sir," the barangay captain grins again. "At least here, we survive. Unlike in the province where there is nothing to eat, nothing to see and nothing to enjoy."

"Why, which province are you from?" Destino ventures further, noting the president relax on his cigar.

"From Gipason, Southern Leyte, Sir."

"I am sure the President will be interested to know how you survive here, as you said..."

"You may believe this or not, Sir, Mr. President, but we earn no less than P100 a day, more if the dump trucks come with broken toys, discarded kitchen utensils and the like. My children are very aggressive—they jump and mount those dump trucks before they could even disgorge their load. Of course, Sonia here, my wife, could not assist now. She has to take care of our latest darling baby."

"Capitan, did you say your family has a combined daily income of P100 on the average?" the secretary of Social Welfare and Development asks.

"Yes, Ma'am, on the average, but more as I said, if the dump trucks deliver items other than plastics. But with plastics, they're okay. What we do, is first rinse them in that basin, then cut them to size as specified, load them in that cart and take them anytime to that building over there. They are then weighed and we are paid in cash, by the kilo. Pak-Li is a good businessman. One kilo here, two kilos there, he pays in cash. No questions asked."

"What do you see and enjoy here?" the president asks, smiling and winking, obviously intrigued with Capitan Cura's high spirits.

"Mr. President, there is really nothing to see and enjoy in this mountain of garbage, although at times, I confess, I like the company of the people here. I also like our meetings where we share common problems like drunkenness, theft, sometimes stabbings and the like. Rape cases are rampant here as well as drug problems. But Mr. President, compared to the province where we come from, our life here is a blessing. We do not only survive, during Saturdays and Sundays, we have picnics at the nearby mall. It's air conditioned and we can see a lot of people in all sorts of colorful attire. Sometimes we see a movie."

It is time for the photo-ops. At the signal of the CPO, Barangay Captain Cura and his wife are positioned along the president and the first lady out front. The cabinet secretaries and heads of concerned offices maneuver themselves at the back, in the process stepping on some unmoving unmentionables on the ground. But they don't care because for sure their faces would land again on the front pages the next day.

"Mabuhay si Capitan Cura! Mabuhay ang Presidente!" all shout as cameras click and as TV lenses zoom.

It is time to go for the next stop. It is still 0800 hours in the morning. Nine more designated stops, four more to the top of the garbage mountain and five more on the way down. The sun begins to get scorching hot as the fumes of Smokey Mountain rise to their level of heat and stink. "God," the president mutters to himself, "What have we done to these people!"

As the memory of the president's first visit to Smokey Mountain faded out, Destino recalled with awe that in just five and a half years, the Rosales administration had transformed that bane of humanity into a "very unique concept." The project not only directly addressed both the garbage and squatter problems but also promoted a master-planned onsite urban development and preservation of the environment program. Representatives of foreign governments and international NGOs who came to visit were convinced by the innovative approach and the political will of President Rosales in tapping the private sector to make the dream come true.

Tasked to coordinate the president's "sentimental" return in two weeks' time, Destino conducted meetings and caucuses with the management of the project, the various leaders of the new community that was zoned according to its livelihood projects and various NGOs that were involved in the development of the community. As he made his last inspection of the route the presidential party would take along the well-polished second floor of the dormitory-type housing units, Destino noticed some pile of fresh garbage in front of some doors. Unable to contain himself because of the stench, he called for the housing unit manager and inquired. Without hesitation, the man simply told him the children living in the units were responsible for "smuggling" the garbage at night. "They've been so used to its smell they couldn't sleep without it. But don't worry, Sir. We'll have them removed in time for the President's visit."

Presidential Adviser Destino was so shocked he couldn't react. As he rushed down to the ground floor, he remembered what the president had said during their first visit— "God, what have we done to these people?" Now Destino asked himself— "God, what have these people done to their children?"

The betting was heavy. The manager of the Kumpare Barbershop raised his ten fingers sky-high, brought them down then raised one arm with only the index finger up. "Ten to one!" The crowd around him oohed and aahed. That meant ten pesos against one peso. At stake—who was going to be number one senator in the forthcoming May elections? The bets—ten pesos for Humphrey Bogart Putto, the comic of the noontime TV show "Goodah" as against one measly peso for any of the other 76 senatorial candidates. This was the first time Putto ran for any public office as against the other 76, most of whom were veterans in the nation's political battlefield. Some were crackpots, of course. But the contested 12 senatorial seats hankered for were not wanting in quality candidates. Some were reelectionists, educators, businessmen and former cabinet secretaries.

The betting was held in a sidewalk fronting the dying Kumpare Barbershop of Mang Tiago at the corner of Espana-Constancia Streets along the northern boundary of the City of Manila and Quezon City. The crowd was composed of Mang Tiago, Bosing Picklat, the boss-man of the jueteng foot soldiers in the area, about a dozen or so sidewalk vendors, some curious bystanders and Patrolman Bruno Pawis, the policeman on the beat in the block.

"Mang Tiago," one of the cigarette vendors asked, "you have to explain to us why ten to one? The margin is just too wide!"

"You're just a kid, that's why!" Mang Tiago lectured. "Now look, all of you. There's no way they can beat Putto. He's on everybody's menu every lunch hour. He's the most popular. Even more popular than Mahal! You eat lunch in front of the TV to watch Putto and to laugh with him, right? Look at my barbershop. Because of my TV, it's full every lunch hour from Monday to Friday, whether people come for a haircut or not. It's hard on the floor and the barbers but that's okay. I'm for Putto because he is the most popular. Goodah! Goodah!"

Mang Tiago or Mr. Santiago Delata was some kind of an institution in the area where his barbershop stood since the bowlegged Japanese imperial army occupied Manila in the early forties. In his late seventies, he was regarded as a professor of sorts in his domain where hawkers and vendors converge, after their long and hardy walk selling their wares along the entire stretch of Espana. It was always intriguing to hear Mang Tiago predict the last two numbers of the winning sweepstakes ticket, what basketball team would win, who was going to be the next mayor and so on. His was not only the voice of experience but also the voice of wisdom.

"What a shame," Bosing Picklat said. "Are you telling us, Mang Tiago that we vote for Putto simply because he is popular? What will he do in the Senate? Tell jokes and sell commercials? Grimace like a cat then snore as the important issues of the day are discussed because surely he is ignorant about them? It's high time we change our thinking about the kind of leaders we should have for this country, otherwise this country will forever be mired in dog shit!" Bosing Picklat was a sturdy man of 58 who got his nickname for the ugly scar that adorned his left face. His left arm was shorter than his right. Its biceps bore the tattoo of Eve, her mouth open, ready to catch the apple from the fangs of the serpent.

"Now Bosing, you have to watch your language, pronto, or else you would have no more jueteng bets to collect," the manager of the barbershop warned. "Remember Bosing, the issue here is who is going to be Number One, not who is qualified for the Senate."

The crowd that now swelled nodded in agreement, except Bosing Picklat.

"Okay, I bet P50 to your P500," Bosing Picklat said, etching those figures on the ground with his extra-long manicured thumbnail. "Chief Pawis here is my witness. He'll collect your P500 for me after all the votes are counted."

His authority invoked, Patrolman Pawis winked at every one, patting the holster of his service .38 caliber revolver. "Deal?" he grunted, lowering his eyelids on Mang Tiago.

Patrolman Pablo Pawis looked too short for an officer of the law. And he had a body that perspired even in cold weather. Those who dared talk behind his back, loved to say the perpetual perspiration of the patrolman was caused by his guilty conscience. He had too many cases including murder, theft, robbery, rape and other forms of unpleasantness. That he managed to stay out of jail was anyone's guess.

"Deal, *ultimo!*" the manager of the barbershop nodded.

"Now, this is really something," one of the vendors observed, grimacing at Mang Tiago. "Now, Mang Tiago, if you are definitely sure that Putto will be number one, then why don't you raise your ten pesos to P15 to my one peso?"

"No problem," Mang Tiago shrugged. "I know your limitations, my son, *mi hijo.*"

"Okay, I bet P20," the "son" wrote the figure on the ground with the cap of his ballpoint pen. "Chief Pawis will then collect from you, for me, P300 if I win. Right?"

"No problem," Mang Tiago shrugged again. "That is quite logical," Mang Tiago grimaced.

"Now, wait a minute. Wait a minute!" Bosing Picklat protested. "That simply now means that for my P50, I'll collect P750 if I win, right?" Bosing Picklat looked at Patrolman Pawis for support.

"*No nada,* no you don't!" Mang Tiago shot back.

"But the issue is the same and the person is the same!" Bosing Picklat exclaimed.

"No, they're not the same." Mang Tiago said, dismissing Bosing Picklat.

111

"What? Not the same? Who's number one? It's the same joker, your Putto, your hijo de puta Putto, right?"

"*Que horror!* It's not the same. And be careful with your filthy mouth. Putto is not a joker. He is a comic!"

"What dog shit are you talking about? Putto is both a dog shit comic and a dog shit joker!" Bosing Picklat now stood over Mang Tiago who remained seated on his stool.

"Then our bet is off," Mang Tiago declared. "Because you're *loko-loko*, crazy, that's why."

"What did you say, that I'm crazy?"

"Yes, you're more than crazy. You're a lunatic and a *hijo de puta!*"

Before any one could move or intervene, Bosing Picklat had whisked an ice pick from inside the long sleeve of his shorter arm. With five swift motions of his right arm, he had stabbed Mang Tiago in the neck once, in the breast twice and in the pit of his stomach twice. And as he turned to vent his final fury on the young cigarette vendor who cleverly anted the bet over him, Patrolman Pawis, his service revolver now drawn and aimed a few inches from the back of Bosing Picklat's head, pulled the trigger. The blast sent every one scampering for dear life as human gore and blood splattered on the sidewalk.

It was seven o'clock in the evening, another Wednesday. Almost all those with TV sets were glued to "Truth or Tale", the most popular talk show in town.

VITO   Welcome once again to "Truth or Tale", the most talked about talk show in town. Is it the truth or is it a tale? Is it a true story or a tall story? Tonight, we have for our guests the paranormals, which in our understanding includes the psychics, the clairvoyants and the fortune-tellers. Paranormal doesn't mean abnormal, let me qualify immediately. Paranormal means beyond the normal, meaning beyond scientific explanation, beyond what may be established as scientific fact or evidence. Tina?

TINA   Thank you, Vito. That is right. Our viewers will remember that two years ago, two paranormals predicted a plane crash, the sinking of two passenger ships and the eruption of a volcano. Well, their predictions came out to be true because all of those happened last year. That's really scary, isn't it? In other words, these paranormals have the ability or gift to predict the future.

VITO   Anyway, I am sure no such thing will happen tonight, because tonight we will not be asking our guests what disasters will happen soon. On the other hand, we will be asking them to predict who will become the next President of this country.

TINA   That's correct, Vito except that people can avoid predicted disasters by not taking the plane or the ship. But certainly, what if a certain candidate is predicted to win and indeed wins, he will still be the President for those who did not vote for him because obviously they don't like him!

VITO   Ha! Ha! Ha! You got me there, Tina. You really got me there! Very clever. Now, before we finally introduce our guests, let's have a few words from our sponsors.

TINA   Please stay with us… we'll be back.

As the scene of the studio fades out, the boyish face of Kidd Batuta, the prince of local movies and darling of commercial ads looms on screen, taking a big round bite of his favorite jumbo sandwich, his dimples flashing.   Then Luningning Morena, Miss Universe 1st runner-up and local supermodel, glides on the fashion ramp, her eyes glistening their cutie, little stars as her oh-so-slim body displays the latest lingerie above and below her open midriff.   Then, Steve Karate, the bone-cracking martial arts villain-hero and international movie star, withdraws the glass of sparkling liquid gold rum from his lips as he intones—"Only in the Philippines…"

TINA   We're back and welcome to "Truth or Tale", the most talked about talk show in town. Vito?

VITO   All right, here we go. As a matter of courtesy, we shall first introduce our lady guest. You can see that she has a white turban with a medallion at the center that looks like an eye drooping in half-sleep. She says she can predict the future through the eye of her vision, that is, if it comes to her at all. For the record, she had predicted the election and reelection of Clinton, the election of Wahid in Indonesia and so on. Please welcome, Madame Carla Madonna Omen.

TINA   Our second guest is the man with a Ho-Chi-Minh type of goatee and who, as you can see, is not wearing any footwear. There, he is wriggling his toes. Well, the reason he doesn't wear any footwear, he says, is because to wear them is to desecrate the earth, since Adam, the first man, he says again, was created from the earth. He carries soil particles all the time and applies them on the soles of his feet when he is about to step on concrete or steel but not on wood or stone which are natural parts of the earth. He says he can predict some events from the feel of his feet on earth. For the record, he had predicted the eruption of Mount Pinatubo in Zambales. Ladies and gentlemen, let's welcome Professor Hagibis del Yuta. By the way, the professor earned his academic title from the University of Liboria in Africa which he now and then visits to lecture—getting there and returning here literally on his feet.

VITO   Our third guest, the last but certainly not the least, is only 16 years old and just graduated valedictorian of his class.

TINA   I understand he got accelerated twice, didn't he, Vito?

VITO   That's right, his name is Sonny Boy Profeta. Beside him is his elder sister, Melinda. Melinda is a registered nurse.

VITO   Sonny Boy is quite different in the sense that while the medium of Madame Omen is her vision; that of Professor del Yuta's his feet on earth or is it earth on feet; that of Sonny Boy's is his whole body which reacts like a barometer to some objects or materials. So that the stronger the reaction to a particular object or material, the more likely that object or material is "it". Am I correct, Sonny Boy? Oh, Sonny Boy is pointing at his sister... Am I right, Melinda?

MELINDA Actually it is not just any object or material. Sonny Boy only reacts to living things or their representations like pictures, images on TV, their voices, the names of people written on paper and something like that. Gold, diamond and the like, his body doesn't react to, so far.

VITO So there you are folks. Let's have a word or two from our sponsors.

As the scene of the studio fades out, Luningning Morena, Kid Batuta and Steve Karate breeze through their commercials, Karate ending his rum sale with his classic sigh: "Only in the Philippines."

TINA We're back and welcome once again to "Truth or Tale", the most talked about talk show in town.

VITO Okay, here we go. The question is simple enough—who among the six official presidential candidates will be elected President of this country in the coming May polls? Let's start with Madame Omen. Madame Omen, please.

OMEN Since your representative invited me to appear here some weeks ago, it struck me immediately that the date of the visit might have something to do with the name of the candidate, an association that helped me make some accurate predictions in the past. Say, if I were visited April 29, the date 29 if spelled out would have 10 letters. I then consulted my tarot cards and my crystal ball but no candidate's name appeared in there that would somehow establish some kind of association. Then for three successive nights, a candidate's surname appeared that corresponded with the date of the visit and vice-versa. Both came very clear in my 'one eye', as my two natural eyes were closed in their sleep at the time, until I woke up. You see, my 'one eye' opens only when my two natural eyes are sleeping. Heh, heh.

TINA Madame Omen, what do you mean when you say your one eye opens only when your two natural eyes are sleeping? Am I following you?

OMEN Yes, I think you are. By my 'one eye', I really mean the eye that gives me this vision of seeing in the dark, not the eye on my turban because that is only a symbol. See, it's sleeping because my two natural eyes are open right now. Heh! Heh!

VITO Was this vision or revelation or whatever you call it similar when you predicted the victory of other presidential candidates before?

OMEN Yes, in the case of Clinton of the U.S. When I was asked a similar question some six months before the American elections in November, I always saw, I mean my one eye always saw the number seven which is the number of letters in Clinton. It was different with Wahid over Megawati in Indonesia. Instead of numbers, my one eye repeatedly saw a kris, the Muslim dagger strike a heart. But you know the heart did not bleed, not a drop. That probably explains why although she lost, Megawati still became vice-president at the time. Heh! Heh! Heh!

VITO   We are on to the next suspense. Professor Hagibis del Yuta, it's your turn, Sir.

YUTA   Thank you. Actually, the answer to the question, 'who?' was revealed to me after exactly 14 days of walking the earth around the six residences of the six presidential candidates. I don't like to mention this, but I almost got shot by the security guard in the first residence, chased by big dogs in the next three, almost brought to the police station in the fifth and bodily thrown out of the premises by two burly men in the sixth residence. I had already gone around the world on my feet but I had never met such difficulty as in my visits to these six residences.

TINA   Oh, I'm sorry… Why, why did all that happen?"

YUTA   Well, I think the answer to your question is obvious. After I pressed the buzzer and they saw me with my long hair, my goatee, my beads and my feet without shoes, they probably thought I was a bum, a beggar or a hermit.

VITO   Didn't you tell them your purpose?

YUTA   I didn't have a chance in the first three but when I did in the fourth, aside from my appearance, they called me all types of names like crazy, nuts, weirdo and so on.

TINA   Oh, no… to be honest and not to flatter you professor, you look very decent to me and I am sure with Vito, too.

YUTA   Thank you. You are the first person in the world to say that to me.

VITO   Please continue, professor.

YUTA   As I said, I could not get inside so I had to walk the earth around the residences. Please note that these residences had high concrete walls and the pavements around them were also concrete so it was more difficult for me to look for soil fragments in the immediate vicinity to apply to my soles. Anyway, to cut the long story short, it was around the last residence that my feet felt those volcanic vibrations.

VITO   You said in the last residence, your feet felt those volcanic vibrations. Would you please describe that further for us?

YUTA   I got lifted up my feet four times, at every corner of that residence. Each jolt was such that I had to brace my arms against the wall and really push my feet downward to steady myself. By the way, I also felt some sort of vibrations with the other five but not as intense compared to this candidate's residence.

VITO   Professor, would that mean the residence of the candidate with the least vibration would get the lowest vote?

YUTA   I cannot really tell. I hadn't had the experience of comparing the differences by degrees. It was always the strongest vibration that told me this was it!

VITO   So professor, you are now sure the candidate whose residence your feet felt those volcanic vibrations will become the next president of the country.

YUTA I never say I'm sure about my predictions. I just describe what my feet tell me.

TINA So that's it for the professor. Let's just wait later, until our own feet will feel the professor's volcanic prediction.

As the scene of the studio fades out, Kidd Batuta, Luningning Morena and Steve Karate breeze through their commercials.

VITO We're back folks. Welcome again to "Truth or Tale", the most talked about talk show in town.

TINA You know, Vito, our telephone lines have been very busy in the last half hour. Hundreds of callers with all types of reactions are coming in by the minute. Gosh!

VITO Well, that just goes to prove that our people are agog who's gonna be the next president. And it's time to go to our youngest guest, Sonny Boy Profeta. Now, our viewers must have noticed the only decor that we have on top of this low table is a box and this flower vase which I will set aside right here on the floor... there. Now, let me tilt the box a little bit so the cameras can show its contents to our viewers.

TINA In the box as shown are six pieces of rolled paper containing the candidates' names. Sonny Boy will not move the box in one way or another. He will only pick one piece at a time, as he goes along. And lastly, Sonny Boy will not open the piece of rolled paper to see, much more read, the name of the candidate written on it.

VITO Okay Sonny Boy—are you ready?

TINA There, Sonny Boy is now extending his arm. There, he just picked one. He draws it closer to his face—his eyes are concentrating gosh, gosh... Sonny Boy is shaking... gosh Vito, Vito!

VITO Wow! What was that? Two, three, four fractions of a second? Okay, let's relax. There, Sonny Boy just dropped the rolled piece on the table beside the box. Now... he is on his second pick.

TINA As before, Sonny Boy is now drawing the second piece of rolled paper to his face, his eyes concentrating... ops... he drops the piece on the table... no reaction?

VITO No radioactivity, Melinda? Yeah, Melinda nods. She agrees.

TINA Now, Sonny Boy is on to his third pick. There, now he draws it to his face, his eyes on it. Now, now, Jesus Lord... Sonny Boy is hit... is hit! Vito, Vitoooo!

VITO Madame Omen, Professor, Out of the way! Out of the way!

OMEN Eeeekkkk! Eeeeeeeeeeekkk!

YUTA This is terrible! Terrirrrble! Terrrribblllle!

VITO His body, his body is contorting!!! His legs are kicking!!!

TINA His eyes, his eyes are bulging!!! They're rollllinnng!!! Helllpp!!!

VITO Melinda! Melinda!!!

MELINDA Let him be.

116

TINA   My God! He's falling off the sofa! He's convulsing!!!

OMEN   In the name of the Father, the Son and the Holy Spirit...

MELINDA   All right, all right... Sonny Boy. Do you hear me? It's me, Melinda. Now, let's get back to your seat. There... it's all over, Sonny Boy. It's all over. It's all over. He's back to normal now. That's it folks. Sonny Boy is okay now. Just like before. Just like nothing has happened.

VITO   Where's the piece of paper?

MELINDA   It's inside his fist. Now. Sonny Boy, open your fist... Here it is!

VITO   Kindly put that on top of the table out front... there. Thank you, Melinda. Tina? Tina!

TINA   Wait a second... let me breathe... Gosh!

VITO   Melinda, when do we get to the fourth pick?

MELINDA   It's over. That was his seventh intensity, in his third pick, the highest in his scale. I'd say that, that was as far as his physical body could take. It's over.

VITO   Let's have a station break.

Out of camera range, Melinda produces a face towel and starts wiping the beads of perspiration on the face, neck and back of Sonny Boy while a studio hand gathers the pieces of broken crystals that were once the flower vase. Madame Omen starts to redo her make-up as she had unwittingly smeared her face with her trembling fingers during her bouts of panic, Professor Hagibis del Yuta eyeing her with ultimate sympathy and understanding. "There's no way that you can redo that face, lady," the professor hears himself whispering to no one.

On TV, Kidd Batuta, Luningning Morena and Steve Karate breeze through their commercials, Karate ending his rum sale with his classic sigh, "Only in the Philippines."

VITO   That was incredible! So we're back folks—and to the moment of truth—or is it tale? Tina?

TINA   Yes, yes, Vito. But before, ah, ah before, gosh—we go to the real who, may I just ask one question before that?

VITO   Okay. But just relax...

TINA   Is who, a man or a woman?

OMEN   A man.

YUTA   A man.

TINA   Sonny Boy is whispering something to Melinda.

MELINDA   Sonny Boy says it's a man.

TINA   Wait a minute. I think I will ask another question.

VITO   Please hurry...

TINA   Why is it that Sonny Boy never says anything direct...

MELINDA   He's like that immediately before, during and after. I think it's the impact on him. That's why.

VITO All right. And now to the final question: based on your revelation, or would I say, what has been revealed to you, who will be the next president of this republic?

OMEN I've written the name on my left palm as instructed. Here, I'll spread my palm out for everybody to see the name.

VITO Camera please… there. Can all of you out there read the name? Is it clear on your screen?

TINA It's Mahalina!

VITO It's Mahalina! Professor del Yuta? How about yours?

YUTA I've also written the name on my left palm as instructed. Here, I'll spread my palm out for everybody to see the name.

VITO Camera, please—there. Is the name clear on your screen?

TINA Very clear. Again, it's Mahalina!

VITO It's Mahalina all right. And now, to Sonny Boy. Wait—Sonny Boy is pointing at the piece of rolled paper on the table, the one out front that Melinda earlier had gotten from out of the fist of Sonny Boy. Let me pick that up myself. Here it is! I'll open it slowly—there it is—camera please! Can you read it now in your screen?

TINA Again… it's Mahalina! Unanimous!

VITO That's right. All three of our guests say it's Mahalina!

TINA Before we start entertaining our callers…

VITO Just a minute Tina… We still have to open the other five pieces of rolled paper to check if the names of the other candidates are indeed written on each of them. Okay, folks. Let me start with the other two that Sonny Boy took out of the box and are now on top of the table. Okay here they are. Camera please. Let me open one. Can you see it now? Let me open the other. Can you also see it now? Okay, it's confirmed. They contain the names of the other two candidates, not Mahalina's.

TINA And may I pick the other three rolled pieces of paper still inside the box? Camera please. Let me open the fourth, the fifth and the sixth. There… can you see them? It's confirmed. No name of Mahalina. These are the names of the other three candidates, aside of course, from those that Vito already showed earlier.

VITO That completes all the candidates and all are accounted for.

TINA Right Vito and you better believe this. Right at this moment, we have exactly 2,756 callers. Can you believe that? This is the first time that this has ever happened in our show!

VITO Wow! So where do we begin?

TINA The honorable Senator Santolan has been…

DICK Then put her through.

VOICE This is Senator Naomi Ganzon Santolan…

VITO Magnify! Magnify the audio!

SANTOLAN candidate for president of this republic. Let me tell you immediately that I am totally enraged by your inane, impertinent and idiotic show, thus I am filing charges against all of you, including those apostles of

118

quackery and prophets of necromancy that you so conveniently call your guests. Let me also tell you that any elementary school pupil can discern that you are using your piggy-brained show to actually campaign for an equally piggy-brained candidate, you know who. And because of your evil scheme of things, you had actually maligned me as a person and as a respectable senator of this republic. Your malicious and libelous intentions are lucid. The mere fact that you asked first if it was a man or a woman, was already prejudicial to my candidacy since every voter-citizen in this country knows that I am the only woman candidate. So right from the start you attempted to eliminate me. And do you think you succeeded? Of course not! And that is your misfortune because once my asteroid comes zooming in and I am declared President, you will all be swallowed by fire in Dante's Inferno including your show and your quacks. Meanwhile, look for the best lawyers you can hire because I am filing a multi-million-damage suit against all of you. See you in court!

VITO   Let's have a station break.

TINA   Please don't go away. We'll be back.

At Home
Apartment No. 201-A
243 New York Street
Cubao, Quezon City

Dear Angela,

It's been three weeks! Well, for your information, I've finally visited your two daughters last Saturday, stayed overnight at your mother's and came back one day late for work. Both are very much okay, with your eldest calling your mother "Mama." Looks like she won't recognize her real Mom anymore, what with your prolonged stay abroad. Your youngest was indifferent to my stories that you are about to come home with a truckload of chocolates. Let me assure you however that your darling daughters are voracious eaters, never cried when I was there and always throwing things that your dear mother seems to relish. They're active, that's why, your mother keeps on telling me.

Your mother pleaded with me to tell you to write her. Yes, your checks have regularly arrived, no problem with that, but a letter from you, she said, would be better appreciated. Hmmm... once a mother always a mother.

Election time is still far away but the usual mudslinging and character assassinations are already in full blast.

Which reminds me, that old goat of a mayor of our town has to be replaced! He has been there in that seat for so long he couldn't stand anymore what with his arthritis and all. And besides, our clan has to vindicate your father's untimely death. He's my uncle Waldo, too! I'm sorry.

Did I tell you in my last letter that I've been taking lessons in ballroom dancing? I've never realized that of all the dances, the cha-cha-cha is the dance of conquest, that is, if you know how to do it. Either you go forward with as many steps for the kill, backward for as many steps for more seduction or come-on, or sideward for demure-

evasion. Unlike the tango that is macho-dominated or the disco blast that is pure and simple aerobics, the cha-cha-cha presents so many possibilities. After mastering the fundamentals, the body language follows. You know what I mean, do you?

I am now writing my master's thesis. I should have done this much earlier as you advised me before. There is really no substitute for intellectual growth. And you know what? Anita Cosme, you will remember her of course, wrote and urged me to apply for a teaching job in the state university near our hometown where she now teaches. Who knows, I might land a job as an instructor after my master's program. Wow, that reminds me of our hometown again. I really like to be back to our hometown what with the traffic, pollution, garbage, etcetera here in Manila.

Promise me you'll write as soon as you get this letter. Your childhood friend and cousin who really miss you very much, I am...

Love,
Fili

4
WHO ARE WE

When the Davide campaign was launched, the legions of volunteers during the Rosales campaign, prodded by their fellow volunteers who were awarded appointments in the Rosales administration, again volunteered. But this time there was a big difference.

"What kind of a place is this, Tim? The toilet drips, the beds are full of roaches, the shower smells of mud. The whole place stinks!"

"The linens are unwashed!"

"What is this? Are we running a presidential campaign or a *sari-sari* store?"

"Give us our refund and we go home!"

Timostocles Sipula just arrived straight from the airport. He hadn't slept or eaten. Despite all that, he looked neat in his white shirt and his colorful tie, his thick black hair well scrubbed "iron pressed," according to Ligaya and exuded a confidence that was hard to dispel, especially in times such as the core group of volunteer coordinators was experiencing at the moment.

"What's going on, Tim? The last time we met, the campaign manager assured us of the release. What we got were streamers and sample ballots!"

"And where would we hang the streamers? Around our necks?"

"Our headquarters are empty and we're behind in rentals by two months now! What shall we do... close shop?"

"Okay, guys. Keep your cool, okay?" Sipula pleaded. "That's why I have to fly here to find out what we can do about this whole mess."

"Just a minute, let me explain," Pascual Candoy, Region VII RSAC (Regional Sectoral Affairs Committee) chair interrupted. "First, I was the one who called Ligaya, for this emergency meeting. Second, we've got to have a common stand and National HQ should know about it. Remember, election is two weeks away. Third, I chose my own Cebu because it is the most accessible whether by plane or by boat from all the regions in the country. Fourth, I'll advance the refund of your food and accommodations here. I'm sorry about the water. We've got water shortage and we're getting only a few barrels from Bohol. I hope you understand and bear with me. I have to take this initiative for the sake of President Rosales and, of course, our Boss. So, I beg you that we listen to Tim first. We've done this before, during the Rosales campaign and I do think that we can do it again if we stick together. Tim, why don't you tell us everything so that we will understand and come out with some alternatives?"

When Candoy spoke, everybody listened—primarily because he sounded as if he believed what he was saying. His loud voice and his thick Visayan accent guaranteed full attention. Candoy was the president of the biggest federation of cooperatives in his region.

"Thanks, Pasqui," Sipula said, adjusting his tie. "Okay, I got Ligaya's call the other day that the RSACs were on their way here. I was in Laoag, up north, trying to track the CM for three straight days but I couldn't find him. I was told he was on the campaign trail with Davide. Obviously, he has suddenly become inaccessible. I had two appointments with him at HQ but when I got there, I was told he was somewhere else attending to 'more urgent matters', quote unquote. Our Boss made those appointments with the CM. Our Boss was in New York at the time. Before I took my connecting flight from Manila, I called the Boss and told him of my failed meeting with the CM. He assured me he'd exhaust everything to get to the CM or if that were no longer possible, he'd talk to President Rosales."

Sipula paused. He was beginning to get hungry. He felt for his handkerchief and realized that in his hurry, he forgot to tuck one in his pocket.

"For the sake of the President, we have to stick together. We're not like the local pols whose loyalty is equal only to the amount of money given them. That's who we are, in contrast to who they are. I assure you the Boss will be back and he'll meet with us within the next five days. This is all I can say for the moment. By the way, I need not tell you what my wife of three months is saying to me about this whole mess, except to say she is absolutely mad at me."

The line about his wife struck a familiar chord among his listeners.

"Well, Tim, let me tell you this and Pasqui, too," Tito Palson, Region II RSAC-Chair interrupted, his hand vigorously swatting a fly that wanted to land on top of his bulbous nose. "Let's not talk about our wives, okay? Because if we do, I might be forced to tell you that because of this miserable campaign, my wife has started throwing plates all over our place. Luckily so far, I've not been hit."

Groans could be heard from the others. They had their own stories to tell.

"I hope you understand," Palson continued, swatting but missing the big black fly. "I think the situation bottoms down to this. We have lost our credibility in our respective regions. In my particular region, let me tell you, our own close allies have already abandoned us. You will remember how difficult it was before to convince them, knowing that our candidate is that hard to sell to the public. And now this!" Palson exploded. He had smashed the persistent fly on top of his bulbous nose with an open palm.

"Not only that!" Region VIII RSAC-Chair Joey Loberizan joined in the attack, scratching his oversized belly. "We were assured that we could not possibly lose because we are the party in power, that we are loaded..." Loberizan lifted the plastic cup of coffee before him. Finding it cold, he drained it in one gulp and crumpled the empty cup in his fist, uttering an unprintable expletive. Loberizan was also the president of the Rotary Club of his district whose projects for the poor were legendary.

"What's really going on, Tim?" Roland Palanca, RSAC-Chair for the National Capital Region asked, his eyes looking sidewise toward his companions. Palanca was also the chairman of the federation of NGOs in his region. "Is it true that some of our VIPs are making money out of this, that monies intended for the campaign are ending in their own pockets?"

"Now, I think we have to be careful about that, Roland," Sipula interrupted. "It is not fair!"

"What careful?" Joined in Region XI RSAC-Chair Rac Castan, his thick eyebrows swerving up as he threw his words. A lawyer by profession, he was also the president of the biggest urban poor organization in his region. "It's being talked about openly now that the CM, that the…"

The tension rose and a full minute of hostile silence passed.

"By the way Tim, what's the Boss doing in New York, in London? Is he on a holiday or something?" Region XII RSAC —Chair Mario Cabellos asked, aggravating the hostile silence, his voice full of sarcasm. Cabellos was also the chairman of the biggest farmers cooperative in the whole of Western Mindanao.

"I think Mario you're going out of bounds!" Sipula shouted.

"Who's going out of bounds?" Cabellos retorted. "You were the one who just told us the Boss was in New York, right?"

"You shut up, Mario, or it's time we all go home. I don't like your insinuation!"

"What insinuation?"

"Didn't you imply, the Boss was on a holiday? Weren't you insinuating that like the others, he is also making money out of this campaign? Isn't that what you are insinuating?"

"You said it! I didn't!"

"May I have the floor, please," Region III RSAC-Chair Claire Napole was almost on the verge of tears. The only lady in the group, Napole was also the president of the biggest foundation in her region whose micro-lending program for the poor had won several international awards. "Gentlemen, please. As the only woman present here, allow me to speak, okay? I appeal that we take this in a very sober way. I need not remind ourselves that we are all volunteers here. The sacrifice we had to undergo is already up to our necks. I don't think it's worth throwing all our gains no matter how small… in the wastebasket."

Napole paused, her eyes getting moist. "May I suggest, Tim, that we go to the root of this problem in a very calm and sober way, without getting mad at each other. We've been together for a long time now. Let' s move forward, not backward," Napoles paused, wiping her eyes. "By the way, if no one has noticed yet, we are only 11 here instead of the 15 RSAC chairs. Does that tell you anything? Well, you were talking about your wives. I need not tell you my husband is totally shocked at my involvement in this campaign. The first time he called me crazy, I asked him why. You know what he said? Well, he said, if I were sane then I would not have joined this campaign for Davide, who he further said, only crazy people would ever think of voting for President of this country."

Her companions bowed their heads. Claire wiped her eyes again. Silence followed for a long time.

"Thanks, Claire, we'll all remember what you said," Pasqui said, blowing his nose into his handkerchief. "Now Tim, shall we start again?"

Sipula suddenly stood, pulling his trilling cell phone out of his belt. "Yes, yes, 'Gaya… okay… okay… you sure about that? Okay… yes, 11 out of 15. Yes… kindly… yes. Please don't stop till… okay, we're fine so far. Yes. Keep in touch, bye."

"That was Ligaya," Sipula told the group. "She called to say the Boss is definitely arriving on Saturday... Gaya said he'd be glad to meet with us on Monday, lunchtime, at the usual place. Gaya is preparing your plane tickets and reservations right now." Some heaved a sigh of relief.

"Okay, let's start again." Sipula continued. "Two newspaper columnists have already written about the rumor on the President abandoning Davide. The rumor on our Boss has hit the front page of one newspaper. Expect this thing to escalate a few days from now which means hell will break loose from hereon to election day. Now, shall we add more fire to all this?" Sipula paused, loosening his tie.

"I guess we have no other alternative but to wait until our meeting with the Boss on Monday," Sipula said, shrugging his shoulders.

"No other alternative?" asked Candoy.

"Yes, I guess so," Sipula said dryly. "On second thought, I guess we have to use our best effort as we go back to our respective regions. By that, I mean, we institute some kind of damage control as far as we can go without spending additional amounts because we don't have that right now."

"How do we do that, Tim?" Mario Cabellos cut in. "Without additional amounts to institute damage control against these rumors? You must be joking! You know, every time we go to our local radio station, we spend. Every time we go to the local newspaper, we spend. Even if we do it by word of mouth, we spend. Why? Because we have to order beer, gin or what not to squelch the rumor. But as often as it goes, a few bottles of beer or gin would start another rumor! Gad, this is simply insane!"

"Okay, let's not quarrel over this again. Let's just wait 'til Monday."

"How about our fare home? We only had enough to get here!"

"Okay, how many of us here have no cash to get back home?" Candoy asked.

Four raised their hands.

"That means, one plane fare, three fast craft fares, plus bus fares for home." Pasqui went over the faces that represented the four regions and did some estimates. "Okay, I'll take care of the plane fare for one, the five others including Tim, shell out from your own pockets to take care of the three boat fares and bus fares."

"Thanks, Pasqui," Sipula said, removing his tie. "Okay, let's pack."

"How about snacks along the way?" somebody asked.

"And meals?" another followed.

"How about a present for the commander-in-chief?" he meant his wife.

"Let's get out of here..." Pasqui said as everybody laughed.

They hugged, shook hands and parted in silence.

Once alone in his room, a member of the group hurriedly pushed buttons on his cell phone. "Hello," he kept his voice down, eyeing the door. "I've got something for you. Here's the latest." He went on to monitor his report. His voice started to choke. Something in his discomfort pricked an inner corner of his conscience.

"A little more pressure on the right, that's it! Some more... ugh, ughhhh, whew!" the man lying flat on his whole front body groaned. Except for the freshly scented towel on his torso, he was naked from head to toe. After a while, he asked. "Hi, partner, you okay?"

No answer.

The occasional low creaking of the small bed, the low snore, the light chopping of tiny hands over flabby flesh, the fresh scent of lemon, the soft whirl of the air conditioner, all these were just appropriate, for the moment, to rest and to think.

"Hi, partner, you okay?"

No answer.

"Honey..."

"I'm not Honey. I'm Sharon."

"Hi Sharon. Is my partner okay?"

"He's asleep, Sir. I think he's okay. He's got a lot of air bubbles inside his shoulder blades, though. I'm trying to put pressure to get them out," the girl on top of his partner said.

"He okay?"

"Yeah, I think so."

"Kindly apply more lotion, sweetheart. Thank you. A little more pressure... uggh, ughhhh, whew!"

"I'm not Sweetheart. I told you I'm Sugar," the girl on top of his back said.

"Okay, Sugar. I think I'll go to sleep, too. Kindly wake us up after 30 minutes, okay?"

"Yes, Sir."

Silence.

"Is this your first time here, Sir?"

"Yeah. Nice place, nice girls especially you, Sweetheart, I mean Sugar."

"You really mean that, Sir?"

"Of course, I mean it, you, especially."

Silence.

"What's your name, Sir?"

"Mr. Lonely."

The occasional low creaking of the small bed, the light chopping of small hands over his back, the right pressure of her fingers against the flesh between his ribs, the sweet fresh smell of lemon spray, the regular low whirl of the air conditioner and the weight, yes, just the right weight of Sugar's hot young body on top of his back—all these were just right to rest and think. The days ahead were murky but a decision had to be made. The latest monitor from his sources, including one in the inner circle of presidential adviser Destino, told him that decision had to be made, now or never. Congressman Racleto Albanos, the majority floor leader of the House, adjusted his head on the pillow. A slight smirk surfaced at the corner of his mouth as he started to slide into sleep.

"Everything okay with you, Sir? You look completely reinvigorated, so with Congressman del Prado," the attractive manager of the Suzukisan Massage Parlor smiled suggestively.

"Yeah, perfect massage and a 30 minute nap are just the right balm for us, poor public servants," Congressman Albanos grimaced, winking at his partner.

"Were the girls courteous?"

"Very."

"Glad to hear that. Okay, your companions are waiting on the second floor, so with your favorite Suzukisan treat and drinks, Sir. Gladys here, will escort you."

Bowing like a geisha, the kimono-clad Gladys led the two guests through the carpeted stairs down to the second floor. This was the back route only VIPs were privileged to take.

"Hi, Gladys, you look just great in that garb," Congressman del Prado, the younger of the two said, attempting to place his right arm around her waist.

"Thank you, Sir," Gladys replied, expertly avoiding the move. "This way please." Gladys bowed again, smiling demurely, pushing the massive door of thick leather over foam.

"Now, speaking about the devil!" the seven men in the room cheered.

The feast was vintage Albanos treat: everything Japanese, including the pretty kimono-clad waitresses, except the drinks which were changed from rice wine to Remy Martin gold and Johnny Walker black.

"Okay girls, you have to leave us for a while. And please close the door behind you," Albanos clapped his hands imperially, motioning the girls to leave. "We have important things to talk about and we don't want to be disturbed." He patted his bulging stomach. "Squatting on my ass after that hearty meal is simply too much," he joked. His companions chuckled.

The girls in kimonos exited. His colleagues moved closer on the floor toward Albanos, adjusting the cushions on their posteriors.

"Partners, I think the hour has come for us to make a decision together. Forget the other six, they're absolute suckers to Davide," Albanos addressed his companions, taking another sip of his Johnny Walker Black. At 69, Albanos was the quintessential example of a traditional politician: sure of himself, sure of what the other politicians stood for as against his own and sure where the wind was blowing in the political waters. He was also what others would call a walking jewelry store. He was adorned with gold, from the pen in his breast pocket to the pin in his tie, to the rings on his fingers. Around his neck sparkled a gold necklace that he touched now and then. Around his left wrist was a gold Rolex watch that he also fondled now and then, purely for effect.

The rest also took their drink, except one, the Region X party chairman, Congressman Ruperto Candelabra. He had anticipated this agenda but he did not like the tone of the majority floor leader.

"Partner," Candelabra said as calmly as he could. "I fully agree that there has to be some kind of a decision. All I ask is, we have to think this through very thoroughly. For one thing, there is Pin Davide that we have to consider. Whether we like it or not, we owe the man a lot. And of course, there is President Rosales. What would he say?"

The majority floor leader took his first double of Johnny Walker. The rest looked at each other.

"You're right, partner," Albanos said, lighting a cigarette. After taking a few luxuriant puffs, he continued. "You're damn right. We have to think this through thoroughly. And that's precisely why we are here. That's precisely why I took the initiative that we meet here because I want us to take a common stand, after thoroughly thinking it through."

Albanos fondled his necklace, apparently satisfied with what he just said. Then he asked, "Would anyone like to say something?"

"First of all," Governor Rolando Cerilles, party chair of Region VII, said, pouring another shot of Remy Martin. "I would like to say here without any reservation that Pin Davide has been with me through thick and thin. And I think this is also true for the rest of us. But frankly, you and I know very well the presidential fight today is a different ballgame. True, he is running for President and all of us here are running for reelection. But my reading is simple. Pin can afford to lose, I, for one, cannot. You, too, I think, cannot. But for Davide... win or lose, he gains. You know why? It's because the stakes are too high up there. He may lose the votes and perhaps even his pride, but he gains everything in the end. That's not true with me, with us. Once we lose, we lose everything: votes, pride and money. I'm sure you know what I mean and we need not be hypocrites about it."

Cerilles gulped his shot, poured another one, swallowed it like water and lit a cigarette. Everybody understood what the governor was trying to say. If he lost in the forthcoming elections, he would be a goner forever. The cases filed against him by the Ombudsman were full of hard evidence from construction of farm-to-market roads to irrigation facilities.

"Careful there now, partner," Albanos laughed, taking another gulp for himself. "We are still in Phase Two. You might not be able to get it up—in Phase Three!"

Everybody laughed except Candelabra.

"Well, I might sound too cocksure about this whole thing," Cerilles observed, "but I'm just being practical."

"May I add something?" Congressman Josue del Prado, Party Chair of Region V said "I'm not really bothered about Pin Davide. If there is anybody who knows his politics, it's him. If anybody knows about his business, it's him." He gulped another shot. "What I'm bothered about is President Rosales. You know the old man. He doesn't say much, but when he's sore at you, wham, you're dead! How can we look him straight in the eye, if, after tonight, we shift?"

Everybody knew what the congressman was talking about. In one party caucus, President Rosales had berated del Prado for failing to account for party funds allotted to his region. According to reports earlier that undoubtedly reached the president, the good congressman had used the money to build a new vacation house for his mistress in the resort town of Tagaytay. To del Prado, he had not done anything that any other politician had not done; he had just been caught, that was all.

Fondling his Rolex, Albanos looked at his colleagues. Then he clapped his hands as a girl in kimono came in. "Sweetheart, give us some hot towels and steaming hot coffee pronto, please?"

As he pressed the hot towel on his face and around his neck and took sips of the hot steaming coffee with three drops of Johnny Walker black, Albanos felt his insides stir and his thoughts refreshed.

"I believe our esteemed partners from Regions V and VII have expressed a universal sentiment. But let me make some elucidations." Albanos paused, relishing the moment. Obviously, he was now in his element. "On Pin Davide, we know him. As you know, I've been with him in politics much, much longer than any of you. And I agree, he's been with us through thick and thin. But as Partner Rollie here said, Davide is running for the presidency to gain, win or lose. And my gut feel tells me he's running for the presidency to lose in order to gain." Albanos paused to let that sink. "So, there is really nothing unusual about it all. In the end, whether we back him or not, that is not his problem. It's all part of the business. You know when you run for the presidency, you really have no constituency, in the sense that we have our own constituency, whose names we know, whose families we know, whose towns we know and what bridges and kilometers of roads and budgets we are accountable for, every day, every week, every month. For the presidency, it's nice to hear that the whole country is the President's constituency, but when the votes are counted, it's us who know who voted for whom. Davide knows this very well, that is why he knows his politics and his business. In the end, he really doesn't have any pride at all."

The majority floor leader paused again, feeling his adrenalin rise, gulping another double of Johnny Walker on the rocks.

"Now to President Rosales. All of us here and the majority of our colleagues in the House have nothing to say against the old man but he will no longer be President after June 30. And he knows that, too. So, where does that leave all of us?"

Albanos paused, believing his logic was well anchored politically. He sounded very persuasive, too. Then he played with his necklace.

"What about the party, the party, partner?" Congressman Rosetti asked, gulping the double in his glass.

"What party are we talking about here? In contemporary politics, the party only emerges immediately before elections and dies a natural death after elections!" Albanos averred, scanning the faces of his colleagues. They knew his politics, didn't they?

"So, I repeat, where would all this leave us? Pin Davide is running for President and he knows and we know, his chance of winning is as nil as squeezing juice from a dry leaf. So why is he running? We already know that. He knows his politics and he knows his business. President Rosales had done his job very well, in fact, done it beautifully. But he will no longer be President after June 30. So, where would that leave us? Where, would, that leave us!"

Albanos shrugged, stretching his open palms, the kind of gesture that told his listeners there was nothing else to consider.

"The answer, Partners, is clear and simple—we would be left alone to paddle our own canoe, to fight for our own survival and to be left miserably alone, to spend our own limited resources, because Pin Davide has not delivered, except for that

128

measly sum that Claudia, God pity her, handed over to us like we were beggars. And I tell you, if we do not decide now, we will end up losing our own identity, who we are, wretchedly defeated, our own personal funds vanished, our own constituency abandoning us and our own self-esteem gone with the wind."

After once more looking at the faces around him, Albanos asked, sounding impassive while fondling his necklace. "Are we ready for the vote?"

Albanos punctuated his coup de grace with a theatrical shrug of his shoulders. Loud silence followed.

"There's no need for that, I agree," Rosetti said, gulping another double.

"So, where do we go from here?" Congressman Reynaldo Cusia, party chairman of Region VI asked, sipping his nth double, his eyes at the door.

"As I told some of you over the phone the other day," Albanos said, now grinning heartily. "Fatso is simply waiting for my return call. Note carefully that it was Fatso who gave the offer first. Not me, not anyone of us. The offer is 25 times over what Davide promised but failed to deliver."

"And when will that come?" almost all asked.

"As soon as I give him the return call and my word."

"That's good!"

"That's great!"

"So... what's phase three?"

"Aha! So, you still remember!" Albanos guffawed. "Phase three, my friends, is on the 17th floor. They're all behind the one-way mirror, all first class, all sweet and gentle, all the way down." He was now bursting with laughter, his face reddening like fried lobster. "Just state the number that's pinned to her left breast and you'll have her. If after awhile, you won't like her, change her anytime. No extra charge. Courtesy of the house!"

Albanos struggled to stand and after steadying himself, took what looked like a small matchbox from his inside coat pocket. Raising it up, he declaimed: "Do you know what's inside this matchbox? It's the great V for testosterone power, for those who can't get it up!"

All oohed and aahed as hands were extended toward him, palms up. "Not yet, my friends. Let's have a toast!" All cheered, pouring more refills, then raising and clinking their glasses.

"Toast to Pin Davide who knows his business, to President Rosales for his goodness and to Mahal, the next President of the Republic! To Love!"

"Cheers!"

"And a toast to the wound that never heals!" Andales bellowed, emptying another double. Withdrawing his glass, strands of saliva dripped from the corners of his mouth. Albanos then dropped one great V on the extended open palm of the governor.

The queue was short. Each finally got his light blue miracle pill, Albanos laughing like a stallion along the way.

U p in the mountains, there was stillness except for what sounded like a song.

Edey, edey andaman—
Ne imensad keg daben
Nepenga' su limbutung
Yampa' be tambeden dan
Su bayadaw ki menginey,
Yampa' deketayen dan
Su dea' ki menihanlek,
Ken' neketambed kew
Tenyagew ke yekbasan,
Ingsu nekedeketey kew
Dagwat nu gintamuwan
Ne begubegu nakluwas
Yampa' si mendamagus

The language was indigenous but the tone of voice was familiar, pulsating in lyrical waves. Then it rose to a limpid pitch while the mountain breeze softly caressed the skin.

The climate could be somewhere between 14 to 15 degrees centigrade but Katrina Avila just sat there, almost mesmerized, listening, her eyes fixated upon the source of the voice: an old man, squatting Gandhi-like at the end of the wooden porch. He was naked above the waist and his ribs protruded out of his gaunt, dark brown skin. As he raised his arms now and then in a prayerful pose, Katrina noticed the long uncut nails, like the talons of a monkey-eating eagle. She couldn't see the eyes because they were covered with bark-like eyelids. His hair was long, wholly gray and uncombed, its ends reaching the wooden floor upon which he sat. He must be over a hundred, she thought.

"What is he singing?" Katrina asked her young host.

"He is not singing but chanting. The old man is a *talaulahingan*, a chanter. He is chanting the sacred story of our people, of our great, great ancestor Agyu from his sojourn as a *naraneen*, a man of earth, his adventures, his battles against adversaries and his journey to *Nelendangan*, our paradise. The *talaulahingan* has been in that position in the last 35 hours, non-stop chanting, except for a few minutes to chew on the betel nut inside his mouth. His chanting right now has something to do with Agyu's warriors preparing for battle. You will notice the beat in his chant follows lyrical forms and musical structures."

Katrina and her crew were totally awed. Forewarned not to use a camera flash as this would disturb the chanter, they just sat there silently, unmoving. Now and then, unintelligible sounds would come from his throat as he paused, then chanted again. His eyelids seemed to vibrate, the concentration intense, the voice high pitched and sustained, perspiration flowing from his face and unto his neck.

"He is describing the make and type of weapons the warriors used for combat," the young host said, nodding his head toward the chanter. "He says that these are

130

very attractive with no equal, so alluring without compare, interwoven are the fabrics of the cord of the dagger and the girdle of the sword and so on."

"Why, are they preparing for battle? For what and against who?" Katrina asked.

"The sacred story of our people, the *Ulahingan* epic is full of battles against our adversaries from giants the size of mountains to rocks full of evil spirits. Our ancestors had to go through many hardships as a test for them to enjoy *Nelendangan* afterwards."

"Sounds like the Iliad or the Odyssey of Homer?"

"Yes, to some extent, in the sense that our epic also went through generations of oral renderings. As you can see, this *talaulahingan* is chanting the epic from memory. It's all oral transference, from one generation to the next. We believe our epic predates that of Homer. For one thing, the oriental civilization precedes that of the west."

"This is really amazing!" Katrina could not help but raise her voice in wonder. Then she asked "How is this chanting related to the death of the Supreme Datu?"

"The chanting of our epic transcends the death of anyone in the House of Agyu. It is our link to our glorious past. But eventually, the death of the Supreme Datu will be part of the epic in the distant future. The epic is a dynamic one. It is enriched by additional episodes through the centuries. But for the epic to remain dynamic, it will require chanters to pass the story from one generation to the generation. What is sad is our younger generation does not appear to appreciate our sacred story."

Edy nud menge yumbed,
Dew nud menge meyali,
Ken' te ikka'insa
Myamis hitayen
Te igdagandan ne dagmal
li' hu igkepenateng
Libas bibitayuen
Idasun ni sa ngalan
Kuna be yandan lalag
Di nu yandan maluwa
'Salamat nengentaydu
Tedun anaya ana ta
Untung negihyeyabaw
Dun bes si manah ta

"The *talaulahingan* says the warriors of Agyu are now gladdened the enemy has landed, for their weapons and their courage are ready for battle. Thanks to the Highest *Diwata,* our Supreme God".

Katrina stood and leaned against a tree. In her many assignments for TV Channel 6, she had not seen nor witnessed anything like this. Scanning the mountain range above her, she felt the freshness of her surroundings and began to be conscious of the strong presence of the future supreme datu of his people, his conviction, his love of his culture and the deep black eyes that pierced her when he looked her way.

"Shall we go now to my uncle's wake?" Her host asked as he guided her up the porch and to the inner foyer. The wailing, the crying and the fainting inside startled her. Somewhere outside, the beating of the native *agung* (gong) reverberated, its indigenous sounds eerie and strange.

"Don't be amazed," the young man beside her said. "This is all part of the ritual. The seven sounds of the *agung* you just heard is a call to all our people in the mountains and by the riverbanks of the death of our leader. It will again be repeated now and then until we take his remains to the burial grounds."

Katrina Avila, two-time journalism awardee for investigative reporting of many death-defying encounters in the past, felt her legs limp. Squatting on the floor, she braced her elbows against her knees to support her head. The spirits of the mountains had engulfed her and her eyes began to moisten, as the wailing, the crying and the fainting continued in their divergent vibrations. Inside the hollowed space of the big round log of hard wood in the middle of the mourners, the remains of the Supreme Datu stayed still and serene.

"How come you are the only one not in native garb?" Katrina asked her host later, out on the wooden porch. For the first time, she noticed his faded blue shirt that seemed too small for his bulging muscles, the tight pants that clung to his slim waist and legs like they were part of his rough-hewn skin. The beak nose that curved like that of a hawk. And the deep black eyes that pierced her, sharp and unblinking like a forest animal's on the hunt for a prey.

"I just came from the city to notify the new administration that the House of Agyu has nothing to do with the government anymore. After the burial ceremony, the council of elders will proclaim me as supreme datu. From there, I will implement my plans in accordance with our tradition and the instructions of the council of elders." The deep black eyes left her as the taut face turned toward the sinking sun.

"Are you saying you will also be preparing for battle as the *talaulahingan* chanted?"

"Yes, to some extent. But we are not ready for that yet. Most of our people are ignorant and find happiness only in alcohol. Our young people are illiterate. So, my first step is to get our people educated." The young man paused, looking up toward the darkening skies. "That most of us are ignorant and find happiness only in alcohol is actually the consequence of a deliberate effort of the government to make us so, just like what the European colonizers did to the North American Indians. And that is the lesson that I will not forget. It will take years. It might not even happen in my time. But I will implement the beginning with the blessing of our ancestors and the Highest *Diwata*, our Supreme God."

Completely lost in her own thoughts, Katrina asked, "Are you thinking of schools to educate your young, your people?"

"Yes, something like that. But we have to begin somewhere. Schools will need teachers and teachers will need instructional materials. Where would we get those? So we have to begin with what we have. We have rich resources here, we have gold, all types of minerals, we have great trees. We have fowls, wild pigs and all sorts of flora and fauna. We can tap all of these, to begin with."

"Do you have any message for the government, what you intend to do?" Katrina asked, her gray-brown eyes seeking his.

"Yes, I have," he replied.

"Can I tape them and can I have some camera shots… of you?" Katrina asked again, her gray-brown eyes never leaving his.

"You may… if you want," he answered, gradually looking away.

At the other end of the porch, the lean old man with his eyes closed, his face toward the sky, continued chanting.

Ew edey mengey din en man su
Sina' ne pengulendem,
Ew edey manda'an ne-
"Eyan en te inlulud
Yan en te hinulud nu."
Ne yan la binasabasa,
Ne yan en pinanumanglit,
"Ne nelugey ne ulangdan
Te dulwung te Gebunen
Ne idan nu itung baley
Te subang te Mudan'udan,
Ne yampakan te belayen."
Ew edey manda'an su-
Ada diyan ikem din,
Te muntug alimugut din
Te baying ne tambeleng din,
Ne keduwag keapu din,
Ne kempat te pundada din.

(O, goes the chant and we proceed—
"Oh, all that is in my mind,
The sincerity of my thoughts,"
Oh, goes the chant-
"He is indeed your father
And truly he is your parent."
And this then can be said,
And this we may contemplate
"That for many long years,
In the realm of Gebunen,
This is the only visit he has made
To the land of Mudan'udan
And the only appearance
To the portals of this house."

Oh, goes the chant—
He can hardly notice
Dimmed eyes cause failure to recognize
The multitude of his children
And also of his grandchildren,
As well as of his great, great grandchildren.)

Timostocles Sipula concluded that if Dr. Meandro Destino failed to meet the group, the consequence would be irredeemable. It was quarter past one. Everybody didn't have the appetite even if it was native cuisine in a *kamayan* (eating with hands) restaurant, everybody's favorite during past eating sessions. Ligaya was busy on her cell at the far corner of the restaurant, trying to make contact.

"The Boss is on the way!" Ligaya finally announced, rushing in and taking her seat. "What a relief!" she said aloud, filling her plate with her choices. She started eating with relish.

"I'm sorry guys," Dr. Destino said as he came in, taking the vacant seat between Pasqui and Tim. "Why don't we have a round of beer while I'll eat with 'Gaya."

"That's great, Boss." Tim said, signaling the waiter. Everybody became alive again.

"No problem, just one round," Dr. Destino said, admiring the dishes in front of him. "After this, I have to go. This campaign is draining all of us. No sleep, no nothing."

The 13 bottles of cold beer arrived. Ligaya ordered a Cali Shandy for herself.

"Okay, I think, we're all here to solve some problems. Ligaya already briefed me about them, same with Tim who updates me on things almost every day. Where's my beer? Oh, here it is. Thank you." Destino wiped his mouth with a napkin, nodded to the waiter, then sipped his beer. The rest followed.

"Let me go straight to these problems, offer my explanations, then let's have your reactions, then let me go, Okay? I'll be with the President at four." Destino lighted a cigarette.

"One, I just came back from abroad on a special mission of a confidential nature. I was not on a holiday. The President never sends you on a holiday. It was a special mission of a confidential nature, so I cannot go beyond that. I'm sure you understand. Two, it is not correct to say the President has abandoned Davide. Perhaps, the word should not be 'abandoned' but something else that might tell us of the President's inner concern. The reason here, as far as I know, is the President wants Davide to stand on his own, to project himself as a presidential candidate in his own right and not as a clone of the President."

Dr. Destino paused, sipping his beer.

"Three, the rumor that some people at the highest level of the party are making money out of this campaign is true—is true as a rumor. However, to prove this is next to impossible. You will not only be casting aspersions on certain individuals, you will also be exposing campaign money contributors, most of whom would not like to be known. That the President knows about these rumors is true. As far as I know, the President has already called on some people to get to the bottom of this. What the President has found out, I am not privy to. What he would do after that, I also do not know.

"And fourth, the last, the amounts promised you by the party through CM Malasuerte is no longer there. I finally had a long talk with him Saturday morning, that was the other day. He told me many things, which again, are confidential in nature but which I already relayed to the President. But as far as this problem is concerned, you need not worry too much. The President has taken care of two-thirds of that, from his own funds, not from the party. Half of the rest, I will raise myself. Give me 78 hours. Ligaya will release the President's donation at the office before you leave for home. As an aside, Serafin Davide assured me on the phone that he would pay all the debts of the party after elections—win or lose. But that is no longer your concern and we should not bank on that."

"How about the four other RSACs who deserted us?"

"The same, 'Gaya will also pay their debts, those that were incurred in the name of the administration party—when they were still with us."

"I think we still have time for another round of beer, Boss," Tim suggested, seeking the support of the others.

"Right," Destino said, after checking his watch. "I also need another one. I'll just take my nap in the car. 'Gaya?"

"One Cali is enough for me. I'll order cold tea instead."

"Boss, I have a bottle of Chivas in my car," Sipula said. "Would you like me to get it?" Sipula knew the brand of his boss.

"Not at this time, Tim," Destino quickly said. "I will be with the President at four. And you know I only start drinking firewater after five."

Everybody laughed.

"Boss," Roland Palanca of NCR asked. "What is really the score on our candidate? Do we have any chance at all?"

Nobody said anything for a few minutes. The silence grew heavy.

"You mean to say, Boss, that..." Palanca hesitated, his eyes meandering somewhere else, "that the presidency is in the bag for Mahalina? This rumor is spreading like wild fire and it started from the palace itself."

"Well, as we all know Malacanang leaks like an old toilet," Destino said with a chuckle, emptying his bottle as he slowly stood. "And for all I know, we may be a part of the leak. Anyway, please don't condemn us. These are desperate hours."

"I have one question Boss and I hope you won't take it personally," Napole asked.

"What's that, Claire?"

"Did you or did you not make a lot of money in this campaign, as rumored?"

"I didn't, Claire. And I don't need to explain that. It will be self-serving. Thanks to all of you. See you soon."

"This is all bullshit!" Palanca blurted out as soon as Destino was out of the door. "What did he mean when he said that we may be a part of the leak? Was he

135

insinuating that one of us here is playing Judas? I cannot stand this. Why are all of you looking at me like that? I'm leaving! I cannot stand this."

The chapel amid the squatters' settlement was full beyond its capacity. The crowd in fact spilled out to all sides. Supported by eight 4 x 4 posts, four to each side, the chapel's rusted corrugated roof shook, every time one brushed a post or leaned on one. And this was neither Sunday nor was Father Francisco around to offer mass. This was, in fact, a Saturday afternoon and the unusually big crowd was here to attend what newspaper reporters commonly refer to as an "indignation rally."

Seven speakers already delivered their speeches. The last, Priscilla Batungbakal, squatter-activist leader of the Association of the Urban Poor Homeowners' Coalition based in Caloocan City, about to end her fiery delivery, shouted at the top of her voice: "Our time has come, our tiiiimmme has come, brothers and sisters! It is time we get the attention we deserve! For the first time in our sufferings, we now have hope. We now have hoooope! Let us go for Mahal! He loves us and we should love him in return. The past administrations promised us many, many things but all we got, all we got are sad memories of broken promises. Our timmme has come, brrrrothers and sissssters!!!"

The five other leaders, representing their respective organizations in the coalition shouted back in agreement, their fists in the air. And so did their members. Years of waiting for nothing had become too much to bear. Instead of houses and lots, they were now threatened by the local government to convert their squatters haven into an industrial zone.

"The government had not been fair to us," continued Batungbakal in her shrill voice, her small eyes ablaze, her frail body shaking with anger. "Why was Smokey Mountain the only one, the only one developed? As an exhibit for tourists? We have more people here than those in Vitas, Tondo! Mahal is our only hope. Mahal is our only hooope! Do you agrrrree? Are we ready to support and campaign for Mahal? Are we rrrready for Maaaahal?" the veins in her throat swelled as her voice cracked.

"Yes! Yes! Yes!"

Wiping off beads of perspiration from her face, neck and arms with a small, soiled brown towel, Batungbakal then jumped from the platform to the ground floor. As she did, the table on the makeshift platform bearing the statue of the Virgin Mary shook a little, as those out front mumbled *"Susmaryosep!"* and quickly made the sign of the cross.

Simeon Sempron shifted the sack of corn over to his left shoulder. One more kilometer, he told himself as he pinched the ache at the base of his neck. The drought had caused it all. Instead of harvesting 15 sacks of corn, he only had this one sack, his aching neck and hurting feet. He couldn't even buy a new pair of sandals. The milling cost, the jeepney fare from the highway to town and back, plus the kilo of dried fish that he had to buy means there would be nothing left!

Sempron dropped the sack of corn when he got to the barangay hall along the highway. Looking at the sun, he estimated he still had one hour before the next passenger jeep would pass by.

"Hello there, Compadre," Pablo Tabile, the barangay captain, greeted him. "How is Comadre Petra? Actually, I was going to call a meeting of the council this Wednesday. But since you are already here, I might as well tell you of the latest development."

Sempron was one of the seven councilmen of Barangay Kadugay in the municipality of Lo-oc. At 38, he looked 58. He was the typical upland farmer, gaunt and haggard looking. The earthworm-sized veins at the sides of his forehead and at the back of his legs looked like they were about to burst anytime soon. His hair was unkempt, he had tattered nails, tattered toes and tattered clothes.

Tabile drove the goats out of the hall as he led his friend to one of the bamboo benches.

"Compadre, this is still a secret but the good mayor instructed us to support the candidacy of Mahalina," Tabile said, his voice low and guarded. "We have to shift loyalties. There is no way, according to the good mayor, that our administration candidate will win." In contrast to Sempron, Tabile looked citified. He wore a long-sleeved striped shirt open at the front and a pair of khaki jeans. His eyes were covered by dark shades he bought from one of the Muslim sidewalk vendors in town. He also had on a colorful pair of imitation Air Jordan shoes and cap.

Sempron remembered. He heard in his portable radio that the mayors' league had been meeting and debating whether or not to shift to the opposition. He remembered, too, that his portable radio needed a new set of batteries. He needed the radio not only to keep him awake while tending to a farmland he had acquired under the comprehensive agrarian reform program. All in all he had a three hectare farm but could only cultivate half a hectare. He didn't have the means to cultivate them all.

"I guess, we have no choice, Compadre. We have to survive. We are simply too far away so that our voices can be heard. So whatever the good mayor tells us, we follow."

Sempron could not readily agree. Of the seven councilmen, he was the most vocal against subservience, against kowtowing to the whims and caprices of politicians. And he believed in President Rosales even if he had not met the man. He was completely sold to people empowerment, that beautiful concept President Rosales had been saying in many of his radio broadcasts.

"Compadre, the good mayor has promised to deliver. Here is your part of the advance. Don't you worry about it. Nothing personal."

The barangay captain pulled out his wallet, extracted a P100 note and inserted it in the empty pocket in front of Simeon Sempron's heart.

With both palms covering his head, his elbows on his knees, Simeon Sempron stared at the dusty floor of the passenger jeep, groaning noisily on the highway toward town. His first stop would be the rice and corn mill about one and a half kilometers from the market.

The house sat amidst sweeping lawns and a groove of tall mahogany trees. It was a picturesque two-story edifice with French windows painted white and blue and a stately front porch. It was not a mansion but it was opulent in every way. It stood elegantly in the middle of about 2000 square meters of prime real estate, each square meter costing around P25,000, the equivalent of the basic monthly salary of the president of the republic. To the economists and demographers, that same amount is the equivalent of the combined income of a family of six, engaged in menial labor somewhere between seven to eight months and, therefore classified as living below the poverty line.

The open garage, seen from the front, displayed three imported cars, a black Ford Expedition, a pale beige Jaguar convertible and a scarlet BMW. Nobody really knew how many lived in the house but some of the closest neighbors did: only two, not to count the two drivers, four maids and two gardeners. At least once a month, usually in the middle of the night, a black Mercedes Benz 560 would visit the place, escorted by a convoy of three vehicles, one at the front and two at the back. At the start, most of the neighbors were asking themselves who the nocturnal visitor might be. But this was Forbes Park, the enclave of the rich and the super-rich. And so the curiosity died a natural death, as most residents of the park were more concerned with their money than with their neighbors.

"Mom," the young man hollered from the wide foyer of the house. "You really think Dad would be happy if I go into politics?"

"Jason, you've been saying that a lot of times but you haven't done anything yet, not even told your Dad about it."

"How could I do that? I told you he's too busy!"

The mother came in from the kitchen to join her son. Jason Angelo was now 24 years old and the spitting image of his father, except for the *moreno* color of his skin—which was his mother's trademark when she was still in her prime. The others were all fair in complexion and she was the brown beauty.

"What are you reading?" Mom said as she sidled beside her son.

"Nothing"

"C'mon, Sonny Boy!"

"It's a script, Mom."

"Script, for what?"

"A movie."

Mom remembered with some emotions her movies in the past. She was a movie starlet, the most adored starlet at the time and Jason's father was the lead star.

"What's the title?"

"The Son Also Rises."

"Oh, I remember now. Ava Gardner was the lead female star and was it Clark Gable?"

"Ha! Ha! Ha! No, Mom, don't get confused. That was the 'The Sun Also Rises' written by Ernest Hemingway. That one was a movie about love and war. This one is about a son who also rises after his father's fame. They're different, miles and miles apart."

"Hmm... so this is original?"

"Of course! My buddies and I thought and wrote about it in our cinema class."

"Jason, are you saying that..."

"Yes, Mom. I'm going to use this movie as a vehicle for my plans to go into politics. The story line is kind of pure and simple local but the episodes are world class. It simply tells of a son who is abandoned by his father but who despite all the odds, rises to fame and fortune, until both son and father are reunited in the end. Beautiful, isn't it? What do you say, Mom?"

"Gosh, Sonny Boy. I think it's time we see your Dad and tell him all about it. I am sure he will like the idea very, very much." The mother gushed with pride, lovingly hugging her son.

The regular Wednesday monthly meeting of the honorable councilmen of Barangay Kadugay in the municipality of Lo-oc started their session almost two hours late. This was because the barangay captain and presiding officer, Pablo Tabile and three other councilmen had to pay their social obligations by staying longer than necessary after the banquet in honor of the newly weds, for whom they acted as sponsors. "One for the road!" In Barangay Kadugay, that oath was always broken.

Barangay councilman Cardo Roque was fuming in his seat in the barangay hall. He was the chairman of the finance committee. His arithmetic told him there was no way the barangay could raise the money to fund the lavishly planned coronation night, the most awaited activity of the forthcoming barrio fiesta. Roque had expressed his apprehension during the last meeting. To his great surprise, the barangay captain with his usual show of arrogance, told him "...to produce the funds since you are the chairman of the finance committee."

The more Roque thought about the lack of funds and the arrogance of Tabile, the more he fumed. And the louder he fumed, cursing this time when he saw Tabile and the three other councilmen stagger inside the hall, obviously inebriated, shouting expletives while making excuses that they had to walk the seven kilometers of rough road so as not to be late in this meeting. *What impertinence!* Roque cursed again.

"I am now calling this meeting to order," Tabile announced, slamming the table as soon as he found his seat.

"I'll order a Coke," said one councilman at the far end of the table.

"I said, I'm calling this meeting to order, not for you to order Coca-Cola!" Tabile snapped, scanning the faces around him and snorting at the councilman.

The honorable councilman who ordered Coca-Cola was a notorious ignoramus. Obviously, he had not attended the seminar on parliamentary procedures, a favorite among local legislators. It was commonly known that because of their expertise in the Robert rules of order, half of the sessions in the august halls of local legislatures in the province were stuck in debate, whether one was in order or out of order. Thus, for lack of time, the main agenda were always deferred for the next meetings.

"Now, what is our agenda?" Tabile asked, signaling a woman far into the hall for a cup of coffee.

"We have only one item in the agenda," the secretary said.

"That's right," Roque, the chairman of the finance committee blurted out immediately. His anger earlier had somehow ebbed, now that he found his opening.

"And what might that be?" the barangay captain asked, facing the secretary.

"It's the funds for the coronation night, your honor, "the secretary replied, looking furtively at Roque.

Roque fumed again. He felt the barangay captain had deliberately ignored him. But this was not the time, he cautioned himself. The funding problem must be resolved now or he would be blamed later. There was so much at stake. A successful coronation night would bring him closer to the town mayor who was scheduled to crown the beauty queen, not to mention the hundreds of votes he expected to get in the next barangay election. He was not appointed chairman of the finance committee for nothing and the barangay captain and his drunken buddies better remind themselves of that fact.

They should also remind themselves that he was once a town policeman who knew no fear, who had four deep notches on the butt of his .38 Smith and Wesson revolver. He had been accused but acquitted of murdering the political rival of the incumbent mayor for a fee.

Roque smiled to himself as he remembered the mayor whisper, immediately after his acquittal, that he had political plans for him in the future.

"All right," Tabile said. "Ladies and gentlemen, we shall now hear the honorable chairman of the finance committee present his bright ideas for the forthcoming coronation night."

Roque's ears tingled. He didn't miss the sarcasm of Tabile. Hold your temper, Roque again cautioned himself.

"Thank you, Mr. Chairman," Roque found himself saying. "The forthcoming coronation night will never be successful if there are no funds to finance it…"

"We already know that!" Tabile cut him off. "Why don't you go straight to the point!" Gesturing to the woman at the far end of the hall, he almost shouted, "More coffee!"

The interruption hit the ears of Roque like hot coal. He felt his fists tighten under the table. But to his surprise, his head stayed on the level.

"I'm sorry, Mr. Chairman," Roque again found himself saying. Then he continued, "My total estimate for a successful coronation night is P180,000. We still have P20,000 left in savings out of the total budget allotted for the fiesta."

"P180,000 less P20,000 is P160,000," Tabile said, looking straight at Roque. "And where will you get the P160,000?"

"I don't know, Mr. Chairman. Please note that the P160,000 is the cash requirement. Over and above are donations in kind…"

"P160,000… that's equivalent to 16 sturdy carabaos!" Councilman Simeon Sempron exclaimed. This was his first statement of the day. "At P10,000 each. That's a lot!"

"May I hear from the others?" Tabile asked, ignoring the side comment of Sempron. "May I ask how we can raise the P160,000 since the chairman of the finance committee claims he does not know…"

Silence followed.

Sensing that he would not get any, Tabile continued. "While you are still looking for bright ideas in your heads, may I announce that the good mayor is reminding us of the resolution that we have to pass unanimously, that is, endorsing Mahalina for President. The mayor made me understand that all the barangay councils in the entire province would do the same, so with all the municipal councils."

After the prolonged silence, Sempron said: "Don't you think we should first consult our respective constituents before…"

"I don't think we have time for that," Tabile snapped, looking at Sempron with daggers in his eyes. "The matter is considered urgent by the governor and all the mayors. We really have no choice."

"But…"

"There is no but. Mahalina will win anyway. Why waste our votes to losers. Davide has no chance whatsoever. He's a tradpol from ear to ear. Santolan, the once famous crusader is a has-been. The rest are pretenders. Even if you combine all the votes of all the other candidates, they won't even get to 20 percent of the total votes of Mahalina. That's the hard reality that we cannot get away from." Tabile concluded his speech with a smack of his open palm on the table.

"I think you are grossly exaggerating," Sempron said, scanning his colleagues for support. "You have forgotten that President Rosales is backing up Davide. And even if you think that Davide is a tradpol like most of us anyway, he will win if President Rosales wants him to win."

The other councilmen were suddenly awake, some of them nodding their heads in agreement.

"I have never underestimated President Rosales and I have all the respect for him," Tabile said, suddenly lowering his voice. "But he is no longer the candidate." Then he raised his voice. "And Davide is simply not marketable. And let me tell you this—you cannot just force people to buy a kilo of fish in the market that is obviously rotten. In fact at times, I have this suspicion President Rosales was simply forced to endorse Davide because there was no one else to endorse. President Rosales really had no choice."

"I think those are harsh words, Mr. Chairman." Sempron said, his voice quivering. "I suggest they be deleted from the minutes."

"I want them in the minutes!" Tabile blurted out. "And I will also put in the minutes that you, Councilman Sempron is objecting to the wishes of the mayor!"

After making sure the secretary wrote that in the minutes, Tabile stood and turned toward Sempron. Lowering his voice but making sure that everybody heard him, he said: "Would you like to bet one carabao to my ten carabaos, one goat to my ten goats, one fighting cock to my 10 fighting cocks, one box of rum to my 10 boxes of rum or one box of beer to my 10 boxes of beer that Mahalina will garner more votes than all the votes of all the other presidential candidates put together?" Tabile paused, to make sure his dare sank. Then leaning close to Sempron's startled face, he howled: "If you won't take the bet for any one or some or all of those I mentioned, then you are joking, joking, joking!"

Councilman Sempron bowed his head in total humility. He didn't even have a goat. That would cost around P800, he estimated in his head. Beer? Rum? He stopped drinking a long time ago. He had really nothing, except his firm belief that President Rosales would make Davide win.

Councilman Roque did not bow his head. He was staring over the top of the coconut trees and far beyond, toward Kadugay Bay and its sparkling waters. When Tabile challenged Sempron and offered his bet, an idea sparked in Roque's head. He had seven sturdy carabaos, a herd of goats, 11 good fighting cocks and enough cash for the other items.

"Mr. Chairman, I call," Cardo Roque said nonchalantly. "I'll take your bet on all the items."

That sent all the councilmen looking at each other. Even the woman in the kitchen stretched her ears to make sure she heard it right. But there was no doubt Roque called the bet; he was dead serious. Everyone knew, too, Roque was Kadugay's most famous gambler, a reputation he shared with Tabile.

"Aha! So you are taking the cudgels for Sempron, is that it?" Tabile ejaculated.

"No, I'm not," Roque retorted. "I'm simply interested in making sure we have a successful coronation night."

That sent the other councilmen looking at each other again.

"And how is this betting related to the coronation night?" Tabile asked incredulously.

"To raise the needed funds for the coronation night," Roque simply said. "Now, I'm taking your bet however with just one small condition and this is: if I win, I will donate all my winnings to the fund, less my original bet, of course. On the other hand, if you win, you donate all your winnings, plus half of your own bet, to the fund. And…" Roque paused, then delivered his bomb, "a pledge from me, witnessed by all our colleagues here, that I will not run against you for barangay captain in the next election."

Roque pretended to fondle his long hair, slowly looking around. Then he stared at Tabile. "Deal?"

Tabile stared back at Roque. Their eyes locked for a long time. No one blinked. Then nodding his head slowly with a smirk on his face, Tabile said, "Yes, sure. It's a deal."

The close encounter between the two local political hotshots became the fertilizer of the soil of idle talk and gossip in the fields of work and *sari-sari* stores selling alcohol—morning, noon and night. Barangay Kadugay in the municipality of Lo-oc would never be the same again.

Ruperto del Pardo, president of the Asian Consolidated Bank and chairman of the board of the Metropolitan Business Club (MBC) warmed at the thought that the club finally decided to stay neutral in the forthcoming presidential elections.

The banging of tables, the vulgar language and the threats of resignation came in the middle of the debate when the club was confronted with the question who to finally endorse among the six presidential candidates.

"The truth that had been established in this heated debate is the fact that all candidates, I repeat, all candidates have both good and bad records. The sad thing however is, the bad exceeds the good by a very wide margin. In short, all the candidates fall miserably below acceptable standards."

This time there were no debates. Instead, low voices began to surface among seatmates around the long mahogany conference table, but their words were indecipherable. The chairman's throne was at the end, near his desk and before him on the table were stacks of paper, glossy pictures of indiscretions and other effects. It was known in high places that the MBC had an intelligence arm that was more extensive than the intelligence arm of Malacanang Palace. It had on its files useful information on ambitious politicians, their assets and liabilities, their virtues and vices, incriminating or not.

The MBC was the most powerful business group in the country. As a matter of policy, the Club adhered to the principle that there is no economic progress without political stability and there is no political stability without economic progress.

"Now, considering the situation we are in right now, I propose that the only option left for us is a compromise—the MBC will not at this time endorse any of the five official presidential candidates, in a unanimous vote of staying neutral. However, this compromise agreement shall not deprive any member of the club to exercise his individual right to make his own choice and campaign for his own candidate at his own time, if he so desires, provided that he does not use the name of the club for the purpose."

The chairman had muscled in. The die was cast.

It was newscast time on Election Day, six o'clock in the evening. People were glued to their television sets. Broadcasters Fred and Gina were on the air, on TV Channel 4.

FRED And now to the latest on Election Day... Who is our first reporter in the field, Gina?

GINA It's Pompey Alcuna in Sorsogon, Sorsogon. He reports it's generally peaceful out there except for a minor accident, a result of a quarrel between bettors or something. Pompey, you're on.

POMPEY Thank you, Gina, Fred. It's generally peaceful here in Sorsogon, Sorsogon where the polling places closed at around four o'clock this afternoon. The conduct of the elections was generally efficient. Voters easily found their precincts and knew where to vote. There was, however, a stabbing incident just in front of this restaurant you can see on your screen. According to witnesses, a certain Crispin Pantol, a fan of Mahalina, stabbed another Mahalina fan by the name of Nestor Bukerol. Pantol stabbed Bukerol because Bukerol would not concede to Pantol's claim that Mahalina would get no less than 90 percent of the votes in the entire province of Sorsogon. And that started the unfortunate incident.

FRED My gad, Pompey, did anyone die?

POMPEY Happily, no. The doctors at the hospital where the victim, Mr. Bukerol was brought said the guy was lucky. The knife used was somehow blocked by a lower rib. This is Pompey Alcuna reporting for Channel 4, live, from Sorsogon, Sorsogon.

GINA Thank God, for that! And now, we go to Davao.

FRED Johnny Paraiso is our reporter in Davao. Johnny, you're on.

JOHNNY Thank you, Fred, Gina. It's generally peaceful here too, Fred. Polling places closed here at five this afternoon, with most people saying Mahalina would surely be number one. Rusty Kapunan, former secretary of interior and local government and now campaign manager of presidential candidate Marshall Dimalasa, whom we accidentally bumped into at the APO View hotel here claimed, however that nothing is over until it's over. He was, of course, referring to Dimalasa as the surprise winner. "I have full confidence that the people will rally behind the Moral Crusade," he said. "That means more votes for Dimalasa. Just wait until all the votes are counted and you'll see," Kapunan assured his listeners. This is Johnny Paraiso, reporting for Channel 4, in Davao City.

FRED I really like the guts of Kapunan, Gina. Hope he is right this time.

GINA What do you mean?

FRED Never mind... And now we have an interesting development from the palace of His Eminence Cardinal Pedro Alingasa. Cecille Rustan, our reporter is there. Cecille you're on!

CECILLE Thank you, Fred, Gina. His Eminence, Cardinal Pedro Alingasa, the powerful voice of the Church, known at times as more of a politician than the man of the cloth that he is, lashed earlier today at what he calls "the massive fraud that characterized the present presidential elections." Here is a clip of my interview with His Eminence, at four-thirty this afternoon at his palace.

CECILLE Your Eminence, what do you think of the presidential elections that were just concluded today?

HIS EMINENCE It was characterized by fraud, massive vote buying and all sorts of foolishness. Compared to past presidential elections, this one is unprecedented. It must be the work of Mammon. For at this time, gambling lords, drug syndicates and economic saboteurs are involved. I, together with our brothers and sisters in Christ must condemn these highly condemnable acts. As in the 2nd Epistle of the Book of Peter in the Holy Scriptures, Chapter 2, Verse 22, 'The dog is turned to his own vomit again and the sow is washed to her wallowing in the mire.'" This is Cecille Rustan reporting from the Palace of His Eminence Cardinal Pedro Alingasa for Channel 4.

GINA We sought all presidential candidates for an interview about the conduct of the elections but unfortunately not one, repeat, not one could be found by our reporters.

FRED I think there is only one explanation to that, Gina. The rigors of the campaign must have exhausted all their energies. In war, they call it "battle fatigue."

GINA Right. But anyway, we are still lucky to have been accommodated by one of the most attractive yet humble personalities in this campaign. She is Claudia Palomos Davide, the wife of presidential candidate Serafin Andolana

Davide of the administration party. Roxanne Cortez was there at the Davide mansion in Forbes Park.

ROXANNE Ma'am, so very nice of you to accommodate us.

CLAUDIA That's ok with me, Roxanne. Pin is with his party mates in a caucus right now. If I can be of help, I'll try.

ROXANNE Thank you, Ma'am. What do you think of your husband's chances, right now?

CLAUDIA As his wife, I feel confident that he will make it. But if it's God's will that he won't, then I will accept it.

ROXANNE You have been deeply involved in your husband's campaign. You must be exhausted although I can clearly see that you aren't. You look absolutely fresh and young as ever!

CLAUDIA Thank you for your compliment. Yes, I was really deeply involved. But I've been used to that, you know. When you get to assume that role someday, my advice to you Roxanne is make sure you get sleep regularly even on the road and always drink a glass of milk at breakfast time.

ROXANNE Wow... Thank you Ma'am, I'll remember that. Would you like to say something, anything at all especially to our viewers?

CLAUDIA Yes, thank you. To all our friends who believe and voted for my husband, I thank you very much for casting your votes for him. I've been with Pin Davide for many years and I can say with great pride that he is a kind-hearted man who never forgets his obligations to his family and his constituency. Thank you again.

ROXANNE This is Roxanne Cortez reporting for Channel 4 in Forbes Park, Metro Manila.

GINA This is an update on the violence three days ago, along Congressional Road in front of the gate of the House of Representatives where 13 demonstrators died and two police officers were killed. Robin Bagis is our reporter on the beat.

BAGIS Thank you, Gina. The leaders of the demonstrators last Thursday are very indignant and have accused the authorities of police brutality and murder. I am in front of this funeral parlor for the wake of the 13 dead demonstrators. As you can see, the whole population of the metropolis seems to be in mourning and angry.

FRED How about the two police officers that died?

BAGIS That is the mystery in this tragedy, Fred. Nobody in the police department seems to know where their bodies are. My interviews along this line proved to be an exercise in futility.

FRED Have we established who started the shooting or is it a bombing?

BAGIS No reliable report on that too, Fred. We confirmed shots came from all directions after the police sprayed water cannons at the demonstrators. Immediately after, came the body count... 13 demonstrators and two police officers confirmed dead. But as I said earlier, the bodies of the two police officers are nowhere to be found.

GINA Any new information about the bombing of the demonstrators against charter change?

BAGIS Nothing on that too, Gina. We interviewed the police director of the Metropolitan Police Force who said they are still in the middle of their investigation. He assured us though that they are doing their best and everything is under control.

GINA Fred?

FRED It appears there is no end to all these demonstrations, Gina. In Mindanao, people are demonstrating for an independent republic. In the Visayas, they are demonstrating against central government dominance. Here in Luzon, people are demonstrating against almost everything, from graft and corruption to traffic and what have you.

GINA It looks like we can never move forward, Fred. It looks like it's always backwards for us. Well, what else is new?

FRED From the chaos in our streets, we shall now move on to the peace and quiet of our mountains. To all our friends in the indigenous community, we offer our condolences to the passing away of the Supreme Datu of the House of Agyu. The Supreme Datu Josephus Sibugong died yesterday at around three o'clock in his sleep, in his abode in the high mountains of Mindanao. He was 97 years old.

GINA For those who are not familiar with the Supreme Datu of the twelve tribes of the House of Agyu, he brokered many peace pacts between some of his tribes and the government and between some Muslim rebel groups and the government. Datu Josephus Sibugong was a colorful figure in many Malacanang affairs in the past that honored him for his peace initiatives and wise rule over his people. The House of Agyu is the center of power and arbiter of tribal conflicts among all the indigenous peoples that thrive in the mountains and the riverbanks in Mindanao. Katrina Avila filed this report last night.

KATRINA It took us practically four and a half hours on horseback to reach this beautiful mountain where the kingdom of the House of Agyu sits and where the body of Datu Josephus Sibugong now rests. The coffin in which his remains are temporarily laid to rest is actually a hard, round log, cut in half and hallowed in the middle. According to their tradition, the Supreme Datu just like any man in the tribe will be buried facing east so he could see the sunrise and let his soul come back to his farm in the early morning. The mourners you see around the coffin are some chieftains of his many tribes and close relatives. The wailing and shouting as you can also see and hear are part of the ritual for the dead. Some fainted earlier. Beside me is the heir of the Supreme Datu, Datu Tomasing Labaongon. He will be crowned the next Supreme Datu of the House of Agyu by the Council of Elders after the burial. Sir, could you tell us of the legacy that your uncle left you and your plans for your people?

LABAONGON The Supreme Datu of the House of Agyu was a man of peace but he died a very frustrated man. Immediately before he died, he felt that his people had been treated worse than the Indians in North America. While most of Indian lands were treated as reservations, ours are claimed by land grabbers and taken away from us, with the help and consent of the government.

KATRINA I am sorry to hear that, Sir. So what are your plans in the near future for your people?

LABAONGON My uncle told me immediately before his death, that the House of Agyu must not allow itself to be used anymore by the government.

KATRINA We've been informed that you were invited to grace the inaugural of the incoming president on June 30. Will you pay the courtesy at least in honor of your uncle who had always been invited and attended all inaugurals in the past?

LABAONGON That was the glorious past—today is the miserable present. From here on, we will not honor this government, the Moros whom the government had treated like spoiled brats, the land grabbers and the capitalists here who felled our trees and grabbed our lands. We will declare all these lands our own patrimony, the heritage from our great, great ancestor Agyu, the Supreme Datu of all supreme datus before he ascended to Nelendangan, our heavenly paradise. That is his will and legacy to us—passed from many generations, with the blessings of the Highest Diwata, our Supreme God.

KATRINA This is Katrina Avila with her crew reporting for Channel 4 from the House of Agyu in the mountains of Mindanao.

GINA Let's have our station break. Don't go away, we'll be back.

Both sides of the road leading to the ancestral home of Mahalina were clogged with all sorts of vehicles, bumper to bumper. A traffic gridlock alert was declared in the entire area. Cameras were everywhere. A news helicopter hovered above. Well-wishers of all types and persuasions lined the street with their placards and streamers, proclaiming victory and congratulations. In the foyer and in the wide lawn, refreshments flowed endlessly while entertainers from the movie industry regaled the victor with their songs, dances and antics.

At a corner of the wide foyer, Mahalina in his undershirt slouched on a large leather chair. He had a heavy lidded look. A big burly man was massaging his back. In front of him, on her shorts and knees, a woman in spaghetti top, large dangling earrings and lips painted dark red, was pedicuring the toenails of his right leg on top of her lap. Mahalina's left leg was strung over the arm of his big leather chair.

Around him was his task force with their folders and pens on the ready. Fatso Santos, who had been briefing Mahalina on the latest election results, was beginning to get jittery. The cheers and applauses outside were getting louder and more frequent. Mahalina was getting distracted.

"Mr. President…" Fatso Santos almost shouted above the din.

"Sonnamagun. Tell those people there to shut up!" Mahalina barked. "And get me another shot!" One of the burly men behind him darted out of the premises.

"In Eastern Visayas, it's 73 percent, Sir. In Western Visayas, 78, in Central Visayas, 67 percent, Sir, all in your favor, Sir."

"Hmmm."

"In Northern Mindanao, it's 86. In Southern Mindanao, it's 89 percent, all in your favor, Sir."

"Metro Manila?"

"I already reported that, Sir."

"Metro Manila?"

"89 percent, Sir, as I reported earlier."

"Northern Luzon?"

"Yes, Sir, as I also reported earlier, it's 82 percent for Northern Luzon, 78 percent for Southern Luzon, yes Sir, as I already reported earlier, all in your favor."

Silence.

"Sir, have you reviewed our proposal for the final line-up of your Cabinet?" Fatso's voice was on guard.

"Go."

"Actually, Sir, the last proposal was for the second batch. You already approved the first batch."

"Hmmm."

"For the second batch, Sir, for the position of Secretary of Trade and Industry, we propose Dr. Aristotle Tongas of the International Investment House. He has a Ph.D. from Wharton School of Business."

"Wharton?"

"Yes, Sir. Wharton, one of the top..."

"Never mind."

"For the Secretary of Finance, Ferdie Tancho is nominating..."

"No problem."

"Ferdie Tancho is also nominating Winthrop Lopez to the position of Secretary of Environment and Natural..."

"No problem."

"Robustiano Toledo is also being nominated by Ferdie Tancho for the position of ..."

"No problem."

"Sir, but not until one year later..."

"What?"

"Because according to law no defeated candidate could be appointed to..."

"Explain that to Ferdie."

"Pardon, Sir?"

"I said, explain that to Ferdie Tancho!"

Silence. Mahalina raised his left hand to receive a fresh glass wrapped in tissue paper. He handed over the empty one with his right.

"Our third proposal, Sir, is in the folder before you, marked 03 which lists the big investors in this campaign. Opposite their names are the business opportunities they would like to go into during your presidency. The amounts..."

"Leave that to Ong."

"Ong?"

"Tancho's link to me," Mahalina growled, motioning for another glass. When this was handed over to him, he emptied it in one gulp. Standing up, he staggered and almost fell back on the chair if not for an aide who took his waist and arm to steady him. Wiping the streaks of saliva in his mustache with the back of his hand, Mahalina scanned the faces around him, without a flicker of recognition, as if they were another bunch of anonymous insects from outer space that had ventured in. Placing an arm over the shoulder of his aide, Mahalina ambled out.

When they saw Mahalina approach, the crowd erupted in applause. The conductor's baton suddenly rose in the air then swooped down, as the local singing ensemble sang Mahalina's favorite love song, "Love is a Many Splendored Thing."

As soon as Mahalina was out of earshot, Pangilinan clicked his fingers. "That's one big pro-factor for the President. No hassle, no argument, no debate. Fast, fast, fast decisions especially when he's tanked up!"

No one noticed the sneer on Pat Gan-Alfonso's face. Cheers of congratulations and high fives filled the wide sala. Even Pat forgot all about Pangilinan's remarks, overwhelmed by the accolades for her plum position as Secretary of the Cabinet and Head of the Presidential Management Staff. As for Fatso, he was now the "Little President."

"Okay, your excellencies," Fatso quipped, turning to his colleagues in the task force. "Again my sincerest congratulations. It goes without saying this country needs you as Mahal needs you. So, back to our assignments tomorrow, same time, same place. Main agenda, the inaugural."

Pat Gan-Alfonso felt for the key in her purse after punching the button for the 27th floor.

Hastily, she opened her purse and looked at herself at its tiny mirror, flipping a few strands of stray hair upward. Smiling at what she saw, Pat got out of the elevator, inserted the plastic key to Room 2704, got in, bolted the door, then hollered, "I'm home!"

"I'm in here! I'll be with you in a minute," Noli de Leon hollered back from the bathroom.

Kicking off her heels, Pat slumped on the sofa, felt for her Virginia Slims and lighted a stick.

"There you are!" Noli emerged in his bathrobe and sidled beside Pat. "You must be tired, brainy beauty. Let me massage your neck, your shoulders and your hmm..." Noli sidled closer, playfully running his fingers on Pat's back.

"Yeah, a little tired. But the massage could come later," Pat said, adjusting herself on the sofa and brushing the running fingers aside. "By the way, where have you been in the last four days?" Pat blew a smoke, inhaling deeply.

Noli did not answer as he stood to get his own Winston on the study table. Lighting one, he strode over by the window of the condo facing the lighted boulevard below.

"Well, didn't I ask you where you were in the last four days?" Pat asked again.

"Well, I thought I'd made myself clear, that I am obligated to make this monthly ritual of visiting the kids..."

"The kids? Or is it Lucy?"

"C'mon, Pat. We don't have to go over this again, okay? Otherwise, if it is Lucy, then why are we here in this condo for the last eight months?"

Pat didn't answer. Crushing her cigarette butt in an ashtray, she stood and switched on the coffeemaker in the kitchen. *Why take up this issue all over again? Is it because of Lucy? Why, I don't really care about the bitch. What do I care about? Noli de Leon?*

"Pat," Noli whispered, cupping his hands around her breasts, his front pressed against her rear. "Let's not quarrel over this same thing, okay? What's important is that we can make our own fires burning together, eh?"

Pat stared at the ceiling. It was some 25 minutes ago when Noli really burned her, again and again. *And now he is snoring like the big fat pig that is his belly. He was not like this before. I mean his belly. He was trim. Haven't I pointed this out to him? But he always says with a chuckle his belly is not his virtue...it is his ability to make a full woman out of me! And he is right. Isn't he?*

But aside from the burning side of it, Pat readily acknowledged that it was Noli de Leon who taught her how to maneuver in the intricacies of the bureaucracy. And not only that but also in the art of power play, long before they got themselves together in bed. True, she was a magna cum laude graduate in psychology from the exclusive Jesuit institution in the country, but as Noli kept on reminding her, it was not the psychology of it but the actual exercise of power that must be observed, analyzed and taken by the bull of its horns.

"Are you still awake, brainy beauty?" Noli rolled over, his fingertips tiptoeing over her.

Pat looked at herself in the bathroom mirror. She wasn't exactly ravishing but she was "brainy beauty," a rare combination highly regarded with awe and envy and sometimes fear in the bureaucracy. And didn't she have a voice that everybody found inviting, not to mention her ability to articulate in plain language complex concepts and issues? Once fully dressed and on her usual two-inch heels, she was still the woman most men would like to bed. And that was her great advantage. While they waited for some signs of entry, she used them.

"Hey, brainy beauty, what's taking you so long in there? C'mon, its breakfast time!" Noli hollered.

One of the advantages of modern life was—you could have your meals delivered to your front door any time of the day by just a phone call. No more knife to slice a bulb of onion or a piece of tomato. No more cooking. No more husband to tell you what kind of breakfast or lunch or dinner he would like you to prepare. And by gad, wasn't that the reason why she had to split with her husband? Why, wasn't marrying that spoiled brat the biggest mistake of her life?

"I'm sorry for the outburst last night," Pat said, sipping her hot chocolate.

"Which outburst? The outburst about Lucy or the outburst in bed?" Noli winked in mischief, swallowing a piece of pancake dipped in syrup.

"The outburst about Lucy, you pig!" Pat wagged her tongue, pinching Noli's thigh under the table.

"Ouch!" Noli uttered an exaggerated cry, pressing her hand upward. "So, what's the latest?"

Pat finished her chocolate as she lighted a slim.

"It's this Fatso and this academic that are really getting on my nerves."

"Well, I know about Fatso. But how about this academic?"

"Well, this academic... he thinks he's the greatest thinker since Plato and keeps on concocting jokes about Mahal that really get my goat."

"Why, is he in a position to threaten yours? I think that should be the fundamental question." Noli swallowed another slice of pancake.

"No, I don't think so. He's new in the game, that's why I think he won't last. He's actually just trying to attract attention."

"So what about Fatso? What's his latest scheme?"

Pat dragged on her slim. "Want some?"

Noli de Leon shook his head as he reached for another Winston.

"Well, to my surprise, he invited Ong to our meeting yesterday. They were exchanging furtive glances all the time as we were discussing sensitive issues. Ong, I understand, represents the Chamber."

"There's a lapse in analysis there, Pat. Nobody represents the chamber in the political ballgame." He lighted his cigarette. "In commerce and trade, yes, but definitely no, not in politics."

"What makes you think that?"

"You know, the chamber of short names is a very united group when it comes to wheeling and dealing in commerce and trade, both here and abroad. It is also a kind of syndicate that extends unlimited loans to its members. But when it comes to investments in politics, it is, to each his own. In fact, individual members try all the time to outdo each other when it comes to making political connections and collecting their own chips afterwards. Believe me, we'd studied this long time ago and President Rosales himself knows about it. He knows too, how Tancho wormed himself around and managed to have access at the top and stayed there."

"Is that why the President is able to control each one of them, contain them?"

"True, true, true." Noli de Leon nodded. "In the same manner you cannot control the chamber if it comes to that. As I said, to each his own in the political front."

"So, you are saying Ong is acting on his own, independent of the chamber, but in conspiracy with Fatso?"

"That could be the only explanation," Noli de Leon said, crushing his cigarette in the ashtray. "What about Fatso? Has he given any sign that Mahalina knows about Ong in your group?"

"Beyond what I said so far, I could not tell. But I heard many times Mahal say that when it comes to financial matters, he'd be on top of it."

"Hmmm," Noli de Leon hummed, lighting another cigarette. "Will I be free to monitor this info to President Rosales?"

Pat thought about that for a while.

"Just a moment, Noli... What's your personal plan?" Pat asked, lighting another slim.

"Well, I decided to go into private practice after President Rosales and probably some small business venture on the side."

"What about us?" Pat asked, flipping ash.

"My brainy beauty! I'm totally amazed...that such a question should come from you!" Noli said, incredulously. "Pat, you know you are more in love with your own career than with anything else, that is why you can't have a lasting relationship with anybody and I mean with any man. That is why you are separated. That may be true with me, too..."

She pinched him again on the thigh. Both of them cackled.

"Well, I think there is no harm," Pat said after a while. "You may tell your Boss. Anyway, your President will soon be out and mine takes his place."

"Thanks Pat. I owe you one."

"No, Noli. We're now even," Pat smiled, reaching across to wipe some morsels from the lips of Noli with the tip of her forefinger. Closing his eyes, he opened his mouth and extended his tongue.

It was five o'clock in the morning in the presidential study. President Rosales read on.

> After the shortest count in the history of presidential elections in the country, the COMELEC last night declared Juancho "Mahal" Mahalina the winner over five other presidential candidates. Mahalina garnered 14 million votes, nine million votes more than his nearest rival Serafin Andolana Davide, the administration party candidate.
>
> "It was the shortest count," the COMELEC Chairman said. "Mahalina simply ran through the race with nobody immediately behind him except his own dust."
>
> Asked after the declaration, Mahalina, obviously without sleep but totally euphoric, simply exclaimed— "Love conquers all!"
>
> As the news of Mahalina's victory were aired on TV and heard over radio, throngs of people mostly of the D & E crowd began to troop toward the ancestral home of Mahalina. Asked, one said, he needed a job. Another said, 'Mahal promised us three meals a day. I brought my family along to witness that promise come true.' Another said, 'I just want to see my idol.'
>
> Mahalina ran for president as the champion of the poor, the downtrodden and the marginalized. "Mahal is love for the people," was his battle cry. "Elect me President and I will give you my love."
>
> Meanwhile, feisty Naomi Ganzon Santolan railed and ranted. Interviewed as she was leaving her campaign HQ late last night, the erstwhile only woman presidential candidate vowed to file charges against the COMELEC. "Those harebrained sanctimonious scum bugs," Santolan declared. "They ought to go back to elementary school for their lapses in arithmetic. All they know is addition, addition and addition for others but subtraction for my votes." Santolan further raged. "I was cheated again," she sneered. "But this time they cannot get away with it just like that. There will be no stopping my asteroid until Naomi Ganzon Santolan becomes President of this republic!"

In his mansion at the plush village of Forbes Park, Serafin Andolana Davide also raged. "The COMELEC came out with numbers that are impossible to reconcile. How could I, the administration candidate, with most of the congressmen and mayors supporting me, get as low as only a little over three million votes? And nine million votes behind Mahalina? I have received all kinds of calls from hundreds of thousands from friends here and abroad asking me what I would do next and they said they would support me 1,000 percent. In the following days expect millions of my supporters to march to the COMELEC to file their protest on my behalf."

Efforts to locate the other presidential candidates proved futile until press time. Perennial presidential candidate Vicente delos Ajos, "Lolo Inting" to his fans, interviewed in his home simply said: "The only reason the COMELEC disqualified me is because I am the only man who could beat Mahalina. Everything was pre-cooked, that's why. (*COMELEC/ p. 18*)."

Before he could turn to page 18 of the banner story, President Rosales noted the headline at the top right column— "Putto tops Senatorial Race." The president read on.

Comic Humphrey Bogart Putto topped the senatorial race over 75 senatorial candidates; the COMELEC announced last night. Putto, of the popular TV noontime show *Goodah* has been predicted all along to top the race. The actual count showed his votes went beyond the wildest of expectations. For every 100 votes counted, he garnered no less than 85 votes. That makes Putto even more popular than the new President-elect Juancho Mahalina."

According to the COMELEC, Putto and the ten others who topped the polls will be proclaimed within the next two days. The twelfth slot is currently under protest. This is being protested by senatorial candidate Rudirico Salazar who claims his votes from his town alone would more than offset his rival's lead of 885 votes. These votes are also under protest.

Former executive secretary Robustiano Toledo of the Rosales cabinet, many are surprised, is at the tail end of the senatorial derby. Like Putto, Toledo also ran under the party of Mahalina but unlike Putto whose noontime show had been consistently number one in the ratings, Toledo's alleged life-story as a rebel hero of some sort, depicted in a quickie movie flopped at the tilts. Obviously, no one associated the rebel-hero Commander Ruby to the real former executive secretary and senatorial candidate Robustiano "Ruby" Toledo. (*Putto/ p.18*).

Was it his karma or was it simply bad luck for Toledo? President Rosales muttered silently, shaking his head in disgust. Leaning forward, he pressed a button.

"Yes sir!" An aide poked his head at the door. "Call PA Destino and please tell him to organize a transition team for a smooth turnover, ASAP but NLT 1200 hours, Friday, the 10th."

"Anything else, Sir?"

"That will be all for now."

K a Lulu, a.k.a. Task Force Commander Lourdes Dalisay once again looked at the map pinned to the wall beside her. "Is everything clear to all of us?" she asked, addressing the seven men and another woman in front of her. This was the ninth day after her meeting with Ka Roger and Ka Alex at the Luneta Park. Five of the men were directly under her, the sixth represented Ka Alex of the People's Watch Brigade and the seventh, was Ka Piccio, the assassin and point man of Ka Rollie. The woman, Ka Vangie was a former classmate and now her aide. The place of meeting was a safe house in Montalban, Rizal.

"Why don't you go over it again, Ka Lulu," Ka Piccio suggested, "just to make sure?"

The rest nodded in agreement as Ka Lulu laughed.

The laughter came out in innocent little spurts, like those of a grateful child after a feast of mother's milk. It was the kind of laughter that signified assent, in recognition of the fact that nothing should be left to chance and, therefore, there was no room for impatience. She knew these men were hard and brutal, but all that, should be reinforced with a clear understanding of the mission at hand, if that mission were to succeed.

Ka Lulu went over the details again. After some 45 minutes, she reminded her hearers: "Never forget that I'll be timing everything. If for one reason or another, you won't hear my three signals, that simply tells you that we may still have a few seconds 'til the next green light. From there, we proceed, as in the first scenario. Got it?"

There was no doubt from the hard and brutal men in front of her that Ka Lulu was a master of her craft. The details she described earlier were exactly the same.

"What about you and Ka Piccio? Would you have..."

"You'll be surprised, Ka Berting," Ka Piccio interrupted. "Ka Lulu can drive that thing like Evel Knievel."

Ka Berting who was worried earlier now laughed with the others.

"What's the cargo, Ka Lulu?" except for Ka Piccio who knew, everyone wanted to ask the same question but it was Ka Polding who finally did.

"I have strict instructions from the Chairman to keep it to myself. This is one delivery that should be treated 'on a need to know' basis. I hope you understand, Ka Polding."

Silence followed. Ka Lulu then ripped off the map from the wall and rolled it swiftly in her hands, Ka Piccio lighting its other end with his cigarette lighter. As the roll of Manila paper burned halfway, Ka Lulu slowly dropped it on the floor.

Everyone watched as the rest of the map consumed itself and as Ka Lulu pulverized the ashes with her boot.

T he new lecture hall was filled to capacity. By special request addressed to the department chairman, another public address system was installed outside so those who could not be accommodated inside would be able to listen to the last part of the lecture series in "Contemporary Politics and Politicians."

Outside, non-enrollees of the course, professors, instructors and the curious who heard of the interesting lectures, came and found themselves squatting on dry grass and sitting on benches under the acacia trees that hovered above Romulo Hall, the new lecture hall that was "borrowed" for the occasion.

"Good afternoon, class."

"Good afternoon, Sir!"

"This afternoon is the last session of the series of seven lectures on the subject entitled, 'Contemporary Politics and Politicians.' As your professorial lecturer I must say my experience with you has been a most enriching one. I hope you also feel the same way. My only regret is we don't have enough time. "Contemporary Politics and Politicians" is such an intriguing subject, it never dulls the mind. Your incisive reactions further deepened our understanding of its complexities.

"I will focus my summary today on the subject by looking at the institutional backdrop against which contemporary politics and politicians operate and the necessity of conflict to establish a state of dynamism or 'stagnancy" among the protagonists representing the five aspects of politics as you revealed them to me."

The professor paused, scanning his notes.

"To begin with, let us backtrack a little to the five aspects of politics and see first their original aims and ends. The aim of Governance, our first aspect, is to institute control otherwise its end is chaos or revolution. Thus, when governance is shaken, the usual alibi of politicians is 'everything is under control.'

"The aim of Business, our second aspect, is money, otherwise if there is no money, its end is impoverishment or bankruptcy. Thus, when business slumps, businessmen worry, knowing that 'if there is no money, there is no honey.'

"The aim of Armed Force, the third aspect, is to kill the enemy, otherwise it ends being killed by the enemy.

"The aim of Religion, our fourth aspect, is heaven, otherwise its end is hell. Priests and pastors schooled in old traditional religious doctrine always preach of heaven or hell as a reward or a punishment after death. The more contemporary ones are advancing the idea that there could also be heaven or hell on earth.

"The aim of Entertainment, the fifth and last aspect, is amusement but it seems to have no end in contemporary times. The clown of olden times who failed to make the king laugh ended up with his head cut off. But in contemporary times, laughter and sorrow have become one and the same. People pay their way to the theatre, plus automatic charge for 'amusement tax,' please note, to be entertained or amused even if the movie or film shows a virgin being slapped, kicked and raped. But note immediately, that the spectacle just shown is all make-believe and the people viewing the spectacle know that. They also know that the sexy starlet acting the role of the victim is paid handsomely for her talent. So, everybody is happy and amused. As those in Tinseltown would say, 'That's entertainment!'"

The professor scanned the faces of some of his female students, apparently to appeal for their understanding, fully aware that at this time and age, women have become overly gender-sensitive. He didn't see what he was looking for. Some nodded their heads, some pretended to write, some exchanged whispers, about what, he wasn't sure.

"So far, I attempted to draw a very simple description of each aspect of politics in the hope that you will always remember them outside of this classroom," the professor continued. "If we can associate as quickly the aim and end to each group, force, party, whatever, then I think this will lessen to a great degree some of our mental meanderings at times," the professor paused. No reaction.

"More often than not, it is in the process of moving from aim to end or what happens in between that we cannot anymore be simple, that we cannot help but be confronted with complexity. For example, Governance whose aim is control or its end is chaos, has set up a massive infrastructure of control known as the bureaucracy, which if seen from the national perspective, starts with the president, vice-president, governors and mayors, not to mention the many 'vices' in between. Don't forget the justices and judges and the senators and congressmen, who are all part of the same bureaucracy, parallel vertically and horizontally on both sides of the totem pole. Religion is no different. The Roman Catholic Church for example, is a bureaucracy that is even tighter and more rigid than any government bureaucracy, so far on earth. From the Holy Pope, to the cardinals, to the bishops, to the priests, they are all under tight and rigid control by the Vatican.

"Business is also no different. The recent mergers of giant corporations are establishing mega-bureaucracies patterned after OPEC, WTO and the like to corner and control global commerce and trade. Armed Force represented by the military establishment of any country, is another bureaucracy that demands rigid discipline, following the chain of command from the top brass of generals down to the foot soldiers or its dogs of war.

"However, please note: the more rigid and tighter the control, the more ineffective the bureaucracy will become. And if no damage control is applied, the system becomes sick of bureau-pathology and will be suffering from bureau-pathological woes. If not further checked, it will end in chaos, that is, if it is not yet comatose.

"Now, compared to the other four, Entertainment is some kind of a mutant. For by its very nature, it is individualistic or ego-centered. Associations like actor's guilds and similar such groups never become strong or influential because of the giant egos of its individual members. Anyway, it is not surprising that the only solid organizations or groups associated with Entertainment are those that give awards, which is obvious, isn't it?

"As I stressed in past lectures, the major force binding all bureaucracies is the system of rules that practically cover every conduct and behavior of their members. In Governance for example, if you break the rules you either end up in jail or you don't get elected or reelected. In Business if you break the rules, you either lose your creditors or you go bankrupt. In Armed Force, you either get court marshaled or in olden times sent to die by musketry. In Religion either burned at the stake in olden times or threatened with excommunication in modern times.

"In Entertainment, there are no rules to rationally explain the process from aim to end. Because it is the masses, I repeat, the masses who make the unwritten rules or emotional judgments. Once the masses are no longer amused by your antics, they'd soon stop buying tickets to your movies or cease viewing your TV show or listening to your radio drama.

"Now, all this leads us to the question—how will all these groups become associated or related with politics?"

The professor paused. No reaction.

"Looking at all this from the larger society as a whole, the answer to the question is intrusion or intervention that causes the connection. Business, for example, once it intrudes or intervenes in governance and influences the latter, Business starts becoming an aspect of politics. When Business wheels and deals to get a contract from Governance and Governance grants the contract, then Business becomes an aspect of politics. When the military-industrial complex puts pressure on Governance to buy more arms and Governance provides the money, both become aspects of politics. When Religion requires its faithful to vote solid for one candidate and the latter once elected provides some concessions, then Religion becomes an aspect of politics. When Entertainment takes advantage of its mass appeal and let actors and actresses run for public office, then Entertainment becomes an aspect of politics.

"Please note immediately that any of the other four only becomes an aspect of politics if and I say if, there is a positive response from Governance. The positive response could lead to either a happy union if the majority of the voters will benefit from it, or to a conspiracy of some sort, if the majority of the populace suffer as a result. If there is no positive response and the pressure continues, then conflict arises.

"Conflict is healthy if it strengthens Governance but it is fatal if Governance could not contain or control conflict, otherwise any, or some or all of the others will dominate and take control of Governance."

The professor paused. "Any questions so far?"

For the first time, the professor noticed no hands were immediately raised. Either the students were asleep (but most were staring at him) or stunned by his statements. Maybe they were still trying to put heads and tails in their proper places.

"Oh, yes," the professor acknowledged the student in crew cut over some seven others who finally raised their hands.

"Sir, I am Wilfred Alaban. I am intrigued by the way you simplify the concepts of aims and ends of the five aspects of politics. They are easy to remember and hard to forget. However, if they are really that simple, then how come they have become so complex?"

His classmates roared.

"That is why you are intrigued, so with me, so with your classmates, that's why they just roared." Laughter followed. "Do you know why Plato's *Ideal Republic*, conceived some 200 years before Christ, is up to this day still easy to remember and hard to forget? The answer is simple, because Plato made it simple. If you recall, the *Ideal Republic*, according to Plato, should only have five types of citizens, each with a very clear and simple function. The philosopher-king to govern, the businessmen to undertake commerce and trade, the slaves to do labor, the soldiers to protect the state and the women to bear children. Plato really had no choice because his concept was confined to the city-state of only about 2000 to 3000 people during his time. Brilliant as he was, Plato failed to anticipate the Malthusian theory of population explosion, no doubt perpetuated by the women whom he assigned to bear children. Although, I say immediately there was really nothing new to that since the mandate to multiply the human race had been given as early as the Old Testament. Thus, when the republic is expanded to millions of citizens with their own varied needs and desires, you really have no choice except to expand the apparatuses of Governance or things will get out of control and chaos or revolution sets in.

"Sir, Sir!" arms shot up in the air.

"Sir, I am Mercedez Alvarez. My question is this. Can Governance not regulate TV, theatres and radio stations from sappy, corny and inane presentations? Can Entertainment be encouraged instead, to advance education-oriented programs to minimize the masses from becoming totally obsessed with the world of make-believe?"

"Now, that is kind of difficult because it is the masses that dictate what the TV, theatre or radio should air or show and not the other way around. I don't want to sound cynical but there is some kind of truism in what one wit has said: that TV is for the lazy, movie is for the lonely and radio is for the barrio. On the other hand, there is some sense in considering the high ratings that, what you call, the sappy, corny and inane presentations obtain all the time. The People's Republic of China is very strict about all these things but it appears this is not our bowl of rice over here. Oh yes, I agree with you fully of the need to go into educational programs but I see no light in the horizon that can make that happen in the immediate future, unless the masses themselves change. On the other hand, it is not farfetched to say that a great number of the so-called educated class also find amusement in the sappy, the corny and the inane."

"Sir, I am Lita Ocampo. Which of the four aspects outside of Governance is best prepared to establish a sort of happy union with Governance or if Governance itself becomes totally comatose, as you mentioned earlier, could take over and establish some kind of stability if not dynamism in politics?"

The professor paused for a few seconds before he answered.

"It's kind of difficult considering the many variables to be factored in. But generally speaking based on what we have learned so far, we can say those in Business, Armed Force and Religion are better prepared because they know where they are in the bureaucracy and have been trained to respect authority. You cannot say the same for those in Entertainment. In that department, everyone is a star."

"Sir! Sir! Sir!"

"Okay, one last question," the professor declared after checking his watch. "We have a few minutes left. Okay, the young lady in pigtails is recognized."

"Sir, I am Marisse Rayosin. Sir, before I ask my question, let me say, on behalf of our class, that your lectures are really very enlightening and very entertaining. Thank you, Sir."

Her classmates roared in approval.

"Thank you, too."

"Sir, if I may ask... what is your technique in making complex issues sound so simple? As one of my classmates said earlier, they become easy to remember and hard to forget?"

Her classmates roared again.

"Sir," the young lady continued as the fracas subsided. "Sir, I'm not flattering you, huh. Anyway, we don't get grades in this class..."

"Let's give Sir an A-plus!" a voice hollered from the back, as others laughed.

"Okay, I don't give grades but I am required to certify to your attendance equivalent to one credit unit."

"Hurrah!" the students cheered.

"So, Sir?" Miss Rayosin persisted.

"All right, to be honest I don't really have any technique. It's just that I like pursuing issues especially with young and eager students like you. However, while I don't have a technique or a methodology, I have a formula."

The professor then went to the board and wrote the following: "From KISS to KISS."

"The first KISS means 'Keep It Simple, Stupid!' I know most of you are familiar with this kiss. This one is some kind of an admonition for people who refuse to see things in their natural, unadulterated and elegant state. Worse, some people make simple things complicated. The original eventually becomes a fake, that is, what used to be a natural beauty is transformed into a mask of make-up. Many quarrels ensue because some people make mountains out of a molehill. This is the context around which the first KISS may be better understood. The second or the next KISS stands for 'Keep It Sizzling, Sweetheart!' When things get muddled, issues befuddled, or relationships entangled, it always pays to go back to simplicity, to the basic, to the classic, to the undress, to the chaste, to the natural state of things and keep it there, steaming hot, sizzling as in sizzling steak, sizzling kiss, sizzling love. Taken altogether, that is what is meant by From KISS To KISS, come rain or come shine."

Pablo Tabile turned off his transistor radio. He had surfed through the local station, four Mindanao stations and two Manila stations. He had read the four national two-day old newspapers on top of his sofa table that he bought from his last town visit. All reported that Mahalina won by a landslide and had in fact already been proclaimed winner by the COMELEC.

Tabile smiled to himself, the kind of a wicked smile that spelled victory. He had councilman Cardo Roque finally between his fingers. *The fool..., he thought, I would not call his bluff.*

Tabile stood as he tightened his knuckles. *What does he think of me, another fool?*

Tabile continued pacing the floor. *The bets on carabaos, goats, fighting cocks, rum and beer are nothing. It is his promise not to run against me in the next election—that is the clinching point. Whether he meant that or not and I am inclined to believe he was only faking, I don't really care. It's in the minutes of the meeting. If he won't comply with that, then it's between him and me. And I'll see to it that he eats grass from thereon.*

Tabile peered from his back window to his yard below. Seven of his fighting cocks were ready for the coming fiesta derby. *If he thinks he's a gambler, then let him enjoy that delusion. I had called his bluff and he must be squirming in his balls right now. Well, I have to admit he got more votes than me in the last election and am sure he has raised a lot of funds to fight me in the next. But does he really think he can beat me if he runs for barangay captain?*

Tabile wasn't sure of the answer, as he paced the floor again. *Well, why don't we cross the bridge when we get there? In the meanwhile, why don't we celebrate?*

"Diego!" Tabile hollered as his aide came running from the backyard, circling the house toward the front.

"Yes, Sir!" his loyal aide of 18 years, replied. Diego was about 39, had long ponytailed hair. He had bulging muscles and a long scar that stretched from his right ear to the underside of his Adam's apple and farther down to his torso.

"Prepare the jeep, we're going out."

"Where to, Sir?" Diego asked, as he mounted the driver's seat, adjusting the large army type dagger at the small of his back.

"We'll go to 'Kadugay's Happy Hour' to celebrate," Tabile said, smiling his wicked victory smile. "We'll fetch our friends along the way."

Diego knew who these friends were. They were the three constant companions of Tabile in weddings, cockfights, drinking sessions and in the town's sing-along bars and seedy places. During council meetings, they were inseparable, along with Tabile, of course. They sat on adjacent chairs, they agreed as one, for or against and cast their votes as one, for or against. "Kadugay's Happy Hour" was an extension wing of councilman Cardo Roque's house. This was Roque's version of the town's restaurant, cum bar, cum sport's center where at the middle stood a single billiard table. The bar was located at the far end wall, the seven tables with their chairs, immediately before the bar. It was about three o'clock in the afternoon. Except for two youngsters practicing their skills on the billiard table, there were no other customers as yet. When the local political kingpins arrived, the two youngsters left in a huff.

"Ten beers and two servings of *pina-paitan* (heavily spiced half-cooked meat)!" Tabile bellowed, as soon as he alighted from the jeep. "Dog or goat, Sir?"

"Dog," the four companions chorused, taking their seats with Tabile around one table. Diego took another table, at the back of his master.

"Where's councilman Roque?" Tabile asked the girl serving them.

"He went to town, Sir. He said he'd be back before six o'clock."

160

"Toast, to our victory, my friends!" Tabile raised his bottle. His companions did the same.

It was almost six o'clock. They've each consumed 11 rounds of beer, three servings of *pina-paitan* and several packs of cigarettes.

"One more round!" Tabile ordered.

"I'm sorry, Sir." the girl behind the counter said. "We've run out of beer. But we still have a lot of rum."

"Okay, two bottles, long neck," Tabile drawled, his eyes drooping, his head dangling.

The two large bottles of rum disappeared as swiftly as they came.

"One more round?" Tabile asked, turning to his companions. One head was flat on the table. Another dangled from left to right.

"I think Cap, we have to eh, go. I'm tanked up," his third companion said, gripping his throat to keep himself from vomiting.

"Waiter, eh, waitress," Tabile gestured to the girl. "How much?"

The girl readily handed him a piece of paper.

"Only this much!" Tabile said, sounding incredulous, showing the bill to his companions. "Chicken feed... charge it to my account!"

"But Sir, Councilman Roque's instruction is, all credit is good but we need cash. Please Sir, otherwise, he will deduct this from my salary..."

"You tell that son-of-a-whore boss of yours, I am charging all our orders against what he owes me. Is that clear?" Tabile started to stand. Diego, at his back, took hold of his shoulders, to prevent him from toppling over.

At this point in time, the jeep of Roque screeched to a halt at the front of the place, just before Tabile's jeep.

"What seems to be the problem?" Roque yelled, alighting from his jeep, eyeing Tabile and sensing the predicament of the girl. Roque was obviously inebriated himself, judging from the way he staggered inside. His nostrils flared.

"Oh, my, my saint of the holy dog, my friend, Councilman Cardo Roque, the brilliant chairman of the finance committee!" Tabile bawled. "Just in time, glad you came on time... I just told your waitress here... to charge my orders here against what you owe me!"

"What dog shit are you talking about?"

"What you owe me, my friend."

"Owe you?"

"Remember? You owe me carabaos, goats, fighting cocks, boxes of rum, crates of beer, remember? Mahalina won and won overwhelmingly!" Tabile grinned, his wicked grin of victory, trickles of saliva squirting from his mouth. "And what we ordered here... is chicken feed against what you owe me!" Tabile spat on the floor.

"I think, you're full of dog shit," Roque said, his eyes boring in at Tabile's. "Everybody knows there is nothing official yet about Mahalina winning the presidency. He has not even taken his oath of office!"

"You're more than dog shit yourself!" Tabile bellowed, reaching for one of the empty long neck bottles beside him.

But before he could do what he wanted to do, Roque had swung his left arm around Tabile's neck in a stranglehold, his right arm simultaneously whisking the .38 Smith and Wesson revolver from underneath his front shirt, its muzzle rammed directly against Tabile's temple. "You move and you're dead!" Roque said, his voice even.

Nobody moved. The girl who was directly behind the counter testified later, that Diego who was behind his master, swiftly grasped the long hair of Roque, yanked his head upward then downward as he whisked the army dagger from behind the small of his back. Pressing the dagger's serrated blade across Roque's open throat, Diego then hissed into Roque's ear: "You move or you're dead!"

When the girl screamed in panic, she saw the barangay captain's head jerk, an automatic reaction to her screams. That was the precise time Roque pulled the trigger, she said. "The blast was deafening...blood splattered all over the place," the girl continued. "I saw the barangay captain drop on the floor like a log. At the same time, I also saw Diego push and pull his dagger several times across the throat of councilman Roque, like he was sawing the neck of a struggling rooster. Dark blood squirted out in all directions. It was horrible!"

She blocked out immediately after that, she said in her testimony and didn't know what happened next.

The atmosphere was friendly and jubilant when Meandro Destino entered the Third Floor Annex Conference Room of the New Executive Building in the palace compound. This was the second meeting of the two counterpart committees tasked to plan a smooth transition from the old to the new administration. Finding the room filled to capacity, Destino stood by the door, behind some people who were also standing before him. And then he saw her. There at the head table, seven rows from where he stood, Destino could not believe his eyes. *Marissa...what are you doing here!*

Pretending to read through his copy of the program, Destino now and then peeked over the backs and napes of the rows of people in front of him, wondering, *What is she doing here? What is her role here? She's at the head table. Is she representing the new administration?*

"I think, that's about all," Noli de Leon, presidential assistant for internal affairs announced, looking and smiling at 'Marissa'. "Have we missed anything that needs to be looked into?"

"Yeah, I think that's about all, as far as the major items are concerned," 'Marissa' said. "Though we still have to agree on the final guest list and the reception that follows."

Something is amiss here... Destino mumbled to himself. *While the voice is definitely Marissa's, the face, the spectacle, the hair cut too short, the manner of speaking—they're different. Marissa speaks fast. This one talks deliberately with a distinct accent and cadence.*

Destino flipped back to page four of the program. Opposite the name of Noli de Leon, was the name Patricia Gan-Alfonso, chairperson of the committee representing the new administration. There was no Marissa among the nine members indicated therein. *Could I be mistaken? What does that hyphen after Gan indicate? Is there a connection somewhere?*

"I see your point, of course," Noli de Leon spoke to the woman beside him. "Why don't we schedule those items in tomorrow's meeting? Our last, I hope."

"Fine with me," the woman said. "Any objection from my team? Okay, there seems to be none, so let's agenda the remaining items for tomorrow."

"Let's give a hand to Chairperson Pat Gan-Alfonso and her team," Noli de Leon announced, smiling as he stood, shaking the woman's hand.

Meandro Destino could not believe what he just heard. His first impulse was to leave immediately, but his curiosity took the better part of him, until he found himself heading towards Noli de Leon and the woman.

"Hi, there Boss," Noli greeted him. "Fine so far, Boss. Meyan, this is Pat, Patricia Gan-Alfonso, chairperson of the counterpart transition committee, representing the Mahalina administration and the incoming boss-lady of the presidential management staff. Pat, this is Dr. Meandro Destino, Meyan to friends, Mean to non-friends. Dr. Destino is first presidential adviser to President Rosales."

"Hi!" the woman greeted him first.

"Hi!" Destino greeted the woman in return.

"Is there really such a thing as 'first' presidential adviser?" Pat Gan-Alfonso asked, pulling down her glasses, her eyes glistening at Noli de Leon and then at Meyan Destino.

"Not really," Destino replied. "I don't know why they've affixed that qualifier to my official title."

"That's because he's A-1," Noli de Leon said, winking at Destino.

"Must be, otherwise he won't be first, right?" Pat acknowledged Noli, smiling as she did.

"Why don't I leave both of you?" Noli de Leon suggested. "I'm sure you would learn from each other, that is, if both of you open up. By the way, Meyan, I'll submit my report after our last meeting tomorrow. I've got to rush." With that, he gathered his notes, stuffed them in his briefcase, smiled at Pat in a certain way, then left.

"Another cup of coffee?" Meyan Destino asked, looking at the empty cup of Pat, after he poured one from the coffeemaker just beside the table.

"Sure," Pat agreed.

"By the way," Meyan said, not too sure if he was going towards the direction in his mind. "By the way, do you have a sister or a twin, perhaps?"

"Yeah," Pat sipped her coffee, sitting back on her chair. Meyan sat down too, on the chair vacated by Noli.

"Many say she looks just like me or I look just like her, though she's taller by some two inches and likes to wear her hair long. No, she's not my twin. She's my half-sister, three years younger."

"Is her name... Marissa?"

"Why, do you know her?" Pat took another sip, eyeing him exactly the same way Marissa would under the circumstances.

"Not really," Meyan replied, hesitating. "I met her in a symposium," he added, sipping his coffee.

As Pat drew a cigarette from a pack in her bag, Meyan readily flipped his lighter for her after which he lighted his own cigarette.

"Symposium, eh?" Pat observed, puffing on her stick. "Yeah, that's the kind of diversion Marissa finds herself in now and then. She's so intelligent, did you know she graduated summa, she does not know what to do with her life!"

Meyan let that pass for a while, puffing on his cigarette. But he had to ask her. "Would you know where she might be... at the moment?"

Pat did not answer immediately as their eyes locked. "I'm not really sure. But a month ago, she called me from London, telling me she was on her way to Tasmania. She was joining, she said, a project the late Princess Diana used to be heavily involved in, something to do with malnourished children. As usual, Marissa would never leave a specific address or even a telephone number. So, how would I know!"

Meyan puffed some more.

"By the way," Pat broke the silence, flipping her cigarette's end on the ashtray in front of her. "You sure, you only met her in a symposium, did you say?"

"Why do you ask?" Meyan said—finding himself caught. *I shouldn't have said that!*

"Well, Mr. First Presidential Adviser," Pat said, emitting a naughty laugh. "I'm not exactly blind not to see what's behind all the inquisitiveness!"

Both laughed heartily.

"Well, I got to be going," Pat said, gathering her things on the table.

"Will you tell me... if she calls?"

"If she ever will," Pat said, shrugging her shoulders. "Be in touch. Bye for now. See you later." She left, smiling with a practiced charm.

My Dear Angeling,

This is my first email and I thank you for bugging me to learn it. It isn't really hard, is it, having been used to my Olympia all my life. It's just this mouse whose tail is an arrow that confuses me at times, what with all the boxes of instructions above and below the screen. But it's really amazing what this PC can do! I have to walk to this Internet Café, a block from my pad, just to get here. Well, this is much, much better than waiting for your letter through the snail mail for days. Did you say we could chat in this thing, with a videocam to boot? At least now we could communicate faster and let flow our sorrows and our... joys.

Well, how are you, dear cousin? Surprise, surprise... guess who's taking dance lessons with me? It's Senator Naomi Santolan, the great acidic tongue in person. And let me tell you—while all of us wear leotards, she wears those short, short hot pants that display those stunning legs of hers. I have to admit, she's got them. Ha! Ha! Well, probably, she's into ballroom dancing to get rid of her excess energy and if I may venture to say, to get away from her devastating defeat in the last election!

Your mother called and said your kids are okay.

I think I have become thoroughly politicized. It's probably the master's program I'm taking and the influence of this professorial lecturer in contemporary politics and politicians. I sat in three of his lectures. And by gad, I could not help but marvel how he can explain complicated political concepts and issues in the simplest of terms. In the last lecture I attended, he challenged his students to think and act From KISS To KISS. I'm sure you know the first KISS (Keep it Simple, Stupid!) while the second KISS reads— "Keep it Sizzling, Sweetheart!" as soon as you discover that to be simple is to be true. Wow!

Anyway, how come our compatriots over there seem not to be interested in our presidential candidates over here? Did you say all you get when you asked them is a yawn? That's sad, isn't it? I'm not surprised your preference is Santolan, but as you said, she won't make it anyway.

Angeling, I'm seriously considering our clan's plan for me to go back home for good. And besides, Tony Boy really needs me. He is getting stronger, faster and taller in both mind and body. I am glad to know the university near our hometown, just 11 kilometers away has a good elementary school. Lolo Didong also assured me the west wing of our ancestral home will be renovated and ready for occupancy by the time I get back home.

Oopsss, I've been stuck here in this internet café for almost an hour now. I'll come back and check my email three days from today.

Bye for now, Angeling. From KISS to KISS,

Love,

Fili

5
WHERE ARE WE

The debate on whether or not President-elect Mahalina was to go through a dress rehearsal for his inaugural address was fought between his advisers like his presidency and the republic depended on it.

Those against it, particularly his high school classmates who were now in the "short list" for plum positions in the new administration, his drinking and gambling buddies and his friends from the entertainment industry, believed the whole exercise was humiliating for Mahalina. They also averred this was not necessary, the president-elect having been used to the camera during his days in the movies. Besides, they claimed, the president-elect simply needed a break from the rigors of the last campaign.

Rickie Balete, the Most Exalted Brother of the Brotherhood of Faith in Jesus Movement and newly designated spiritual adviser, made no comment but quickly cited Colossians chapter 4, verse 5: 'Let your speech always be with grace, seasoned with salt, that you may know how you ought to answer each one.'

Those for it, headed by Pat Gan-Alfonso, the proponent in fact of the controversial dress rehearsal, was backed by Raul Pangilinan, newly designated chief of staff, who said there was a "profound wisdom" to it; and Randolf Patis Cruz, newly designated press secretary, who said such an exercise had great value for media. The loud silence of Fatso Santos, newly designated executive secretary was understood as favoring the proposal. Gan-Alfonso argued the dress rehearsal was necessary and, therefore could not be avoided.

"First," she pointed out, "the inaugural address is a media event that would be beamed not only locally but all over the world. One major mistake in pronunciation, lapses in memory, misreading of words, wrong pauses in between and the like, would cause damage to the presidency. Remember," Gan-Alfonso said, removing her glasses from her nose, "the President will deliver his address in English."

"Second," Pat continued, returning her glasses and turning to her listeners, "the President will have to familiarize himself with the teleprompter. Nobody delivers his inaugural address solely dependent on his memory without a mistake. That is what the teleprompter is for, unless you were Abraham Lincoln delivering the Gettysburg Address. And please, don't forget, what the President will deliver is a basic official document against which he will be assessed for his performance in office."

"Third," Pat Gan-Alfonso paused, sensing she now had the full attention of her listeners, "the President will have to wear the same Barong Tagalog and bullet proof vest during rehearsals and during the inaugural. The studio where he will rehearse will be set in approximately the same degree of heat at the Quirino Grandstand on inauguration day to acclimatize his body."

Most of her listeners were temporarily stunned.

Pangilinan filled the interregnum. "Will he also be wearing the same pants for the inaugural?" he asked, his tongue pushing his gums, his manufactured grin purely for effect.

"That's up to the President," Pat Gan-Alfonso quickly retorted, aware of the mischievous interruption. "He may, or if he prefers, just wear boxer shorts and his slippers. Anyway, he will be behind the rostrum all the time."

Pangilinan almost swallowed his dentures as the rest guffawed.

When Mahalina was asked later if he was willing to go through the dress rehearsal as proposed by Pat Gan-Alfonso, he simply said: "Sonnamagun. Let's go, go, go!"

At three in the afternoon the following day, the dress rehearsal began. "Okay, roll it!" Pat ordered with a theatrical wave of the hand. The technicians in the studio raised their thumbs-up in acknowledgment.

"Five, four, three, camera, action!" Pat directed, nodding at Mahalina.

"The Honorable Chief Justice of the Supreme Court, the Honorable President of the Senate, the Honorable Speaker of the House of Representatives, Excellencies in the Diplomatic Corps, the Most Exalted Brother of the Brotherhood of Faith in Jesus Movement, Distinguished Guests, My Countrymen."

Mahalina paused, looking at Pat. His opening lines seemed okay to her. She was sitting on a solitary chair, directly out front, below the rostrum. He did not miss her intense look at him, a copy of his speech on top of her lap.

"Today marks the beginning of doing what I vowed to fulfill some 45 years ago when as a young man, I realized that hopelessness is the most depressing of all human deprivations. Since then and throughout the years, my understanding of the feeling of hopelessness among the young children who could not go to school, among the mothers who could not feed their children, among the fathers who could not find work and among the citizens of this country who have lost faith in their government, gnawed deeper and deeper into my heart... as it was revealed at the same time to me... that the only force that could entirely cast away hopelessness was and is still love. Pat! Pat! The tele-prompter... my eyes... they hurt... Sonnamagun!"

"Cut! Cut!" Pat Gan-Alfonso ordered.

Rubbing his eyes, Mahalina got down from the rostrum. "I cannot, cannot stand tele-prompter! My eyes hurt. Cut speech... too long." He lighted a cigarette.

"Mahal, I mean, Mr. President," Pat couldn't help but smile. "It's not possible. This speech has been cut down a lot of times already. This 25-page document before you is barely able to accommodate all the major elements of your program of government based on your major campaign promises. Take one out and what will the people say, that you easily forget? But you need not worry. We'll have the lights on the teleprompter adjusted. Okay?"

"Sonnamagun!"

While the technicians worked on the lights, the speech coach sat down with Mahalina, Pat Gan-Alfonso hovering from a discreet distance. At about that time at the San Francisco International Airport, a tall mestiza in her middle forties wearing extra large dark shades was urging her companion, a young lady of about 23 to hurry inside the terminal building.

"Just cool it, Mom," the young lady gasped for breath, pushing the cart of travel bags in front of her.

"Yeah, cuz if we miss this flight, your Dad will be really pissed off," the tall mestiza hissed, pushing her own luggage cart.

"Where are we gonna stay over there, Mom?"

Both were now racing toward the ticket counter.

"Your Dad bought us a new townhouse," the tall mestiza said, handing over their plane tickets to the man behind the counter.

"Are we really gonna attend the inaugural?" the young lady asked again.

"Now Jessica, clam up, okay? Your Dad will take care of everything, okay?"

In the living room of the modest mansion in Forbes Park, where in its open garage were parked a black Ford Expedition, a pale beige Jaguar convertible and a scarlet BMW, mother and son were engaged in conversation.

"Ma, do you think Dad will allow me to go into politics?"

"Why don't you ask him?"

"But he's too busy! I don't think he has enough time to even listen to me."

"Now, now Jason. Don't ever say that again. Your Dad will always have time for us but do not expect that to be everyday, every week. As you very well know, if he cannot come to visit us, he calls."

"Even now that he is already President?"

"Why, didn't he call me and ask for you immediately after he was declared winner? He has always been like that son, ever since. I have never, never reminded him for us, for me, for you."

"You think he will allow me to go into politics? You know I'm already 24 years old. I can start as mayor, then up. Who knows I might be like him someday?"

Silence followed for a while.

"Ma, you said you already showed him the script. What did he say?"

"Your Dad asked to give him more time. Some people are reviewing it for him."

"Really, that's great, Mom. Am sure glad to hear that."

"Five, four, three, camera, action!"

"The centerpiece of my program of government is Mahal for the People or Love for the People. In specific terms, this means three meals a day for the great majority of our families, schooling for their children, housing for their families and jobs, jobs, jobs for the parents to sustain the family's basic needs. The next, the next—Pat—Pat! What happened to bankruptcy—the paragraph here. Why not here?"

"Cut... cut! I'm sorry, Mr. President. We discussed that last night and we thought that it is not necessary."

"Not necessary! Who discussed?"

"Fatso, Randy Ong and I felt it is not necessary because you might sound weak, blaming the past administration this early. And besides, citing bankruptcy of the past administration would require statistics and that would need a lot more paragraphs, Mr. President."

"I don't care. Put that paragraph here. The people must know. The past administration spent all the money. That is why government is bankrupt. Put that here. Sonnamagun!"

"Yes, Mr. President. Give me ten minutes."

"I don't care if ten hours. My classmates are waiting outside. I'll be back."

"The President doesn't follow my suggestions," the speech coach complained. "He doesn't pause and there is not enough breathing between sentences. He tends to roll over them like he's gurgling some whiskey."

"Okay, okay," Pat Gan-Alfonso sneered at the speech coach. "Just indicate your comments in red on your own copy and show them to me later. Okay?"

While Pat Gan-Alfonso reviewed her notes, referring to some folders now and then from her brief case, Rickie Balete, now spiritual adviser was also reviewing the draft of his prayer for the inaugural.

Looking at his advanced copy of the speech, Balete concluded that its centerpiece message was love for the people—the deprived, marginalized, hungry, unschooled and jobless. *Aha!* Balete cheered, lifting the pen from its holder. *I found it! It's the Beatitudes, in the Gospel of St. Matthew, Chapter 5, Verse 3. Blessed are the poor in spirit for theirs is the kingdom of heaven.*

Balete pondered on that passage for a while. Jesus in his Sermon in the Mount did not refer to the poor people but to the "poor in spirit." That meant people with low vitality, lost vivacity, weak batteries, unfulfilled hopes, paled enthusiasm and people of little faith, rich or poor. Most priests and pastors of this or that denomination or diocese wittingly or unwittingly failed to make the distinction, thus practically abetting the poor to remain poor because anyway, theirs was the kingdom of heaven. If the poor in spirit should be made distinct in the president' speech, Balete told himself, he would not only gain more followers from the poor but also open alliances with the rich—the rich who are poor in spirit.

As soon as he thought he had put the final touches to his prayer, the spiritual adviser instructed his secretary to call a number.

"I think this is okay. Only one paragraph, eh? I told you so."

"Thank you, Mr. President. There's a little revision in the preceding paragraph. Your spiritual adviser just phoned and I took the liberty of inserting his suggestion," Pat Gan-Alfonso explained.

Gan-Alfonso noted the president puffed vigorously on his cigarette, after which he said: "I think this is okay, too, except this line about rich people. Idea is good. But let us wait for proper time. The poor, they might misunderstand me."

"Okay, we delete that. So the sentence will end with the poor. Right?"

"Okay, delete. Already inputted?"

"Yes, Ma'am," the computer technician nodded from inside the booth.

"Okay, Pat. I hope this is last revision. I'm getting tired of this piece of paper. Whoever invented teleprompter must be crazy. Why can't we simply rely on memory or speak from heart? In movies, once you forget lines, you adlib. Why can't we do same here?"

"Mr. President, Mahal, please. Even Clinton uses a teleprompter. This is the start of the greatest performance of your life. This will..."

"Sonnamagun! Shall we start again?" the president cut her, sauntering toward the rostrum.

"Five, four, three, camera, action!"

"The centerpiece of my program of government is Mahal for the people or love for the people..."

Mahalina paused, looking away from the teleprompter as Pat below crossed her slender left leg over her right. When she looked up, their eyes met.

"All these we shall do without the least hesita-sation, he-tisi-tion, he-sit-ta-sion and without let-up..."

"Cut, Mr. President," Gan-Alfonso interrupted. "I'm sorry, but you've got to get it right." Turning to the speech coach, Gan-Alfonso said. "Take note of that, please. If the President can't pronounce that right, change the word later."

"Sorry, Pat," the president-elect said. "I was just distracted."

"That's okay. Shall we start again, from Line 21? Okay, five, four, three, camera, action!"

"All these we shall do without the least hesitation and without let-up. Much as we desire to push for other programs, we cannot possibly do so, for as I repeatedly mentioned in the last campaign, the past administration had caused this government to go bankrupt through profligate spending on programs that do not pay dividends for our people and national development. But let me remind them. My administration will prosecute those responsible and if found guilty, I will send them to jail."

Mahalina paused again, as Pat below crossed her slender right leg over her left. The long pause caused Pat to look up, one stem of her glasses still in her mouth. Their eyes met and locked.

"There is no hidden agenda in my administration. To begin with, in the spirit of transparency, the gates of the palace shall be open... Pat... Pat! I cannot stand heat... cannot stand heat!"

"Cut! Cut! Very impressive, Mr. President!" Gan-Alfonso exclaimed, standing and holding on to the script. "But what's the problem this time?"

"The problem... I cannot stand heat!" the president-elect cried, unbuttoning his collar and rolling up his sleeves.

"Careful now with your get-up, Sir. It won't look good in the next shots."

"Sonnamagun...get another one!" Mahalina ordered, lighting a cigarette. He then came down from the rostrum and asked one of his aides for a drink.

"Four pages more, Mr. President," Pat Gan-Alfonso gasped with pride. "The heat in this studio is set at a high of 30 degrees centigrade that approximates the heat at the Quirino Grandstand on Wednesday high noon, when you deliver your inaugural address."

170

"Okay Pat. You are really a genius. You think of everything."

"Thank you, Mr. President. I am completely overwhelmed."

"And what about this vest? You'll be cooking me in sweat, in perspiration!"

"The bulletproof vest, you cannot also do without, Mr. President. On cooking you in sweat and perspiration, well, let us just pray there will be enough breeze from the bay to fan my President's discomfort when he finally delivers his speech."

"Sonnamagun, Pat. You are not only a genius. You also think like my mother."

While Pat Gan-Alfonso viewed the clips of the president's delivery for editing and premier viewing for close friends and advisers Sunday evening that was three days from the inaugural, the officers of the United Workers Movement, the Urban Poor Federation, the National Confederation of Small Farmers and Fishermen, the Integrated Homeowners Association of Metro Manila, Women for Equal Rights Movement and many other non-government organizations and peoples organizations were busy finalizing their agenda for the inaugural on Wednesday. The atmosphere in the large auditorium of a Jesuit university in Quezon City was euphoric as the day's convenor, an ex-seminarian steered the deliberations with just enough verve, reminding all that the day had finally arrived for the poor, now that Mahalina was president.

Everyone's attention was suddenly brought to the gigantic screen of the auditorium as the four-point agenda of the discussions were projected: 1. More jobs and higher pay hikes; 2. Poverty alleviation; 3. Homes for the homeless and 4. Action now or never.

"Those in favor, shout... Yes!" the convenor's voice thundered.

"Yes!" the auditorium erupted in agreement.

"Those not in favor, shout... No!" the Convenor's voice thundered again.

Silence.

"Approved!" the Convenor banged his gavel.

"My friends," the Convenor addressed the crowd. "Before I call the overall chairman of the committee of our super-coalition 'March to the Palace' for Wednesday, the subject being last in our agenda for today, may I project on screen the draft of our cover letter to the President to introduce our demands. I have to admit I drafted four formal letters but rejected them all, knowing the President doesn't read letters, much more long formal letters. So I have to think of something different, something unique that would immediately catch his attention. I hope you understand. Here goes..." On the gigantic screen onstage, the following lines loomed:

M - ore jobs hasten
A - lleviation of poverty and
H - ousing for the poor.
A - ct now, Mahal and
L - et us live in love.

"Wows" and "OKs" erupted in thunderclaps. The juxtaposition of letters in the magic name with their basic needs, gave lucid meaning and wholeness to their cause. The voice of the people, by the people and for the people once more rose in wild applause.

The convenor's voice thundered again: "Any objections?"

"Approved!" the assembly thundered back.

The convenor ended the meeting with his final statement: "My friends, we are doing the march to the palace because Mahal promised to love us, he would uplift our lives because he loves us. We voted for him because of that promise. Our march to the palace is a reaffirmation of our faith in President Mahalina and a simple reminder of his professed love for us. We pray that he won't forget his promises to us. Let us now live and make love!"

"Five, four, three, camera, action!"

"So far, I had enumerated to you the four major problems my administration will be facing in the next six years and my plans to resolve them. But there is another major problem that I think most of you are aware of by now. I refer to the renewed hostilities in the southern bowels of Mindanao, perpetuated by Muslim extremists and separatists.

"My countrymen, I was elected because of my love for the people of this country. These Muslim extremists and separatists think otherwise and intend to disrupt my agenda of love for the people. Let me remind them today that Mahal was not born yesterday, that Mahal would never blink at the first sign of a threat and that Mahal would never run away from a good fight, whether that fight be fought with fists or with guns. Pak—Pak—Pak!" As Mahalina delivered the last three bullet-sounding cracks, he simultaneously took the classic boxing stance, right hand extended, left hand cocked for the knockout punch, dancing back and forth, spinning quickly.

"Cut! Cut!" Pat Gan-Alfonso cried. "Mr. President, why, why did you bang the rostrum with your fists? Took the stance of a boxer? And did all that with your pak, pak, pak! Those are not in the script!"

"Sorry, Pat... I got carried away."

"Okay, let's start from my countrymen again, line l4. Five, four three, camera, action!"

"My countrymen... I was elected because of my love for the people of this country. These Muslim extremists and separatists think otherwise and intend to destroy my agenda of love for the people. Let me remind them today that Mahal was not born yesterday, that Mahal would never blink at the first sign of a threat and that Mahal would never run away from a good fight, whether that fight be fought with fists or with guns. Fatso, Fatso, Santos! What's up, my friend!"

"Cut!" Pat Gan-Alfonso snapped, turning her back to see the intruder wave his arms, acknowledging the president's loud greeting.

"I'm sorry, Mr. President, Pat for the intrusion but this thing could not wait. I tried to sneak in but..."

"What thing?" the president and Pat asked almost at the same time.

"It's about the Muslim problem in your speech."

"What?" both asked again almost at the same time.

172

"We've got a For-Your-Eyes-Only message from the Southern Command. It says Commander Ahmad Jamil desires to negotiate in peace with your new government, Mr. President."

"So?" Pat asked, this time unable to hide her contempt.

"The implication is," Fatso Santos lowered his voice, "there might be a need to temper that portion of your speech."

"No way!" the president snapped.

"Mr. President, my understanding is Commander Jamil has preempted our moves. If you reject his proposal now, get on with your speech and the media finds out later, you will look bad and belligerent. On the other hand, if you reveal in your speech Commander Jamil has sent you a message of peace, then that will be a big ace in your leadership, on the very first day of your assumption into office. I'm sure both the local and international media will lap it up. 'Confidence in the new presidency assured even from extremists groups…' I can imagine the headlines, Mr. President."

After a few drags from his cigarette, the president asked,

"What do you say, Pat?"

"I think Fatso here has a point. But I also think there is a need to look at it more objectively. Why not tonight, Mr. President? We postpone the premier showing of your speech for tomorrow night. We still have two days after that, before the inaugural."

"Okay, contact Southern Command right away."

"I already did, Mr. President," Fatso Santos smiled, looking at Pat Gan-Alfonso with pride. "General Napoleon Cornelio will be arriving at Camp Aguinaldo at 1700 hours, this afternoon. He will take your orders from there, Mr. President."

In Camp Khadapi, in the deep jungles of Mindanao, Commander Ahmad Jamil reread the document before him and concluded it was authentic and bore the marks of the chairman of the People's Watch and Revolutionary Army.

The proposal was to merge the forces of the PWRA and Jamil's forces to fight the government and assure victory within a short period of time. But while its assumptions had their basis in fact, they were not feasible from the strategic plateau upon which his armed force and those of the PWRA stood, one from the other.

In the first place, the PWRA's strategic aim was to install a communistic government in the country. Jamil's ultimate aim was to establish a separate state within a state. The rationale of the PWRA chairman was to introduce a foreign ideology to entirely change an ineffective government. His, Jamil's, was to claim some territories of land, the legitimacy of which was substantiated by the fact his forebears had ruled these territories hundreds of years before this government even took its present form.

Commander Jamil stuck a new cigarette in his long gold plated cigarette holder and lit it with the table lighter. He continued with his musings. First, he told himself, Communism that used to be a world force was now reduced to ashes. The four remaining communist countries were in serious trouble: China, Cuba, North Korea and the Soviet Republic.

Secondly, the communist movement in the country was a spent force with no guns to fight a lasting battle. On the contrary, his, Jamil's army, was armed to the teeth with the latest weaponry, fully supported by sympathetic countries, its military commanders closely working together as brothers and comrades-in-arms.

Finally, the Communists were pagans, the children of Satan and the curse of Islam. Why, Jamil asked himself why he even read the document from the pagan of them all? Recognizing his transgression, Jamil picked the document before him, dug his long nails into its pages and tore them to shreds, then threw the rubbish in the waste can beside his desk and spat into it.

His musings took a sudden turn. The communists were not really the enemy. "It is the Americans," Jamil spat the words, remembering, feeling the hatred in his heart. He recalled how the Americans massacred the Muslims in Jolo during the Moro-American wars, how the Americans invented the .45 automatic pistol solely for his grandfathers and grandmothers, so they could not even crawl after its first blast. For the Americans: "The only good Moro was a dead Moro."

Just as his rage began to rise again, one of his aides by the door announced Task Force Commander Tausug wished to see him. Immediately, Commander Jamil felt complete calm. Tausug was not only his classmate then at the University of Cairo. He was also one of his most reliable field commanders. Four years his junior, Tausug proved not only one of the fiercest fighters under his command but also one who used his brains to confuse the enemy.

After their brotherly embrace and having taken their seats, Commander Tausug immediately reported on his mission.

"Winthrop Lopez had already flown to Manila. He assured me he would see the new President immediately," Tausug said.

"Hmmm. What's the latest on this?"

"Our informant confirmed that General Napoleon Cornelio suddenly left for Manila. It is also confirmed he was summoned by Malacanang. I think Winthrop has done his job as you desired."

"Hmmm."

"My Commander," Tausug broke the silence. "Considering the timing, I think we should now implement Oplan Sarimanok." Commander Tausug was referring to the targets marked red on the map by the sidewall of Commander Jamil's desk. "Except for one minor change, if you will agree, my Commander."

"And what is this minor change?"

"My Commander," Tausug said. "One of our assets in the PWRA reports they will deliver a surprise package for the new administration, similar to ours during the inaugural."

Jamil remained silent. Tausug continued to relate the details of his report, including the names of those who would execute the surprise package.

"How reliable is this asset?" Jamil finally asked, his eyes straight at his younger comrade.

"Very, my Commander. Our asset was a classmate of Commander Lulu during their college days. Both of them also majored in chemistry. Our asset is now directly under the command of People's Watch Brigade Task Force Commander Sawa."

"I see," Jamil nodded slowly, looking with admiration at his younger comrade. Truly, he told himself, Tausug was an invaluable asset to the cause of the Almighty Allah. "What is the possibility," Jamil then asked, "of us assuming what they have in mind, without them knowing about it?"

"A big one, my Commander. I have already drawn up the blueprint. It can be done without any difficulty," Tausug said with pride.

"Tell me."

In the next hour, Tausug outlined the operational details of the blueprint.

"Will the American ambassador be there?"

"I was informed he will surely be there, including the rest of the American embassy."

Jamil slowly nodded his head. "Okay, let us do it."

"*Insha Allah!*"

"As God wants."

They had been in his kitchen for five hours now. The food was good, the brewed coffee was good and the remembrances were good. They were both assistant professors at the National State University some years ago, when, in the pursuit of their academic careers, they also consulted each other who to date and eventually who to marry. But those were not the focus of their friendly conversation at the moment.

"I've packed my bags, my friend. I'm ready to go. My return ticket is in my breast pocket," Raul Pangilinan said with finality, his tongue pushing his dentures against his gums.

"No, my friend. You are not leaving yet." Pedro Abaya said, coughing. "Our agreement is you will have to stick it out with him for at least one year. Remember, he has not yet even taken his oath." Abaya coughed again.

"I know that. But the evidence is clear. He's not sober. His attention span doesn't go beyond a few minutes. Matters of state are completely alien to him. I don't think I can live with that for one year. My five months with him were entirely wasted."

Pedro Abaya, Raul's friend, decided to use a different tack. "What did you say in your latest book, my friend?" Abaya coughed again. "If I may quote what you wrote in Chapter VII: 'It is, therefore, the responsibility of men of knowledge to teach all, both the ignorant and the eager, on level with their current state of mind and in accordance with their call with destiny.' Didn't you say that? Or, are you saying now that theories of governance as propounded by academicians are not compatible with those who actually exercise power?" He coughed again.

Abaya and Pangilinan were both 66. The similarity ended there. While Pangilinan was thin, Abaya was fat, in fact almost puffy in both face and body. While Pangilinan had this habit of pushing his dentures against his gums while talking, Abaya kept on coughing while talking. Pangilinan wore false dentures while Abaya had a bad case of asthma.

"Well, thank you my friend for remembering that line. But my assumption is the ignorant and the eager are teachable. Your man isn't. You can't put him for one minute in a classroom and engage him in intelligent discourse. His mind is simply outside of any classroom. He is unbelievably incapable of original thought. He simply isn't teachable and you know it!" Pangilinan was more excited now, pushing his tongue harder and faster against his dentures.

"Perhaps, what you've been trying to teach him, he already knows or thinks he knows!" Abaya was also getting excited, coughing all the more. "Why not teach him something he doesn't know yet, something completely new to him?"

Pangilinan shrugged. "Now my friend, that's rather sublime, coming from you. Well, let me just ask you one thing. How come you don't do it yourself? We're practically in the same field and our theories of governance practically run in parallel lines. Yeah, why don't you do it yourself?"

"Well, you know the answer to that. I'm his uncle." Abaya coughed again, his face bloating.

"Then the more reason you should do it!" Pangilinan's dentures almost jumped out of their sanctuary.

"No, I can't. I tried that several times before but he just wouldn't listen."

"Is it his refusal to listen or his inability to understand?"

"Search me!"

"So there you are, my friend," Pangilinan said in dismay. He remembered how he had hankered to be chief of staff of the president of the republic. It would have been a memorable moment to have his oath of office at the palace, the event covered by media, the pictures to be shown to his family, friends and colleagues abroad.

The ex-future chief of staff of President Mahalina then said: "Let's just put this as another bad day of an academic, correction, another bad day for two academicians. Bye, my friend. I'll email you when I get back home. Perhaps between now and then, I can think of, what did you say, something new, to teach the non-teachable."

It was already two o'clock in the morning. Still, the president-elect sauntered from the room to the sala and back. In the room were his newly designated National Security Adviser, the Chief of the Presidential Security Battalion, the Chief of Staff of the Army, Southern Command General Napoleon Cornelio, Fatso Santos and Patricia Gan-Alfonso. In contrast to the frail and slender body of Pat Gan Alfonso, others were robust men with big egos.

In the wide sala were Mahalina's classmates of high school days and his drinking buddies, all happy-go-lucky guys, all committed to the proposition that life was to be enjoyed and the sky was the limit. While the discussions in the room were on matters of national security, those in the sala were on love and the fountain of youth. While those in the room were serious and heated, those in the sala were boisterous and loose. While endless cups of coffee were served and consumed in the room, endless bottles of whiskey were served and gobbled up in the sala.

The arguments in the room revolved around one either-or proposition—either the president in his inaugural address wage war or offer peace to the Moro separatists and extremists. As the minutes and the hours wore on, the arguments became more heated, the discussions leading nowhere. There was no presiding officer as the president-elect appeared fewer times in the room and more and more times in the sala.

"I appeal for your understanding," Fatso Santos removed his glasses, wiping them with a handkerchief. This was the nth time he did that. "Once the President wages war, there will be no end to it. That means, I repeat, bloodshed on one hand and sacrifice of the priority programs of Mahal's administration, on the other."

"There is no question about that. We understand the situation very well. But you also have to understand our position. Jamil's scheme is obvious and devious to us. He talks peace as he prepares for war. He wages war then retreats when he is cornered, then talks peace. It's a vicious cycle. He's playing Jekyll and Hyde," the Chief of Staff of the Army countered, sighing deeply as he finished.

"I find this offer of peace by Jamil a sham," the SouthCom General declared. "Let's look at the map." He then stood, removed the pen from his front pocket and positioned himself beside the map that was pinned to a small board with a stand. Using his pen as a pointer, he began. "This here is the highway which I said earlier, traverses the three provinces in question. Here, south of it is the location of Camp Khadapi. From this camp, to the crossroad here where the three provinces trisect— is a distance of 13.7 kilometers. The tunnel which I said earlier had been reported to the high command some two years ago connecting the camp to this portion of the highway, is now actually a network of tunnels leading to the three provinces, all heading towards each provincial capitol site. No wonder for every encounter, the enemy just disappeared on top or along this highway. And, if I may add, this network of tunnels was definitely not built for a day. They have been at it for years."

"Wasn't that how the Vietcong beat the hell out of the Americans?" Pat Gan-Alfonso asked, obviously intrigued.

"Yes, the same network of underground tunnels the Vietcong used to beat the hell out of the French years earlier."

"Why are you up so early, Mom?"

"It's already four in the morning, Jessica. I have to rush and see Bruce Kundiman," the mother pointed out.

"Bruce Kundiman?"

"He's the couturier. He's the best!"

"What do we need a couturier for? We would look weird in the inaugural!"

"There's a little change, Jessica. We're not going to the inaugural. We're going to the reception instead, at the Manila Hotel."

"Wow, Mom, that's great, really great!"

At the American Embassy fronting Manila Bay, three men in white long sleeves and pin-striped suits sat around the breakfast table. Having finished their meal of buttered toast with tuna and fresh, cold pineapple juice, they were now taking their brewed coffee. Only Dick Martin was smoking.

"So what's the assessment of the agency?" Rushmore Stockman, the resident ambassador queried, looking at Martin. Stockman was a giant of a man, 6'4" tall with a gargantuan nose that curved down like an eagle's. Everyone in the embassy called him "Stocky," not only because that was short for his family name but also for the tons of flesh he carried on his body. Originally from South Dakota, he was named after Mount Rushmore where the huge heads of Washington, Jefferson, Lincoln and Roosevelt were carved out of the mountain of stone.

"It's still early to say, Stocky," Martin observed, scratching his beard. "The situation is volatile."

"So there is really nothing from the old man, huh," Marvin Reed, the consul, said, apparently unconvinced. Reed was as tall as Stockman except he was as thin as a reed, his family name. That was why everybody in the embassy called him "Stick." Born in Mobile, in the southern state of Alabama, the Consul was a former bomber pilot who flew bombing sorties over Vietnam in his B-52. He made several kills and he was proud of them.

"It's difficult to say, Stick," Martin said, shrugging his shoulders, "although there are a lot of rumors."

"What rumors?" Rushmore Stockman said, standing while loosening his belt.

"We're checking on them."

"What fucking rumors?" the resident ambassador persisted.

"One, there will be bombings, really big ones this time, courtesy of Ahmad Jamil or the PWRA or some others, what the hell. Two, there will be riots instigated by the leftists. And three, there will be a coup of some sort."

"C'mon, Dick. You know all these are boring old tales," Stick snapped, looking at Stocky. "Why don't you cut all the bullshit?"

"That's why I said these are rumors... they need to be verified. Only that in this fucking country, rumors are almost always the precursors of truth." This time Martin looked at the consul with some kind of derision, nodding his head repeatedly toward the resident ambassador as if saying, "Don't you fucking see the point?"

"Yeah, I do see the point," Stockman sighed, unzipping his fly as he headed toward the kitchen.

"Where you goin'?" Martin asked, chuckling.

"To the john..."

"To do what?"

"To take a leak, you snoopy, fucking spy."

The consul guffawed in total amusement, his funny bones obviously tickled to the hilt. Martin chuckled louder while the resident ambassador of the U.S.A. wriggled in his discomfort, ambling out in his great weight. Like all men of all races, the American ambassador was no exception. He also had a bladder.

The explosion at the office of the secretariat of the March to the Palace Coalition took four lives and wounded nine. Father Tim, the ex-seminarian and convenor of the coalition was one of the first to go. His head was blown to pieces and if not

178

for his laminated plastic ID inside his wallet in his pocket, he would not have been recognized. The dead bodies of the three others were so thoroughly mangled, the medical team had a very difficult time reassembling their body parts which were strewn all over the office floor and walls. The wounded were too shocked, the medical team had to drive away investigators and nosy reporters until some signs of recovery were evident, an understatement really considering the extent of the physical damage and the psychological trauma that would soon follow.

The outrage from the members of the coalition was one of mad frenzy and called for revenge. "The perpetrators of this barbaric and heinous crime must be caught and hanged," they shouted. Vowing to proceed with their march to the palace with greater resolve—to demand their four-point agenda, they now also sought redress for the victims and their families.

The politicians immediately followed suit. Some declared they would join the marchers. Some proclaimed they would not only join the marchers but would in fact call for an investigation of the atrocity in aid of legislation.

No statement came from the police except to say they were still following leads.

"The signs of the times call for sobriety," His Eminence, Cardinal Pedro Alingasa pontificated before media. Citing St. Peter in Chapter 5, Verse 8, the Cardinal continued: 'Let us be sober, be vigilant because our adversary the devil walks about like a roaring lion, seeking whom he may devour.' It was another of his press conferences. "But it is the kind of sobriety that should bring about swift justice to the victims of injustice. For if that justice is not swiftly given while on earth, that justice will surely be rendered swiftly and without warning from heaven. For as it is written in 1st Thessalonians, Chapter 5, Verse 3: 'The Lord shall at his own time come like a thief in the night.'"

Except for Pat Gan-Alfonso, the five big robust men suddenly stood at attention as the door to the room swung open. Obviously inebriated but somehow still sober, the president-elect theatrically slammed the door behind him while humming his favorite, "Love is a Many Splendored Thing."

"Shiiit down, I mean sit down. Hik!" Mahalina gestured as he took his seat by one arm, reversed it, sat down and held the backrest with both arms. He was using the chair as a rocking horse, coaxing it back and forth with his ample buttocks. Humming again, he scanned the faces of the men and Pat Gan-Alfonso in front of him.

"So?"

"Mr. President," Fatso spoke, taking off his glasses and wiping his eyes. "We discussed the whole gamut of the so—called Commander Jamil initiative. We also went into the details, the pros and cons. But in the end, we could not agree."

"Gamut... medicine? Is Jamil sick?" Mahalina asked, looking at Fatso.

"I'm sorry, Sir," Fatso said, grinning uneasily. "Gamut means the range or extent of Jamil's initiative."

"Sonnamagun!" Mahalina snapped. "Don't try to impress me with words I do not know." Then looking all around him, he asked: "Why you no agree?"

"Our strongest objection, Mr. President," the Chief of Staff of the Army pointed out, "is Jamil's duplicity. He offers peace when he's cornered, but in the process prepares for war. The latest evidence is the discovery of a network of tunnels by the SouthCom."

"Yes, Mr. President," General Cornelio of the SouthCom connected as he stood beside the map, using his pen as pointer. As before, he showed the network of tunnels on the map and its clever design, pointing out to Mahalina how the rebels outwitted government military forces at every turn.

The humming and the seesawing stopped. From General Cornelio, Mahalina's eyes settled on Fatso.

"So?"

"Mr. President, "Fatso Santos spoke again, putting back his glasses at the tip of his nose. "General Pecson and I recognize the serious implications of this discovery. But since it is not yet publicly known, the Mahal administration can play poker with Jamil for a while—projecting the image that Mahal is indeed a man of peace, for love cannot thrive in war."

"In short, Mr. President," General Pecson, the presidential security battalion chief-designate seconded Fatso Santos. "Talk peace in your inaugural address without necessarily mentioning Jamil or his tunnels. Then, let's wait and see. At the first sign of deceit, you drop your bombs."

Mahalina drew a cigarette, flipping his lighter. Every one noticed his hands shaking. It took him two tries to finally light the cigarette.

"So?" Mahalina asked after two simultaneous puffs. All exchanged glances but no one spoke.

"So?" Mahalina asked again, now raising his voice.

"Mr. President," the National Security Adviser said, clearing his throat. "We still maintain that if your inaugural address is coached in love and peace, you open opportunities to one and all that includes the extremists and separatists. There will be no bloodshed at the start of your administration. The international press will surely dub you as a man of peace. And..."

"Sonnamagun!" Mahalina erupted, throwing his cigarette on the floor, smashing it with his right foot. "Sonnamagun!" He erupted again, kicking the chair in front of him. That sent the chair reeling against the low table as coffee cups and spoons went tumbling down the floor. "What did I hire you for? To give me more headaches! You spend hours talking and talking to give me more problems? When you talk to the President, you talk as one, not many, or you confuse me crazy!"

"Mr. President, please..." Fatso Santos pleaded.

"Out, out all of you! You are useless, useless! Hik, Sonnamagun!"

As the five elephants stampeded out of the room, Pat Gan-Alfonso who was silent all along started gathering her notes and headed for the door.

"No, no Pat... you stay," Mahalina called after her.

Pat slowly turned around and leaned against the door. With her folder and leather bag clasped around her arms against her breasts, she stood there not knowing what to do, as the president picked up the chair and set it erect on the floor. Sitting down at the edge of the low sofa, Mahalina leaned backward as he slung a leg over the sofa table and then pressed his temple with his left arm.

"Headache, Mr. President?" Pat ventured.

"No, no headache," Mahalina said, fishing for a stick out of the pack of cigarettes he just got out of his pocket. Then he felt for his lighter. "Sonnamagun, did I throw that one, too?"

"I got one, Mr. President," Pat hurriedly walked back to where she was seated earlier, put back her things at the end of the low table and fumbled inside her bag for her lighter.

As Pat leaned over to light his cigarette and as Mahalina also leaned forward and clasped her extended arm with both his hands, Pat felt there was more to the touch than just to steady her arm for the light. As the electricity hit her, Pat clumsily withdrew her hand as the lighter fell on the floor. Instinctively, she picked up the lighter as she went down on her knees to gather the spoons, cups and saucers that were strewn all over then placed them one by one on the low table. As she was doing this, she felt Mahalina's gaze on her exposed knees. The tips of her ears tingled.

"You want me to leave... now?" Pat blushed, standing, doubtful if that was what she wanted to say.

"No Pat. You stay. I need you here."

Pat flushed. Did Mahalina mean what he just said?

"Sit down, please," Mahalina waved her toward the chair beside him, inhaling on his cigarette. "Want some?" Mahalina extended his pack to her.

"No, thanks, Mr. President. It's Virginia Slims for me," Pat said, fumbling for her pack in her bag. She had to steady her hands as she lighted her own stick. And she knew that he noticed.

"What do you think?"

What do I think, about what? Pat asked herself. But quickly, she remembered what she thought while standing with her back to the door as the men scampered out.

"I think you have to be angry, really angry with your big boys more often, Mr. President." Pat said, feeling some kind of relief. "That will always keep them on their toes even until dawn."

"Oh yes, oh, yes, it's twenty to five in the morning," Mahalina suddenly shook in uninhibited laughter. "But that is not what I meant!"

Pat Gan-Alfonso almost panicked. And the more the president laughed, obviously teasing or was it taunting her, the more she felt vulnerable. *Vulnerable?* Racing against her thoughts, she noted the president slowly grind his cigarette butt in the ashtray.

"Okay, let's be serious," Mahalina said, leaning forward, facing Pat.

"Serious... Mr. President?"

"Serious."

"What do you mean, Mr. President?" Pat Gan-Alfonso was about to burst.

"I mean, is it war or peace? Is it love or hate?" Mahalina said, gazing in her eyes.

Pat Gan-Alfonso closed her eyes. *Did I misunderstand you?*

"Well, what do you say?" Mahalina asked softly.

"Mr. President," Pat said, inhaling deeply, slowly opening her eyes. "I was listening carefully to the arguments between the hawks and the doves in your team," Pat continued, feeling in control again. "Since you asked what I think about it—this is my position. Go for war! Your image as a fighter to protect the oppressed is deeply ingrained in the hearts and minds of the people, who overwhelmingly voted you into office. You are not a diplomat, you are not an academician and you are not a freak. You are a fighter and that means you love to fight to redress a wrong, because you hate abuse and all its cousins and relations. The campaign for the presidency is over. You won and you won overwhelmingly. Now that you are President, you have to act decisively, not because you want the people to love you more but because you love your country most."

As Pat Gan-Alfonso finished, she felt immediately exhausted. She had to stand and inhale and exhale more air to prevent herself from crying.

"Pat," Mahalina stood, clasping both her hands in his.

"Mr. President, please..."

"No Pat. Look at me. I go for war. You put all of what you said in my address, okay?"

"Thank you, Mr. President," Pat now burst into sobs as Mahalina slowly drew her to him, pressing his lips deeply on her brow. Then he hugged her gently, then tightly.

"Mr. President, please..."

"Okay, now you know I need you," Mahalina said after a while, slowly releasing her. "Remember to put all you said in my address. That's an order!"

"Thank you, Mr. President," Pat heaved, wiping her face with a piece of tissue and putting on her glasses.

"Oh, there's one thing more, Mr. President," Pat remembered, reaching for a folder inside her bag.

"What is that?"

"This is the four-point agenda demand of the coalition 'March to the Palace.' It is addressed to you."

"What about?"

"It's their demand of your campaign promises to provide more jobs and higher pay hikes, poverty alleviation, housing and what they call, action now or never. There is an additional demand, that is, redress for the death of Father Tim and the others in that bombing the other day."

"I agree. Include all that."

"One last thing, Mr. President. I suggest we delete that portion in your address where you promise to open Malacanang at all times to all the people. It's rather very risky right now, under the circumstances."

"Do it."

"Would you like to read this?"

"Keep it."

As she turned to go and was about to open the door, Mahalina called after her. "Pat, you take care of yourself. Remember, I need you."

Pat Gan-Alfonso slowly turned her face but did not answer. She slid out of the door, softly closing it behind her.

"Listen, Mother. That's the 24th applause. The guy is really great, huh!"

"Now, you listen Jessica," the mother said, looking over her shoulder, adjusting the straps of her new gown. "He's not just the guy. He's your Daddy and he is the President. Now if you don't mind, why don't you come here and unzip my back. I think Bruce Kundiman really did a terrific job."

"Now, Mother, will you please shut up for a while," Jessica said, punching a button on the remote to increase the volume. "There again. That's the 25th! Boy, this is exciting!" Jessica exclaimed, motioning her mother to come near her.

With her mother's back to her, Jessica slid the zipper down, pulling her mother's face toward her.

"Now, kiss," she quickly buzzed her mother's cheek, her eyes still glued on the TV.

"I'd like to see you again in your gown."

"Now, Mother, please listen. There it is again and again. That's the 26th and the 27th! And look at that crowd—there must be millions out there!"

"Okay, after that speech, okay?" the mother went back to the wall mirror and took another look at herself. Holding the gown at the back of her neck, she went inside her room to change.

Meandro Destino stood by the window of his apartment, his eyes on the TV. He was also listening to the speech but his eyes were not on Mahalina. They were glued on Pat Gan-Alfonso who was directly behind the president, now and then looking at something on her lap, no doubt a copy of the address, following every word of the president. Had she heard from Marissa? Destino asked himself, slipping a cigarette out of its pack, tapping it against his wrist, lighting it and knitting his brow, without once taking his eyes off Patricia Gan-Alfonso, the sister of Marissa Gantuico.

"Swordsman to Scabbard One... do you copy?" Gen. Pecson, Chief of the Presidential Security Battalion, whispered into his handheld radio.

"Scabbard One to Swordsman, Roger."

"All Scabbard stations on yellow."

"All Scabbard stations on yellow, Roger, Sir."

"Over and out."

Behind the rostrum with the seal of the Office of the President gleaming out front, stood President Juancho "Mahal" Mahalina. Gulping for a little more saliva, he scanned the crowd immediately before him with the largest streamer out front that read, "Mahal is Love and Love Means Action Now!" Below was printed 'March to the Palace Coalition.' In red T-shirts, this particular crowd was some 1,000 men and women across and 24,000 in depth.

Mahalina was now soaked in sweat as he moved his body around a little to loosen it from the bulletproof vest that engulfed him. He looked at the bottom of the page before him. He was now on page 12. He was half way through. Gulping another squirt of saliva, he scanned the crowd, inhaled deeply and continued.

"There is no hidden agenda in my administration. In the spirit of transparency, the gates of the palace shall be open to all those who in love, in peace and in good faith—seek audience with the President. (Applause) Palace officials shall make themselves available at all times so the problems of the people, especially the poor and the aggrieved shall be attended to immediately with dispatch. (Applause) A new office to be known as 'Mahal Action Now Center' shall be created to coordinate all activities and will be directly under the direct supervision of your President." (Prolonged applause)

"**M**om," Jessica hollered from her seat. "That was the 37th applause!"
"Am listening, Jessica... am listening!" Her mother hollered back from the kitchen as tears began to fall down her pallid cheeks. She shook a little and more tears flowed.

Mahalina leaned a little, focusing his eyes at the teleprompter. The heat of the sun was at its height and he had difficulty distinguishing the words in front. To the crowd immediately below him, the impression was the president was looking directly at them to show his concern. That short pause led somebody to shout "Mahal!" The chanting reverberated throughout: "Mahal! Mahal! Mahal! Mahal! Mahal!"

Remembering what Pat Gan-Alfonso told him, Mahalina straightened his body, manufactured a smile and waved his right hand. He was now using the same arm as a baton, beating to the beat of the chant. The crowd roared.

"**S**cabbard One to Swordsman... Do you copy?
"Roger, what's up?"
"Scabbards Two to Seven are asking what's going on?"
"It's just the crowd chanting. Anything else?"
"Just asking, Sir. No, nothing else."
"Standby on yellow as before. Over and out."
"Standby on yellow as before. Roger, Sir."

His adrenalin rising no doubt from the thunderous response of the crowd, Mahalina adjusted his glasses, the words in the teleprompter coming out clearer. He continued:

"My countrymen, topmost in the programs of this administration is my program of 'Mahal for the People.' Priorities under this program are to provide jobs for the jobless with higher pay scales, poverty alleviation and housing."

The roar of the crowd exploded in several thunderbursts in the high noon heat. Those immediately in front were jumping in euphoria, the chant booming all over again: "Mahal! Mahal! Mahal!"

As the president raised his right arm for silence, the thunderous applause gradually subsided.

"You got them now. You got them now, Mahal." Pat Gan-Alfonso cheered to herself, her heart thumping faster.

"For those of you who are in dire need of these priorities, I say do not make demands on your President. It is your President who will make demands on himself. For Mahal, it is action now or never!"

When Mahalina spoke those lines, the crowd exploded into a deafening roar, like the roar of a hundred and one jetliners taking off. The earth shook. "Mahal! Mahal! Mahal! Mahal! Mahal! Mahal! Mahal!"

"Scabbard One to Swordsman May Day! May Day! Do you copy? May Day! May Day!"

"This is Swordsman, what? Repeat, Scabbard One, Repeat…"

"Scabbard Seven reports bombing of La Mesa Dam. I repeat, Scabbard Seven reports bombing of La Mesa Dam. Scabbard Six reports bombing of government TV Station Channel Four. Both bombings occurred two minutes ago. Do you copy?"

"Two bombings occurred two minutes ago? Did you double check? Do you copy?"

"Roger, Sir. Both bombings are confirmed."

"Sound off all Scabbards—Red Alert, Stage Two is on. I repeat, Red Alert, Stage Two is on. Do you copy?"

"Roger, Sir, loud and clear. Red Alert, Stage Two is on."

"Over and out."

General Pecson grabbed another handheld radio from his aide. "This is Swordsman. Secure periphery. I repeat, secure periphery!"

"Roger Sir."

Handling back the handheld radio, General Pecson then lowered his head, whispering to the hidden microphone inside his sports jacket. "Prepare Casanova exit. Repeat, prepare Casanova exit."

Some 15 plainclothes security on stage pretended to scratch their ears or straighten their lapels where hidden high-tech miniature devices received the order of the general.

"Roger, Sir," was the simultaneous whispers that followed.

Fully focused now, Mahalina took a deep breath. As soon as the chanting subsided, he continued, raising his voice to a higher pitch.

"So far I have enumerated to you the four major problems this administration has inherited from the past administration and my plans to resolve them."

The president paused, looking at the margin and then raised his voice a little more.

"But there is another major problem I think most of you are fully aware of by now. I refer to the renewed hostilities in the southern part of this republic, perpetuated by Muslim extremists and separatists."

This time the president raised his voice much higher.

"My countrymen, I was elected President because of my love for the people of this country. These extremists and separatists think otherwise and intend to disrupt my agenda of love for the people. Let me remind these authors of deceit and perpetrators of bloodshed, that Mahal was not born yesterday, that Mahal will never blink at the first sign of threat and that Mahal will never run away from a good fight, whether that fight be fought with fists or with guns."

Looking at the margin, he changed the tenor of his voice.

"Let me apologize immediately to the ladies and gentlemen in the audience who had been schooled in the language of culture and refinement, for I tend to be rough sounding and unpresidential."

Then he raised his voice to full throttle.

"But in situations such as what we are experiencing today in Mindanao, your President will only talk in the language the enemy understands. And this is my message: You want war? You get war. You want peace? You get peace. But you cannot have both."

The president paused, his eyes now misty, his whole body shaking a little. He looked at the margin. He lowered his voice.

"I am not a diplomat. I am not an academician. Neither am I a freak. I am a fighter because I want to redress a wrong... because I hate deceit, I hate abuse and I hate all types of aggression."

Mahalina paused, inhaled deeply and raised his voice to full throttle again.

"The campaign for the presidency is over. I won and I won overwhelmingly. Now that I am President, I must act and act decisively to obliterate the enemy from the face of this republic. I will do this not because I want my people to love me more but because I love my country deeply than most."

He paused, counted three as instructed in the margin and then raised his head toward the blazing sun.

Bowing, he whispered: "May God in his infinite mercy bless us all."

The VIPs on the front row stood to shake the hand of the president as he went back to his seat. Just then, Rickie Balete, the Most Exalted Brother of the Brotherhood of Faith in Jesus Movement and the president's spiritual adviser, strode toward the center of the stage and raising his handheld microphone, intoned, "Let us pray..." as all those on stage stood and bowed their heads.

"Almighty Father in heaven, creator of the universe and author of all faiths and creeds, we thank you for the blessings you have bestowed upon us, by granting to us President Juancho "Mahal" Mahalina, the new leader of our nation.

"As we bow our heads in gratitude, we see in the horizon many hopes and many fears: many hopes because President Mahalina fully understands the plight of our people, many of whom are poor in spirit; many fears because our nation is confronted with many problems.

"But as you have taught us, Almighty Father, in Chapter 3 in the Book of Ecclesiastes, there is a time for every purpose. In verse 2, a time to be born and a time to die, in verse 3, a time to kill and a time to heal and in verse 8, a time to love and a time to hate, a time of war and a time of peace. Almighty Father, through your son the Lord-Jesus, we invoke your divine wisdom to guide our beloved President Juancho "Mahal" Mahalina to pursue his course of action, to raise our hopes and to assuage our fears. For again as you said in the same book, in the same chapter, in verse 13, all men should eat and drink and enjoy the good of all their labor for all this is the gift of God to them.

"Father in heaven, please accept our offering of love to you as the faith's One Thousand Voices Choir renders our closing prayer in your name."

From both sides of the gigantic stage, one third of the choir of One Thousand Voices took their places between the Most Exalted Brother out front and the first row of VIPs headed by the president from behind. The rest took their formation on the improvised steps fronting the stage below.

"Go, go go!" General Pecson whispered to his pocket microphone as he quickly strode toward the president. The close-in security detail of 15 jumped cat-like on their feet and cordoned off the president in three seconds flat without knocking off seats or chairs in between.

The spectators seated on the bleachers above the stage gasped, some stood and leaned over some heads but immediately went back to their seats. The gaze of General Pecson and the swagger stick he lifted in his right arm gave them the signal to keep still.

"Mr. President," General Pecson said as he held the upper right arm of the president. "We have to get you out of here, now. Bombs have exploded and this area might be next."

Pat Gan-Alfonso froze in her seat. She heard what General Pecson said and she saw the worried look of Mahalina as they whisked him out of her sight.

The VIPs and guests on stage parted in the middle as the close-in presidential security detail rushed out backstage, covering the president from all sides.

In the parking area, handheld radios cackled, car doors were yanked open and slammed shut. The motorcycle escorts leading the presidential limousine and the cars behind in red plates gunned their motors, switched on their headlights, turned off their blinkers, moved on and veered west. This convoy was the decoy. Meanwhile, the heavily tinted big black suburban with security plates veered east with neither blinkers nor headlights. Three cars went ahead of it and four cars followed. This convoy was the security detail escorting the president. Inside the suburban, General Pecson gave the details of the bombings. The president cursed, unbuttoned his collar and lit a cigarette.

The One Thousand Voices Choir of the Brotherhood of Faith in Jesus Movement, their hands clasped before them, their heads bowed, their gowns immaculate began with a hum. Then its four harmonious voices: soprano, alto, tenor and bass gradually rose and cascaded in the air as it worshipped the omnipotence of the Almighty. The crowd suddenly went still in silence and meditation.

Our Father who art in heaven,
Hallowed be thy name,
Thy kingdom come, thy will be done,
On earth as it is in heaven.

"Ma'am, message from the Swordsman," her security escort handed her the handheld radio.

"Swordsman to Nightingale, do you copy? Over."

Pressing it on her right ear, Pat Gan-Alfonso whispered, the harmonious blending of 1,000 voices soaring over the bowed heads of millions in the noon heat, "Copy. This is Nightingale, over."

"You are to fly to the Eagle's nest, ASAP. Casanova is waiting. Do you copy? Over."

"Nightingale is on her way. Over."

"Over and out."

At about the time Pat Gan-Alfonso was hastily led by her aide and two bodyguards towards the rear exit of the Quirino Grandstand, some 300 meters away, a large canvas-covered truck was stopped by the police officer manning the traffic flow along Roxas Boulevard fronting the Manila Hotel. The large motorcycle navigating in front of the truck also stopped.

"Heh, Mister!" the police officer yelled, approaching the truck driver's side, his right hand resting on his service revolver. "You are supposed to take the right lane!"

Before he could finish, the motorcycle rider at the front of the truck twisted the bike's throttle as the rear wheel spun and shrieked furiously. Like the head of a striking cobra, the front wheel went up as the bike's full power kicked its whole body out of the pavement, headed straight ahead and rammed the police officer's front torso. Doing a swift U-turn, the bike stopped just below the truck driver's side, as its engine roared three times. At that same instant, the truck driver leaped from above, landed cat-like on the pavement, leap-frogged and took the backseat as the motorcycle roared and zigzagged through the open spaces, between the lines of cars and vans behind the truck, spewing burnt gas and black smoke.

The police officer totally caught flatfooted, picked himself up from the pavement, wiping off the dust on his arms and uniform. He groaned as he felt the impact of the motorcycle's front wheel on his chest. Then he remembered. A red alert was sounded just some four minutes ago. The La Mesa Dam was bombed. The government TV station was bombed.

Looking at the commuters that started to gather around and the motorists who were honking their horns as well as some of those who were already out of their vehicles, the police officer suddenly took several steps backward, staring at the truck, his mind on the fleeing motorcycle and the truck driver on its back. With one swift motion, the police officer drew his service revolver, fired successive shots in the air, shouting while pointing at the truck with his left arm, "It's a bomb! It's a bomb! Run! Run! Run!!!"

On stage, Rickie Balete, the president's spiritual adviser, turned his face toward the sky as the choir's 1,000 voices soared through the peak of the hymn's eternal exaltation:

For Thine is the kingdom,
And the power,
And the glorrry foreeever,
Aamen."

"Praise the Lord Jesus!" Balete roared, the crowd roaring back, "Hallelujah! Hallelujah! Hallelujah!"

Rickie Balete roared again, "Praise the Lord Jesus!" Balete's head was up, his eyes closed, his arms spread-eagled toward the sky, his whole body shaking, feeling the mighty spirit of the Lord upon him. But before the crowd could roar back, the bomb inside the abandoned truck, some 300 meters away, exploded into a thousand and one thunderous eruptions, as pandemonium broke loose.

All eyes were glued to "Truth or Tale", the most talked about talk show in town. It was seven o'clock Wednesday evening, the sixth day after the bombings. Like most events that capture national headlines, the bombings generated their own blasts of tall stories and morbid jokes, not unusual in a country where rumors and gossips mushroom after every tragedy. Still, people wanted to be updated about the bombings, the latest national whodunit. The well known guests of the show were expected to provide the answers in a more objective and comprehensive manner, in contrast to the isolated if not emotion-laden news reports and radio broadcasts that only added more confusion to the mystery.

Thus, people's eyes were glued to their TV sets. Vito Sta. Dolores, the male host was already midway in his introductory statements.

VITO   And now, to the question, how come until today, which is the sixth day, no one has claimed responsibility for the bombings, which is unusual, isn't it?   And so, to answer some if not all our questions and to assuage public apprehension, we have in our panel the Honorable Randolf Patis Cruz, Press Secretary representing the Office of the President; the Honorable Renato Barbason, Chairman of the House Committee on Public Order and Security; newspaper columnist Feliz Salamanca who has been writing about the bombings in her usual incisive ways; General Ricardo Valdez who is on top of the investigation team; and last but not least, Mrs. Dorcas Marcelino, a private citizen who was right in front of the stage during the inauguration day. Tina?

TINA   Thank you, Vito. And thank you, too, for our guests. We are deeply honored. To our viewers, you may call us for your reactions on the telephone numbers you see on your split screens, while those in the studio may just raise their hands later. Let's have a word or two from our sponsors. Stay with us.

On TV, the prince of local movies and darling of TV commercials, Kidd Batuta looms on screen as he takes a big round bite of his favorite jumbo sandwich, his dimples flashing. Then Luningning Morena, Miss Universe 1st runner-up glides on the fashion ramp, her eyes glistening their cutie, little stars as her oh-so-slim body displays the latest lingerie for women of all ages above and below her open midriff. Then Steve Karate, the bone-cracking international martial arts champion and villain-hero movie idol, his macho grin ever so cool, withdraws the glass of sparkling liquid gold rum from his lips as he intones, sighing with satisfaction—"Only in the Philippines..."

VITO   We're back. Tina, I think we should first ask Mrs. Dorcas Marcelino what she saw and heard and what she did as soon as the bomb exploded. Mrs. Marcelino?

MARCELINO Well, I'm telling you that I am still nervous not just because of that bomb but because I'm here. This is my first TV appearance and I didn't know...

TINA   That's okay, Mrs. Marcelino. I am sure our viewers will appreciate hearing your experience on inauguration day.

MARCELINO Thank you. I was in the 12th row, I recall now, fronting the stage when Brother Rickie Balete started jumping at the center of the stage and shouting Praise the Lord Jesus! Praise the Lord Jesus! when I heard the explosion. Suddenly people were shouting 'Bomb! Bomb!' When I heard that, I suddenly remembered what my father used to remind my brothers, sisters and I when we were young that when inside a movie house and somebody shouts 'Fire! Fire!', never make any move until you know what's really going on and where you want to go. So when I heard Bomb! Bomb! I just stayed in my spot, held on to my two kids who were with me. And that's it.

TINA   And then what happened next?

MARCELINO Well, as I said, I just stood there holding on to my two kids while people were shrieking and scampering toward the sides because they could not move forward. The massive stage was in front, you know.

VITO   Did you see President Mahalina on stage while this was going on?

MARCELINO No, I mean, I stretched my neck to look for President Mahal on stage but the stage was now empty except for Brother Balete who was no longer shouting, Praise the Lord Jesus. He just stood there, alone on stage, as if he was praying again. Though, on second thought, he might have just stood there because he was too stunned to move.

TINA   Mrs. Marcelino, from where you stood, how loud was the explosion? Was it just loud or very loud?

MARCELINO It was really very loud. And the shrieking and shouting all around me made the whole thing terribly deafening.

VITO   Just to clarify. Mrs. Marcelino, you said you stretched your neck to look for President Mahalina on stage. Why did that occur to you at the very moment when everybody was already in panic?

MARCELINO   Well, it was kind of automatic. It struck me, if anything happened to my idol the President, my whole family, our entire barangay who voted for him will naturally be devastated.

VITO   Tina?

TINA   There you are folks. If only people will learn what Mrs. Marcelino did in the middle of a panic, then I believe fewer people will be hurt. Remember folks, when somebody shouts 'Fire!' or 'Bomb!' never, never panic! In the meanwhile, let's have a word or two from our sponsors. Please stay with us.

Off camera range, the Honorable Press Secretary stands to shake the hand of Mrs. Marcelino. "You did very well, Mrs. Marcelino or shall I simply call you Dorcas? President Mahalina is doing all he can to catch the perpetrators of this horrible deed. Be assured he will hear what you just said about him."

On TV, Kidd Batuta, Luningning Morena and Steve Karate breeze through their commercials.

TINA   We're back on "Truth or Tale", the most talked about talk show in town. Vito?

VITO   Thank you Tina. I think at this time, our viewers are very eager to hear from the honorable Press Secretary, what the President feels about this whole thing. Secretary Randolf Patis Cruz, please.

CRUZ   Thank you, Vito. As most people already know, President Mahalina acted immediately by ordering the police authorities to catch the perpetrators of this horrible deed and send them to jail. That order...

SALAMANCA   I'd like to remind the Press Secretary that that order was given six days ago, when the police was given by the president 48 hours to solve the bombing. Today is already the sixth day!

CRUZ   That is correct except that the deadline had to be extended. No one has claimed responsibility for the bombings and that makes it doubly difficult to pinpoint the perpetrators. I am sure General Valdez here would be in a better position to give our viewers the details. But before he speaks, may I assure the public that President Mahalina is trying his best to solve this problem at the soonest time possible, under the circumstances.

SALAMANCA   Soonest time possible! This is already the sixth day! Why can't you just tell us where we are right now to set the record straight?

CRUZ   And if I may add... in the most expeditious way, under the circumstances. President Mahalina has appealed to the public not to panic and pleaded for their understanding.

VITO   General Valdez, as head of the investigation team, may we ask you how far have you and your team gone into the investigation and how soon is soonest?

VALDEZ The Press Secretary was correct when he said the deadline set by the President had to be extended, for the simple reason that no one has so far claimed responsibility for the bombings. It is really very difficult if you start from scratch since everybody becomes a suspect. In addition to that, the NBI has not, as of today, given us any hint on the make or type of the bombs used. All they've told us, so far, was that they are having difficulty, that the bombs could be of some new type and kind.

SALAMANCA In that case, why don't you ask the help of the FBI, Scotland Yard, if you and your people cannot do it?

VALDEZ In fairness to the NBI, they've already sent fragments of the bombs to the FBI for further analysis

TINA When do we expect the FBI to get back to your team?

VALDEZ I cannot really say but in cases like this, the FBI has always been very responsive.

CRUZ I would like to add that it is not only the police that are in this thing. All intelligence services, including the Presidential Security Battalion are also involved. President Mahalina has outstanding orders...

SALAMANCA All intelligence services, my eye! No wonder, this case has dragged for six days now. Too many cooks spoil the broth. No wonder the public is getting furious!

VITO This is getting to be interesting. Let's have one or two words from our sponsors.

TINA Don't go away. We'll be back.

As Tina's face fades out, Kidd Batuta, Luningning Morena and Steve Karate breeze through their commercials.

Off camera range, the exchange between the panelists continues. The press secretary appeals to the lady columnist to please temper her comments as these might lead to some breach of national security. "Shit, what breach of national security are you talking about?" The lady columnist raises her voice. "What you are saying is pure and simple canard. When bombs explode in public, that, Mr. Press Secretary becomes a matter of public concern! Or are you hiding something?" "Feliz, I didn't mean to upset you," the press secretary says, "What I really wanted to say was..." Vito cuts them off.

VITO Welcome back to "Truth or Tale"—live. So far, we've asked two of our guests to help us with some answers the public had been asking all along about the unsolved bombings, with Lady Columnist Feliz Salamanca giving some reactions in between. Now, may we ask the Honorable Congressman who chairs the House Committee on Public Order and Security, Congressman Renato Barbason. Sir, please...

BARBASON Thank you, Vito. We in the House are very concerned about this. That is why as chairman of the Committee on Public Order and Security, I have already urged my colleagues that the committee conduct an investigation ...

SALAMANCA Another investigation? Oh my God, oh my …
BARBASON in aid of legislation. Feliz here knows that we need to tighten our security apparatus in the interest of public order and security.
SALAMANCA In aid of legislation or in aid of grandstanding for reelection?
VALDEZ Feliz, I… I… I fully agree with the honorable congressman. To be honest about it, the police force is in dire need of manpower, modern equipment, weapons and of course, higher pay scales. We need all these to effectively combat crime and terrorism.
TINA In short, you are thinking of passing a law…
CRUZ Actually, President Mahalina supports that idea.
SALAMANCA Just a minute, just a minute! What has all this got to do with the immediate problem? The public is in furor, the bombers are on the loose and another bomb or bombs might just blow us up to kingdom come, anytime. And here we have high government officials talking about something else!
VITO Feliz, if you were the President what would …
SALAMANCA Now Vito, don't be naughty. You know…
VITO I mean just for the sake of picking on your brains. You seem to have a good idea what to do…
SALAMANCA Hunt down those bombers, tie them up and then line them up against the wall!
TINA You know President Mahalina used strong language when he delivered his inaugural address. He said something like if you want war, you get war, if you want a good fight, you'll get it whether with fists or with guns. Did he really mean that? I mean, apply the same in this situation?
CRUZ The President was specifically referring to the Muslim extremists and separatists.
TINA What if the bombings were the handiwork of these people?
CRUZ Now Tina, that's highly speculative. That is why we are conducting an investigation.
BARBASON That is why in the House, we would also like to do our share.
VITO What do you think? Why, why until today, no one has yet claimed responsibility for the bombings? Isn't that rather unusual? In the past, it only took some hours after and then…
TINA Excuse me, Vito. We have a very important caller. It's the President!
VITO Magnify the audio! Magnify!
PRESIDENT Good evening, Vito. Good evening, Tina. Good evening all. Hik! I know why there is no claim. There is no claim because the bombers are cowards. They are cowards because they hide. Sonnamagun! You cowards, you come out! I fight you with fists or guns. Pak! Pak! Pak! If you don't, then I hunt you. Then I line you against wall. Right Feliz? Hik! Vito, Tina, tell all. Tomorrow, I take over. All investigators report direct to me. Sonnamagun! That is all. Good evening to you all. Hik!
VITO Yes, Sir, Mr. President! Well, you've heard the man. Let's have a station break.
TINA Don't go away. We'll be back.

As the studio scene fades out, Kidd Batuta, Luningning Morena and Steve Karate breeze through their commercials, Karate ending his rum sale with the classic sigh: "...Only in the Philippines."

VITO We're back folks. Tina?

TINA Yes, Vito. We've got hundreds of callers reacting to the President's statements earlier. Shall we take some of them now?

VITO I am not surprised. The President surely hits back hard when provoked. And when he does that, most people love it, err, probably a few don't. Anyway, I think those calls can wait. We have plenty of time later. But we still have to call on Feliz Salamanca, not as an inquisitor at this time but as a member of the panel. Feliz, please.

SALAMANCA Inquisitor! Anyway, Vito, before I say my piece as a panelist, may I just ask a few questions which I would like to direct at Mrs. Marcelino? Would that be okay?

VITO No problem. She's yours.

SALAMANCA Mrs. Marcelino, let us go back for a moment to the inaugural ceremony before the bomb explosion. Do you recall the choir that sang the Lord's Prayer?

MARCELINO Yes, it was so touching. They were all in white gowns. And they sang like angels! My hair stood on end.

SALAMANCA From where you stood, you said you were some twelve rows from the stage front, did you see clearly what was going on at that time on the stage?

CRUZ What's the bitch getting into? Don't turn your face. Just whisper.

VALDEZ I'm not sure, Sir, but definitely...

MARCELINO Every thing was clear. The sun was very bright and very hot but just at the back of my head. As a matter of fact, while I was deeply touched by the singing, I was also...how do I say it... kind of disappointed because I could not anymore see my idol, President Mahal. He was covered from the front by the thousand singers.

VITO Now, Feliz, what's going on?

SALAMANCA Please Vito, this is important. Now, Mrs. Marcelino, you just said that you could not see the President at the moment, because he was covered by the curtain of singers from the front, from your line of vision. Right? Okay. At that precise moment, did you also see the people at the top of the bleachers overlooking the stage below?

MARCELINO Yes, yes. Now I remember because all of a sudden some of those people at the top of the bleachers suddenly stood and started pointing their fingers toward where the President was, behind the curtain of singers. In fact, it occurred to me at that very moment that something was happening to the President, but that was only for a few seconds because those people up there suddenly went back to sit on the bleachers as the singing of the Lord's Prayer went on.

SALAMANCA Thank you very much, Mrs. Marcelino.

VITO I'm totally intrigued. Now, what gives, Feliz?

TINA I am too. In fact, I'm in pins and needles right now!

SALAMANCA Actually, what Mrs. Marcelino just told us confirms what some people on top of the bleachers also told me—that the President was bodily whisked out of that stage by his security people, immediately after he, the President was covered by the curtain of singers from the front.

CRUZ What are you saying?

SALAMANCA I am saying the President already knew a bomb was about to be exploded before, I repeat, before the bomb actually exploded.

BARBASON So?

TINA So?

VITO So?

SALAMANCA I'm saying the people should have been forewarned! What appears now is the President of this republic ran away to save his own dear life and abandoned his people to the mercy of the bomb! That 23 innocent civilians including a police officer were directly hit and killed, that hundreds of other people broke their bones and one old man died because of the stampede that followed was bad enough. But for the President of this republic who professed love for his people, who said he won't blink at the first sign of danger, who in his inaugural address orated he would fight with fists or with guns... to run away like a scared rabbit at the first sign of danger is simply beyond the comprehension of ordinary mortals like me. This is a classic case of a self-proclaimed fighter who fled! I'm not saying President Mahalina is a coward but some people are already saying he has no balls! I believe...

TINA My God!

VITO Jesus Christ!

BARBASON Oh, my God!

CRUZ Feliz, I'm warning you!

VITO Let's have a station break.

TINA Don't go away... we'll be back.

Dear Angeling,

Thank you for your last email. Wow! So, you've finally found your ideal man. That's really great and I am very happy for you. Imagine, hitting the proverbial two birds with one stone. You got not only your new love but also your new Boss! By the way, how much is he paying you a month, eh? What did you mean when you said that he is so big and so tall and yet so tender? Is it because he is already 65 years old? Or is it because he really cares for you? Or is it both? Well, the mere fact that he proposed marriage is a sign that he is serious. Anyway, if I know you, you would not just plunge into something if you weren't sure about it. Okay, we all make mistakes but who doesn't? I am definite that with our mutual sad experience in the arena of love or marriage, we can't afford to make another big mistake. In my case, I fell in love but didn't marry but I have my son Tony Boy and that's compensating enough. In your case, you fell in love, got married to Reynante, then broke up with him but you have two lovely daughters.

So what is there to fret about? Well, my advice to my dearest friend and cousin is to simply wait for say—two months. Anyway, if he is that persistent, two months aren't really that long. You met, did you say, five months ago, so that makes a total of seven months. I think that is just right, Angeling. Overall, that will also tell him that you are not that easy. That's how we maintain the balance, right? It's like the cha-cha-cha. Parry and thrust, thrust and parry otherwise if you allow him to push and push you, you'll have no more space to move forward but backward and backward you retreat, as he dominates. Got it? Ha! Ha!

Just make sure the wedding should be in our hometown and Fili is your Maid of Honor. The mere fact that he also told you he'd marry you anywhere in the world, is already an assurance that he is that sure and sincere. But again, don't be in a hurry. Just two more months, Angeling and believe me, everything will be all right. Do write me about this by next email. Promise?

Our old folks at home, especially Lolo Didong want me back to our hometown for good, after I finish my masteral studies. Since you had been definite not to come home anymore, much more run for mayor, Lolo Didong and our clan have decided it should be me. The clan, he says, has decided that I run for mayor not only to vindicate the murder of your father (am sorry to mention again the death of Uncle Waldo) but also to redeem what we as a clan lost in pride and prestige.

In addition, Lolo Didong says I am the only one left of age (just like you), the only one who finished college (again, just like you) and the only one who showed political promise as early in high school (also just like you). That's what they say, the rest of our close relatives with potentials are much younger and still in school.

So I am really seriously thinking about all this. What do you say? Besides Angeling, I'm really getting pissed off by the situation here: escalating prices, pollution, traffic, demonstrations, crime, floods and what have you.

The dismal political situation is another. Believe it or not, the bombings until now have not been solved. A month and a half passed and still no solution. What is ironic is that according to the authorities, the problem has become more complicated because two groups have already claimed responsibility, thus the authorities have to first determine who between the two groups really did it. Isn't that the most stupid of all inanities? Why don't they just go after the two groups and line them up against the wall? That was what Mahalina said he would do many times over, on TV and everywhere else every time he opens his mouth. What makes it worse is that the media is making mincemeat out of his unfulfilled campaign promises and has dubbed him as an inutile president.

The people are beginning to be restive and the communists are getting active again. The war between the government and the Muslim rebels are getting worse day after day. It's kind of scary nowadays to go to the malls, not to mention government buildings and big business offices because of talks and threats of more bombings and sabotage.

The street demons are at it again. Demos here, demos there. It seems that every issue is worth dying for in the streets. I don't know. Some say, all this is an indication of our crab mentality. Others say, they're tired of the presidency, thus the move to break away from imperial Manila. Still others say, losers can't accept they're losers so they vent their frustrations in the streets. On the other hand, I remember in "Truth or Tale", one said people join demos for the "fund of it" You know what that means? Well…

Please don't forget to tell me more about your new love and Boss. You promised to send me pictures. Better still, have it posted on your web page. Oh yes, your mother called the other day.   Your two daughters are as usual robust and in the best of health.

Shall I break the news of your forthcoming wedding to Mother Dear or will you just surprise her two months from now?   Ha, ha!   Bye for now and my best regards to your new love.

From KISS to KISS,

Fili

6
ARE WE HERE

Simeon Sempron sat on the fallen log bordering the northern portion of his farm lot at the top of the hill of barangay Kadugay, in the municipality of Lo-oc. The sun at three o'clock was scorching hot. The leaves of trees did not move. Only the sound of distant birds stirred, a sign that no matter how faint, the world around him was still alive. Thirty-eight days had gone and still no rain. Most of his new corn stalks were wilted. He and his wife Petra prayed hard in the early mornings but apparently the Good Lord had not heard their prayers, their pleadings for just one torrent of rain.

Two more days and it would be school opening again. Three of their seven children would be back in school and on foot, negotiate the five kilometers of rough terrain to and from the Libertad elementary school. And he had not bought the new rubber slippers he promised them. Their school uniforms were still good for another year, Petra, his wife, kept on assuring him, so there was nothing to worry about. Just the new set of notebooks and pencils, the daily *baon* (ration) for lunch and the new rubber slippers, of course.

Sempron examined his feet. His toenails were cracked and the calluses around them as hard and stiff as those of a carabao hide. The varicose veins at the back of his legs now looked like giant earthworms. Sempron had no rubber slippers but he had sandals fashioned out of what was left of an abandoned tire he found at the back of the vulcanizing shop along the highway, his favorite spot to relieve himself after three kilometers of hiking from his farm. His three kids used to laugh at him as he limped in his sandals. He had at the start used some discarded electric wires, again courtesy of the vulcanizing junkshop, to tie them around his feet, but they dug into his ankles after some walking and that made him limp. He had since changed them into strips of rubber and no more laughter from his sons came after that.

Sempron was stripped of his seat in the barangay council after he returned the P100 the barangay captain slipped in his shirt pocket sometime during the last presidential campaign. In fact, Simeon Sempron had delivered a speech before the council, saying his conscience bothered him. In that speech, he minced no words as he declared he could not just shift loyalties, that the bribe money was an insult to people empowerment. In the verge of tears, he concluded that progress in the barangay could never be achieved if public officials like him and his colleagues in the council would allow themselves to be corrupted. Everybody listened to him. But after one week he was stripped of his seat. He was an appointed councilman, not elected.

Sempron was the only high school graduate in the council. Two went as high as second year, another two finished elementary grades and the rest did not. Simeon Sempron used to think it was his duty to share with his colleagues the virtues of holding on to principles, much more that they were all holding official duties in their barangay.

But what happened? Months passed and the council had yet to be convened. Since the violent deaths of Barangay Captain Pablo Tabile and Councilman Cardo Roque, there had been no peace in Kadugay. An OIC had been designated but could not bring together the two warring groups: the supporters of Tabile, on one hand and those of Roque, on the other. Diego, the suspect, could not be found. People were on edge.

As he saw the sun slowly dip in the west, Sempron again thought of the rubber slippers for his three children. The honorarium he used to get as a councilman could have taken care of the slippers. And now the young stalks of corn were wilted.

Sempron stood and stretched his back. As he headed for his nipa hut, he wondered if indeed his family could eat his principles, an admonition that Petra, his wife, kept on nagging him about.

Priscilla Batungbakal, mother of six, president of the Integrated Homeowners Association of Caloocan City and newly elected overall chairperson of the march to the palace coalition, stood as she acknowledged the wild cheers of the crowd before her.

"My friends," Batungbakal began, her voice shrill, her eyes angry, her right fist clenched, her left gripping the standing microphone in front of her. "We should thank ourselves for working our butts off in the last nine hours to come out with two resolutions for immediate implementation. First: for President Mahalina to immediately deliver to us his campaign promises. Second, immediate arrest and incarceration of the criminals and murderers who bombed and took the lives of four of our officials headed by Father Tim and the nine others wounded two years ago. The President again promised he would not allow criminals to go unpunished, that he himself would pursue them, if the inutile police officers fail to do their duties.

"But my friends, as we thank ourselves for agreeing on these resolutions, so should we also condemn ourselves for acting like bureaucrats, writing our demands on paper like run-of-the-mill type of complainers and whiners and for playing the role of beggars in the streets all the time. Why? Why is this? Whyyyy?

"It is because we have allowed ourselves to be used as prostitutes, prooostitutes! The only difference is that prostitutes earn everyday because they are used everyday, everrrryday! We? The politicians use us only during elections and forget us until the nexxxt elections."

The crowd began to groan. Some snickered.

"Let me tell you. I am now 46 years old. My eldest is 22, high school graduate, now a professional janitor in that mall at North EDSA. My youngest is five. I have nine children in all. Ninnnne! Now, where did all of them come from? From here—herrrre!" she thumped her navel. The crowd winced. "And where did they come out? Here, herrrre between my legs!" she spread her legs. The crowd roared.

"Now, why am I telling you this? Why did we bear many children? It is because the politicians, pooliticians promised, proommised us the good life, education for the children, good paying jobs and a house and lot! So we organized

200

our group into what those government agencies want to call homeowners association. Our association became known as the Caloocan City Integrated Homeowners Association. That was 18 years ago. Eighhhhten! What do we have today? We still have the association but no homes. No hommmes! No jobs! My husband works only four hours a day at the North Harbor because there are so many without jobs to be accommodated. I stopped long ago looking for low paying jobs. I was the first to put up our own *sari-sari* store but now every shack in the neighborhood has its own *sari-sari store*! So no more sales! [The crowd laughed] Home lot? The local government and that Chinese are now negotiating to convert our claim into a mall! Malllll! So, no more house and lot. Home? Homeless! So, homelessssss association. So what do we have?"

Somebody shouted "children!"

"Coorreecct! Children! Chilllldren, plus of course, my husband. My husband, I had him vasectomized." The men groaned. "And he insisted I be ligated so we will be equal! So, I was *ligatized. Ligatizhashunn. Tubally ligatizazazhunn*!!!" The crowd howled and bawled.

"So why am I telling you all this? Because I am fed up, fed up! My family is fed up. We are all tired of politicians, pooliticians and their proomises and for making us prooostitutes during erections—opsss... elections!" The crowd thundered.

"How about you, Mr. Tirol and your association?"

On the makeshift stage, Percival Tirol, chairman of the Metro Manila Association of Tricycle Drivers and Operators fidgeted in his seat.

"Has the price of oil gone down as promised to you two years ago?"

Below the stage, the delegates of the association bawled, 'No, No, Noooooo!' as Tirol vigorously nodded his head.

"How about you, Mrs. Loreta Amatong and your urban poor coalition, have you got your house and lot as promised two years ago?"

On stage, Mrs. Amatong, president of the National Urban Poor Coalition shook her head as her delegation below shouted, 'No! No! Nooooooo!'

"How about you, Mr. Cuarisma and your Metro Manila Vendors Federation, have you got your stalls installed or were you instead driven out of the sidewalks and your livelihood? Did you get what you were promised two years ago?"

On stage, Eutaquio Cuarisma, president of the Metro Manila Sidewalk Vendors Federation stood as he shouted 'No!' His delegation below echoed, 'No! No! Nooooooo!'

"How about you Brother Vic Taglen and your national organization of small farmers, has this administration increased your production in the last two years?"

On stage, Vicente Taglen, president of the National Federation of Small Farmers and Fishermen raised the thumbs-down sign as his delegation below cursed. One shouted, 'Forget it!' and followed that up with expletives.

"How about the rest of our groups here representing the women, the youth, the rural workers—has anyone of you been the recipient of any government grant as a result of the flowery promises of this administration in the last presidential campaign?" Loud cries of 'No! No! No!' reverberated throughout.

"And let us not forget this," Batungbakal suddenly leaped forward to the edge of the stage, carrying with her the standing microphone. "Let us not forrrget this, where is Father Tim now? What about the other three that died with him? They are six feet below the ground. Six feeeeet below the grrrround! And what are they doing there? They are squirming in their graves, squirrrrming in their graves! Why? Whyyyy? Because until now, no one has been caught, not even a suspect, not even one sussspect! And what did Mahalina say? 'I will pursue them, these criminals. I will line them up against the wall. I will fight them. I will hang them.' Fighhhht them? Hannnng them? Lord in Heaven! Lord in Heaven! *Susmaryosep! Susssmaryosep!!!* Ugh, ugh, ugh. [Batungbakal clasped her face with both her hands as she groaned] I'm sorry but I could not hold my tears anymore. Ugh, ugh, ugh, ugh." Some women in the crowd openly cried. Some men rubbed their eyes.

"I'm okay now... All right, what do we do now? What do we doooo now? What do we do nowwww? Do we stay here forever? Foreeeever? We cannot. We cannnnot!

"I suggest then that we stop this foolishness of marching to the palace, this foooolishness of writing resolutions, resolutions, resolutions, resolutions on paper or toilet resolutions! We will only be wasting time, wasting saliva, wasssting saliiiiva because the occupant of the palace is deaf, deaf, deaffffff!

"I suggest therefore that instead of marching to the palace and submitting our toilet paper resolutions, we go on hunger strike, hungggger strrrrike! Yes, hunger strike because most of our families are hungry anyway. And we will not stop. We will nnnnnot stop until Mahalina comes to us and delivers what he promised us!!! If Mahalina does not come to us, we will not stop, until we join Father Tim and our three other friends in their graves!"

It was about nine o'clock in the evening. Awakened from their early sleep, the big, round black flies started buzzing loudly around the stench of uncollected garbage, at the back and sides of the makeshift stage where Batungbakal shouted her tirades against injustice and broken promises.

S enator Humphrey Bogart Putto had another hit, not in the form of a landmark legislation the Number One senator of the republic might have sponsored in the august halls of the Senate, but on TV. Unlike the most popular noontime show "Goodah" two years ago where he acted as a comic with an eye for beautiful women, his current new hit, a one-hour show immediately after dinner time featured the deeds and misdeeds of psychics, paranormals, fortune tellers, witch doctors and all types of weirdos and "weirdahs."

Entitled, "Gottah Go, Lab Yah", the show always ended with his signature parting words, the senator winking at his viewers, his thick mustache quivering like a walrus'. It was his signature parting words and his viewers loved it. "Gottah Go, Lab Yah!" became the unofficial parting words in the streets, malls, piers, bars and school grounds as friends, acquaintances and lovers made promises to see each other again. Senator Humphrey Bogart Putto was the show's actor, commentator, interviewer and broadcaster rolled into one.

In one episode, a witch doctor from the hills of Antipolo was Putto's guest. After the camera shots of his abode in the hills, his daily chores of doctoring the sick, the possessed and the afflicted in the hills, the dialogue went this way:

Senator Putto Doctor Witch, who did you vote for in the last election?
Witch Doctor Humphrey Bogart Putto.
Senator Putto Thank you. Only me?
Witch Doctor You and, of course, Mahal.
Senator Putto How many votes did I get in your barangay?
Witch Doctor All our votes went to you and Mahal.
Senator Putto No doctoring?
Doctor Witch Doctoring? Of course not, no doctoring. I swear.
Senator Putto Ha! Ha! Hah! That's it folks. This is your host, Humphrey Bogart Putto, saying Gottah Go, Lab Yah!

At one time, the honorable senator himself became the subject in an ambush interview. He just came out of the august halls of the Senate.

"Mr. Senator, we've been wanting to interview you in the last five sessions but you were not around. Busy elsewhere?"

"Definitely yes, conducting hearings elsewhere, in aid of legislation."

"People are asking why in the last two years, your voice had never been heard in the halls of the Senate and you have the lowest attendance record so far..." They didn't dare say the honorable senator was known as the chairman of the committee of silence in the senate.

"That is not correct. Even though I am not in attendance, I am doing my job as senator."

"Doing your TV show?"

"That's part of it. The people who voted for me are hungry for new information and, and... entertainment, of course."

"What hearings are you conducting in aid of legislation?"

"Many. Among them, for example, are hearings on paranormals. You know, I got this idea from "Truth or Tale", which featured the paranormals. I have been asking myself how come they were able to accurately predict the victory of Mahalina? So that set me going into this, recognizing that there must be a lot of God-given talent in this type of people. And you know, these people need the encouragement and support of the government. They do not only help the poorest of the poor, they also amuse them, give them hope by predicting their small fortunes for the future. If the government gives regular salaries and allowances to artists, authors, writers and so on, why can't it do the same to these people?"

"You mean similar to the National Artist for the Arts or Literature?"

"Definitely. We can start with the barangay, like the Barangay Witch Doctor, Barangay Fortune Teller and so on. Don't you think this is something innovative?"

"I don't know!"

"Well, just watch until I file my first bill. Gottah go, lab yah!"

The sleek, immaculately dressed men began to loosen their neckties and close their folders. It was quarter to five in the afternoon in the executive boardroom of the Metropolitan Business Club (MBC). "Other matters, please," the Chairman tapped the table with his gavel. All heads suddenly turned to the speaker.

"Mr. Chairman, let me congratulate you again for your foresight during the last presidential elections," the president of the largest export-import company in the country, Ziegfred Campos began. "Your brilliance in breaking the impasse by convincing us to stay neutral solidified our club and I think, most of us have been very happy, that was, after we wondered how you did us in just like that, of course. (Laughter.) But times have changed abruptly since then and today, we are faced with some crisis. The economy is down and we are wondering if a turnaround is possible within the next two quarters. The peso has nose-dived against the dollar, the lowest in the last 12 years, unemployment rate is at nine percent, the highest in the last six years, agricultural production is at its lowest, foreign investments are at their lowest, because of cronyism, corruption and nebulous economic policies which, according to the World Bank are the causes of foreign investors' no-confidence in governance. This is not to mention the war in Mindanao and the People's Watch and Revolutionary Army which is getting active again..."

"What's your point, Zieg?" Ruperto del Rosario, Jr., president of the Asian Consolidated Bank and chairman of the board of the Metropolitan Business Club, asked.

"My point, Mr. Chairman is this. Despite staying neutral during the last presidential elections, don't you think it is now time for us to extend a helping hand to the administration, under the circumstances?"

The chairman of the board turned to his colleagues. Everyone seemed to be in deep thought.

"May I hear some comments?"

"Comment here," Leonel Bustamante, president of the Allied Savings and Loans and Investment House, said. "I think the point raised by Zieg is laudable... except that it may put the Club's integrity in some kind of jeopardy later on."

"What do you mean jeopardy?" asked Campos, his tone adversarial.

"I mean, here we are, indifferent before and now suddenly friendly and pat. It stinks!" Leonel Bustamante knew he just spat a stinger. He pretended to examine his notes in his folder.

"What do you mean, stinks?" Ziegfred Campos's voice went up. "Mr. Chairman, all I wanted for this board to consider is to lend a helping hand. What's wrong with that?"

"In what form will that helping hand be, Zieg?" the chairman of the board asked, his tone reconciliatory.

"For example, we can propose to President Mahalina that we extend a helping hand to the thousands of poor people who are now on the 11th day of their hunger strike. My wife keeps on nagging me about this. 'You businessmen should have a social conscience!' She keeps telling me, day in and day out, since the hunger strike started."

"Is it because," Leonel Bustamante cut in, "the hunger strikers are sitting right on top of your property where you intend to put up your new 39 story building?"

"Goddammit!" Ziegfred Campos shouted as he stood, gripping the edge of the table as if he had been electrocuted. "How could you be so goddamned insulting, Leonel…"

"Please sit down, Zieg. Let's cool it, gentlemen," the chairman of the board said, appealing for sobriety.

"Mr. Chairman," Conrado Dimagueba III addressed the presiding officer, after some seconds of silence. "Mr. Chairman, I was just thinking about Zieg's suggestion," the president and CEO of the International Electronics Corporation, continued. "Assuming we decide to extend a helping hand, why do we go through President Mahalina? Why don't we just go direct to the hunger strikers, that is, if that is the direction we would decide to take?"

"Zieg?" the chairman of the board addressed the original proponent.

"If we go direct to the hunger strikers, President Mahalina might be offended," Campos said, his voice quivering. "You know how sensitive the man is. And besides, he knew we did not support him when he ran for the presidency."

"Because you leaked it to him? Because you wanted your brother to get the government contract for that multi-billion peso construction job in Subic?" Leonel Bustamante shouted as he stood.

"Goddammit!" Ziegfred Campos also stood, shouting. "I never leaked any of our agreements in this club to anybody! And goddammit, my brother's construction company got the contract through legitimate means. He was the lowest bidder!"

"Lowest bidder or crony?" Bustamante asked, his voice soft as butter, his tone full of venom.

"Gentlemen, I think I have to declare a break of five minutes," the chairman of the board said, softly tapping the table with his gavel.

On top of the hills of Daly City, overlooking the glittering evening lights of San Francisco, the city by the bay, stood a two-story edifice where on its balcony, a young lady was gazing at the panoramic view. She had been standing there in the last hour or so and the slightly cold wind was beginning to gnaw at her skin.

"Jessica, why don't you come in here? It's freezing cold out there!"

Jessica got inside, closing the partially opened sliding glass partition behind her. She went straight to the sofa, placed two cushions on her lap and sank her elbows on them.

"Jessica, I think we really have to go this time," her statuesque mother said, placing back the fashion magazine she was reading on the low table beside her. "We missed your Daddy's inaugural. We have to attend his second anniversary as President this year."

"Same as missing the reception at the Manila Hotel after his inaugural, right?" Jessica said, leaning back on the sofa, her eyes rolling and mocking.

"Now, Jessica, don't fuck with me. We didn't miss that. It was the bomb that cancelled the reception at the Manila Hotel and not your Daddy. He had to be whisked out of danger, if you still remember. He is the President, you know."

"Yeah, fuck the bomb, fuck the Manila Hotel."

"Jessica, don't use that word on me, Okay? I'm your mother. You heard your Dad on the phone. He wants us to be present this time. Our reservations from Frisco to Manila are already fixed. I just checked Northwest."

"Mom, please I don't wanna go."

"Why is that Jessica? Why is that?" the mother's voice rose.

"Okay, I'll level with you, Mom. I don't wanna be embarrassed... I don't wanna be embarrassed!"

"Where did you get that idea?" the mother's voice rose higher.

"Mom, please don't fu... Mom, please. I heard Dad on my extension line. He said he'd introduce me to my brothers and sisters. I don't have any brother or sister. I'm your only daughter, Mom! Isn't that, right!" the daughter's voice quivered.

The mother slowly stood and headed for the ref where she poured two glasses of cold fresh orange juice.

"Okay, Jessica," she said, sitting down beside her daughter, handing her the other glass of juice. "Let's talk about this in a very rational manner. Okay, I'll level with you."

The daughter didn't say anything nor did she touch the glass of juice in front of her.

"Okay, I was your Daddy's first. I swear to God, I was his first. He proposed marriage to me but I refused because I was very young then and besides my reign as Miss Asia Pacific was one full year. And one of the rules was to strip the beauty title-holder of her title if she got married within the year. I was also looking forward to a career in the movies because since I won, the offers from the industry were just too many and too juicy to ignore. We became intimate and as a result... you were born, here in Daly City, because I had to go incognito. As you know, your Dad was present during your birth. You saw the pictures."

"The others can also claim the same, that they were also his first?"

"I won't contest that. That's human nature."

The daughter's eyes darted from the ceiling to her mother. "And are you happy with this kind of arrangement, Mom?"

"You know what? Because I love him and I know he loves me. And we both love you."

Jessica slipped her elbows out of the cushions and straightened herself up.

"The others can also say the same..."

"I won't contest that. That's human nature."

"You know Mom, I really find this whole thing weird. You claim you are happy but his wife, I mean the woman he married, appears not happy at all. I've been looking at her pictures in the newspapers, her appearances in the boob tube. I haven't seen her really smile, not once! She's the first lady and all... why do you think she's like that?"

"You know Jessica, that's where I think your mother is luckier. I would have hated to be a first lady, going through all that hypocrisy of attending socials here and there, shaking the fucking hands of people you don't know from Adam, sponsoring social projects just because you are expected to sponsor them even if you don't like them and all that hypocrisy. If she isn't smiling, well, it's probably because she is too exhausted or she simply hates the whole baloney. You know if you really go into it, I mean go into the nitty-gritty of what a first lady does, I think you can summarize it in one word... servant, public servant! Thank God, I've been spared of that humiliation."

"Or is it because she knows Dad is also regularly visiting his other paramours and his other sons and daughters? Gosh, what a harem. It sucks!"

"Now Jessica, a harem is a place where the sultan and his wives and concubines stay in one place."

The daughter took her glass of juice then finished it in one gulp.

"I gotta go, Mom. Last exam in two hours," Jessica stood, kissing her Mom's cheek.

"Drive carefully," the mother said. When Jessica opened the door, her mother hollered after her.

"So, we're flying over to see your Dad, okay?"

"I said, I don't wanna go, Mom. Bye." Jessica hollered back, closing the door behind her.

Dick Martin crushed his cigarette on the ashtray. Rushmore Stockman, the resident ambassador seemed unconvinced over his assessment. Recent events told him governance in the country was in jeopardy.

"So, what do you think of this *jihad*? Is this for real or is this just hype?" Marvin Reed, the consul asked while wiping his mouth with a table napkin.

"No, Stick. I don't think its bullshit," Martin said, sounding serious. "On the contrary, to the Moros, a declaration of a holy war is no simple matter. A declaration of a holy war or *jihad* is a declaration for Allah."

"So, why did it take them eternity to declare a holy war?" the ambassador asked. "They've been fighting this government for hundreds of years, so why all of a sudden this *jihad*?"

"Why don't you ask them that, Stock?" Martin said, as he lit another cigarette. "But if you are asking my opinion, I'd say the answer to your question may be gleaned not from here but within the context of a global Islamic movement. Its aim is to establish Islamic states all over the world."

"Oh c'mon, Dick," the ambassador said as he raised his bushy eyebrows. "I think a lot of people are making capital out of that shit. All these are plain fucking excuses for terrorism." After hungrily puffing on his cigarette, he asked, "Are you saying our embassy here is in some sort of fucking danger?"

"No Stock, I'm not saying that," Martin said, sensing the ambassador's discomfort. "Not in the next few months. Note that the declaration of a *jihad* against this government is not a declaration of total war or conventional war. The declaration of *jihad* against the Mahalina administration is a declaration of a protracted guerrilla war. Only when that is launched and its operations getting some success along the way, will they consider your imperial embassy as a possible next target."

207

"The fucking bastards," the ambassador cursed, inhaling deeper on his cigarette.

"What's your agency's assessment of the war in Mindanao?" the consul asked Martin, eyeing the ambassador.

"I told you, what I'm saying here are my personal views. I still have to file my official report. I'm just opening my mouth as a gesture of courtesy to His Honor, the ambassador here who has recently been inviting me for breakfast. Ha! Ha!"

"C'mon, Dickey, what are friends for?" the consul said, grinning.

"Out with that fuck, Dick," the ambassador said, grimacing, winking at the consul. "Nothing comes out from here!"

"No shit?" Dick asked.

"No shit." the ambassador and the consul said, one after the other.

"Okay," Martin said, shrugging his arms in surrender. "The war in Mindanao has devastated the camps of the rebels. But, and this is a big but, only the physical infrastructure. When the government military forces got inside, they didn't find the bastards except some guys who were left behind, probably the dishwashers and the no-pork cooks. Their biggest camp contained some 30,000 people but when the government armed forces got in, not a fucking soul was there. Everybody just disappeared, hightailed to nowhere. That simply tells you the bastards must have prepared for it right from day one when the Mahalina administration announced they'd raze everything out there..."

"Why the fuck did they announce they were going to raze the whole civilization?"

"Search me!" Martin was himself startled by the ambassador's query.

From their seats by the table, the morning panorama of Manila Bay glistened through the thick wall of bullet—proofed glass. The glass had a slight greenish tint. It was five inches thick and would stop an antitank shell. Now and then, splashes of seawater would strike the wall from the outside as waves splashed the rocks above the shoreline. At a discrete distance, a patrol boat disguised as a yacht was anchored. Inside was a contingent of American marines on 24-hour alert, ready to protect the U.S. Embassy along Roxas Boulevard from the sea.

"So, what's the latest on the diplomatic front?" Martin asked, lighting another cigarette.

"I think some people in the diplomatic front are working to gradually freeze new loans, tighten control over exports and the like..."

"Hmmm... and what else?"

"And a host of other disincentives and scenarios..."

"Like for example?"

"That's all the morsels I can tell you, Martin. I know your fucking agency has more info than the whole foreign services put together. So butt off, okay?"

Martin chuckled. The consul chuckled louder.

"So the cowboy is in for harder times?" Martin said, stroking his beard.

"What the fuck are you talking about, Dicky? Harder times, did you say? This is the worst of times! The town's in debt by more than $50 billion, budget deficit for the year is more than P50 billion, the fucking Moro rebels have declared a *jihad* and that means killing everyone who didn't belong to Islam, which includes you and me, Mr. Martin, Sir. The moribund communist guerrilla assholes have suddenly risen from their graves and are killing people again. How would agriculture thrive in this kind of a setting? And, what is agriculture? It's food, right? What would cowboy and his folks eat after, grass?"

"What about Martial Law?"

"Martial Law? Never again! Either this cowboy stays within the bounds of democracy or he gets kicked in the ass. Or, if he's nuts and there are people who are saying he's nuts, then he can go Islamic or communist. And if he does that, you can bet he's in for another desert storm."

"I think you're intruding in the internal affairs…"

"What the fuck are you talking about, Martin? Did you say internal affairs? You still believe in that crap?"

"What about a coup?"

"They tried that again in Oplan Twilight Zone but it was a good thing President Rosales thumbed it down. Besides, I don't think something like that would work right now. The generals and soldiers are still battle scarred from the Mindanao fighting, not to mention those Communist guerrilla assholes that are resurfacing from their graves. No, I don't think a fucking coup will work at this time."

Scene: Ceremonial Hall, Malacanang Palace. Subject: Oath taking of New Members of the Administration Party and Photo-Ops.

"Thank you, Mr. President," chorused the 39 mayors. Each one tried to outdo the other in shaking the hand of President Mahalina who tried to hide his contempt with a manufactured smile at each handshake.

"Welcome to the Party," the president grunted, accompanying each handshake with the greeting. Cameras clicked and flashbulbs popped.

"May I request the honorable mayors to please leave the stage now," the Chief Protocol Officer (CPO) intoned into the microphone. "May I now request the honorable governors to please rise from their seats and move upstage? Thank you."

Ceremonial Hall was packed not because the president was going to deliver his SONA (State of the Nation Address) but because of the relatives, close friends and sponsors of each politician who wanted to have a picture with the president. "May I request the honorable governors to form just one line with the President, in the middle of the stage please, since there are only seven of you, please." The CPO had to make the request since each governor wanted to be on the immediate side of the president.

Cameras clicked as flashbulbs popped.

"Thank you. May I now request the honorable governors to please leave the stage?"

"Thank you, Mr. President, thank you for taking us into your fold."

"Mr. President, your party will be the strongest ever!"

"Mr. President, just say anything you want from my province and I will deliver."

As each governor said his one-liner, no doubt previously rehearsed while maneuvering to get closer to the president for that pose of poses to win more votes in the home front, his own photographer from the side also maneuvered nearer to take the picture. Not everyone was lucky. Security had to bar any one from coming too close.

"May I now request the honorable congressmen to please rise and take their places on stage, please..."

The shorter ones from the second to the fourth rows raised their heels. Some were not lucky. When their knees buckled down, the cameras clicked as flashbulbs popped.

"Mr. President," Congressman Racleto Albanos whispered. "I engineered the mass defection of these people. We are at your service, Mr. President." Shaking the hand of the president for the second time, Albanos maneuvered his body and that of the president toward the front. His own photographer clicked and clicked.

"May I request the honorable congressmen to please leave the stage now. Thank you."

Four senators rose from their seats and mounted the low platform, the "stage" referred to by the CPO, along with their wives, children and relatives.

Senator Naomi Ganzon Santolan was the first to reach the hand of the president. Leaning over, she extended her left cheek as the president buzzed her. Faster than lightning, she withdrew a millimeter away then extended her right cheek as the president buzzed her again and as she returned the kiss, her arms suddenly around him in a sweeping bear hug. The lady senator just executed the "beso-beso", that form of greeting among the rich and the famous. To some sidewalk sociologists, the "beso-beso" had recently become quite common amongst social climbers although its execution needed some refinement in grace and movement. Cameras clicked and flashbulbs popped. Then the senator whispered in the president's ear.

In a millisecond, the president signaled the CPO to approach then in a low voice gave some instructions.

"May I request that since we only have four senators, may I request," the CPO groped for words "... may I say, that it is the President's wish to have a photo-op with each honorable senator and his or her entourage. Let us start first with Senator Santolan. May I then request the three other honorable senators to temporarily step aside please. Thank you."

Senator Santolan then took over the scene, directed her three siblings to stand in front, her husband to her right side, her parents to the left of the president and the rest of her cousins, in-laws and others, numbering 27 in all, to form a semicircle at the back.

Cameras clicked and flashbulbs popped. Sure that her own photographers had taken the best shots, Senator Santolan then edged closer to the president and whispered "Mr. President, it took me days and days to finally decide, after some soul searching and consultations with my family and colleagues, to join your party. Would you like to know why I finally decided to? It's because I realized you are a good man." The senator then took the arm of the president into hers and gently squeezed it.

The following day, broadsheets ran the story of the defection, practically reliving the presidential campaign two years ago. Two tabloids ran pictures of Senator Santolan, one with a caption quoting her as having said that the phenomenal Mahal campaign was nothing but "a juvenile syndrome over a mustache." The other picture showed a shrieking Santolan dancing the boogie-woogie on stage with her husband, the camera shot zeroing in on her stunning legs. Another picture showed the majority floor leader of the House, Congressman Racleto Albanos with some of his colleagues inside a Japanese restaurant, toasting their glasses. The caption read 'To Mahal with Love!'

One newspaper column was subtitled, "For every season, a butterfly." The article sounded like a dirge, a lamentation. "It's back to square one," the column ended the dirge.

U p in the mountains, the afternoon breeze began to sway the leaves of trees as the fog floated, then alighted and blanketed the valleys below.

Ey de edey Andaman,
'intud neg ledewanan,
Kebaya su lilang ni,
Ey edey Andaman;
'Amang kun su gempa,
Te belagwey enganen nu.
Ma'an le te belebe
Te tindeg penguna'an nu,
Yan nu da ma nenudi,
Ka pennumag sil'utan ka
Te pegsilung nu ne yambun.

"What is he saying?" she asked. "The chanter seems so sad, his voice so low and deep…"

"You want me to translate it word for word?" he asked, looking far down the valley.

"Yes, please."

I have long before this wished
What a great delight it is,
Oh, oh, so goes the story,
Concerning your dignity,
Your own personal belief,
About dignity and pride
Of your own unique being
This is what you bear in mind,
Whenever you are oppressed

211

By your own peers or others...

"The chanter's voice is gradually going up", she said.

E yan nu da lintu'usi,
Ku dew sug tibeba'an ka,
Amambe yan din agi,
Yang ka egseylut,
Ne yang ke egtibeba,
Kena nyu ed iteda,
Ne kena nyug sinendaya,
Nenge iling ne pul'ung,
Sen'unga ne sibelang.

He interrupted. "The *talaulahingan* is saying:

You should be calling to mind
Whenever you are provoked,
In a situation like this,
So refrain from striking back
For you too, turn oppressor,
Do not behave as they do,
Do not ever be like them.
These words are so important,
This advice keep in your mind.

"Why is he saying that?" she asked again.

"The *talaulahingan* started chanting non-stop, two days ago, on a new episode. He is chanting the story about Tigyekuwa Meyumang, the first wife of the king, who saved the kingdom from total ruin. The story says the enemy set the kingdom on fire but Tigyekuwa Meyumang somehow got a bottle of sacred oil from above the heavens as she prayed:

To you most reverent oil,
Oh most sacramental oil,
I pray you turn into rain
Into a water deluge.
Once her words are spoken out
Rain instantly falls upon
All over the land...

"I'm not too sure now," he sounded apologetic. "But it sounds something like that. The immense towering flame is finally doused and the kingdom is saved."

The voice of the *talaulahingan* rose to a new pitch. The birds above the trees seemed to hear him as they perched on the branches, their wings folded, their heads peering down below.   The voice rose much higher now through the mountain breeze.

Agi tew te manubu,
Sangka sinuddanan din iney,
Sigin sigin ne'agi'u'a,
Ne lenaya ne megulang,
Nu iyan basa te nekem,
Ba si'iman ne timpu,
Penayaw te linendem
Te heg deninuddanan din
Ne penelew neg gintas.
Su delantag pengenda'an
Te be se inan ne timpu,
Ne tegel nelibabas
Su lumpad ne sinudanan din,
Ne yan buyawan be nekem
Te di kaey ikewg hipati,
Su lalu'uy te nakem dey
Di Keyg tuligbani'en
Kawang te belegwety dey,
Su wed be lalew pulus dey
Pinelangga dey teydu
Kulendem dey beya'an
Ne ingbe gelun,
Pinuklew dey yeyabew
Tinde nu penguna'ane

"What did he mean by that?   His voice sounds so sad, so full of emotion! While I do not understand a word, yet I could feel the *talaulahingan's* chant inside me." Katrina Avila inhaled deeply as she stood over the cliff, viewing the gorge below and the mountain range beyond that separated the House of Agyu from the rest of the world.   She had strayed this far, away from the *talaulahingan*, unable to hold together the vague feeling inside her.   She had returned here from faraway Manila, on top of this mountain to film a new documentary on the new Supreme Datu and the House of Agyu, a sequel to the first documentary that Channel 6, her TV station, aired in three series a year ago "I can translate that portion with confidence," the young Supreme Datu of the House of Agyu said.   "I've actually memorized it by heart."

"Please... "was all Katrina could say as she looked at him, her gray-brown eyes searching.

"I'll also chant it myself.   Here goes:

The ways of the Manobo,
Unknown to the younger generation,
My dear ones gathered here,

Honored ancestors of ours,
I now make this conclusion
That in times like now,
I am sure of the belief
That to this coming generation
A change will take place.
As the world moves forward
In these present times,
We are miserable and weak
We, of the older generations,
Hold us dear in your mind,
Do not forget us
For indeed we are helpless.
Do not ignore our plight,
This wretched situation of ours,
Poor and useless as may be
We have cared for you truly
Hold you foremost in our minds.
It is our expectation then,
That you would value us in return
Deep within our own selves.

"It's amazing! Really, I had the feeling the *talaulahingan* is sad over the fate of his people, over their misery. But why did he say earlier, that you, the younger generation, should not respond in kind, should not feel provoked, otherwise you would also be like the aggressor?" Katrina Avila observed, feeling she had somehow gotten deeper into some of the nuances of the epic.

"As I said earlier, the saving of the kingdom by Tigyekuwa Meyumang, the first wife of the king, one of the many sons of Agyu, is only one of the thousands of episodes in the *Ulahingan* epic. Episodes vary in story of course. There are adventures against the enemy on earth, the strife that ensued, the suffering that followed, their love life in between, then their final ascension to *Nelendangan*, our paradise, that is, for those who have passed the tests of the Highest *Diwata*, our Supreme God. One of the recurring themes in all episodes is giving up or surrender because of the intense suffering encountered during these adventures. In the particular episode you just heard, the *talaulahingan* reflects the common cry of the people in the kingdom, their cry of anguish for they were not only routed by the enemy but also set ablaze by fire. The advice not to act like the enemy, the aggressor, reflects the voice of the sober Council of Elders."

"What about the lines—to the coming generation, a change will take place... as the world moves forward?"

The young Supreme Datu of the House of Agyu, Tomasing Labaongon did not answer. He stood there unmoving, his eyes transfixed toward the red ball of fire that started to sink into the gap of the mountain ranges to the west. At a distance, beyond the trees, the voice of the *talaulahingan* rose and fell, in regular beats like the beating of the *agung*, its cadence like the flow of water deep down the gorge below.

"The coming change as the world moves in our time," the young Supreme Datu said after awhile, "begins with so much difficulty, as I told you the first time you visited us. The beginning is education for our young children and the change of attitude among our people who are always drunk. It is easy to say that but hard to do. I'm practically alone although I have a lot of confidence to undertake this mission. Again, it might not happen in my time but I will do it. I have to start somewhere. It will be my legacy."

Katrina Avila did not say anything. Feeling her legs shake a little, she sat on a fallen log as she picked a stick and started writing some doodles on the ground. The stick suddenly broke and she threw it away as far as she could, down to the gorge as she sighed deeply.

"May I just call you Tommy?" Katrina Avila suddenly said, surprised at herself. "Your name and title is too long and I feel like I'm one of your servants when I address you with that," she blurted out, again surprised at her bravado.

"My classmates in law school also called me Tommy. I don't think there is any problem, for as long as you don't call me Tommy in front of my people. I don't really mind especially if it is just between the two of us."

Katrina Avila suddenly stood, thumping her feet on the ground. Why was she beginning to be angry with herself?

"Tommy, would you like me to help you start an education program for your people?" she finally said it, feeling relieved. But her excitement grew.

"How did you come to know of my feeling? I wanted to ask you about it the first time you visited us, but I was afraid you'd turn me down."

Katrina Avila could not believe her ears. "Tommy, would you say that again, please?" her voice was almost pleading, her gray-brown eyes searching for some signs.

"I said I wanted to ask you the first time I met you, the first time you visited us, to help me, our people start an education program. That is why when you said it first, I was most surprised why you came to know about my feeling."

"If that is really true, then how come you did not even write me? That was over a year ago. And if I did not come back, how would I know and how could I help?" Katrina Avila's voice almost cracked.

The young Supreme Datu of the House of Agyu lifted his face towards the sky, inhaling deeply. "I was afraid I would be rejected. Pride is very high in my veins, as much as I wanted to tell you, to ask you, to begin my mission with you. Truth to tell, I drafted many letters, one I almost mailed. But I tore them all. I don't want to be embarrassed. No one in the House of Agyu wants that to happen to him. But I am a little educated to understand that you belong to another society, you are famous in that society and your face and voice on television are the envy of many. That is the real reason why I tore up all those letters. This place is not your place."

"Oh Tommy," Katrina's voice now cracked. "I swear I want to help. I swear to God, I want to help. I want to start a new beginning, too. I'm tired of all the glamour, the parties, the politicians, the TV shows and almost everything in my society. I've found this place and I want to stay here, that is, if you... if you want me to... if you want me to begin your mission with you."

The birds in the trees flapped their wings and bowed their heads. For warmth, they nestled together as the fog below the valleys rose and embraced the leaves and limbs of the mountains. The early evening breeze began to caress the skin.

His Eminence Cardinal Luigi Toscanini of Bologna, Italy slowly rose from the canonical throne, strode in measured steps toward the pulpit and stood there for a long time, his deep blue eyes peering through the thick lenses of his glasses toward the white casket draped in velvet cloth.

To the jampacked crowd of mourners, the Cardinal from Italy looked like a living ghost. His hair was blond, his eyes were sunken, his cheeks were hollow and his Adam's apple bobbed prominently up and down below his pointed jaws.

He scanned the crowd. Out front, right pew, sat the president of the republic, President Juancho Mahalina. He could not be mistaken. The face had a mustache, he had a thick forest of black hair and he had a bulky body. The woman beside him could be his legitimate wife and the rest occupying the pew, must be some of his sons and daughters.

On the front left pew, sat the former president of the republic. *What is his name now? How could I forget? Now I remember... Rosales, yes, former President Sergio Rosales.* His Holiness remembered him during his last visit to this country. And the Pope said President Rosales was a Protestant. Wasn't that paradoxical in a country of 87 percent Roman Catholics? But then His Holiness also observed that President John F. Kennedy was a Roman Catholic in a Protestant country, the United States of America. God's sense of balance was truly beautiful and most of the time, beyond the comprehension of man, he remembered His Holiness say as an afterthought, as His Holiness blessed him for his safe sojourn to this country.

And who is the small woman beside former President Rosales? Isn't she the former lady president, Caridad Anilao Castro? Why is she sobbing so heavily? Oh, now I remember, His Holiness told me the former lady president was one of the closest to Cardinal Alingasa. Bless her, oh Lord.

His Eminence Cardinal Luigi Toscanini took off his horn-rimmed glasses and wiped them with a ball of cotton he had concealed between the insides of the huge ring in his finger. All he could see now were the figures of people in white robes, the bishops, priests and the nuns of the Church. *Bless them, Oh Lord.* His thin lips murmured. Beyond, he could see foggy silhouettes of people. Surely, he thought to himself, his friend, his Eminence would be truly missed by his flock.

With his glasses back on, the Cardinal raised his head toward the ceiling. The chandeliers were truly exquisite. And he prayed as he again looked at the casket.

"Brothers and sisters in Christ," the Cardinal began. "I am here because of a very personal request of a dear friend. In the last two years we had been corresponding with each other, he always kept on reminding me that when it was time for him to go, I should come and say a few words before his burial."

The voice startled his listeners. It was a voice that contrasted fully with the frail figure. It was a voice that rang above the sepulchral silence inside the massive cathedral.

"Two years ago, when we met at the Vatican, he again reminded me. And I said to him, my friend, what if I am the first to go, would you be obliged to come and say a few words before my burial? My friend whose body is about three times as mine laughed so loud I was afraid he would awaken His Holiness for it was very early in the morning. And you know what he told me? My friend, he said, I am sure that I will be the first to go. One, my body is three times bigger than yours so I am more vulnerable to high blood pressure. Two, the problems in my country are also three times bigger than yours. The first problem is political. The second problem is political. The third problem is political."

His Eminence Cardinal Luigi Toscanini paused as he heard the slight snickers. Truly, the flock of his friend appreciated a good joke.

"And so, brothers and sisters in Christ, here I am to say a few words before the burial of my friend, our friend, His Eminence Cardinal Pedro Alingasa. His Eminence always found time to say a few jokes after serious discussions of religious dogma and I will never forget most of them. One time, he said his name Pedro stood for the ordinary folk in his country; at another time he would say Pedro stood for St. Peter, hence he had the keys to heaven and that included my rite of passage. He said his family name Alingasa means in one of your dialects, Visayan, he said—uncomfortable warmth, a consequence of the intense summer heat which compel most women to fan themselves even inside the church. Oh, I can see that some of our sisters have stopped fanning themselves. That is okay with me. Please continue with your fanning. That was my friend Pedro's joke, not mine. Thank you.

"To continue with my friend's jokes, he said, the meaning of Alingasa as uncomfortable warmth became 'uncomfortable pest' to politicians because of his homilies and pastoral letters. Now I am beginning to realize, probably that was what he meant when he said the number one, number two and number three problems of his country are political."

The Cardinal paused. He was now sure everybody was enjoying his homily, including those who had lost their political fortunes and seemed mildly cheered that at last, they had triumphed over his friend's dead body. For sure, some of them were inside this great cathedral. He wanted to say something about that as his eyes slowly scanned the crowd, though he knew he would not be able to identify them. He decided not to make any joke about that.

"Brothers and sisters in Christ. In the last two years of our letter writing, I was struck by my friend's new focus on this new branch of science known as emotional intelligence. His interpretations went something like this. Emotional intelligence springs from the heart as mental intelligence springs from the mind. As popularly known, EI says that the deepest yet the clearest but the most tender of all human emotions is love. And because love is indeed the most tender, it needs a force to strengthen it. And that force my good friend said is friendship. Most marriages by

217

the way start with love and to sustain that marriage, both husband and wife must be friends. Otherwise, without friendship, marriage that starts in love may end in hate.

"His Eminence, my friend Cardinal Pedro Alingasa has always written me of his love for his flock. In two letters, however, he wondered why his love for his flock had made more enemies than friends! When I wrote him back, I asked, who are these enemies? Naturally, I had to ask him. When he wrote back, he told me he has made three enemies: one, the politicians, two, the politicians and three, the politicians."

A swell of snickers flowed throughout. The Cardinal grimaced.

"He's got the teeth of Bugs Bunny!" a small boy whispered, pulling the ear of his mother.

"Shhh... you behave!" the mother whispered back, pinching her son's inner thigh.

"Ouch!" the boy shrieked.

"Shhh!" the mother hissed again.

"There is no doubt in my mind that my friend was sincerely concerned with politicians—they also being one group of his flock. To His Eminence, everyone was part of his flock. And he was concerned with politicians because he felt they were the only ones who did not believe him. And also, he felt they had misunderstood him. In one of his last two letters to me, he asked me to pray with him to ask forgiveness that if he was misunderstood, it was not his intention. It was his abiding love for his flock that inspired him to remind them if he felt that they had gone astray, to bring them once again to the fold before they could be devoured by the wolves.

"Brothers and Sisters in Christ, I find considerable difficulty in expressing the thoughts and feelings of His Eminence whose life has just ended, who I am sure cannot hear what I am saying because he is already at peace in the bosom of his Creator. Nevertheless, I feel elated his passing away somehow inspired me to share with you what I feel and what I think at this moment.

"The Holy Scriptures is quite clear on the matter of the relationship between church and state. In the book of St. Luke, Chapter 20, Verse 22, the Son of God says: 'Give unto Caesar the things which are Caesar's and to God the things which are God's.' Jesus Christ made that declaration in the context of paying taxes to the governor of Judea but this was not meant to be absolute, because the same Son of God said later that you could not serve two masters at the same time, that is, God and Mammon. All of us believe, whether we are Christians or Muslims, that there is only one king, one master, one God. Even if some call God by some other name, it is the same God, our Creator. God has created man and man, because of the many talents that God bestowed upon him, has also designed and devised many inventions to give order and meaning to his life on earth in praise of God. And one of these is government, the state.

"When the Son of God said to give unto Caesar the things which are Caesar's and unto God the things which are God's, He did not mean that God and Caesar are equal. He was only reminding us that while we give Caesar what is due him on earth, we should not forget that we have our Creator to reckon with. Paying tribute to Caesar or the government is in recognition of man' s respect for what he himself created. In the process, man should not forget that God is his one and only Creator.

"Perhaps, it is the misunderstanding of these truths that His Eminence Cardinal Pedro Alingasa had been misunderstood and it was because of this that my friend asked me to pray for him for forgiveness.

"Sometimes I think if religion were not treated as an institution, the controversy between church leaders and politicians would not have emerged. I had on several occasions confided this thought to His Holiness and my understanding is the Holy Father himself had been thinking about it. To me religion is belief, belief in God as our Creator and Heavenly Father. And that might as well be for the Church. When the Son of God Jesus Christ referred to Saint Peter as the Rock upon which to build the church, He was referring to the rock as the pillar of strength that would propagate the sets of belief that the Lord Jesus had instilled upon his disciples. What happened thereafter was clear—the church was built by man in his material world but the spirit behind it is God's.

"One of the favorite passages of my friend, His Eminence Cardinal Pedro Alingasa is found in the Book of John which I think most of us are familiar with. 'For God so loved the world, he gave His only begotten son that whosoever believes in him shall not perish but have everlasting life.' When Cardinal Alingasa treats everyone as part of his flock, he was simply acting as the Good Shepherd, very much concerned that no one goes astray on the path toward God.

"President Mahalina, immediately before I came to say my last farewell to my friend, His Holiness told me his heart is always with you and your people. His Holiness also told me he is always praying to God to forgive whatever transgressions His Eminence Cardinal Pedro Alingasa might have committed upon his flock."

The Cardinal paused again, looking at the casket with his somber eyes.

"So my friend, I have followed your request, to say not only a few words but many words. I am sure you must be laughing very loud now; not only have I met my friendly obligations but also I have expressed things you might have left unsaid when you were still with your flock. We all pray for the eternal repose of your soul, in the grace of our Lord Jesus Christ, the only Son of God."

Never, never before in the history of the country had there been one like it. For the first time ever, people of all types and persuasions, the young and the old, the rich and the poor, all but for a very few, moved in one direction—to see again and again the movie 'The Son Also Rises,' starring Jason Angelo Mahalina and Charlene Divina.

Jason Angelo Mahalina played the role of Jason Angelo Mahal who, as the plot went, wanted to prove to his father that he too, could rise to fame and fortune. Living alone with his mother, he was regarded as a bastard son and he had to live with the condescension of his classmates and the eagle-eyed members of high society in the exclusive village of Forbes Park. Unable to bear it any longer, Jason Angelo left the country and squandered everything he had in drink, in women and in song. Empty and impoverished, he worked as a bus driver in Hong Kong, a waiter in Los Angeles, a pier hand in the docks of Rome and a potato peeler in a ship that plied the sea route from Copenhagen in Denmark to Upernavik in Greenland where the temperature went from below zero to hard frost.

Bored to death along the lonely route, Jason Angelo joined a troupe of Romanian entertainers based in London, doing road shows and specializing in comical skits and zoo animals. During the day, he fed the monkeys, the lions and the boa constrictors, along with his tent neighbor, a big bosomed woman who looked like a Teutonic dishwasher and who kept calling him, "Mah dahling 'Ason." During the night when the comical skits were staged, Jason Angelo acted as one of the clowns who got slapped exactly 17 times per show. Humiliated, he left the troupe, then bummed and begged in the cities of Paris, Frankfurt, Rome, Oslo and Geneva until he realized he was wasting his life away.

Coming home, he persuaded his mother who was all too happy to welcome him back, to venture in the business of entertainment: by contracting starlets, singers, comics and their ilk to do personal appearances and road shows in the cities and towns of the country. He was sure he could make a lot of money out of it, as that Romanian troupe in London, he told his mother, less the humiliation he suffered which he could not share with anybody. His mother, a former starlet in the sixties was fascinated by the idea and used her connections.

The venture prospered. But what surprised Jason Angelo and his mother the most, was the attraction the crowd had on him. As assistant manager of their venture, Jason Angelo did the emceeing at times and took some parts when one of the entertainers got sick or could not make it at the 11th hour. It did not take long for everyone to find out that he could also act and sing. Every time he did his impromptu act, the young girls shrieked and the women swooned, as each performance ended with shouts of 'More! More! More!' Until the name of Jason Angelo Mahal became the talk of the town—mayors, governors and congressmen competing with each other to get a booking of his shows for entertainment during town fiestas and all types of celebrations and anniversaries.

Aside from his new discovered talents, no one could say that Jason Angelo Mahal didn't have the looks. His thin mustache, thick black hair, *moreno* skin, his shy boyish smile that sparkled in his eyes and innocent-looking face and his height of five-eight and a half simply sent the crowd agog as the young girls shrieked and the women swooned.

One of his entertainers was Charlene Divina, formerly Charlene Divinagracia of the CyberRockets, the young sultry singer who started her singing career in political rallies with her hit 'Limme, Limme, Limme.' Now she had grown into a woman whose body, from face to neck, from torso to legs, as aficionados of the female form would say, one could easily kill for. She stood five-five on her bare feet. In spaghetti tank top and hot pants, she was a knockout. Her walk was totally riveting, a casual, bouncy yet natural walk. And she had the talent.

Her voice could soar up to the heavens in a millisecond and come down to earth in another. After a few practices, Jason Angelo and Charlene did their duet and the crowd, mouths agape, contorted, jumped and burst in excitement and euphoria. The reporters covering their road shows dashed off their superlatives.

The love-team of Jason Angelo Mahal and Charlene Divina assumed the role of the one and only love-team. 'The Son Also Rises,' became the one and only movie. The love-team and the movie of the new millennium had arrived.

To a few, the plot of the movie was corny, sappy and inane but not one and no one could argue that the movie as a whole was picture perfect, each shot, each frame, a living postcard, the work of experts in cinematography. The shots in Hong Kong, L.A., Rome, Paris, London and those in the country were done and edited by the cinematographers of Kevin Costner in the "Dances with Wolves" and those of James Cameron in the "Titanic."

The movie was a "super-megahit", its stars the "super megastars", terms of idolatry crafted by media and immediately sensationalized by the millions of fans.

In the metropolis alone, queues of screaming movie fans lined the ticket booths. In some places, there were riots. In one occasion when the stars did a personal appearance in a theatre lobby, traffic stopped along the avenue and side streets. Screaming fans ignored the long lines of cars, trampling over them from hood to hood and from bumper to bumper as car, van, truck and bus horns hooted and tooted. Within three weeks, the fans started wearing shirts, blazers and caps with "Jason Loves Charlene" or "Charlene Loves Jason."

In the squatter area in Caloocan City, Priscilla Batungbakal, the fiery chairperson of the march to the palace coalition and chief instigator of the hunger strike, struck the last nail to hang the one-meter by five-meter streamer above the front wall of her recently renovated shack. Printed in big bold letters, the streamer emblazoned "The Son Also Rises Sari-Sari Store." Asked where she got the money for the renovation of her shack and her new, well-stocked variety store, she simply said, "I have to survive." She earlier resigned as chairperson of the coalition and abandoned her companions in the hunger strike after she had a long talk with the wife of business tycoon Ziegfred Campos, the owner of the land on which some of her companions had remained mostly emaciated now, still waiting for President Mahalina's unfulfilled political promises.

There was no stopping the excitement and the intoxication the "The Son Also Rises" and its stars had wrought upon the populace. And as the excitement and the intoxication rose, so did the ticket sales. At the end of its sixth week, estimates of gross sales rose from three fourths of a billion to P1.2 billion.

Production and sales figures were closely monitored by the financial wizards of Ma'am, the mother of Jason Angelo. Reports of fake items were also monitored but Ma'am had a heart of gold. "Let that go on for awhile. This is also one way of helping the poor in our society. For as long as we are making a little of our own, we can tolerate the imitators and their imitations."

Exactly one year on the day the super-megahit movie was first shown, the TSAR (The Son Also Rises) Film Astrodome stood resplendent in the sun by day and luminescent in the dark by night at the top of the hills of Antipolo, overlooking the whole of Metro Manila. Financed by the taipans of business and industry and the "friends" of Ma'am, the mother of Jason Angelo, the super-mega structure loomed like a gigantic egg at its center, surrounded by steeples that seemed to hug the clouds in the sky.

Inside, at the center of its gigantic stage, stood President Juancho "Mahal" Mahalina, a cordless microphone in hand, obviously enjoying himself. He was delivering his monologue. He scanned the crowd of some 5,000 smiling and boisterous faces, sitting around tables stuffed with all types of stateside libations and spirits. "So I asked my son, Jason Angelo, hik! Why me?"

"Dad," he said, "remember, I wrote the script for you."

"For me!" I said.

"Yes, Dad. For you, because I want to be like you Dad."

Wows and whistles.

"See, my son wants to be like me!"

Applause.

The president took a few steps toward the edge of the apron of the gigantic stage, where directly below, Senator Naomi Ganzon Santolan sat, one shapely leg over the other, her breasts thrust forward, her jaws up. Sensing the president was ogling at her, the lady senator crossed her legs outward the table, toward the direction of the president.

"Hi-hi, there, Madame Senator! I thought it was Betty Grable with her million dollar legs! Hik!" The senator stood and bowed as the crowd roared.

"To be serious now, I like to announce that starting tomorrow, eh, it's already one fifteen, I mean, at eight o'clock today, my first lady, hik, I mean, the first lady executive secretary, the one and only, Patricia Gan-Alfonso. [Standing ovation as Gan-Alfonso stood and acknowledged the accolade.] I said Pat Gan-Alfonso will take over Fatso Santos' job."

"Fatso, where are you? Hik! Oh, there you are! [Laughter] You know what? My friend Fatso said to me, 'Bosing, please accept my resignation.' I said, why? Then Fatso, my friend said, 'I have to prepare.' Hik! Then I said, prepare for what? Then he said, 'I am running for senator.' [Hoots and applause] Then I said that's still three years away! Then he said, 'Bosing, I don't have your charisma!' [Applause] Then, I said, that is all right. I fully understand." The crowds snicker.

"Where was I? [Laughter] Oh, let us not talk about politics. [More laughter] If there is anybody to blame for the lousy economy... [The crowd mooed] Okay, I'll not talk about bankruptcy anymore. [Applause] Hik! So, I asked my son, Jason Angelo... [All right! All right! The crowd agreed] what's the title? Then he said, 'The Son Also Rises'. Then I said, the sun will always rise. [Laughter] Then he said, 'No, Dad, it's me, your son who will also rise like you.' Then I thought for a moment [Giggles and laughter] this guy is okay! [Applause] Sonnamagun, this guy is really like his father! [More applause] Jason, where are you? Oh, there you are!" Jason stood from the table below and waved his arms, the crowd standing and applauding.

"That's enough. You all shut up! [The crowd sat back] No, Jason, please rise again. [Laughter] Turn around my son. There, isn't he the spit-ting image of his father? Sonnamagun!" Jason's body slowly stiffened, struggling for a handkerchief. As he stood, his whole body shook as he wept unashamedly, muttering and crying.

"Thank you, Dad... Thank you. It's so nice to have a daddy!" Charlene beside him also stood, trying but unable to hold back her own tears. "Jason, love, you are now vindicated. Your Dad just said so in public. Jason, please..."

As they both sat down, the crowd stood and chanted, 'Jason, Jason, Jason!'

"And so my friends, I'd been asked by my son, Jason Angelo to be present tonight," he looked at his watch against the hanging chandeliers. "I mean last night and this morning [Laughter] to dedicate this building, I mean this super-mega-structure [Applause] in the name of Mahal which means love, because love is a many splendored thing," the president started to hum a few bars of his favorite love song, the crowd humming along.

"To the millions who found happiness, hik, in 'The Son Also Rises', starring Jason Angelo Mahal [Applause] and Charlene Divina, the Tsar and Tsarina [Standing ovation] of the new millennium in the filmdom of this republic, I thank you very, very much. Tsup, tsup, tsup..." the president threw his kisses; the crowds roar in mad frenzy.

Sauntering down the stage toward the presidential table below, Mahalina spread his arms, Jason Angelo rushing out to meet him, as father and son hugged and patted each other's back.

"Mr. President, thank you for your inspiring dedication in the name of Love," the Honorable Press Secretary Randolf Patis Cruz announced. "And now, ladies and gentlemen, we now go to Part II of the first anniversary of the TSAR, 'The Son Also Rises'. May I now call on the number one senator of the republic, the Honorable Senator Humphrey Bogart Putto and the brains and legs of the senate, the Honorable Senator Naomi Ganzon Santolan!" Cruz scratched his throat. He had emceed Part I from eight o'clock last night. He could now concentrate on his Remy Martin.

From their separate tables, the two honorable senators of the republic raced toward the stage: Senator Putto all in white; Senator Santolan all in red. The crowd roared, the drumbeats boomed and the trumpets blared in alarum from the CyberRockets Band and Orchestra as the revolving stage got into position. When the two senators got to their spots on stage in front of their respective microphones, the beat of drums and the blare of trumpets stopped.

"Ladies and gentlemen," Putto began in his deep baritone, bending his head over the microphone: "This is Humphrey Bogart Putto, your host, who ain't gonna go home yet to Momma 'cuz he's in love with yah!"

Laughter.

In her distinct, riveting accent where consonants smacked and vowels hung whole, the lady senator began: "And this is Naomi Ganzon Santolan, your hostess, whose legs have no equal except those of Charlene Divina's."

Hoots and whistles.

"Ha, ha, hah!" Putto guffawed. "Ladies and gentlemen," the baritone now boomed. "Welcome to Part II of the first year anniversary of the super megahit of the new millennium, the one and only 'The Son Also Rises', starring the super megastars, Jason Angelo Mahal and Charlene Divina!"

"Yahoo! Yahooo! Yahooooo!" Santolan shrieked, the crowd echoing her. "And to start the ball rolling, the much awaited ballroom dancing begins! Ladies and gentlemen, the CyberRockets! Maestro, go, go, go! Dance for all!"

Santolan yahooed, her legs shuffling, her arms swinging, her hips gyrating to the first boogie-woogie of the CyberRockets' 'Take the A-One Train.'

Putto swayed, clicking his fingers, his mouth babbling along with the beat: "Tadada, tadada, tadada, tadada, go!"

The rambunctious mix of instruments and the clapping and thumping of hands and feet of the singers of the band suddenly filled the enclosed dome. From all sides, some 1,000 pairs hit the dance floor, gyrating to the dizzying beat of the boogie-woogie: bodies swaying, arms flying, waists twisting, skirts flapping, down and around, heads swirling, eyes rolling and legs buckling. On stage, Putto and Santolan did their thing, leading the pack of animated dancers.

Then the Reggae, then the Swing. "Ladies and gentlemen!" Santolan announced, dragging the lanky Putto beside her before the microphone. "Ladies and gentlemen, the Tango! All the movie stars, cabinet members, the senators, the congressmen and their partners are decreeeed to dance the tannngo! Maestro, Hernando's Hideaway!"

The throng of movie stars and politicians hit the dance floor. On stage, Naomi Santolan pirouetted around Putto whose lanky frame was now bent, his stilt legs stretched far apart, his breathing pushing his torso up and down, the caterpillar below his nose wriggling in protest. In step with the beat, Santolan again circled Putto, then once in front of him, flipped her head back, stretched her right leg between Putto's legs, then yelled, "Come on, Macho Man!"

Feeling the tip of Santolan's toes scratch his crotch, Putto stiffened. The classic intoxicating metrical beat of the tango reminded him of Valentino, the great dancing king, his idol. His adrenalin suddenly rose. Clasping Santolan's slender waist, he drew her to him as their bodies locked and stood erect, his face to the left, her face to the right. Then along with the 1-2, 1-2 and 1-2-3-4 beat, he bent backward as far as he could go, Santolan on top of him, her left leg wriggling like an inverted periscope. After swiftly turning around with her like a spinning top, he bent forward as far as he could go, executing the great Valentino dip, his whole front glued over her, his jaws landing on top of her cleavage, his face to the right. She clung to him from under, her bent right knee supporting his abdomen like a jack, hair touching the floor, arms spread-eagled, her tongue out of her mouth, her face to the left. Those familiar with the great Valentino's vintage tango maneuver oohed and aahed. The crowd went wild.

On the dance floor below, the movie stars and the honorable government officials swayed and tried Putto's maneuvers. Some succeeded halfway. The rest simply laughed off their failure. The tango was not their dance.

At the presidential table, President Mahalina and Pat Gan-Alfonso were whispering at close range. A new bottle of whiskey replaced the last one in front of the president. A waiter in bowtie poured another glass of champagne for Pat. Some of those who surreptitiously eyed the two felt there was some confidential powwow, a private one-on-one concerning sensitive matters of state between the two most powerful personalities in the politics of the republic.

From the tango, the CyberRockets band and orchestra shifted to the mambo, then the samba and then the twist. On stage, the lanky frame of Putto was now seesawing from side to side, trying to keep up with the beat. Opposite him, Santolan bent low, her torso and her hips rising up and down like a mini-twister, a baby tornado. Putto now grunted and grunted, his brush of a mustache twisting and wriggling, like a caterpillar about to be dislodged from its moorings. Santolan shrieked and shrieked, her jaws jutting backward and forward, her nostrils vibrating like the struggling gills of a *Tilapia nilotica* temporarily out of the water.

"Ladies and gentlemen!" Santolan gasped for air, shrieking before the microphone, her right arm fastened around the left arm of Putto whose lanky frame was now bent like a capital C, his knees knocking at each other, his hair and mustache dripping with sweat, his eyes drooping, his tongue hanging.

"Ladies and gentlemen, by special request we shall now dance the Cha-Cha-Cha!" the crowd roared. "The President and the First Lady, [Santolan gasped for more air] the one and only First Lady Executive Secretary Patricia Gan-Alfonso shall lead the dance, to be followed by Jason Angelo and Charlene Divina! Dance for all! Cha-Cha-Cha!" the crowd roared the more.

From the rambunctious twist and twist mix, the CyberRockets Band and Orchestra went to the standard classic beat of the cha-cha-cha, beginning with the come-on beat and sound of 'Oye Como Va'. As the president took the hand of Pat Gan-Alfonso and as Jason Angelo stood and took the hand of Charlene, the crowd roared. As both pairs hit the middle of the dance floor, the crowd thundered.

Then somebody shouted from one of the hanging boxes above. "Putto and Santolan to the dance floor!" This was followed by shouts from below until the whole roar became a frenzied chant. Santolan dragged Putto down the stage to join the president and Gan-Alfonso and Jason Angelo and Charlene in the middle of the dance floor.

"Mr. President," Pat Gan-Alfonso gasped amid the roar. "I can only dance the sweet!"

"Now, Pat listen," Mahalina clasped her left hand tighter down to his side as Pat's right arm clang to the president's left shoulder. "All you do is follow rhythm. Okay, one step forward as I go backward, gyrate. I go forward with my right, you go backward with your left. Gyrate. Now, we go, there. Hmmm. I forward, you backward. Good. Hmmm. I backward. You forward. Good! Hmmm."

Pat Gan-Alfonso was a fast learner. As she moved with the president, she was also eyeing Santolan's maneuvers to her right, who was now on the top of her elements. Santolan was doing the head work, bust work, leg work and foot work, forward and backward while egging Putto, taunting Putto because his legs were now stuck to the floor. Putto struggled to respond but his body was now bent like an inverted U, his shoulders pointed downward, his head, the only part of his body jolting now and then, like he'd been hit by a series of tics. From his looks, it was abundantly clear that the spirit was willing but the flesh was already weak to dance the cha-cha-cha.

Pat Gan-Alfonso easily executed the fundamentals, now swaying with the president, one step forward, gyrating, two steps backward, gyrating. As "Tea for Two" sprang from the end of "Oye Como Va", Pat took the role of the aggressor. Shuffling two-in-one steps forward, then two-in-two, then more, then more, Pat couldn't be stopped. Pat accelerating in momentum, her partner dancing backward and backward, laughing boisterously, exuberant that Pat had mastered her footwork in such a short time.

His laughter didn't last long. Shuffling backward the fourth time, trying to keep in rhythm and the onrushing push of Pat, the inebriated presidential left leg got entangled with the right as the presidential buttocks hit the marble floor with a thud. Before Pat could utter a gasp, the president, his arms braced against the floor, pushed himself up but could not. The tons of whiskey in the system had softened the presidential muscles.

"One!" the crowd of dancers immediately converged around the president and counted. The president, pale as a white sheet, again pushed himself up, his body shaking, his mustache quivering, his eyes about to leap out of their sockets. He didn't make it.

"Two!" the president didn't make it.

"Three!" cries of "Oops, Ooppps, Oooopppssss!"

Like a wounded bull, Mahalina snorted. He inhaled and exhaled. With all the strength he could muster, he pushed himself up, harder, hardest. More cries of "Ooooppppppppssss!"

Finally, he made it up staggering, balancing himself to stand erect. Slowly turning around and gasping for air, he waved his arms to acknowledge the loud cheers of his admirers.

"Music!" Mahalina hollered toward the CyberRockets whose players had momentarily stopped. Having heard the presidential command, the players went back to their instruments. The itching sound of brass echoed sweetly in the air, the scratching whispers of trinkets over snare drums reverberated gently, the CyberRockets singers swaying to the opening beat. Then in one melodious outpouring that could only come from the heart, the singers hummed then sang the song closest to the president's ears:

Hmm-hmm-hmm-hum-hum-hum - Love
Is a many splendored thing...

As soon as he heard the familiar tune, the president hummed to himself, encircling Pat gently around his arms just a little below her waist. Pat moving in rhythm subscribed, her arms discreetly meandering on the broad shoulders of the head of state.

The rest of the thousand and one animated dancers swayed along the slow, sweet and yearning rhythm of the dance of love.

It's the April rose, that only
Grows in the early spring...

Holding hands, Jason Angelo Mahal and Charlene Divina strode toward the stage as the lights dimmed. Facing each other, still holding hands, the two sang as one.

Love is nature's way of giving,
A reason to believe in,
The golden crown that makes
A man a king...

The clear and distinct voices of Jason Angelo and Charlene blended and rose, the CyberRockets humming, their sound waves lingering in the background.

Lost on a high and windy hill
In the morning mist
Two lovers kissed
And the world stood still...

Holding hands, facing each other, their eyes locked, Jason Angelo and Charlene shifted their decibels and in soft cadence intoned...

Then your fingers touched
My silent heart and
Taught it how to sing

Facing the audience, their eyes closed, their voices vibrating, the duet of the new millennium soared, their golden vocal chords rendering the last two lines of the song of love:

Yes...true love
A many splendored thing.

The spotlight on stage faded. The young and eager bodies of Jason Angelo and Charlene locked, swaying while the deep and penetrating resonance of the alto sax took the refrain. The thousand and one pairs of dancers swayed, their fingers touching, their breathing tightening, their whispers of intimacy cascading, from one ear to another.

One society matron whose menopausal jaws snuggled over the left shoulder of her much shorter partner, a struggling young actor, remembered Yeats. Recalling her favorite quote, she recited her own convenient rendition into the left ear of her partner: "Oh bodies swayed to music, how can you know the dancers from the dance?" Bewitched, she tightened her grip around his waist, pulling him closer to her matronly breasts.

"Love is divine," Jason Angelo whispered.

"And divine is love," Charlene whispered back.

227

"Love is happiness," whispered the president.

"And happiness is love?" the first lady executive secretary whispered back. Giggling like adolescents, the president pulled Pat closer toward him in a subtle and prolonged dip. Pat floated then sank, whimpering.

Swaying alone to the rhythm of the alto sax, Senator Santolan took her eyes away from the glistening chandeliers above, gyrating toward the front of her estranged partner, declaiming her favorite Shakespeare: "Love is not love that alters alteration finds but bends with the remover to remove..."

"Music is the hik... language of the soul," Senator Putto mumbled, his head hanging between his long arms that now got stuck over his bended knees. "Gottah go, I wannah go home to Momma!"

Slowly raising his head and looking at Santolan swaying her hips and twirling her arms to the rhythm of the alto sax, Putto took a step forward but backward and backward he went, until his knees buckled down on the marble floor, his lanky frame back to capital C. "Gottah go, lab yah... hik!"

Up in one of the opera boxes parallel to the chandeliers, overlooking the dance floor below, Ka Piccio, the assassin asked Ka Lulu as soon as she sat beside him. "Are you you sure the package has been detonated?"

"Doubly sure... I did it myself," the bomb and explosive division chief said. Looking down at the dancers below and listening to the splendor of the song of love, she sighed: "Too much damage if it happens here. I am glad the chairman changed his mind." Ka Lulu laughed the laughter of an innocent child, after clinking their glasses of red wine.

"I have to go and relay the message to the chairman," Ka Piccio said, standing and walking stealthily away.

The sonorous decibels of the alto sax rose like wanton whiffs of perfume above the muffled sound waves of the voices and musical instruments of the CyberRockets, lingered above the tingling chandeliers, meandered among the dancing couples and then went around and around the insides of the astrodome, until they found their way out of the air vents and exhaust fans and into the early morning mist and windy hills of Antipolo.

Five days after, a caravan of buses, jeepneys, private cars and all types of vehicles ascended the winding hills of Antipolo and disgorged thousands of demonstrators around the gates of the TSAR Astrodome. Powerful megaphones and bullhorns shouted orders and instructions as the demonstrators raised their placards, banners and streamers, shouting and screaming.

"Down with Mahal!"
"Down with TSAR!"
"TSAR Anniversary—An Anomaly!"
"Down with Drunken Public Officials!"
"The President—A Bad Example"
"Mahal is Blind"
"Truly, Love is Blind!"

"The Son Also Rises"
stands for
"This Sorry Anemic Republic"
in
"The Southeast Asian Region"

They screamed, bellowed and bawled, angry at Mahalina, for his scandalous display of opulence amidst the poverty of his people, his drunkenness and his broken promises and for converting the republic into one monstrous movie madhouse.

Inside the gates stood men in camouflaged uniform, their high-powered rifles on the ready. Up in the turrets, powerful binoculars swept the landscape, their recoilless rifles by their side.

"Down with Mahalina! Down with the President!"

"We appeal to our friends... please disperse now," the loudspeakers from inside the gates cracked. "You have no permit and the president is not here!"

The exchange of insults and curses went back and forth. Pushed by anger, the screaming demonstrators at the front lines rushed to the gates, scaled the iron railings as rocks and all sort of objects flew from all directions. Suddenly, automatic rifle fires cracked and grenades exploded. Bodies hit the ground as cries wailed in the hills.

The uproar in the "Filmdom of the Republic" caused a tidal wave of mightier protests and demonstrations throughout the archipelago.

In the capital cities of Mindanao, Christians, Muslims and Lumads alike lined up, affixing their signatures in support of reviving the old clamor and movement for Mindanao independence. Some signed with their blood. Their rationale: President Mahalina, like all presidents before him, not only abused his powers but was unable to address the problems and needs of Mindanao. The presidency was person-centered, never nation-focused, they said. It was no longer a question of an incompetent or corrupt president running a national government. It was now a question of survival for the people of Mindanao.

In the capital cities of the Visayas, people of all types and persuasions converged in public places where speakers shouted their indignation against an incompetent and uncaring government. The government, they said was Tagalog-biased and started their rallies by singing the national anthem in Visayan.

In Luzon, the Tagalogs in Bulacan, the Kapangpangans in Pampanga, the Ilocanos in Vigan and Laoag, the Bicolanos in Legaspi and elsewhere held their public fora and street demonstrations against an array of political and socio-economic problems exacerbated by a corrupt government.

Happy Valley, Bukidnon

Dear Angeling,

Am finally home and still excited about it. The house is already renovated and Tony Boy is back in school. And my job in the university is giving me a lot of challenge, not to mention renewed acquaintances and new friends. Plus free computer time to write this long letter. Ha! Ha! So here we are, again in our own hometown.

I am glad I decided to leave Manila forever and come home to the province, intact in both mind and body. While I miss a lot of the city's many amenities, there is really no substitute for the province's clean air, unpolluted streets and finally home where familiar faces are always around. Add of course, Tony Boy who is now staying with me. He makes all my despair in the dark disappear. You know what I mean? His birthday is 14 days from now and he will be in fifth grade. Can you imagine that? How time flies!

You remember Anita Cosme? She is now Mrs. Anita C. Varias. Her husband is the dean of the College of Engineering and they are staying in a university cottage where a room is reserved for me just in case I get benighted. Anyway, our town if you still remember, is just 11 kilometers away and if my Volks conks out now and then, I either commute or stay overnight at Anita' s place.

In the political front, I think everybody is to blame. Of course, the first one should be President Mahalina and the people who elected him. And now they are blaming each other. What an irony. As the saying goes, the people only get what they deserve. Painful as that might be for the country, I believe we need some lessons in shock treatment to wake us up now and then.

Did you see on CNN what really happened in that demo at the TSAR Astrodome? Well, some people are relieved that it turned out to be a dud. The firepower and the grenade blasts turned out to be blanks. Yes, nobody died except for the bruises that some demonstrators got after they dove from the high gates and walls to the ground and scampered in all directions, thinking the blasts were real rifle fire and grenade explosions. And by gad, that triggered bigger demonstrations that are now all over the place, nationwide!

230

NOW, to the lighter side. DID I tell you before I left Manila that I had already learned all the steps of the cha-cha-cha, beyond just the fundamentals? The spin, the shuffle, the parry and thrust, the touch and the brush, the side steps, the turn and all types of movements from the head to the toes. One thing more—I never realized the cha-cha-cha has a very close affinity with our own curracha. You know, the old folks' dance of yesteryears. First part is flirtation between male and female, second part is the chase, either male or female initiating the move and then the contest between the two to gain crowd approval.

If I recall right, in curracha crowd approval means money. Money is thrown at the feet of the dancers once they get the nod of the crowd. Therefore, more crowd approval, more money.

I told our DI about this until he, with my help, choreographed a number, with cha-cha-cha and curracha music and the steps in between. The result is simply fantastic and the DI says he'll perfect it and introduce it to the ballroom dancing crowd. He said he'll acknowledge me when the time comes.

I initiated two dance sessions in the university and its president likes the idea of holding regular ballroom dancing every Saturday night. So I now am the DI over here!

And Angeling, you better believe this. I think I finally found my match. This time on the dance floor! Although he is kind of effeminate, the way he moves his hips and his arms, he really dances very well, especially the cha-cha-cha. We are in complete sync! He moves forward, I move backward. I move forward and he moves backward. And every time he holds my hands, I feel electricity. When our hips brush against each other, its double electricity. And the more when he holds my waist and let his arms brush my sides upwards in rhythm with the music. My Angeling, its triple electricity! He is a biology instructor and thus, I think, he knows how to read my anatomy, I mean, how my body parts react and he takes advantage of that. I think I'll have to be serious this time. Only last night, he drove me home in my Volks, his left hand on the wheels and his right arm over my shoulders. He just drove and we didn't talk.

231

When we got out of the car, he held my hand and
then squeezed it as he said good night. Next
time, I'll be the one to hold his hand but I will
not only squeeze it. I think I can do better than
that! Joke only, huh!

Our clan met again last Sunday afternoon.
Things are getting serious now. They're starting
to do the headcount of our relatives who, I am
told, comprise more than half of our town. Some
highlights: the president of the local business
club, our parish priest, the chief of police and
the vice-mayor are all uncles. So how can we
lose, our oldies keep on saying, not to mention
that nine of the 12 councilors are also our
relatives in one way or the other. They also keep
on saying that I have the personality to attract
most farmers and laborers, that I have a master's
degree, etc. The only liability I have, according
to them, is that I am a single mother. So what,
Lola Besing said, I can always marry. But I said,
that will erase my family name and that is what
most people here know and remember about me. Then
Lolo Didong said that's no problem because I could
always hyphenise.

What do you say, Angeling? I really hope you
will change your mind and get me out of these
complexities. Anyway, if you won't I would have
no choice but to follow the wishes of the oldies.
Actually, in my heart of hearts, I also really
want to. Believe me, I can do a lot for our town,
if given the opportunity. Besides, politics is in
our blood, too. The immediate past mayor of our
town, your father, my uncle Waldo, was a Cruz.
The first governor of this province was a Cruz.
Two representatives before in our district were
Cruzes, among many others.

By gad, I forgot. Remember Katrina Avila, that
very pretty, multi-awarded journalist who used to
be cover girl and whose investigative reporting
always hit TV? Didn't you say that she was
engaged to one of the wealthiest scions of an
American-Filipino family in the West Coast? Well,
let me inform you she just got married to the new
Supreme Datu of the House of Agyu. Tomasing
Labaongon, that's his name. Sounds like a song
and a fruit, right? Well, the wedding was held at
the top of the mountain, with all the *agungs* of
the indigenous peoples of Mindanao beating. All
the tribal chiefs were in their native costumes as

their spears hailed the wedding as the sign of many new things to come to their 12 tribes of about 2.5 million people. The marriage reads like a fairy tale in reverse, the man a shy but powerful ruler in nativelandia; the bride, city-bred, magna cum laude from Berkeley, very rich, very pretty and very talented. Unlike 'The Son Also Rises' where Jason Angelo Mahal and Charlene Divina become the love-team of the new millennium because of a movie flick, this one is real and true to life. And by gad, if the Jason Angelo-Charlene Divina love-team is a match that could only be made in the seventh heaven, this one is a match made in the highest mountain of reality.

Lolo Didong and Lola Besing were there to witness the wedding and are still euphoric over it. Lolo Didong, as you know, is two-thirds native and that explains why he has so many land claims that until now have yet to be granted to him by the government. I guess this is his hidden agenda for wanting me to be mayor. Why not if I could manage that for our family patriarch? Ha! Ha!

Please, Angeling give me comforting words how to get through all of this, okay? And also, whether I'm going to marry or not. Don't you think Tony Boy will get jealous? Will it be good for him or not? Next time, let's not schedule your visit any more. As soon as you are free and the weather permits, just fly over and enjoy the rural peace and quiet over here. But please, please promise that during the entire campaign period, you should be here to help me campaign and win the fight—at all cost.

Wish me the best of luck and same to you.

From KISS TO KISS (Come Rain or Come Shine)

Fili

E
EPILOGUE

The view from the beach house is spectacular. White sands. Blue waters. Fishing boats in the horizon. Occasional tiny winged birds crisscrossing, gliding playfully just inches above the pacific waters. Along both sides of the cove, rows of tall and lean coconut trees stand majestically, their evergreen fronds gracefully swaying in the air. A gentle soothing breeze whistles in the afternoon sun.

Out in the extended foyer immediately before the swimming pool, Juan Carlos Enriquez, JCE to close associates, lounges on an oversized wicker chair, luxuriantly puffing a cigar.

"Well, gentlemen, dinner is still one hour and 20 minutes away," JCE reminds his guests, placing his empty glass on the low table beside him. "Meanwhile, why don't you boys take a dip in the pool or take a swim down there in the sea? I think we have all the time tomorrow to finish our agenda." He stands. "The girls must be thoroughly enjoying themselves."

His guests nod and chuckle.

JCE and Pin Davide take off their shoes, descend down the rocky stairs and walk in the sand. The rest agree to take a swim in the sea where the tide is low.

The girls at the moment are admiring the orchid collection of Renee, the wife of JCE. The collection is sheltered from the hot sun and strong wind by green nets that stretch from the back of the beach house up to the foot of the hills, a good kilometer away. Giggles and laughter could be heard now and then, as they move from one orchid bloom to another.

"What could the boys be doing right now?" asks Consuelo, the wife of GDQ.

"Let's forget about them 'til dinner," replies Renee, giggling, her ample breasts swaying marvelously as she leaped over a row of small potted plants. "They have their own agenda. We have ours!"

Unbeknownst to the girls, the agenda of the boys are directed at bolstering three major assumptions: first, President Mahalina would not last long if a sustained attack against him and his corrupt administration will be pursued; second, a credible transition government can be installed to take over the present one; and third, a credible leader can be found to qualify as head of the new government. Oplan TZ was being reviewed again.

It is finally time for dinner. The long table is full of exotic seafood. The three maids are as usual in their immaculate caps and aprons.

"So, what have you boys been doing in the last two days?" Claudia, the youthful and pretty wife of Davide asks, reaching for a fat claw of a crab. As soon as it lands on her plate, one of the maids reaches for what looks like a pair of pliers, clamps the claw between its jaws and squeezes it. Yellow substances come out of its cracked surface as Claudia exclaims, "This is delicious! Thank you." She then dips her fingers in the delicacy and starts eating with relish.

"Yeah, you've sequestered yourselves pretty tight, didn't you," Margarita, the wife of Racleto Albanos observes, winking at Claudia.

"We girls had actually been wondering about your agenda," Renee says, scanning the faces of the boys. "We thought... you were all plotting a coup d'etat or something," she adds, accompanying her side remark with a special naughty smile for the girls.

The boys chuckle.

"We are actually planning to write our collective memoirs," JCE says, still chuckling. "That will be the first part. Part II is our combined proposal for the country on good governance."

"Really!" the girls almost say their reaction together.

The boys chuckle again.

"Do you think, Father Ben that Mahalina will last?" Claudia asks, her question a sudden detour, her tone serious, her eyes peering at Father Morales.

The boys suddenly stop eating. They look at her.

"That depends," Father Ben chuckles, looking at the boys. "Mahalina's current mistresses seem to give him a long and happy life. But I am sure that if he will increase their numbers, he will surely not last long. He will die of exhaustion."

"Really!" the girls chorused, their eyes twinkling.

"My goodness, Father Ben! You being a priest, how can you say that!" Claudia brings up her table napkin and covers her mouth to keep herself from shaking with laughter.

Father Morales roars as the boys also roar.

"Actually, there is a cost for those who live in a high level of tension," Father Morales suddenly turns serious, remembering a philosophical treatise by one of his favorite authors. "Physical parts of the body wear down. Excessive smoking, drinking and lovemaking tax the heart, the liver and the gonads," Father Morales now sounds like the good priest that he is. "Sleep becomes evasive and the mind does not respond to truth and will not invest in trust."

The universe is suddenly still. The mood for reflection has taken over irreverence.

Out in the foyer fronting the swimming pool and the ocean beyond, the crescent moon appears, glistening on the surface of the still waters. At the stroke of 9 o'clock, the three-man combo strikes the inviting beat of "Oye Como Va", JCE and Renee's favorite. In the dining room, all ears are suddenly cocked in the direction of the gazebo, beyond the foyer.

"Time to dance. Let's go!" Renee exclaims, holding on to the arm of her husband.

"Let's perfect our styles," Claudia likewise exclaims, dragging Pin Davide towards the gazebo. Racleto Albanos and his wife, Marshall Dimalasa and his wife, Arturo Tan-Kong and his lady companion follow as Father Morales excuses himself.

They dance to the inviting beat of the cha-cha-cha far into the night.

On top of the hill at the left side of the cove, two men with powerful binoculars rise, gather their gears and sling their knapsacks over their shoulders. "Time to go,

Ka Bert," Ka Piccio, the assassin says. "I'm sure the Chairman will be happy about our findings."

"Damn these politicians." Ka Bert snorts. "And I thought they were enemies!"

"Not really," Ka Piccio says. "They're all friends. They just find it convenient to sleep with the enemy now and then."

Both men take the path down on the other side of the hill as the metrical beat of the cha-cha-cha fades out in the lengthening distance.

Former President Sergio Imperial Rosales puts the final touches on his paper as he sets it aside on the sofa table in front of him. Rubbing his eyes to remove the strain from too much reading, he leans his back on the thick cushion of the sofa in a corner cubicle reserved for him at the Library of Congress in Washington, D.C. He is scheduled to deliver his paper on business investments in Southeast Asia and global terrorism the following day, at Georgetown University. Slowly, he puts back his glasses. Leaning forward a little, he scans the volume of books and magazines lining the shelves before him. Then his stare settles on his country, a series of tiny dots on the edge of a basketball-sized globe illuminated by a lampshade on top of a low table. Former President Rosales sidles toward the table. Then he slowly turns the globe around and around, each turn ending with his country before his eyes. He feels for the tiny dots with the tips of his fingers as his heart aches for home. Then he remembers the cable from GDQ.

Former executive secretary Ruby Toledo used to eat his breakfast of corned beef, two fried eggs, sunny side up and a cup of garlic rice with gusto but since he lost in the last senatorial race, he has limited himself to coffee. As the months went by idly, he drank more coffee as he lessened his sugar until he drank his coffee without sugar. Perhaps, it is the bitterness of it that he now enjoys drinking purely black coffee. After one year of his humiliation, he was offered a cabinet post but he refused, preferring the substantial monthly retainer he is getting from the king of the other central bank of the country. Plus, the promise of the king to fund his next bid for either a senatorial or congressional seat. Toledo made good his deal with the king. The king's tax evasion cases have long been forgotten. As he thinks of his prospects, Toledo sips more coffee and finds a certain undeniable sweetness in it. "Strange," Toledo wonders as he sips more coffee without sugar.

Rusty Kapunan's handsome face has become that of a spent old man's. His thick black hair is now entirely gray, his speech is slurred and his robust confidence gone. He just had a heart bypass. He knows his wife hates him for the deterioration but he doesn't care. What he cares about is how he could put into action his concept of a moral crusade in the politics of the country, an obsession he so loved and nurtured but died in limbo before it could even be launched. Though he heads one of the biggest subsidiary firms of Don Felipe Aboitez immediately after the Dimalasa debacle, he does not enjoy it. Since he took over this firm, profits have nose-dived. He knows Don Ipe doesn't like it. Rusty Kapunan doesn't like it, too. However, his view of the political world is the same. He knows best and anyone who disagrees with him is hopelessly wrong.

In his new camp deep in the jungles of Mindanao, Commander Tausug Ali rises from the floor and shouts in joyful exaltation, *Allah Achbar!* "God is Great!" Seized by the inspiration, he throws his body on the floor again facing downward in complete submission. *Allah-u Achbar, Allah-u Achbar. La illah illa Allah...* "God is greatest, God is greatest. I testify there is no other God and Mohammed is His Prophet. God is greatest, God is greatest, I testify there is no other God and Mohammed is His Prophet!" He repeats the Shahada as he prostrates himself, letting the exaltation embrace him. He now fully believes that the hand of Allah is upon him and the shoes of the Prophet on his feet. His prayer has been answered. The latest news from his big brother Ahmad Jamil from the Middle East has confirmed everything. Tausug is now overall commander of the Moro rebel forces. Jamil is the ambassador, campaigning for support from the Middle East for the cause of Allah in Mindanao. *Insha Allah*! "As God wants!"

Lourdes Dalisay a.k.a Commander Lulu is now head of the People's Watch Brigade of the PWRA. She took over the post after Task Force Commander Sawa was killed in a violent encounter with the military in the hills of Nueva Ecija a year ago. Commander Lulu is listed as one of the ten most wanted persons in the country and carries a P400,000 reward for her capture, dead or alive. She has become a living legend. A movie of her ideological beliefs, exploits and love life in the mountains is in the making. In fact, a multi-awarded scriptwriter had already been hired to portray Ka Lulu as a woman who in the inside is as soft as a rose petal but who in the outside is as headstrong as a bull. But the producers, hungry for authentication, are encountering some difficulty. Commander Lulu has refused to be interviewed or photographed.

Katrina Avila cradles her baby as she guides his mouth to her swollen breast. Tomasing junior looks exactly like his father. He is handsome in his native skin, is long-limbed and has the sharp and unblinking eyes of a forest animal on the hunt for its prey. Katrina feels complete joy, her milk oozing freely into the eager mouth of the heir of the House of Agyu. She feels completely fresh too from her daily morning bath in the mountain spring flowing out of the gargantuan roots of a cluster of sky-high *kamagong* trees, a few minutes walk down the valley from their abode at the top. Katrina used to enjoy the scent of imported perfume after every bath in her condo. Now, she adores the scent of moss after every bath in the mountain spring. Everything has been good so far, Katrina Avila muses to herself, as she remembers promising Tommy to give him all the sons and daughters he wants. And how she loves Tommy, Katrina sighs. It doesn't bother her that Tommy has lately taken to alcohol, a habit he despises as endemic among his people. It doesn't really matter, Katrina admits to herself, as long as he continues to hum to her his endless love and not snore loudly in bed after drinking endless bottles of gin with his tribal chiefs.

The children of the House of Agyu are now beginning to appreciate their three R's. In time, she would ask Tommy for more pencils and writing pads. Next year, she would ask him for a school building. And how about in the years ahead? Looking at the lush mountains before her and the blue skies above her, Katrina in the fullness of her heart, is now sure that by that time, Tomasing junior will finish law school and lead his generation toward a brighter future.

The plates careen like flying saucers, smashing glasses and tumblers on the small dining table. More flying saucers fly, smashing glass-encased cupboards. A small piece of broken glass hits the left ear of Timostocles Sipula but he does not move. His wife, seven months pregnant is in a rage again.

"What's this I hear that you are politicking again, that you are reactivating your so-called national network of volunteer coordinators?" she screams. "Why, will there be elections this year? Aren't those still four years away? What's going on? Haven't you learned your lesson? Grrrrr!"

"But Love, we have to mobilize now," Sipula croaks, his breathing almost suffocating him. "prepare ourselves, because once this administration falls..."

"What administration falls?" she screams again. Haven't your so-called volunteer coordinators been calling us ever since, asking for refund of their expenses, because they'd been in debt since your crazy campaign? Their wives have been calling me, too. You know that? What a shame! Where is your idol Davide with his billions? Didn't he promise to refund all your expenses? Don't you know he was just using all of you? Haven't you learned your lesson? And where is your savior, Destino? Grrrr!"

Still screaming and with all the force she could muster, she yanks the tablecloth toward her as plates, glasses and cups smash each other on the dining table, their shards skittering all over and hitting the floor. His untouched cup of chocolate rolls over and splashes out its hot lava on the front of his shirt. Still Sipula doesn't move. His wife continues to scream like a lost soul. Supporting her overgrown stomach with her arms, she staggers toward the bedroom and slams the door behind her.

The ultrasound assured Sipula that their baby is a boy. This is her second pregnancy. The first ended in a miscarriage when she was four months pregnant. That happened when, beside him at their door, she collapsed when two uniformed police officers told Sipula they had a warrant for his arrest. He was sued for breach of contract and estafa but he didn't have the money to pay. The case: he had signed a contract with a three-star hotel for food and lodging of 300 volunteer coordinators who were whisked to Manila to execute a last ditch effort to help salvage the dwindling Davide campaign. The expenses for the hotel were within his approved budget for special operations. But the money did not come. That was during the last presidential campaign.

What came after was the warrant of arrest. His wife, after her collapse was still in shock, until she started bleeding. The bleeding didn't stop until their doctor said his wife had lost their first baby.

Sipula cups his ears with his hands as his wife's wailing reverberates in the small apartment. She bitched, she moaned, she complained. He is completely devastated. His sense of self-worth and pride was truly self-fulfilling when he was part of the victory of President Rosales before. His sense of self-worth and pride went berserk when he was part of the catastrophe that characterized the Davide campaign. Sipula's dream of tipping the balance now hangs in limbo.

Dr. Meandro Destino scratches his unshaven face as he leaves the classroom. Before, he recalls, he found considerable fulfillment in his lectures at the National State University and enjoyed the challenge to break the resistance among some of those in the orbit of President Rosales to justify unpopular political decisions. He also recalls working with volunteers during political campaigns. Now, he is totally immersed in learning how to prepare the soil, mix rotten leaves with dry animal manure to produce earthworms and plant a fruit tree.

The classroom he just left is one of those in the Kadugay elementary school in the municipality of Lo-oc where during Saturdays, the extension man of the town's agricultural department comes and teaches all those who care to listen, what to plant and how to care for their crop.

Destino had returned to his roots immediately after the term of President Rosales. His neighbors around the small farm he inherited from his parents all speak of the same problems all throughout the year, like his immediate neighbor Simeon Sempron. To Sempron and his neighbors, it is always the problem of what to eat next, where to get water for the crops when the rains do not come and when will God finally answer their prayers.

Now and then Destino wonders what he is doing in this part of the world as he reminisces his past. Now and then he receives word that President Rosales has been looking for him. Now, as he recalls his past, he begins to conclude that it is a lot easier to strategize grand plans with multi-million peso budgets in the corridors of power than plant a tree and make it bear fruit, in a farm in the middle of nowhere. Now and then he also remembers Marissa Gantuico. The last time he heard from Pat about her was that Marissa had joined a band of mercenaries in the Congo, in far away Africa. Nothing was heard about her since then.

"These bastards should be taught how to lick my arse!" Rushmore Stockman explodes like a volcano as his dense eyebrows arch sky high. "C'mon, Stock, keep your cool or your fucking kidney will burst again. Kind of boring to see you go to the john and take a leak again, this early in the morning," Marvin Reed, the Stick, twits his Boss with a chuckle. Both just received official notice of their new postings to the American embassy in Jakarta.

"And what the fuck are you doing here, Dicky, dicky-doo Martin? Still spying for Uncle Sam?" Richard Martin laughs as he sips his second cup of coffee. In his long years with the modern mandarins in the Foreign Service, he has yet to decide whether most of them should be acting on stage or should stay silent behind their desk and plot the next diplomatic move. Dick Martin is sure of one thing about the ambassador and he tells him so: "You know what, Stock? You're really such a lovable fucking bastard." Then he adds, "By the way, what have you done for this poor country so far?"

"To serve Uncle Sam's interests!" Rushmore Stockman snaps. "Why, is there anything more noble and patriotic than that... huh, huh, huh?"

The three Americans horselaugh as they exchange high fives.

Jason Angelo and Charlene got married three months after the inaugural of the TSAR Film Astrodome. But they separated seven months after their wedding, dubbed then as the "Wedding of the New Millennium." Jason could not stand the endless ogles of lust from men on his young bride and Charlene could not stand her young husband's womanizing, especially with the liberated matrons of high society.

There are attempts at reconciliation and Charlene, especially Charlene, wants to. But her last straw, so to speak, comes when she hears Jason himself say the reason he wants as many women as possible is because he also wants as many children as possible. "Altogether," Jason adds with his boyish smile, "that would mean more votes for me when I finally enter politics."

That broke the camel's back, for Charlene. If there is anything she hates, she says, it is the machismo of men, their vulgarity and their pretensions.

She was two months pregnant when she finally called it quits. Some say she had an abortion and disappeared from public view after that. Others say she delivered the baby abroad and definitely would stage a comeback at the opportune time, with or without a Jason Angelo.

Senator Humphrey Bogart Putto knits his eyebrows and smiles before the TV cameras.

"Senator Putto, the clamor for you to run for President is getting hotter every day. What can you say about that?"

The senator mumbles something and cuffs his ears as if to say he has not heard.

"Mr. Senator, would you please raise your voice a little louder?"

The senator manufactures a cute smile as he gently scratches his mustache with a thumbnail. "I'm sorry but some of you had distracted me. Why, what was your question?"

"Mr. Senator, I asked that the public clamor for you to run for President is getting hotter every day. What can you say about that?"

Senator Putto gently massages his temple with his forefinger. "I think it's too early for you to ask me that."

"But Mr. Senator, the presidential election is only four years away. Everybody knows it takes many, many years to prepare oneself to run for the presidency."

"I know that, I know that." the senator does not anymore manufacture a cute smile. His imaginative mind is now light years beyond to meet his destiny.

"So?"

"Did you say the clamor for me to run for President is getting louder every day?" the senator asks, his voice low, his cute smile returns, now glistening in his eyes.

"Definitely, Mr. Senator. Your fan clubs have increased, many businessmen, politicians and the like are gravitating around you. You are the most prominent godfather in most christenings, the most sought-after sponsor in weddings and apparently, the most omnipresent during funeral wakes. This is not to mention that you are also the most visible guest in every prayer rally of the Brotherhood of Faith in Jesus Movement..."

"Well, if that is what the people really want, who am I to refuse?" Despite his suspicion that these flatterers in media are simply leading him on, his adrenalin is now at full throttle. "As the saying goes, *vox populi, vox dei,* the voice of the people is the voice of God. Ha! Ha!" He ends the laughter with a wicked political wink.

"Mr. Senator..."

"Sorry. Gottah go, lab yah!"

Rickie Balete, the Most Exalted Brother of the Brotherhood of Faith in Jesus Movement contemptuously hits the off button on his remote as the large TV screen before him goes blank. These jokers, he mumbles, they should be taught a lesson. Why should I allow myself to be used by them? By that buffoon Putto and his kind? And why do politicians continue to seek my favor? It is simple — it is because of the solid votes of my millions of loyal disciples! My people are correct. It is God's will that I should aspire for the highest position in this land. It is now time for the modern Red Sea to be parted again, time for the new Moses to lead his people out of the rut of this evil world and the tyranny and greed of its Pharaohs.

Rickie Balete paces the floor, pondering his newly revealed destiny. Hastily flipping through the pages of the Holy Bible, his trembling fingers crawl until they find Revelation Chapter 20, Verses 6-7: "And he said to me, it is done. I am Alpha and Omega, the beginning and the end. I will give unto him that is athirst of the fountain of the water of life freely. He that overcomes shall inherit all things; and I will be his God and he shall be my son." Balete cradles the holy book between his two hands and brings it lovingly to his breasts. He genuflects, then slowly raises the Holy Bible above him, bowing his head. Thank you, Lord-Jesus. Thank you. Hallelujah! Praise the Lord-Jesus!

Madame Madonna Omen gazes at her crystal ball. As her eyes scan the mist, fog and skies inside its universe, she raises her palms upward. Suddenly, her whole body begins to shake as her mouth opens in hissed whispers. "I see you now... I see you now... why do you weep, Mr. President? Oh, I see, oh, I see, you are suffering in both your body and in your soul. No, no, Mr. President, I have no power to save you. I only have the power to look at you. Yes, yes, you are looking at me but you cannot see me. You have to look elsewhere, Mr. President. You cannot? Yes, you cannot because the dark clouds have taken over the mist, the fog and the skies of your universe. The dark clouds are clear signs of an impending doom. Weep no more, Mr. President. Your days are going, going, gone."

Sonny Boy Profeta easily reaches the last step of the tree house. He has taken the nine steps in four long hops despite his sister Melinda's shouts from somewhere in the yard. "Stop that foolishness, Sonny Boy... you're bound to trip!" As Sonny Boy playfully jumps from the topmost step of the stairs for the floor, he trips, balances himself but his small, lanky body turns him around and in the momentum he hits the wall. He grabs for the nearest post but instead rips the presidential calendar that is hanging there. Sonny Boy gazes at the torn picture of the man in his hand, then he begins to shake as his whole body convulses, as the tree house shudders like it is shaken by a violent volcanic eruption.

Mount Mayon erupts the same day. Professor Hagibis del Yuta had predicted that it would erupt that very day. He had said so in a seminar of volcanologists at the University of Liboria in Africa four months ago.

In the last two years, "Truth or Tale", the most talked about talk show in town has become the most talked about talk show in the universe (meaning, in the entire country). Vito Sta. Dolores, its male host with the head of an international airport runway that could land a 747 and Tina Gomez Latorta, its female hostess with the voice that slithered in the airwaves like a bewitching musical instrument have become the most talked about TV celebrities in the universe (meaning, in the whole country).

Political surveys reveal that if elections were held today, Vito would easily land second to Senator Humphrey Bogart Putto (meaning Vito could challenge the senator in the presidential race or run as his vice-president) and Tina would be the number one senator of the republic.

It is 15 minutes before the end of the show on prime time TV. Kidd Batuta, the prince of local movies and darling of TV commercials, Luningning Morena, Miss Universe 1st Runner-up and local supermodel and Steve Karate, the international bone-cracking martial arts champion and villain-hero movie idol, already breezed through their commercials and earned their millions.

The most talked about issue of the day is the babel of tongues of discordant voices in street demonstrations that continues to roar and rage throughout the archipelago. Is this history repeating itself, the history of tribal conflicts, ethnic discord, intercultural differences, regional antagonisms that some historians have documented to be the root cause of divisiveness in the republic? Or is this plain and simple political enviousness, crab mentality, the usual whining, bickering and bellyaching of losers who never stop until they themselves are in positions of power? Or is there a deeper rationale for all this?

These issues went back and forth between Vito and Tina of "Truth or Tale" and their guests with endless reactions in between from viewers through the phones and audience participation in the studio.

TINA Wow! It looks like the demons of all DEMONStrations are finally out. Vito, what do you think?

VITO Looks like, Tina. Okay, we only have a few more minutes. May we now call on our guests for their summary statements. Sirs? Madame?

1st GUEST As I stressed earlier, we in Luzon are protesting against this move in Congress to change the present form of government. I repeat, we are for the presidential system. We see nothing wrong with that. What is wrong is electing people who are notoriously undesirable, incompetent and corrupt. Whose fault is that? So instead of spending billions in debate and drowning themselves in political saliva, we in Luzon propose that politicians in Congress legislate a law on voters education and linking this with our formal education system — to ensure that our people will be able to judiciously elect the right leaders for the public good. Isn't this elementary, my dear friends?

2nd GUEST We in the Visayas do not entirely dismiss the presidential system but it should be the kind that gives autonomy to the provinces, similar to the federal system of the United States. This kind of system should encourage local creativity and initiative from our provinces and local governments. What is wrong with our present system is too much power is lodged in the presidency, including the power of the purse. I should know. As a housewife and mother, it is difficult to budget household needs if I don't control the purse. Of course, all of you know we Visayans hate dictatorship in all forms. I need not remind you that Lapu-Lapu killed Magellan because of this.

3rd GUEST Our cause in Mindanao is different, very different. We in Mindanao never, never allowed ourselves to be under any imperialist from the time of the Spaniards to the Americans, to the Japanese. What is tragic is we have a national president but he is never with us, except to make troubles for us. The fact is we supply more than 50 percent of the food that people in this country eat. We have our inexhaustible gold and mineral deposits. In terms of territory, Mindanao with an area of 36,900 square miles, would rank 107th and in terms of population, would rank 48th among 192 nations in the world. We already have our own constitution, printed our own money and have our passports and visas ready for the realization of the Republic of Mindanao. We shall not stop…

TINA Sorry Sir. Thank you, gentlemen and lady for the enlightenment. Vito, what happens now to our country?

VITO Looks like we now have a confused republic, Tina.

TINA Confused republic?

VITO Yes, something like that.

TINA Do we still have hope?

VITO Of course, Tina. For as long as the sun is shining. Let's have a word or two from our sponsors. Don't go away, we'll be back.

At their imposing vacation house by beautiful Lake Tahoe in Las Vegas, Nevada, Angela Cruz-Lester loudly reads on, her husband by her side. "The die is cast. There is no turning back. It's them or our clan. We are pursuing right now three parallel paths to make sure we win the war. One, let the other side withdraw as we pay the operations cost, double the amount we know they will spend for it if they fight us and that includes not touching their relatives who are already employed in the municipal government. We already have the funds for this."

Angela clicks again, as the succeeding paragraph of her cousin Fili's email appears on screen. "Two, match their guns and goons with moral-suasion and campaign relentlessly for clean and honest elections. This is the hardest part but we will do it. Three, triple the expenditures per voter in the last elections. With a voting population of 11,000, this means something like P16.5 million, at P1,500 per voter. This is another hard thing to do but we don't have any choice—times are hard." Bud Lester interrupts again. "Angela, sweetheart, that's small. Tell Filipinas we'll bankroll it. She may take it as a soft loan or as a grant, whatever."

Angela Cruz-Lester loudly reads on: "Lolo Didong and Lola Besing, particularly are very eager for your coming. It was a good thing you went ahead with the wedding even without me as your Maid of Honor. No problem. What is important is you are now Mrs. Bud Lester and we are all very happy for you."

Bud Lester gently squeezes Angela's behind. She responds with her killer smile, clicking and loudly reading on: "Just make sure you'll be here one year before elections. It's the position of mayor of our town or nothing. We are not taking any one little thing for granted. There is only one big thing to remember — to win at all cost.

Best regards to Bud. Your best friend and first cousin, from KISS to KISS, come rain or come shine."

Angela shuts down the computer. She turns on the CD. The tender blast of "Oye Como Va" echoes yearningly out of the 3D surround sound in the background. The cha-cha-cha has become her and Bud's favorite lately, no doubt influenced by Fili's letters about the dance.

Gently, Bud wraps Angela's slim body around his gigantic arms. She slowly turns her face toward him, her eyes locking into his. They clinch. Breathing heavily, his knees shaking slightly, he takes her down on the thick carpet floor as the heart-thumping and lingering beat of the cha-cha-cha sizzles in its rhythm.

***

ACKNOWLEDGMENTS

Grateful thanks to Emilio "Mel" Gonzales, my editor-in-chief and friend. His plan to include this book as one of the features in launching the Dr. Librado I. Ureta Foundation worldwide has encouraged me to no end. The foundation promotes programs and projects based on the three cardinal principles of Leadership, Friendship and Service. Mel is the president of the foundation.

To my daughter Michelle, my associate editor and critic, I am fully indebted. Her incisiveness and critical insights guided me all throughout. At the initial stages, Michelle was expecting her first-born. Jojo, her husband, was fully supportive and gave her all the comfort she needed. In the final editing phase, Jojo ever alert, reinforced Michelle in spotting typos, lapses and came up with critical and significant edits. Exactly on the day I finished the final manuscript, Michelle and Jojo called from Toronto announcing the birth of Jesus Melchizedek. Hearing my first grandson's loud cries over the phone, asserting his presence in this world, gave me complete joy and fulfillment.

To Tess, my wife who gave invaluable ideas and comments, her tolerance and understanding gave me total confidence. She also helped encode revisions at times.

To Melch, our son, my junior who provided technical data and information. Melch also did the final format prescribed by my publisher. He also did the photograph on the inside back cover.

To James Montojo, Jojo's brother who helped in the cover design.

To Tia Elena whose work on the Manobo epic *Ullahingan*, I am also indebted. Some stanzas of the epic are found in this book. I wanted to ask her permission but she had already gone ahead of us a long time ago. I served as one of her research assistants when she did her work on the epic. May she rest in peace.

It would have been impossible to meet deadlines without the use of modern communications technology. Mel Gonzales is based in San Jose, California, USA, Michelle and Jojo reside in Toronto, Canada, and Melch works in Manila. If not for the computer, we would not have the opportunity to exchange ideas regularly and undertake the process more efficiently through email, chat and or by phone.

ABOUT THE AUTHOR

Photo by: Melchizedek R. Maquiso II

Melchizedek Maquiso or Mike to his friends once worked in the Office of the President, Malacanang Palace, Republic of the Philippines. Cha-Cha-Cha is his fifth book, his first novel; the other four, are textbooks or reference materials in higher education. He took his AB and MA at Silliman University and finished his PhD at the University of Alabama as a Fulbright scholar. He lives with his wife on a farm in Kalipayan, Mimbalagon, Gingoog City in Mindanao.

Printed in the United States
18477LVS00005B/244-249